BEYOND
THE
SAMOVAR

Janet Hancock

Beyond the Samovar

Published by The Conrad Press in the United Kingdom 2019

Tel: +44(0)1227 472 874

www.theconradpress.com

info@theconradpress.com

ISBN 978-1-911546-51-1

Typesetting and Cover Design by: Charlotte Mouncey, www.bookstyle.co.uk

Cover features images by Artem Svetlov of RZD steam locomotive Er 774-38 on Flickr and a painting of Distillation of oil Baku by unknown artist on wikimedia

The Conrad Press logo was designed by Maria Priestley.

Printed and bound in Great Britain

by Clays Ltd, Elcograf S.p.A

Strange, is it not? that of the myriads who
Before us pass'd the door of Darkness through,
Not one returns to tell us of the Road,
Which to discover we must travel too.

Edward Fitzgerald – *Rubaiyat of Omar Khayyam* (1859)

Remembering Ken, who made it all possible,
and
to the memory of my Birmingham grandparents:
William Walter Tonks 1862-1926
Gertrude Maud Tonks (née James) 1886-1978
whose story shall never be known

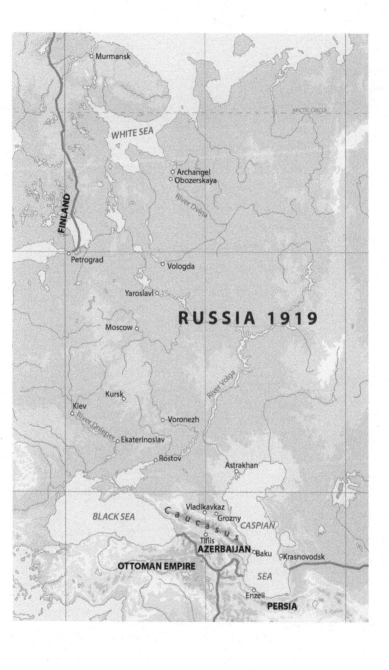

PART ONE

'All the world has gone wrong. The millstones of God are grinding; some sort of flour will come out of it.'

Peasant woman in N.E. Yaroslavl Province, Russia, September 1917

M.P. Price - *My Reminiscences of the Russian Revolution*

ONE

Baku, Azerbaijan, May 1919

'Go home to England?' Livvy echoes as if trying the words for fit and finding them wrong. She is standing behind the kitchen table, something familiar, fingernails digging into the wood, perspiration tickling her wrists and the back of her neck. Peter is washing his hands at the stone sink, lathering carbolic past his wrists after a day at the oilfield. Wind is buffeting the shutters.

She can't believe what her husband's saying. 'Travel?' she repeats. 'What do you mean? George isn't even a month old. This is our home,' she protests, 'the first I've had I can call my own.' She didn't choose anything in this apartment in the Black Town, Baku's industrial quarter: Yefim Aaronovich's first father-in-law, one of Baku's oil pioneers nearly fifty years ago, bought and furnished it as a wedding gift to his eldest daughter and Yefim Aaronovich, his heir apparent, in the last decade of the old century. But since July she has been mistress. She was sure another family would be allocated the second bedroom but the apartment has remained hers and Peter's, their haven, their eyrie, their garden of Eden.

Peter looks at her over his shoulder. 'Darling, we can't stay here. The Russians are fighting each other in Russia and both sides want Baku's oil.'

A tremor of dread, powerlessness, spirals through her at the memory of three days' bloodletting in March last year, after which *bolshevik* revolutionaries seized power in Baku, the only faction who could impose law and order on ancient hatreds between Christian Armenians and Moslem Tartars.

Peter turns from the sink to dry his hands. His light brown hair is flopping over his forehead, where sweat is tracing a course to his shirt collar. She wants to push the hair back but stays where she is, his words distancing her. 'The Azeris will fight anybody who tries to take their independence,' he emphasises. He wiggles dripping fingers. She always has a clean towel for him. It lies on the table between them. Her eyes hold his, falter under their harshness. She lets go of the table, gives him the towel.

'The British Army will protect us,' she says. 'That's what they're here for.' It's a comfort, an assurance of permanence, security, British soldiers on street corners these last six months and their cheerful: Morning, ma'am. And shops reopening, roads cleaned, although since George's birth she's hardly been out, flagging in the heat more than before.

'They're here to shore up Azeri independence but they won't always be.'

'Why not?'

'Some British MPs are against more involvement now the war in Europe is over. Even if the troops aren't sent back, they're needed elsewhere: Egypt, India. We can either leave with them and go to Persia first, or make our own arrangements.'

'Persia?' she shrieks.

'Livvy, the Russia we knew and loved has gone forever,' Peter pursues, rubbing dry his hands and arms. 'We must think of

George, his future, where he is to grow up. Do you want it to be in an oriental Azerbaijan, anything Russian or European a relic of the past? He'll have an Anatolian teacher, and be forced to study Azeri at school and the history of Turkic peoples. As an engineer and state employee, I'm expected to learn Azeri within two years.'

'And from Persia how would we get to England?'

'Overland west till we reached the Mediterranean.'

'It would take weeks. And then as long again on a boat home. I'm not going anywhere by sea. I get too sick. You know I do. I've told you about those frightful five days from Tilbury to Petersburg, retching in the Baltic wind, stomach threatening to propel itself out of my mouth.' She pleads, 'I'll teach George here.' Tears are trickling down her cheeks, over her jaw to her neck. 'I taught Yefim Aaronovich's two small sons, didn't I?' She's round the table, grasping Peter's arm, burying her face in his jacket, inhaling him, the sweetness of crude oil and male odour of tobacco. He's shushing her, kissing her. 'We'll be safe,' she persists, 'this apartment wasn't touched when the Turks were in power.'

But his mouth is over hers and he's pulling at her skirt. They're on the table, their first lovemaking since George's birth, in a wantonness and desperation of which she hasn't thought herself capable and roughness she's never known from Peter.

Afterwards, he carries her to their bed. 'We'll stay as long as we can, darling.' He's caressing her, smoothing stray hair from her face. 'I can't bear you to be upset.'

TWO

September 1919

Peter is already through the door into the outside corridor. She must move, follow him, not dawdle. They didn't tell Masha, their maid, exactly when they were leaving until he emerged from their bedroom with two bedrolls - something you see people with these days for a journey of any distance – and he called Masha from the kitchen.

The Russian girl has come into the hall; her lips part slightly.

You've been waiting for this moment, Livvy thinks. George sleeps in her arms.

Masha holds the door. 'Go well, Livvy.' Blue eyes linger on George before looking down.

Peter's feet, left, right, sound on the stone steps down to the road. 'Thank you,' she manages and is out of the apartment. Go. Just go.

Outside, Peter is several paces ahead. She sets off into hot north wind, the dust fine, penetrating. She settles the muslin shawl, same blue as her skirt, over her head and the lower part of her face: a combination of protection from the elements, and eastern modesty, for since Azeri independence last year people do stare at a bare face. Peter's in working things: black jacket, cap askew. He's worn the jacket nearly every day of the twenty months she's known him, except for their wedding day and Sundays when they used to go to church. It makes him look shabby, ordinary, what everybody strives for since the revolutions a couple of years ago. The only way to stay safe on the streets, he'd say.

Look ahead, not back. Think of survival. Yes, but is it wrong to take with you memories, things you won't, can't, forget? She will always remember the wind in Baku. For three quarters of the year it howls round the city like a genie out of a bottle, bringing a little relief from the heat. But this late afternoon there is no respite. She passes curlicued, wrought-iron balconies and shuttered windows of sandstone apartment blocks like the one she's left. Not even cinnamon water sprinkled on her shawl can mask smells which for her will always be part of Baku: oil, spiced cooking, the perfume of acacia; and fear.

She holds George to her chest to guard eyes tight in sleep and calm her shaking hands. A dog is barking, a baby crying, the city waking from its second slumber of the day.

Peter strides towards the tram stop. Against his legs bounce the bedrolls. Into them she has wrapped muslin squares for George - how soon, where, will she be able to change him, wash them? – one set of clothes each, drawings by Peter's brother and his diary, photographs of her own brothers with her mother in Norwich, both *Princess Royal* hatbands, some valuables for barter, with the few Kerensky and tsarist roubles they managed to hoard. And the white silk stockings she wore the day she married Peter. On a string round her neck, beneath the top button of her blouse, hangs the ring, a Russian triple knot in three shades of gold which he placed on her finger a few minutes after six o'clock on a July evening last year in the English church a mile down the coast. The ring had belonged

15

to the *baboushka* where he'd been lodging, and fitted as if made for her. Without it, the finger feels empty, increasing her sense of vulnerability. She is a few days into her twenty-fifth year.

Under a sky burned white by the sun's glare, she catches up with Peter. He's two and a half years older than she is. She's loved him since the second time she met him – no, the third, really – captivated by the warmth of his gaze and smile in Baku's Tartar Quarter where she'd gone shopping for Yefim Aaronovich's cook. Now, he doesn't look at her as if to meet her eyes might encourage her to voice again misgivings about a two thousand-mile journey across Russia, or even turn back; worse still, make a scene as she did in May. Since his decision to leave the day before yesterday, he hasn't shaved, moustache no longer neat, adding to his unkempt appearance.

The tram to the railway station trundles over the cobbles towards them, drawn by one horse, a dejected creature passed over for military use, the shape of whose bones shows beneath its skin. He clambers aboard the tram, deposits the bedrolls, takes George from her, grasps her hand to help her up and she's off the ground of Baku.

She breathes fumes that cling to anyone working in the oil industry, glances at the few Tartars seated on wooden benches: Moslem descendants of people who for centuries have lived in Baku, in fact all the Caspian coast and inland. She's heard stories handed down the generations, of heroes of resistance to Russian tsarist rule, holed up in the mountains of the Caucasus; bandits, some might say.

She averts her eyes from dark gazes, shivers at the memory of Yefim Aaronovich's ransacked three-storey house last November, in a quiet city-centre street named after the Stock

Exchange at the far end. By then, only the Armenian servants were living there. Did any of these men … these hands … ? And are any of them in the pay of Masha's father, disgruntled at Peter's discovery of his treachery and at being done out of a few Azeri banknotes in spite of a chance to move into the vacant apartment with his daughter? A lunge between the ribs from a *kinjal* is all it would take. She counts the beats of her heart reverberating in her ears like the tolling of a bell.

The tram bowls past distillation plants, factories, refineries. Baku is on a peninsula. She's always thought of the city like an amphitheatre clustering on a hillside above the horseshoe shape of the bay, as if built in a crater. For more than five years she's lived here. She gazes farewell at the line of cliffs, rising land rendered pink in six o'clock sunlight.

There are gaps where buildings, gutted a year ago when the Turks took the city, have been pulled down. New ones are in progress. Tartar workmen squatting in the shade, alerted by the clacking of the horse's hooves and the wheels, turn to stare at the tram. Peter is right, she thinks, there is no future for the two of them in Baku, British civilians, part of a shifting population of a hundred or so oil workers, business people and governesses; visitors who have outstayed their welcome, reminders of perfidious Albion to citizens proud of their capital of an independent Azerbaijan, and fearful of *bolshevik* and White Russian predators now that the British Army has abandoned the Caucasus.

In the station, they stand with the bedrolls on a cracked marble floor. Engraved pillars and a lofty ceiling still give something of the grandeur lavished on the construction in the 1870s. She has not been inside since the morning of her arrival in the summer of 1914.

17

Peter rests two fingertips against George's cheek, loosening the shawl. 'All right, little fellow?' he murmurs, although they have decided the less English they speak the better.

She is about to say, 'don't wake him', but halts, does not want to start such a long journey with don't. George opens eyes that are the same hazel as Peter's, gives his father a gummy smile, and her heart almost floats away.

She lifts George into what she calls his mountaineering position, feet against her left breast as if he might climb over her, head above her shoulder. She keeps her hand against the back of his white cotton bonnet; it has a frill of broderie anglaise embroidered in red stitches fine enough to have been painted. The bonnet was a gift this morning from Charlotte, an English friend whose little house near the church has always been open to Baku's British community. Charlotte and her companion have lived there longer than anybody can remember, with no plans to leave.

She watches the ebb and flow and chatter of human traffic: Russians, and honey-coloured Azeris in loose-fitting garments, women veiled. She wonders who they are, where they've been or are going, and if they would mind very much if she and Peter stayed in Baku. Nobody appears interested in two people with bedrolls and a baby.

Her canvas sandal pushes against cigarette ends and husks of sunflower seeds. 'These wouldn't have been here in the old days,' she tells Peter.

He turns to look at her, a ferocity in his expression she has come to know at times of uncertainty: he's still afraid I might turn back. Peter clicks his tongue, shakes his head. She clamps her lips together as if she would hold back any more English words. 'Darling, we agreed,' he reminds her in Russian.

She nods, fends off the strangeness of the endearment on his lips in another language, and resentment that he had whispered to George in English not Russian, before they curdle with her regret at being wrenched from her home: sofa and chairs with thin legs, padded upholstery patterned in red, green and yellow. As though she would erase having spoken in English, she repeats what she has just said, in her adopted tongue learnt from the Armenian servants in Yefim Aaronovich's house, and Masha who also used to work there; the Armenians were patient, smiling, as she filled her cheeks with Russian syllables, clusters of consonants.

Peter is looking at people waiting at the far end of the station. 'They've started selling tickets,' he says. The republic of Azerbaijan has kept this legacy of a century in the Russian Empire, tickets on sale for half an hour before a train leaves. So the line must be clear, for a while anyway.

He goes to wait in the queue. She breathes out, a long, sweeping sigh, picking over how after months of nothing being said about going to England since that quarrel in May, suddenly the matter resurfaced and here they are two days later on their way. It all centres around Masha.

ɛʍ

The Russian girl started working for them in the apartment at the beginning of the year. Peter knew her father, a foreman at the oilfield. Married six months and very pregnant she, Livvy, was missing four years in Yefim Aaronovich's household, and his small sons' chatter and sudden displays of affection. Grateful for help and company during the day, she accepted Masha's familiar manner. In the old days, when they were both paid by Yefim Aaronovich, she'd always been *baryshnya* to Masha in deference to her position as an unmarried woman, an employee like Masha but one who enjoyed privileges a servant did not such as eating with the family and taking an afternoon siesta. Ten hours a day the girl had scrubbed and polished at the house, to return to a slum in the Black Town and the needs of a father and four brothers.

The morning after news reached Baku of the Tsar's abdication two and a half years ago, Masha turned up for work late at the front door of Yefim Aaronovich's house rather than the kitchen entrance, demanded to speak to his young wife, addressing her by name and the sisterly *ty*, and suggesting a more equitable allocation of household tasks, only to be sent packing.

'Stuck-up sow,' Masha recalled at the beginning of this year.

She drew in a breath of shock to hear somebody, anybody, so spoken of. 'Masha!'

The Russian girl shrugged. 'I got married a few months later, Livvy. Nikolai Antonovich.' Masha savoured the names. 'My Kolya. Drunk with each other and the spirit of revolution, we were. Can you imagine what it meant to people like us? The joy, the utter freedom, not having to watch what we said to those who considered themselves our betters. I lived with him and his family in a flat even smaller than the one I'd left. Never enough to eat. Father still expected me to keep house for him and my brothers. Nine months later Kolyushka was born, named after his papa. He was sickly from the start. Died in July, aged six weeks. Kolya never saw him, killed a couple of weeks before, fighting with the Red Army against the Turks in the swamps at Yeldakh.'

She glimpsed tenderness in Masha's diminutives for her

husband and son in spite of lines at the sides of her nose, and of her mouth, one with a downward tilt, unused to smiling. 'I'm sorry,' she said. It didn't seem an adequate response. She rested a hand on Masha's arm, bony beneath the faded blouse, a touch of sympathy she hoped would be more eloquent than words.

She and Masha were the same age. She shared her darning thread, made sure the Russian girl took home at night a handful of rice, or a slice of sturgeon bought that morning and wrapped in damp muslin.

For weeks after George was born, she'd sit in the kitchen of the apartment watching Masha knead dough; breathe in the warm, yeasty smell, touching the end of George's nose with hers, nuzzling the softness of his neck and tips of shell-like ears, resting her cheek against the down that covered his head, marvelling that he was hers to keep, that no-one was going to ask for him back. In the afternoons while he slept and Masha cooked and cleaned, she rested on the sofa, sewing, waiting for Peter to come home from the oilfield or refinery that used to belong to Yefim Aaronovich, drifting on the rhythm of the days, shutters closed against the heat.

One morning a few weeks ago, Masha said, 'No more British soldiers in Baku before long, Livvy.'

Her stomach tightened. Not this again. 'What do you mean?'

'They'll be away, back where they came from, Persia or somesuch.'

'Surely not. Everyone relies on them to keep the peace.' George was looking at her as though to ensure she was real.

'They may have kept the peace but they've taken our oil, used it or sold it to their friends.' Masha kneaded as if she would impregnate the dough with her distaste.

'*Your* oil, Masha?'

'Russian oil. Baku is Russian, Livvy. The British don't allow oil to be sold to Russia because they don't want the *bolsheviki* to have it. But some ships go to Astrakhan. Azeri port officials don't check.'

'How do you know?'

A blush crept into Masha's cheeks and she bit her lip. 'We hear things.'

She turned George to her shoulder, clasped him, fearful of unknown plans, secret arrangements, a world outside the comfort of the kitchen. She didn't mention the conversation to Peter so that for them nothing would change. We'll stay as long as we can, he'd said. Yet, not telling him hurt, a literal ache in her chest, the start of a barrier between them. What if there were more things to keep from him and the barrier piled up?

About ten days ago, from their first floor window, she saw him talking to Masha in the street. He normally came home after Masha had left. He was taking something from his pocket. Money? He gave Masha some, which she stuffed in her skirt. The rest he put back.

'What were you saying to Masha?' she asked when he arrived indoors.

'I wanted to know how you were. She spends hours with you, lucky girl.'

You were waiting for her. Why did you give her money? She felt the words would choke her yet could find no way to release them.

'Don't we pay her enough?' she managed to throw in.

Peter blinked. 'I didn't think a little extra would hurt.'

When she mentioned it to Masha next morning, the Russian

22

girl protested he'd been making up her wages. She looked out of the window each day after Masha had gone. No Peter. She'd been anxious for nothing. Until it was lost from sight, she followed the muslin shawl in the green of a peacock's feathers which Masha still wore. She'd bought the shawl in the bazaar for Masha at the same time as her own blue one, a couple of weeks after her arrival in Baku, dismayed that neither Yefim Aaronovich's wife nor daughter was inclined to replace Masha's that was threadbare.

A week later, Peter was waiting for Masha again. She watched them talk, her heart hammering. Masha gave something to Peter. He handed her money and they parted.

'What did Masha give you just now?' she demanded as soon as he was back. 'Why are you paying her? It's nothing to do with her wages, is it?' They were standing in the middle of the room, neither of them inclined to move to the comfort and intimacy of the sofa. Whatever he was going to say, she wanted to believe him, fearful of what it would mean if she couldn't.

'Last week, I overheard her father talking to my Azeri assistant about some papers for translation,' Peter began. 'I slipped into his foreman's shack to see what I could find. He's obviously involved in printing an illegal *bolshevik* newspaper. It was all there, inflammatory nonsense: Azeri independence benefits only five per cent of the nation, they are crushed under the heavy stone of capitalism, if all workers unite they can throw off the weight, Russia is the indispensable market for oil. On and on it went.'

Unease dragged at her. Words stuck in her throat but this time she forced them out. 'What's this to do with us?'

'It was too good as an opportunity to miss, darling. I, shall

23

we say, *persuaded* Masha to get us a *bolshevik* travel permit - '

'You what?'

' - she knew that a word from me to the authorities and her father would've been under lock and key before you could say *soviet*. Believe it or not she's quite fond of the weasly individual. Odious little man, he is, always chewing sunflower seeds even when I'm speaking to him. We'll have to go through *bolshevik* Russia at some point and they don't like the Imperialist British. With the permit, as Russian workers, we'll be all right. We can't travel all the way on the oil industrialists' train like in the old days. We'll do it in stages.'

Only then did Peter pause, regarding her as if he were garnering strength, while she stared at him with the feeling of arriving at a performance that had already begun, an adventure in which he was the main player.

'I thought we agreed we'd stay as long as we could,' she reminded him.

'We did. And we have.'

'Have we? Suddenly it seems you've decided for us both. For the three of us. Oblivious to George's safety, or mine. How can you do this?'

'*Because* of your safety, not oblivious to it. There'll be fighting again in Baku, could be any time – *bolsheviki*, White Russians, Azeri Tartars and Armenians - and I want us out before it starts. Now we have the permit there's no reason not to go.'

Yes, there is: I'm happy here. The words pushed their way up, stalling in her chest among layers of alarm. The ones that found voice were, 'You're trying to frighten me.'

'I'm trying to get you to face reality. I don't want to see again – or you ever to see - a man with his throat sliced from ear to ear, or dozens of bloated Tartar corpses bobbing on the Caspian. It was ghastly, those three days in March last year before the *bolsheviki* grabbed power.'

She swallowed. He was right. And worse had come in September, a year ago, when the Turks took control: six thousand murdered, mostly Armenians, Tartar revenge for the three thousand massacred in March. She and Peter had been evacuated down the coast by then. Turkish occupation only lasted until their exit from the war against Britain and Europe at the end of October. Evacuees returned to Baku in November, the city under British martial law, Tartar and Armenian units forbidden.

'Remember Yefim Aaronovich's house -' Peter went on.

' - no!' she shouted. 'I don't need you to tell me to remember. I had nightmares for months after I saw what had happened, didn't I? I shall never forget.'

He lowered his head, eyes closed. Silence settled around them, absorbing their raised voices, their fear and anger. Peter looked up. When he spoke, his voice was calm, firm. 'Livvy, the last British troops have left Baku. Nowhere will be safe and the *bolsheviki* will capitalise on it as they did before.'

'So you've dreamt up a plan, blackmailed Masha, and not discussed it with me.'

'I saw an opportunity but didn't want to tell you until I had the permit; I insisted Masha say nothing or I would cut her money. We'll make for the north coast. Archangel is still under British occupation. Then it'll only be a few days from there on a British Navy ship, more comfortable than the cargo boat you went to Russia on from Tilbury. We must go soon if we're to reach Archangel before the port freezes for winter.

Mrs MacDonell did it over two years ago.'

'Did what?' Mrs MacDonell was the wife of Baku's former British vice-consul and invited her for tea soon after her arrival.

'The journey from Baku to Archangel. With her baby.'

Was travel any more dangerous now than in 1917? she wondered.

'George can grow up with English children,' Peter pointed out, 'go to an English school, know the rest of his family.'

'You won't … wouldn't … have a job in England,' she tried. 'You have one here.'

'I shan't always. I'm working myself out of it, explaining all the processes to my Azeri assistant, showing him how the machinery works. I'll soon find one in England. We can live with my family in Birmingham first. You and Mother'll get on famously.'

'Why? I wasn't a suffragette.'

'No, but you were independent, leaving home at eighteen, going to London, then to Petersburg with the Claytons. And you have the same chestnut hair.'

That didn't mean anything. And she'd left Norwich as an escape, a stranger in the house she grew up in because of her stepmother. But she knew Peter was going to have his way. He'd worked it all out hoping to avoid her becoming hysterical as had happened in May. Why couldn't she simply trust his confidence and optimism; stop pushing against the force of his will, and against armies, factions hungry for power? Because, instead of staying, hanging on to their home, it meant change, discomfort, almost certain danger; and, if they survived that, a sea voyage. When they were evacuated down the coast last September, she spent the twenty-four-hour voyage spewing over the side of the boat. Those five days with the Claytons from Tilbury to Petersburg in 1914 were hideous, clinging onto the rail of the boat, shivering and retching in wind which cut through her coat and all the layers beneath, the certainty that some force over which she had no control was determined to turn her inside out. Lying on her bunk, listening to the wind roaring round the creaking boat, she vowed: I shall never travel by sea again.

Peter moved towards the kitchen to wash his hands. At the doorway he turned. 'We'll have an even nicer place in England,' he promised, 'with our own furniture.'

℘

Waiting for him at the station while he buys the tickets, she hopes they won't have to use the *bolshevik* permit at all. How will they know if they're in *bolshevik* territory? The permit only covers them as far as Moscow, which wasn't what Peter demanded from Masha, and because of that he withheld some money from her. He is convinced something will come up in their favour. Moscow to Archangel might all be White Russian by the time they reach there. His British passport should see them across land held by the Whites. The passport – a single sheet of paper signed by the Foreign Secretary – is folded several times in a cloth bag she has sewn onto a tape under Peter's shirt. She doesn't fear the Whites: not only have they been armed and supplied by the British, but they are loyal to the Tsar, the old order, life as it was and might, just might, be again.

It's the *bolsheviki* who are the rebels, upstarts. Masha she is used to, harmless, all talk and bluster: freedom, bread, land for the peasants. But unknown *bolsheviki* are rough, foul-smelling. Several of them demanded entry into Yefim Aaronovich's house one Christmas afternoon a couple of years ago, hair matted to foreheads and backs of necks, insisting they had orders to search for food surplus to the household ration; the tattered remnants of the tsarist army who'd elected their officers, demobilised themselves and returned home with their weapons after the Tsar abdicated. No more standing in icy mud up to their knees in ill-constructed trenches.

Straightbacked, unsmiling outside the door of her room - where she'd been sewing - she held her head high, eyes on two of the intruders as they arrived at the top of the staircase. Faded grey uniforms hung on skeletal bodies. One of the men was clutching a rifle. She spoke as commandingly as she knew how. 'You cannot come in here. I am a British subject. You have no right to search me or my room and property.'

She didn't understand what they were saying to each other, coarse speech, so stared beyond them at walls covered in cream silk, sweating fingers interlaced behind her back. When one of them spoke to her, incomprehensible dialect, she kept her eyes fixed on the same distant point. '*Izvinite, baryshnya*,' the other apologised, backing away. Perhaps they thought she was mad.

Feet bound with rags, the intruders leapt downstairs. They'd checked every room in the house without taking anything; there certainly wasn't any food. Bravado. Flexing newly found muscles after their comrades' seizure of power in Petrograd a few weeks before even though this had not yet happened in Baku. Now, they will demand to see papers, know the right of any individual to walk on Russian soil and eat food which might be given to others. During the last year, there've been rumours that the *bolsheviki* murdered the Tsar and his family.

But no bodies have been found. Surely no-one would dare, not even the *bolsheviki*.

Can she still speak in the same tone of voice as that Christmas afternoon? Who she and Peter admit to being will depend on who confronts them; maybe a split-second decision. The rest of the time they will be two of the nameless, faceless masses.

She wonders if Masha and her father have already shifted their few belongings to the apartment from their grimy tenement, one of several five storeys high the other side the Black Town where you can lean out and almost touch the hand of your neighbour opposite. Years ago, about eighteen months into the war against Germany, she and Masha dragged a sack of flour along a street of greasy cobbles, avoiding puddles of dirty water, the stink of sewage overpowering that of oil. Up to the top of a winding wooden staircase they struggled, with no banister, straight into a kitchen smelling of stale fish, Masha's mattress on the stone floor. The other room was the province of the father and four brothers, all oilfield workers and therefore exempt from conscription. She steeled herself not to show shock or dismay to diminish or embarrass Masha. The Russian girl, however, had no such qualms.

'Papa hoped for something better from the oil,' Masha admitted. 'Before we came to Baku he at least had a strip of land and a cow. When I was three, my job was to shovel up the muck to fertilise the soil.'

'Yefim Aaronovich believes that one day men of reason will advise the Tsar.'

Masha just looked at her, a stare that said: you don't know anything. The Russian girl turned to find some grubby-looking hessian and they shared out the flour.

Masha and her father must be delighted with the good fortune that has just fallen into their laps: a two-bedroom apartment that used to belong to the man who'd employed them all. The brothers are in the Red Army.

She pictures Masha standing on the Turcoman rug – a masterpiece in terracotta, rose, orange, black - stretching out arms with space to spare; opening the mahogany armoire, trying on skirts and blouses left behind which were bought before the war or stitched from a length of bazaar calico, or given last year by Yefim Aaronovich's wife before the Russian family left Baku for Persia. And preening in her straw hat, which Charlotte's companion decorated with lace for her wedding day.

Not the wedding dress, though, the white voile gown with a lace fichu collar Charlotte found for her to wear with the silk stockings. She took the dress in a cloth bag back to Charlotte this morning.

THREE

Peter returns with the tickets. 'The train only goes as far as the frontier,' he tells her, picking up the bedrolls and starting towards the track. 'After that, it's Denikin's land.'

White Russian territory. 'What do we do then?'

He sighs. She bites her lip, hating his frustration with her. 'Livvy,' he says, 'we use our initiative.'

He is pushing his way into the train, securing space on the lower level, reaching out to help her up. She sits down, wooden planking hard through the thinness of her skirt, bedrolls rammed against feet and legs. George is whimpering. The air reeks of tobacco, garlic, human odours and crude oil. She covers her mouth and nose with her shawl, lowers her glance against the scrutiny of fierce, slanting Tartar eyes. As she did on the tram half an hour ago, she speculates that these could be the sons, brothers, perhaps the very hands, of men who wrecked Yefim Aaronovich's house. When she looks up, one of the men is watching her from under dark, curling lashes. She cannot read his expression. Is it curiosity or a sinister arrogance? Or has he been paid by Masha's father to look out for her and Peter?

Fragments dislocated in time flicker before her eyes, this unknowing girl who'd discovered a sense of adventure, arriving in Baku five years ago on the oil industrialists' train which she and Yefim Aaronovich's daughter Esther had joined at Rostov. Their shared compartment had table lamps with pretty shades;

and soft wide seats upholstered in strawberry-coloured damask which the *provodnik* opened into two beds made up with starched linen sheets in the evening. The adjoining lavabo had hot and cold water. The *provodnik* brought clean towels and soap. When he came to collect their luggage, she was stuffing into a valise a silk chemise and fripperies Esther had left strewn around the compartment; sixteen-year-old Esther was used to having things done for her.

The train lurches forward to skirt the oilfields north of Baku. She cannot see out of the window, does not need to, miles of what look like ghostly forests of burnt out trees, in the middle of which are squat buildings. Beyond, sandy desert, a hummock of camel grass, villages in the distance. Not a flower anywhere. The day she arrived, barefoot children in colourful clothes stood some way from the railway line and waved as the train steamed past. Patches of white, partly dried-up salt lakes conjured memories of Norfolk marshes. A man swathed in shapeless, loose garments the colour of sand, head wrapped round with nondescript cloth, was smoking a pipe, sitting on a trotting donkey. The heat pulled at her like grasping fingers, leaching energy. June it was, and she was here as companion to Esther until the German governess returned from visiting a sick father in Berlin. Her only luggage was a tartan carpet bag lent by a friend in Petersburg; she'd quickly copied the Russian habit of dropping the 'Saint'. She'd left her winter clothes with her friend. How full of hope people were in those days. You could make plans: I'll go to Baku for three months, return to Petersburg, find another job.

The dust has a parched, acrid smell. George's mewling has risen to a cry, innocent, demanding, fists clenched and pummelling the air. She whispers to Peter, 'I need to feed him.' I can't, she thinks. Not here, with all these people, all these men. How soon will she be able to change him? She wants to wee.

Peter remains standing, screening her from the press of people, hands in pockets, her only bulwark against calamity, the abyss. People are clucking soothing noises to George in a language she doesn't understand, not Russian. It does nothing to calm him. She unfastens two buttons of her blouse, pushes towards her shoulder the wedding ring on its string so that it can't be seen. George's lips and gums tug at her nipple. She closes her eyes, life force flowing from her to George, child of her body, of her and Peter's love.

∾

In the rattling train, Peter sits down beside Livvy when she's fed George. People around them push out a space that isn't really there, breathing in as if to make themselves thinner, eyes eloquent in understanding at a baby pacified, asleep against its mother's chest. He gazes at Livvy, his darling, already dozing on his shoulder, a tableau of perfection in a traumatised world. Perhaps George will be like a passport, he thinks, inclining people to help, even share rations with them. Here, nobody has anything to offer. Many of the passengers are women and old men clutching bags and baskets, all of which will be empty but on the return journey may contain some grain, a little cheese or milk, even a scrap of meat. Squashed among them are oil workers released home to Tartar villages. They come to work for a year, lodge in barracks at the oilfield, are replaced by their brothers.

He wants to bend and kiss the curve of Livvy's chin into her neck but stays still, eyes away from her not resting on anybody or anything, his hand on her arm around George. He wishes he could wrap her in silk, keep her in a quiet arbour away from a harsh world, so giving is she of herself, and never to anybody before him. What an amazing wonderful thing that he went to Baku nearly two years ago from Grozny, where he'd been working for more than three years as an oil engineer. The train back after his week's leave in Baku was packed with army deserters, as many clinging to the roof, all shouting for the driver to get a move on and not be a coward. The train was to follow the coast north from Baku for several hours, as it's doing now, then turn inland for about a hundred miles until it reached the fortress town of Grozny, first of a chain the Russians built a century ago to subdue the Caucasus. However, after a few miles the line was blocked. The train returned to Baku amid fickle cheers and lewd singing about the Tsarina and her daughters.

In Grozny, he'd had an English mistress. They would devour each other in snatched meetings between her husband's visits home, each encounter possibly the last, enforced separation an aphrodisiac more powerful than any bazaar concoction. Born of English parents, the husband was a wool buyer for a firm in Constantinople and trekked around remote areas of the Caucasus where he understood the languages and dialects, places no Russian official would dare show himself. But with Livvy, time, the universe, is theirs for the rest of their lives, to discover layer upon layer of pleasure and he now understands the depth, the liberation, of the marriage vow 'forsaking all other'.

He'd been in Baku a couple of months, taken on by Yefim Aaronovich at the oilfield, the line still not cleared, when he met Livvy along the Marine Boulevard one January morning last year. She was with her charges, Yefim Aaronovich's young twin sons, who obviously adored her. Her expression

34

said: I have nothing to hide. Modest blue eyes refused to hold his, blush suffusing her cheeks, lips parted in a smile he never wanted to let out of his sight, so he needed to know what new things would make her smile, things he might say, and had to see her again to find out. Did he know, even then, that he wanted marriage, to offer her stability, security, the possibility of her own children instead of looking after other people's? That the days of clandestine assignations, such as he'd had in Grozny, were over? Almost certainly.

Livvy's afraid of this journey. But they had to leave Baku, before the border is closed, or all foreigners arrested, or any of the things those drunk with seized power decide they can do. And there was that terrible business in the hall of Yefim Aaronovich's house late last year. He'd gone there to visit the servants, check they were safe after the Turkish occupation, and collect some of the bedding he and Livvy had left with them for safe keeping – they thought - during the evacuation. She turned up a few minutes later for the same reason. He tried to stop her seeing the carnage. She had nightmares for weeks afterwards. Best take her home to England.

He edges his hand from her arm to the swell of her hip. Her skirt is damp. Wet, even.

ↄﬞ

She opens her eyes, jolted, dragged up from some fathomless place of sanctuary.

A pistol crack. The rattle of a machine gun like stones on a tin roof.

Screams.

Peter is sitting beside her. In the darkness she reaches for his hand. He clasps hers in reply and her heart lifts, seems to expand.

35

Silence.

The train is stationary, the carriage deserted except for the two of them; and George, safe in sleep. Fear is prickling her skin, crawling across it. Her skirt is moist across her lap, but also underneath, her drawers and between her legs. She winces, a breath of shock, shame. 'Peter,' she whispers, 'I've w – I'm all wet.' The words stutter, wobble. 'While I was asleep, I couldn't help it.'

'Sh, sh,' he soothes her, kisses the soft skin of her temple. 'It'll dry.'

'But the smell - '

' – there's no smell, only of the people who were here.'

'When can I wash?'

'Soon, I hope. We're probably at the frontier, which is what all the noise is about. The train may go on.'

She latches her free arm across his shoulder, pulls him to her, buries her face in his jacket sleeve, breathes him in, her oxygen. 'I can't - '

'You can, you must. We're safe.'

Shouts, and someone unfastening the door from outside. Peter eases her away, stands up, raises hands in surrender. Her eyes fix on the hurricane lamp and pistol carried by the intruder. George sighs, still asleep. She turns his face to her shoulder.

'What are you doing here?' the man barks in Russian. He climbs into the train, lifts his pistol level with Peter's neck. White or *bolshevik*? she has to decide; and Peter, too. The Russian is unshaven. Sunken, hooded eyes regard his passengers. Tousled, sandy-coloured hair touches the collar of a khaki greatcoat which has tarnished silver epaulettes. Half the buttons are missing. Silver epaulettes: not a *bolshevik*. A *bolshevik* would've ripped them off, indications of enemy rank. The lamp casts light on trousers tucked into knee-length boots; clean ones, not scuffed or split. There is a rotten smell about the man: blood. The hand holding the pistol is smeared.

'Answer me!' he snaps, stabbing the air with the pistol.

She watches Peter pass his tongue over his lips; hopes he has arrived at the same conclusion as her. 'We are British,' Peter says, 'and making our way to the north coast.'

'British?' the Russian repeats. 'Passport? Papers?'

Peter fumbles inside his shirt but the Russian pushes his hand aside and rips out the cloth bag containing the passport.

The Russian holds up the lamp to the document, narrows his eyes in scrutiny. Can he read it? she wonders. If he's an officer he'll be educated, familiar with European script.

'Just you,' the Russian observes, 'in 1913.'

'That's right,' Peter confirms.

She has been holding her breath. Her shoulders sag on a long outtake. Yes.

The Russian lowers his pistol, hands the passport back. 'You're safe here,' he says. 'We control all the south except for a strip around Astrakhan and along the Volga. We're pushing north to Moscow and need rolling stock. Those ruffians just now got what they deserved,' he adds with derision, 'trying to load grain onto the train and return to Baku. And their friends at the border letting them have what should be for the Army.' For the first time, the man smiles showing white teeth. 'They won't do it again.'

Grain that is much needed in Baku, she thinks. 'How far are you taking the train?' she hears a woman ask the Russian. Is that her? After the panic of a few minutes ago? Peter blinks at her, smiles: well done.

The Russian turns, acknowledging her existence with a tilt of his head. 'Until there's no more fuel. Maybe Grozny. We are short of many things. The British have been good to us.' He points to his boots. 'We still need weapons, ammunition. Sometimes equipment falls into the wrong hands. We continue to fight for our Motherland, united and indivisible;' the Russian's voice is rising, 'for our Tsar, the glory our country once knew.'

George has woken and is wriggling in her arms. She moves him so he can see who she has been talking to.

The Russian holds out his hand to Peter. 'I hope you get home safely.'

Home. The apartment. Small circular tables with scrolled legs, and feet shaped like animals' claws; vases and candelabra; potted palms, and plants whose names she never knew, exotic things hardy enough to withstand the heat.

The Russian clicks his heels, inclines his head to her, touches the top of George's bonnet. He jumps down onto the ground, shouts along the track, rams the door closed.

George is crying. The train moves forward, gathers speed. The Russian has left a smudge on George's bonnet. She sees the mark as a stamp of approval, the first test passed.

ᕦᕤ

The Russian brings her and Peter water and flat bread as dawn light filters into the carriage, following a second stop and an exchange of gunshots sounding like acacia seed-pods.

However at Grozny, hours later, she reels with shock: the officer, fielding and returning shouts, raises his arm, strikes the stationmaster across the face, knocking him to the ground. After the fetid carriage she is standing by the train under the

38

September noon sun, gulping mountain air; air that cured Peter's bad chest and the winter of sickness he'd had in Petersburg over five years ago, before she knew him. Into a cloudless sky thrusts a wall of razored peaks, proud, glistening, some ice-clad. A foaming river roars, flings itself against rocks. Onto a cart the White Russians are loading boxes of fish and flour requisitioned at the coast with the bread and water.

The stationmaster, short and squat, pulls himself to his feet, starts towards his passengers. 'I remember him,' Peter murmurs to her.

She looks at Peter, love splaying through her veins, marvelling again that he didn't stay here but went to Baku and couldn't get back; that they met, a particle of happiness to have come from world cataclysm. She never expected to meet anybody, for wasn't the war in Europe and against the Turks taking all the young men?

Peter feels inside one of the bedrolls, straightens up, hand in pocket.

'Denikin!' the stationmaster spits, replacing his cap on black, curly hair. Blood trickles from a cut at the side of his mouth. Murder gleams at her from almond eyes. '*Bolsheviki*!' He hawks his contempt. Froth and blood lie in the dust at his feet. He rubs the sleeve of his tunic across his mouth, glares at Peter as if defying him to show sympathy for any Russian.

'British,' Peter says.

The man jerks his head in the direction of the Whites, snarls in Russian, 'They take our land, steal our food, our goods, our oil. First the Romanovs, then the *bolsheviki*, now Denikin. We're not Russian. We're Chechen. He's angry because we have no fuel for the train. It's the Whites who've taken what we did have.'

Ancient hatreds: in a rich, velvety voice Esther once read to her a poem by Lermontov. Inspired by the Caucasus, it told of Cossack children reared on horror stories about the evil Chechens.

Peter slips his hand from his pocket. When the stationmaster has finished railing against all Russians, Peter opens his hand flat to reveal a crimson porcelain egg encased in strips of gold. Her heart bangs against her ribs as she remembers Esther giving her the egg, bought in Petersburg, for the first birthday she spent in Baku, the sort of gift she might keep a lifetime, show to grandchildren. She'd been with the family almost three months, the war in Europe only a few weeks old but delaying both her return to Petersburg and the German governess's from Berlin to Baku.

'So there is no fuel,' Peter commiserates with the Chechen.

The man shrugs. 'They take everything.'

'We need to reach Rostov.'

The stationmaster raises his eyes to the sky, spreads his hands in supplication. 'A train should leave tomorrow morning.'

'We have nowhere to stay tonight.' Peter's open hand still displays the egg.

The Chechen takes the egg, puts it in his pocket. 'Come with me.'

Inside her, a smile billows that the Chechen is not too proud to take a Russian egg; he will barter it for food, grain, perhaps fuel. She follows him and Peter across the *trakt*, a rough road alongside the railway line, to a small, single-storey stone cottage that somebody once thought to paint white. The Chechen is shouting to whoever is inside.

They fill the room with their arrival. She peers into the

gloom, inhales the warm smell of fresh bread. The Chechen must have succeeded in hoarding some grain. She feels a flutter of sympathy, congratulation almost, at this quiet success, this triumph over the big people who fight and determine people's lives the way they have done hers and Peter's.

A woman is dragging a mattress across the earth floor, dark, long-sleeved dress and pale pinafore brushing the ground. A kerchief conceals the woman's hair and forehead; when she looks up she smiles in greeting. The woman pushes the mattress into a corner, moves over to the stove in the centre of the room on which some aromatic soup is simmering. Along one wall is a bench with a table in front of it. A baby is chuckling, gurgling, in a cradle suspended from heavy beams supporting the low ceiling. A small boy in baggy trousers and shirt clutches the woman's skirt.

The stationmaster escorts his guests to the other part of the room behind a stone partition reaching shoulder height. 'You'll be better here away from the stove,' he says.

Peter puts the bedrolls on the hard earth.

❧

Three days later a train crawls into Rostov station. Stiff, exhausted, hurting with hunger, she climbs down to the platform, sick with the stink of herself. The acrid smell of coal mines catches her nostrils, just as it did five years ago when she arrived in Ekaterinoslav, to the north west; a break in the car journey from Petersburg with Yefim Aaronovich and Esther: taking off the veil tied round her hat, unbuttoning her waterproof Burberry driving coat, a gift from Esther; staying with Yefim Aaronovich's parents-in-law, who'd returned to Ekaterinoslav from Paris.

She was aching, dusty, sweaty then as well, the roads after Kiev mud tracks baked by the sun, or soft and sandy, twisting through ripening cornfields of the Ukraine. But all she had to do was hand her clothes to the maid and enjoy hot water, warm towels and *Violette de Parme* soap brought to her room. Her only concerns were deciding what to wear for dinner, and copying Esther, resting her knife on the glass knife-rest at the side of her plate, eating with her fork; and not showing surprise or curiosity when the maid placed in front of each man a glass for tea, mounted in a stand.

The last twenty-four hours have been a nightmare of heat, stench, noise, with just two stops for mountain spring water when people scrambled out of the carriages and off the roof: women in colourful garments, babies at the breast, children crying, murderous-looking old men, wiry and hardy as mountain goats, in fleecy cloaks and tall sheepskin caps. She breathed the knife-sharp air beyond Vladikavkaz, "ruler of the Caucasus", until a few years ago a spa for aristocracy. She relieved herself among boulders, and clumps of grass which she pulled loose to clean herself. Somebody emptied the sewage buckets.

The first night at the Grozny stationmaster's cottage, his shouts woke her, curses and imprecations she couldn't understand, then in Russian: they go, like the night thieves they are! The rumble of train wheels, carrying the White Russians, receded into the darkness. How mean, she thought, not to take us with them. A silver thimble, another gift to her from Esther, may have spurred the Chechen in his search for fuel for the next train. She helped his wife. Caring for babies was the same in any language. She washed George's squares with those of the Chechen baby, wiped herself with a cloth dipped in the small amount of water available. Peter walked into the centre of Grozny but told her on his return that he'd found nobody he knew, only hostile Chechen eyes staring from doorways and street corners at this Russian workman breathing their mild, velvet air. He spent the rest of the time swimming in the river or sitting in the shade of the cottage doorway, until the waning sun tinged the mountains pink.

At Rostov station, soldiers are disconnecting the engine; they're in khaki uniforms so could be British helping Whites. Carts loaded with boxes stand nearby. Soldiers indicate with rifles that the dozen or so passengers should make for the exit. She walks with Peter across the square in front of the station, George asleep against her shoulder.

'I'll come back to the station later and see what I can find out,' Peter says.

'Be careful they don't think you're a *bolshevik*.'

'I'll loiter, keep my distance.'

For now, they need a room where they can wash. She inhales the salty sea breeze along a street not even late afternoon sun can brighten. This is the town Esther's maternal *dedushka*, grandfather, came from nearly half a century ago, wearing his only suit, made by his father, leaving family ties, the rituals, wailings and prayers. He crossed the mountains to Baku where there were fortunes to be made in the new oil industry and being a Jew didn't matter as much as in other parts of Russia. The journey itself must've been an adventure. In Baku, new arrivals spent their days digging out oil by hand and taking it in drums by camel down to the port.

She follows Peter with George past dusty, empty windows which suggest most of the Rostov shops and cafes have been

43

closed for some time. Peter has turned up his jacket collar, pulled his cap over his forehead, slouching along, blending in. Holes in the road, as big as those made by shells in Baku last year, testify to the neglect of years of war. Shabbily-dressed people scuttle past as if reluctant to be out any longer than necessary.

Down an alley, Peter knocks at the door of the first tenement and asks the *dvornik* for a room.

Rheumy eyes peer with a film of suspicion. '*Burzhui*?' the *dvornik* lisps through broken teeth.

'Oil,' says Peter.

She hopes the word carries as much weight as it did in the Caucasus. Best not risk the *dvornik* suspecting they are bourgeois on the run: as well as sweeping the pavement, every *dvornik* is the eyes and ears of his building.

Hands in, out of, pockets; the glint of coin. In exchange for some roubles, the *dvornik* shuffles ahead of them up narrow, airless staircases reeking of cabbage and wet washing, to a room on the top floor. It contains a bed, a table, two chairs, a washstand.

Peter goes downstairs to fetch water then returns to the station. Half an hour later he is back. 'Trains are leaving, arriving, lots of stuff being unloaded,' he reports. 'Armed soldiers cover the entrance. You're right, darling. How do I look to them? They'll shoot rather than take time to find out whether or not I'm a *bolshevik*.'

☙

Three evenings and mornings Peter leaves her and goes to the station yard. Sometimes it is closed. At others, soldiers are loading or unloading crates from a train. This evening, he comes back coughing, bending over as if corralling whatever has got into his lungs. She glances up from ladling into wooden bowls soup brought by the *dvornik* as part of the house ration. 'Coal dust,' Peter wheezes. 'Catches your throat.' He straightens, taps his chest, squeezing his eyes closed. 'Raw.'

She looks at his thickening beard, and eyes that appear to be burrowing into their sockets. His clothes seem too big for the body she clasps each night under the thin blanket, as much for warmth as passion. They sleep dressed in readiness for departure. She wonders if Masha's father in Baku is wearing the suit Peter had to leave, the one he was married in. She pushes the idea from her mind: Baku's about eight hundred miles away; just think of survival.

'I've been to the *traktir* close to the station,' Peter says. 'Dingy place but I thought I'd drink tea and see what I could learn.'

He sits at the table, bringing with him an unwashed smell. She passes across a wedge of hard black bread. 'And?'

'I'm the only young man here. The others are dead, or fighting for the Red or White Russia of their dreams. I came away rather than draw attention to myself asking old men questions.'

She puts the ladle in its bowl and sits down. The soup suggests rotten vegetation and must've been heated twenty minutes ago.

They eat in silence.

Next morning, Peter stuffs soiled Kerensky rouble notes into his pocket. 'These are the last. Then we'll be giving the *dvornik* tsarist roubles or an ashtray.'

She is holding George over her shoulder, patting his back until he burps. 'Do you think soldiers at the station might be less inclined to shoot at a woman?'

'What do you mean?'

'I'll go.'

'I can't let you. Too risky - ' Coughing overtakes him.

'Yes, you can.'

Admiration in Peter's eyes warms her. She will do this, for him, for the two of them. 'I'm coming with you,' he insists, 'as far as the square, at least. And George stays with me.'

FOUR

Several khaki-clad soldiers are moving about. Nobody is standing guard. The muscles in her stomach are tightening as she decides what to do.

She calls from some yards away. 'Excuse me! *Izvinite*!' And again.

A soldier turns, stares at her. He has treacle-coloured hair.

She walks towards him. His shirt sleeves are rolled to above the elbow, a large patch of sweat under each armpit. How does she look to him? she wonders, in her creased, faded clothes, shawl tied round her head. 'I'm English,' she justifies herself.

'What yer doin' here?' The soldier's freckled, leathered face suggests years of exposure to a foreign sun. Lurid tattoos peep through a sandy pelt covering thick, muscular arms.

'Oh, a voice from home! What music! Three of us need to get away, towards Moscow.'

'Three of you?'

'My husband and baby.'

'Moscow's Bolshie, you know.'

'We have a permit. We speak Russian.'

The soldier whistles in amazement.

'Is the train going north?' she persists.

'This one is. Final lot.' She looks at where he is pointing, at things being loaded.

'We haven't any more Russian money;' the lie flows from

47

her; she could be speaking of other people; 'but if we could sit on a crate … how far's the train going?'

'It'll stop to offload stuff for the Whites. Where, can't say. Don't want to cross into Bolshie territory. There're bands of them roaming about. Mustn't fall into the wrong hands. But Denikin's pushing north, determined to get to Moscow.'

'How d'you know if you're in Bolshie territory?'

The soldier lets out a slew of distaste through his teeth. 'You don't, because by then it's too late.' He draws his right index finger across his throat.

She swallows. The soldier turns towards the train as if he has forgotten she is there.

She catches hold of his arm. 'You're not going to leave us, are you? Have *you* got a wife and child?'

He swings round, regards her with hard green eyes that make her wonder what he witnessed in the war: death, suffering, things men three times his age would never expect to see in a lifetime; that no man, or woman, should ever have to see, and smoke-blackened walls of the hall in Yefim Aaronovich's house jump into her mind, and … She shuts them off. Stop it. Leave me alone.

She takes her hand away from the soldier's arm as though afraid of losing it.

'Can't let you on the train,' he insists. 'I'd really be for it.'

'Then speak to somebody who can! When are you leaving?'

The soldier shrugs. 'Difficult to say. Get this lot loaded; end of the morning.'

'My husband and baby are across the square. We'll fetch our bedrolls and be back. About ten minutes, by which time I hope you'll have arranged it. What difference can it make to *you*?'

❧

She stands with George, Peter and the bedrolls on the platform. A man approaches and she notices a small silver crown on both shoulders of his khaki jacket. 'You must be the refugees,' he observes. His voice is brisk. 'There will be armed guards on the train but you understand we can take no responsibility for, or make any guarantee of, your safety. The further north you go the more likely you are to run into Bolsheviks, men who have become separated from their units: desperadoes.'

'It was a risk we knew of, Major, when we started the journey,' Peter assures him.

They walk to the last wagon. Peter takes George into the crook of his arm and with his free hand helps her up. She perches on a crate. A wooden edge jabs against the backs of her legs.

Through the high unglazed window, she can just see the soldier she spoke to stop by Peter. The soldier reaches into his pocket, draws out a green packet. 'Here,' he says to Peter.

'Thanks.' Peter takes the Woodbines, offers his hand in farewell.

The soldier clasps it. 'Got a wife and son in London. Don't s'pose I'd know the little 'un after all these years.' He holds the wagon door. Peter passes George to her, clambers up. 'Hope you get there,' the soldier says. He fastens the door.

Peter puts the packet of five cigarettes into his pocket. 'They'll be useful currency later on.'

❧

The train creaks to a halt. She waits, a tingling of apprehension in her stomach. There were several stops to unload equipment

49

from other parts of the train yesterday afternoon and into the night. All her muscles ache, stiff with chill air. Somebody is opening the wagon. She puts up a hand to shield her eyes from the light of the lamp a man is shining through the doorway.

'Passengers in this one?' There is irritation in the Russian voice.

'British,' says another Russian. 'The officer gave the order. We had no choice.'

George is waking. She holds him close to her chest, his face away from the light, her hand against the back of his bonnet. He is chuntering, almost a melody. She pats his back, hopes he cannot sense her anxiety.

'This is as far as the train goes,' one of the Russians from Rostov tells Peter. 'You have to leave.' The man coughs against the pre-dawn air, bends double.

Peter climbs down. He takes George from her then helps her off the crate. George howls an objection. Peter passes him to her. She shivers in the misty meadow rawness.

'What happens now?' she asks the half dozen Russians.

'The train goes back to Rostov,' one of them says.

'Where are we?'

'Voronezh,' another tells her. He has a cast in one eye.

'How far from Moscow?'

He thinks for a moment. 'Four hundred *versts*?'

Nearly three hundred miles. 'What are we supposed to do?'

'That's your problem. Ours is to get this lot away before the *bolsheviki* find it.'

The Russians are unloading the crates onto carts. 'We've taken Kursk,' one says to his comrade from Rostov. 'Two days ago. The General thinks we can be in Moscow next month.'

She remembers the *dvornik*'s wife in Rostov, the way the

woman's mouth twisted when speaking of the Whites: they're not interested in feeding us ordinary people, only in capturing towns; they're all on the side of the landlords and bosses. 'You don't care,' she shouts now. 'All that equipment the British have given you, and you don't care about us.'

The Russians snigger among themselves, ignore her as if she is just a foolish woman not controlled by her husband.

Peter is looking along the path at the side of the line towards an *izba*, a wooden cottage with a sloping roof. 'Is there a stationmaster?' he asks.

'*Bolshevik*,' the local Russian tells him. 'Shot dead when we took the town.'

'Family?'

'Fled.' The Russian shrugs, pulls at one end of a tarpaulin cover.

Peter glances at her. They start towards the path.

ও

In the main room of the *izba*, cupboards have been built into the corners, painted the same blue as the doors. An ikon hangs on the wall, the tilted female face appearing to look only at her, radiating compassion yet infinite sadness. Muslin curtains cover the little windows. Flowering plants on the sills droop in their pots.

There is a bedroom with one bed and a wooden cradle. Peter leaves her with George and the bedrolls and goes to see what there is outside. At the door he says, 'If anyone turns up, I'm the new stationmaster.'

'You look the part,' she assures him. She smiles at the thought, realises it is probably the first time she's done so since leaving Baku.

He made her laugh when they met that January morning

last year along the Marine Boulevard, when laughter and colour had gone out of life, when even water was rationed; and, wondering who'd make the first move, armed units of Tartars and Armenians eyed each other and the newly formed *bolshevik* Red Guard, who looked younger than her, little more than boys, collar button - if they still had one on their grey tsarist uniforms - left undone as a gesture of defiance, unbothered about a shave or hair cut, sharing their weapons with workmen who had no uniform, held rifles the wrong way up and sauntered along with a slackness no soldier would've dared show in the old days.

She was with five-year-old Jacob and Anton Yefimovich. Every morning, after giving them their bread portion soaked in sour milk, she took them for a walk, an English custom that amused their mother: 'You all three come back hot and dusty and have to change your clothes. What's the point, Livvy?'

'The exercise does them good, Nadia Ephraimovna,' she defended herself. 'Jacob's always less boisterous when he's had half an hour's walk.'

They passed flat-roofed, ostentatious, European-style buildings made possible by oil wealth. Square balconies looked to have been stuck on as an afterthought. She sometimes slept on the one beyond the French windows in her room, under a lawn sheet, edges embroidered by Nadia Ephraimovna, initials entwined in one corner.

The boys were in their English sailor suits, brought from Petersburg three and a half years before when all things English were *la mode* in Russia as the Tsarina was a granddaughter of Queen Victoria. Since then, she'd lengthened and let out the suits, and widened them further with offcuts of material.

Smells of oil, fish, the sea, lingered in the mild air around them. Peter's attention had been caught by Jacob chattering. 'A little boy with such good English,' Peter said to her, lifting his hat. 'You must be Livvy.'

Flustered that he should know her name – she later learnt he'd heard of her from Charlotte: have you met the nice English girl who looks after the two youngest Markovitch children? Charlotte had asked him; had Charlotte, even then, marked them out as suitable for each other? - dazzled by his eyes and smile, she was sure she'd seen him before, in another existence, except she'd been with Esther.

'Petersburg? Yes! The hatband! I still have it.'

'You were going to Baku.'

'You were going to Grozny. You'd been ill, still were, in fact.'

June 1914, her last evening in Petersburg, and his too as it happened, they'd been among dozens of British people strolling along the Neva's granite embankment in the salty breeze to meet sailors from four British ships, there as an expression of good will between King George and his cousin Tsar Nicholas. A sailor from the *Princess Royal* had given his hatband to Esther: just as a souvenir, Miss.

And your friend can have this one, another English voice had added. Not a sailor, his grey suit hung on him as if made for somebody bigger. He was coughing. I'm leaving tomorrow, he explained; it'll only be extra to pack.

Something about the man's heart-shaped face – sadness, illness? – stopped her from pointing out a hatband wouldn't take up much room as he gave it to her. After a few words about being ill he disappeared into the crowd and she never even learnt his name.

Here he was again, certainly not ill. He introduced himself, explained he'd just come from the bank, arranging the transfer of his money from Grozny.

'Talk about obstruction!' Peter spread his hands in a gesture of helplessness. His suit still looked a size too big. She wondered if it was the same one as in Petersburg. He had what Mama would've called a generous mouth. 'Two scruffy individuals in leather jackets informed me they were commissars appointed by the *soviet*. "All money and property in Grozny belong to the people, Comrade",' Peter mimicked in a flat voice.

Her face creased in silent laughter. She put a hand there to conceal it. This was a serious matter. The Baku *soviet* consisted of fifty-two workers. She said, 'The *bolsheviki* are not in power here.'

'Not yet,' Peter conceded. 'But that doesn't stop the *soviet* looking after workers' interests. They invent their own rules.'

'Yes, they've set up a military revolutionary committee with its own court.' She kept meeting his eyes, glancing away because the warmth from his gaze and smile was like the sun, too bright to hold, burning her cheeks. 'Yefim Aaronovich says his desk is covered with papers from the *soviet*: terms under which workers can be hired and sacked, their pay, the number of hours they can work: not more than eight out of twenty-four.'

'So they've got somebody who can write.' Peter was dismissive. 'As soon as I told them at the bank I was an oil engineer, they became more co-operative. They need our expertise in oil, their liquid gold. I still had to wait while they consulted someone else. They came back and informed me that when they could get through to Grozny on the telephone, they'd arrange for the transfer of three hundred roubles a month.

Three hundred!'

'Only a few pounds at today's rates,' she commiserated.

'"It is the order."' Peter adopted the commissar's voice again and this time she allowed the laugh. He smiled. 'Order, my foot. They make it up as they go along.'

'Why did you come to Russia?' she asked him.

'Oh, the romance of it - don't you think so? - this vast, remote country of Pushkin, Turgenev. And in 1913, the Ballets Russes gave the first performance of Monsieur Stravinsky's *The Rite of Spring* in Paris.'

Peter paused, as if allowing her space in which to say something. Pushkin and Turgenev she'd heard of, although knew nothing of their work. The ballet Peter mentioned was new to her. She hoped he wouldn't realise this and think less of her.

Peter went on, 'It's very savage, barbaric, a pagan worship of spring. The girl dances herself to death. There was a riot among the audience. When I read about it, I just had to come to Russia, see the country that had produced such a thing. My twin sister had already left home. She went to Canada the summer of the Coronation and stayed there. So I applied for an engineering job in Petersburg.'

'I hope you weren't disappointed.'

'It all turned out rather differently: bronchitis the whole of that first winter - '

She nodded, remembering what he'd said in Petersburg.

' - bitter cold, damp winds, swirling mists. Who'd build a city on a swamp? The doctor insisted the Caucasus was the place to cure bad chests. All that mountain air. And mare's milk.'

'And you've been all right here on the coast?'

'Never better.'

'Why did you give me the hatband in Petersburg?'

'Not only was I ill, I was homesick; didn't want anything to remind me of Petersburg or England.'

Jacob and Anton were sitting on the cobbles, poking the sand. 'We must go,' she said. 'Up you get, boys.'

They did as they were told. Their boots were laced past their ankles. A dusty car screeched along, decorated with red cockades, exhaust roaring. Five men crouched inside, two more on either step and on the box, a couple lying along the mudguards, propped up on their arms, round each of which was a red band. Flags the same colour flew from bayonets fixed to rifles protruding through a smashed window. A Maxim machine gun was mounted on the roof. Anton gripped her hand.

Jacob stood with legs apart and stared up at Peter. 'That might be Papa's car,' Jacob said to him. 'They stole it. Do you work for my papa? He's a good man and kind to his workers.' Jacob stepped back to Anton and took his other hand. Only in appearance were the twins identical: wide foreheads, dark eyes, their mother's full lips.

Peter patted Jacob's cap. 'He is indeed, young man.'

'We love Miss Livvy,' Jacob told Peter. 'She's my sister's friend. We all love her.'

Peter looked at her. 'That's not difficult to imagine.'

She allowed Peter's eyes to hold hers for a moment before busying herself straightening the boys' collars. She was glad to be wearing her straw hat, not the blue shawl she tied round her head for the port or bazaars.

'We read *Chatterbox* with Miss Livvy,' Jacob volunteered.

'Brought from Petersburg that summer,' she told Peter.

'And *Children's Friend*,' Anton contributed.

'Then we sing,' Jacob enlarged. *'One, two, buckle my shoe -'*

'I don't think Mr Boulton wants to hear this, Jacob.'

But Peter, smiling indulgence, seemed in no hurry to leave.

'Three, four, knock at the door.' With the knuckles of one hand Jacob rapped on the palm of the other. Anton shaped his right hand into a fist, waved it in the air without aggression.

'Five, six, gather sticks,' both boys continued.

Peter said, 'I walked here from the bank to calm myself down. The sea always does me good.' He put his hand on Anton's cap. 'I'm pleased I did.'

He offered her his hand in farewell. It was warm, strong. She looked at his eyes just long enough to say, 'I hope your money comes through soon.'

When she and the twins set out the next few mornings, Jacob enthused, 'Perhaps we'll see Mr Boulton again.'

'Perhaps, Jacob,' she replied. But she thought it unlikely. He had his work to do. Yet, she found herself hoping she would see him, this man who'd come to Russia in search of the romance of Turgenev and Pushkin. She'd just been grateful still to have a job caring for the three young Clayton children after eight months with the family in London. Mr Clayton had taken a three-year appointment as manager of the British-owned Petersburg Waterworks.

What had been her idea of Russia then? Long, freezing winters, bears in forests, and a picture, *Princess in the Snow*, in a book she'd had as a child. The artist had portrayed a young woman swathed in furs, reclining in a sledge pulled by three horses. The snow-covered waste continued as far as the horizon, where stood a church, on top of which were five onion-shaped domes. And she'd learnt about the Crimean War with Miss

Handley for matriculation history: the siege of Sebastopol, the battles of Balaclava and Inkerman ... *into the valley of death rode the six hundred.*

In spite of being surrounded by speech she could not understand, writing she could not read, the reality enchanted her: a rippling Neva, blue and sparkling in Petersburg's May and June sunlight, graceful buildings on either side – grey, pink, blue - reflections playing in the water; silver, gold and black uniforms or the cheerful shabbiness of University students in their bottle green caps and trousers, and black jackets.

She had the most awful to-do with Mrs Clayton when after six weeks she announced she'd accepted a summer job in Baku with the family of an oil industrialist and would be leaving at the end of the week. Mrs Clayton called her a naughty, selfish girl. Mr Clayton offered her a hundred roubles a month, the same as Yefim Aaronovich was going to pay her.

Mrs Clayton, whose pinched, tired face was enlivened in moments of crisis by a patch of red on each cheek, found nothing about Petersburg to delight her: the hard bread, the money - I can't even read it, she complained, holding a one-rouble note between thumb and forefinger as if it would contaminate her - the night, or lack of, for it was the time of the White Nights when a glow of mother-of-pearl and amber illuminated the northern sky and tugboats wailed on the Neva. Then there was the *dvornik*, who took Mr Clayton's passport to register with the police the family's arrival in Petersburg, a miasma of stale garlic and tobacco drifting between misshapen teeth the colour of old piano keys; he bolted the outside door of the building at eleven, even during the White Nights, and expected ten kopeks to open it again. Makes me feel like a prisoner, Mrs

Clayton shrilled, not that she was out after eleven, or at all, after being jostled off the pavement: they smelt, Livvy, onions and drink; they wouldn't stand aside to let me pass; they're all thieves and robbers.

About Yefim Aaronovich's family, Mrs Clayton warned: they could lock you in, Livvy, and have all sorts of horrid, foreign ways.

ॐ

Peter brings in a wooden bucket of water from the well behind the *izba*. 'There's a row of carrots look about ready,' he tells her, 'and a chicken scratching round the yard.'

She straightens up from placing George in the cradle, still smiling at the memory of meeting Peter along the Marine Boulevard. She goes back into the main room, sits on one of the benches that surround the table. Peter puts the bucket down, stands behind her, his hands on her shoulders. She trembles, longing for the feel of him naked.

He kisses the top of her head. 'If I manage to catch and kill the chicken, you can pluck it, take out the insides, make us a lovely meal with the carrots.'

'And soup from what's left,' she says. 'We might be here several days.' She turns her head to him. 'We'll have to get the stove going.' She looks at it in the centre of the room, clay, rectangular, four or five feet across.

'There're piles of brown chunks in the yard,' Peter says. 'Probably dried dung.' He is massaging her shoulders, his fingers gentle, rhythmic. She closes her eyes, drifts. 'What was amusing you just now?' he asks. 'It's nice to see you smile again.'

'Remembering meeting you along the Marine Boulevard, the same person as that last evening in Petersburg, and the boys singing to you.' She stands up, faces him, and they put their arms round each other.

'In Petersburg, I thought you were very grand travelling to the Caucasus by car,' Peter says. He places his hand under her chin.

'And in Baku was I still grand?'

She closes her eyes, gives herself to his kiss, parting her lips beneath his, clinging to him. He is lifting her skirt, stroking her thighs, pushing down her drawers. He fumbles with the buttons of his trousers and she guides him.

She holds him to her long after they are both still.

FIVE

In the garden of the stationmaster's *izba*, she picks not only carrots but lettuce and beetroot. Black soil clings to her fingers, staining, tucking under nails and in the cracks where nails join skin. The leaves of a cherry tree hang as if sensing their end. Hollyhocks, pink and smiling, border a swing: a plank and four lengths of rope fixed to a beam. She pictures children playing here. In every direction the land is flat and verdant, the Russian heartland unchecked by sea or mountain for hundreds of miles, for which people are killing each other. Rooks circle the green cupola of a church, sole relief in a hazy, yellow September sky, their cawing the only sound in sleepy silence.

The *izba* is built of tree trunks, ends overlapping those of the wall at right angles, gaps caulked with oakum. Peter is sitting on the bench outside the door, in the roof shade. He has dismissed any idea of walking the mile or so to Voronezh in search of flour or bread. They must always be ready to leave.

He succeeds in catching the chicken. She stands indoors, eyes closed, lips pursed, wishing she could stop her ears against the creature's desperate squawking and flapping, until a gasp from Peter puts an end to it. The meal she produces, eaten with wooden spoons and bowls from the corner cupboard, is voted the best since leaving Baku. Into smoky, sweetened air of burnt dung, they raise tin mugs to each other, containing clear water.

'Lullaby and goodnight,' she sings to George, as her mother did to her and her brothers.

'Let angels of light
Spread wings round your bed
And guard you from dread.'

George shakes his arms, bunches his fists, gurgling enjoyment. As soon as she settles him to sleep she wants to lift him out, feel his face against hers, inhale the aroma of warmth, her own milk.

With sunset, a gentle nocturnal stillness enfolds the *izba*. Snug from the stove's dying embers, she sleeps fitfully, alert for intruders or the welcome rattle of a train. A wild drake calls, distant, hoarse, and his mate quacks a reply near at hand. Hurried, invisible wings scrabble, whistle in the darkness. She takes turn with Peter as lookout.

In the morning, sun evaporates the dew. She splashes her face with water Peter has brought in. In Baku, distilled seawater was delivered to the house each day in horse-drawn barrels, Tartars prodding the creatures with a stick or dusty foot. The first few weeks she was with Yefim Aaronovich's family, a ginger-haired, freckle-faced Russian lad – Ivan was his name - came in to help the servants distribute water to the bedrooms, which were on the second floor. The rest was for the kitchen. Ivan also carried in wood for the cooking range. When Germany declared war on Russia, he said he'd been ordered to Tiflis, capital of the Caucasus. Sniffing, shifting from foot to foot, bowing, he took his leave of the family from the kitchen doorway into the hall, insisting he'd come back as soon as he could. She noticed his shoes were worn through at the toes.

She never saw him again.

From the *izba* she watches people arrive on the platform along-side the railway line: peasant women in short padded coats, coloured kerchiefs round their heads; old men in faded shirts belted over trousers tucked into leggings that appear to have been made from birch bark. Peter talks to them, acting, a shrug, hands wide. When the sun lowers and shadows lengthen, they drift away only to return with daylight and resume their vigil. She imagines herself, Peter and George staying here some time, cultivating the garden, safe in this quiet corner far from those who need to fight. Most of the time she's known Peter they've lived with the threat of riot, massacre. To be somewhere this doesn't happen, now she's away from Baku, is creating a long-ing, an ache in her bones, in the core of her.

There was fighting in Baku when she and Peter chanced upon one another a couple of months after their encounter along the Marine Boulevard last year. And that time she was wearing the blue shawl round her head rather than the straw hat.

She knew her way through the maze of arms' width streets in the Tartar Quarter; knew which were blind alleys where there was barely room to squeeze between houses; knew where cobbles were more widely spaced, less flat, making her likely to trip. But that morning she'd found all the cupboard-like shops shuttered, no saddles, carpets, rope, laid out for sale, or pots, utensils, gold and silver dishes and jewellery; no trades-men squatting with an abacus for leisurely calculations, hands spread in regret at the small amount of food they had to sell, perhaps some chicken feet and wrinkled peppers; no smells of spices, people, mutton-grease candles, just drains and fear, a few individuals hurrying to some windowless door - such paint as clung to it mellowed by age to terracotta - and the sanctuary of whatever medieval, ramshackle house lay behind it. A man wearing a *papakh*, a fur fez, pointed behind him, the direction in which she was going. From between toothless gums came words she didn't understand while he kept on walking.

With shops closed, streets looked different as if buildings and alleys had clustered for company. It wasn't so easy to find her way. She felt more peril than when jostling strangers and laden donkeys. As soon as she heard the stutter of gunfire and glimpsed soldiers the other end of the Bashennaya she pressed against the cold damp stone of an alley that never saw the sun.

Further up the alley a child ran from one doorway to another which was half open. Brightly-coloured washing flapped in the breeze. A woman's voice, unintelligible, raised in anger, was answered by a wail of protest. A half-starved cat lurked in the corner.

After a few minutes, someone else edged into the alley, a hand first, fingers feeling over stone, then an arm, a man's black jacket. Shivering, sweating, heart beating a pulse of fear, she backed further in. When the man turned and she realised it was Peter, relief surged through her to see a friendly face and the shawl didn't matter. Relief, and also joy, unlike anything she'd experienced, an intoxicating drink, undiluted happiness oblivious to heavy boots along the cobbles outside the alley; to shouts, groaning. To everything.

Peter held her hands against his chest. This time, she didn't look away from his gaze but basked in the sunshine radiating from his eyes and smile, breathing in unfamiliar, masculine smells of soap and tobacco mingled with a whiff of petroleum. She could feel his heartbeat, strong and perfect. She wondered what it would be like if he kissed her. She'd never kissed a man. There were short bristles on his cheeks and jaw, as if he hadn't shaved. He'd come to the Tartar Quarter searching for food for his landlady. Three Tartar snipers on the next roof down were concentrating on the Red Guard at the end of the street. In a matter of months the Red Guard had become a disciplined force.

When more shots came from down the street Peter put his arms round her shoulders, resting her head against his neck. She tried to print the moment on her brain, fearful it would pass and she'd lose it forever.

'We must get you home,' he said against her hair. He eased away from her and she felt a chill of separation. At the end of the alley he leaned flat against the wall. He glanced down the street then back to her. 'They've gone. We should set off now while it's clear. Along the port.'

'It's the quickest way from here.'

He took her hands. The softness of his lips against them sent a ripple of pleasure through her.

At the door of Yefim Aaronovich's house he asked, 'Can I call tomorrow evening, Livvy?' allowing the possibility she might refuse.

'Yes, of course.' She couldn't bear the thought of not seeing him again after a second chance meeting.

Later that day, however, the real violence began: three days of gunfire, the roar and boom of heavy artillery, and flames rising from the Tartar Quarter of the city. In the house, doors and windows locked and shuttered, trying to keep the boys occupied, she kept wondering where Peter was, praying he was safe. She can still see Yefim Aaronovich's bloodshot eyes when he returned home, unshaven, clothes smeared with blood and dirt; and the sour smell he brought with him. Wrapped in blankets, he and Peter had hidden all night in the administration block at the oilfield when Armenians from the city rampaged through looking for Tartars; not one Tartar was left alive there. The *bolsheviki* went to the oilfield to announce themselves as the new masters in the city. They helped bury the dead.

During the weeks that followed, Peter called for her most evenings. The domes of the Armenian cathedral rising behind, they strolled down steep, acacia-lined cobbles, wind whipping dust around them, to the Marine Boulevard which was illuminated by electricity. Sometimes, oil was set ablaze on the water, flaring skyward red, pink, orange as though in premonition of the Day of Judgement. Were they the only people on whom fortune smiled and bestowed her magic, they mused, while the rest of the world tore itself apart? She became fearful that suddenly something would break the spell, let daylight in.

She and Peter would look out at ships of all sizes, lights glowing, bobbing, on the Caspian. The sea might be a writhing plume of white, another day a gleaming sheet of metal. The Caspian had the shape of a sea horse's head, did he know? the peninsula on which Baku stood an indentation in the back of the creature's skull.

No, he hadn't known, looked at her as if anything she might say, even a recitation of *One, two, buckle my shoe*, would be a new enchantment to him. She loved the way his eyes rested on her, as though she were essential to him, and she could gaze at him, too.

Was this what her stepmother Rose felt for Father, and he for her? Was this falling in love: a pounding, overwhelming exhilaration, yes, literally like tumbling; the shock of each other at every meeting; a dawning impossibility of living one without the other; an exclusive feeling of completeness when she was alone with him; shutting out even her, where Rose and Father were concerned?

She told Peter she'd left her two younger brothers in Norwich with their father and stepmother. 'She was insufferable. Made it clear there wasn't room for us both. Yet, I'd been looking after Father and the boys for over two years after Mama died, which meant giving up the Grammar School. I was in my third year there. I had a scholarship.'

Father's eyes, the same blue as hers, had stared from his sombre face when he told her he couldn't afford to keep her at school and pay somebody to run the home and take care of the four of them; his hand was on her shoulder, the same hand that had clasped her to him following Mama's death from diphtheria. Neighbours had been helping out but floors went unswept and one morning Father had left for work in an unironed shirt. This can't go on, she'd told herself, and so her answer was ready: I'll look after us, Papa. It'll mean giving up school, he warned, matriculation, teacher training. Never mind, she hugged him.

'What did your brothers think of their stepmother?' Peter asked.

'They didn't seem bothered. Arthur, just a couple of years younger than me, said: at least she can cook. When I pointed out that I could, too, he said: you know what I mean. I didn't. Boys see things differently. He'd finished school and was at work with Father. Rose suggested I go back to studying. I think she just wanted me out of the house but I did, for two hours a week matriculation coaching. Do you know Norwich?'

Peter shook his head, his expression making her feel Norwich must be the most special place on earth.

'I went to Miss Handley's terraced home on Elm Hill,' she told him, 'a rabbit warren of old streets near the Cathedral. Miss Handley always smelled of camphor.' Peter was smiling. 'It wasn't the same as school and my heart wasn't in it. Even so, had I stayed I'd probably have taken the matriculation exams the following year.'

One morning Rose said: I saw Ernest Walker's mother yesterday - Rose didn't look up from rolling out pastry on the deal table in the kitchen - he's doing very well at Banners. Rose glanced to gauge her reaction; had a rounded figure and a smile that never reached the eyes. Has prospects, Livvy. But she was not going to let herself be married off; and in any case, Ernest Walker had spots and pebble-lens spectacles.

'The final straw was when Rose put photographs of Mama with me and the boys away in a drawer,' she told Peter.

He held her hands. 'That must all have been very hard.'

You shouldn't have moved the photographs, she chastised Rose. When you have one, Livvy, you'll realise a woman likes to be mistress in her own home, Rose snapped. This is my home, Rose ... as a child, yes, Rose interrupted; you're not a child, Livvy. From Rose, she learnt the power of words to wound.

'When I told Father about it,' she explained to Peter, 'he refused to say anything to Rose.'

Let her please herself, Livvy, Father said. Sadness clouded his eyes. She and Father were in the sitting room, which smelt of lavender polish. The window was open, a breeze filling out Rose's chintz curtains like a sail; Rose had had new ones made for every room, chosen from the drapery department of the Co-operative store in Norwich where Father was manager.

But Rose has no right to move our photographs without asking, she persisted. It is her home, too, Father pointed out; I'd hoped you and Rose would become friends. How can I be friends with someone who resents my being here?

While Rose had taught her the power of words to wound, those moments with Father gave her another lesson: injury caused by lack of words. Suddenly she felt alone, cast off into a void from this man whom she'd loved and looked after unconditionally as if they were an extension of each other and from whom she was now separate. 'I felt he didn't care,' she told Peter. 'That was the hardest part. Since then, if I've thought about him at all it's been as Father, not Papa.'

She looked away from Peter. It was nearly five years since she'd left home on her eighteenth birthday, everybody busy with their own concerns. Nobody had needed her or would bother if she wasn't there. She'd taken the photographs and placed in her room a note torn from the middle of an exercise book: *I am going away for a while.* The wound healed, in time, but like an old scar still ached if prodded.

Peter and his twin sister were the oldest of seven, she learnt. Another sister had died as a baby. His father manufactured bicycles in Birmingham.

∽

In Baku, that summer of 1918, the *bolsheviki* imposed a night curfew. Peter wore the wristwatch given to him by his father when he graduated from Birmingham University in 1912, so made sure he was in time to leave her at Yefim Aaronovich's door after the evening walk and climb the hill to his lodgings by ten o'clock. She would see him run along the street. She hated the separation and that she had to share him with people at his lodgings, at the oilfield and refinery.

One evening in early July, standing in the Mikhailovski Gardens in the fragrance of yellow acacia among shadows thrown by spluttering gas lamps, he asked her to marry him. 'I want you with me,' he said; 'to take care of you.'

She looked into his eyes, gave him her trust. 'For the rest of our lives,' she promised. They would always be together, the essence of each other. There would be no casting off.

She didn't write to her father to tell him she was to be married. 'There's been no contact for years,' she reminded Peter; 'he let me go, didn't care.' Was it incomprehension or even hurt she saw in his eyes, as if their marriage wasn't reason enough?

'The longer you leave it, the more difficult it is,' was all he said.

Charlotte escorted her up the aisle of the English Church to marry him later that month. It was in Charlotte's dining room afterwards that English and Russian friends sat down to a meal of shared rations, sturgeon, bread, rice, fruit, and somebody produced a bottle of local wine. And it was in Charlotte's guest room that he unpinned her hair, unfastened her dress, kissing her neck, her shoulders, the dress falling round her stockinged feet on a green, gold and terracotta rug on polished tiles, a bowl of rose petals and herbs infusing the room with musk. She gave herself up to the freedom that was theirs, no curfew, farewell or separation; to the thrill of his touch, rough hair on his skin, softness of lips and tongue, their gasps of delight smothered by Turkish guns booming a few miles away and wind screaming against the shutters.

Their fourth afternoon in the stationmaster's *izba*, hottest time of day even in late September. He is sitting across the doorway, knees drawn up, and can look in at Livvy, something he loves when he thinks she's not aware of him. She's been wonderful this last week, the way she got them away from Rostov with the cargo for the White Russians, the meal she made their first evening here - the chicken was quite tender - and how she's kept George contented. She is on a bench now against a wall, leaning towards George asleep in the cradle. The sun creates a shadow across the earth floor. His breath catches, the stardust of more than a year, and an awareness almost of unbelief presses on him, too much to absorb, all he has been given: Livvy, dearest darling, the tilt of her head on the rare occasions she laughs, that air of slight reserve only he has breached, full lips capable of passion he alone has unleashed.

And George. How devoted Livvy is to their son, created from their flesh. The first time he held George in Baku, baby face puffed and red from crying, the rest swaddled by Masha in white material the Russian way – every evening after Masha had gone, he and Livvy undid the bindings to gaze at this adorable child they'd made, and in the mornings Masha would frown, Livvy used to say, at the clumsy attempt at re-binding which lacked Russian tightness – but the first time he held his son he felt his legs wouldn't support him and George went quiet, looked at him as if to say: we belong together. He drank in this precious new life for which he was responsible, perfectly formed nose and mouth, faint line where one day there would be eyebrows … one day … that was when he knew he wanted his son to grow up in England.

Tears sting the rims of his eyes, that he should have so much, and that it could be taken from him. If this is paradise, must it not by its very nature be transient, a glimpse, not a permanent earthly state? Yet, watching the miracle of his wife and son he could forget there are still nearly a thousand miles to Archangel, with no knowledge of how they are going to get there, or feed themselves, or now, in the next few hours, minutes even, who might arrive at the *izba* and demand entry.

When he walked into Grozny from the stationmaster's cottage last week, leaving Livvy helping the wife, did he hope to see his mistress again? Maybe. Probably not. All he could feel for her then was gratitude for their year or more together, a fire that burnt itself out. Perhaps British civilians in Grozny had been evacuated to Persia. He hopes she is safe and managing a degree of contentment with her husband.

☙

She looks up from the cradle. From the open doorway where he is sitting, Peter blows her a kiss, gossamer wings off his fingertips, then turns to face the path to the railway track.

She returns to George. She could spend hours watching him sleep, the marvel of him, thumb against his mouth. She wonders if her mother felt like this about her and her brothers, if it's the same each time. Of course, there will be other babies but she hopes she can have a year or so with just George. One day she will tell him about this journey. Where will they be?

She wishes she could talk to her mother about George, that Mama could see him, hold him, feel the warm certainty of him. The day her waters broke was a general strike in Baku. Peter had left for the oilfield, nonetheless. It was Masha who helped her to bed, turned her onto her side, told her to take deep breaths and not roll onto her back. Masha fetched *baboushka* Agafia, who delivered all the babies in the Black Town, a toothless muttering crone who greased her and eased out her baby.

She and Peter named him after the King; patriotism, perhaps nostalgia.

She can't share any of this with Mama. She used to go to Mama's grave after Father married Rose, and Rose was busy blackleading the grate and kettle, pink cheeks flushed, curls of blond hair escaping from under a mob-cap. Rose mixed sand, flour and vinegar to scour the outsides of copper pans as if to impress new ownership on them.

She would sit on warm grass, trace with a finger black lettering on Mama's grey headstone: *Victoria Olivia Turner, died 28th November 1909 in her 39th year*. She remembered hair the same chestnut as her own, the piano on Sunday evenings. Another good mark in English, Mama would exclaim, hugging her, and a glow had spread through her, that she'd do well at school if only to please Mama. Don't mind them, love, Mama had soothed when small Arthur and Victor squabbled: they're fox cubs sorting out the territory; they'll grow out of it. She looked up at the wide Norfolk sky. A damp rag dipped in the ashes is good enough for the fender and fire irons, isn't it, Mama? That's what I used, same as you did. Rose insists on emery paper, says they have to have a shine you can see your face in. Why did she have to come here, Mama? We were fine as we were, Papa, me and the boys; and you were right, they don't fight as much. They're building a den in the garden. Neither appears to realise the other thinks he's in charge. Papa seems tired. I hope he's happy. If he is, it can't be because of Rose.

But, she had to admit there were never raised voices, and

sometimes when she was in her room, seething, hating the chintz, she might hear the tinkle of female laughter and the deeper tones of her father's voice.

Fearsome in its intensity those eighteen months with Rose was the question that never budged: what am I going to do?

Peter says she will get on well with his mother. But doesn't it need more than having the same colour hair? Peter's mother was a member of Mrs Pankhurst's Women's Social and Political Union, and force-fed in prison. In the Baku apartment, there was a head and shoulders photograph of his parents, solemn-looking, impossible to imagine them feeling anything. Peter left it there because they will see his parents soon.

She wants to like his mother.

&

Has Peter noticed it, too? A rumbling, disturbing of the silence. 'I heard something,' she says.

Peter is running to the railway line. 'Yes!' he shouts. 'A train!'

She gathers George in his shawl. Peter rushes back for the bedrolls. The train is out of sight, a chugging announcing its approach. The peasants on the platform are scrambling to their feet. The train comes into view and she wants to cheer. But she stays silent like those who are standing with their bundles, expressionless, gaunt-eyed.

She does wave when the train is near. The driver, too, raises a hand. She hears singing but can't understand the words except for *Lenin s Trotskim*, Lenin and Trotsky, *bolshevik* leaders, she remembers. She holds George to her chest, palm against the back of his head, glances at the *izba*, already missing its security like a boat cast from moorings.

The train is stopping, and the singing. Men with rifles are

74

jumping down to the platform, eyes blazing, greasy hair blowing around haggard faces although some are wearing winter caps, flaps up; others, kerchiefs tied behind the neck, while one sports a lady's bonnet. They all have new boots, like the ones the White Russian officer was wearing the other day. They may be Whites, she decides, their song against Lenin and Trotsky. She turns away from vodka fumes and the smell of vomit swirling towards her; from a soldier relieving himself on the track.

'Passengers in the back wagon!' one of the soldiers is directing with authority. His cap is perched to the left side of his head. 'We're going to Moscow!'

His accent she recognises as the lilting speech of the Caucasus she and Peter adopted through years of living there but never expected to hear again.

'Long live the Russia of the *soviets*!' the soldier shouts.

So they are *bolsheviki*. The British officer in Rostov the other day said there were likely to be *bolshevik* bands in the area: men separated from their units, were his words; desperadoes. She wants to go back to the *izba*, to the moments before she heard the train; to the peace, stillness, safety she fears may have gone forever.

She looks at the *bolshevik* in charge as she walks to the back wagon, Peter at her side; suddenly feels her legs are going to give way, as if someone has punched her in the stomach. She keeps George against her protesting heartbeat. She is breathing in long gasps. The soldier has a purple scar from left cheek to jawbone. It sits taut in leathery skin making that half of his face lopsided. The first time she saw it, if it's the same one, it was a livid wound a week old, the day she arrived at Yefim Aaronovich's house in Baku with Esther. His eldest son, Esther's twin, came down the marble staircase to meet them and Esther shrieked: Lev!

In horror rather than greeting.

SIX

In the wagon, she holds George in his mountaineering position. He is asleep, lulled by the movement of the train, his head turned towards her on her shoulder. She is separated from Peter by bedrolls, other passengers. Those who'd been waiting at Voronezh expressed surprise that the stationmaster and his family were travelling, too. I was just a stand-in, Peter told them; they're sending a replacement from Moscow; I go all over the country, wherever they say.

The *bolshevik* soldier might not be Esther's brother, she reasons. Plenty of men must have scarred faces after years of war in Europe and against the Turks, not to mention that most vicious of fighting, between people from the same area, same family even, White and Red Russians.

And yet ... Lev Yefimovich stayed in Baku in June 1914 when his father, sister and the German governess went to Petersburg. He was just sixteen and had one more year to do at the *gimnaziya* in Baku. He was expected to be top of his year and receive the gold medal. A university place was not assured, however: since earlier that year the Jewish quota, ten per cent, had been decided by drawing lots.

While Yefim Aaronovich was away, there was a strike at the oilfield. Lev Yefimovich went there one morning to see what was happening and walked into his father's men marching towards the city to demand better accommodation, shorter hours. Lev Yefimovich joined them. Cossacks rode at them to restore order, make them go back to work, whips tipped with leather and lead brooking no opposition.

When Yefim Aaronovich returned to Baku, his voice and that of his son raised in argument echoed through the house from the ground-floor study. She couldn't understand what they were saying but Esther, weeping with shock and distress, told her Lev Yefimovich was taking the men's side; some had been killed.

At mealtimes during her first week in Baku - lamb roasted with pomegranates, or stewed in sour milk were favourites of the family's Armenian cook – she would look across the table at Lev Yefimovich, trying to avoid the wound; after that first day, it wasn't spoken of nor the reason for it. Nadia Ephraimovna, who'd already done a year's medical training when she married Yefim Aaronovich, cleaned and dressed the wound each morning before Lev Yefimovich accompanied his father to the oilfield or the refinery in the Black Town.

At the table, she regarded Lev Yefimovich with fascination: dark hair curled away from his forehead; new wire-rimmed spectacles, for the old ones had been smashed in the riot, gave him a studious appearance. She'd never met anybody who believed with such passion in a cause. Rona, a friend from grammar school in Norwich, had asserted that women should have the vote and choice of an independent life but had done nothing more than cut her hair.

It didn't seem a lot to ask for, better accommodation, although Esther had warned her there were agitators, sent to make trouble.

'Why?' she'd asked Esther.

Esther had shrugged, her oval face and thin lips unsmiling; her eyes widened, the translucent lids appearing to darken. 'To make trouble, Livvy. Papa's overseen a lot of improvements at his oilfield and built a pharmacy. But some decisions, like hours of work and pay, have to be arrived at by all the oilfield owners together.'

Esther and her brother were three when *dedushka*, their grandfather, was murdered at his oilfield, stabbed by a Tartar workman taking literally the call for a show of force against employers. Yefim Aaronovich, already *dedushka*'s engineer and married to his eldest daughter, inherited everything. The young family moved from the apartment in the Black Town to the house in the centre of Baku which *dedushka* had had built in the 1870s; a strongbox in the corner of the study contained deeds to oil bearing land leased to him by Tsar Alexander the second in 1872. Yefim Aaronovich's new wealth, however, brought another tragedy. His wife, already weakened by the birth of her twin son and daughter, never recovered from her father's murder; she died the following year of typhoid. On her bedside table, Esther had a photograph of *dedushka*; her sole memory was of a serious, unsmiling man whose whiskers and moustache had prickled and smelt of tobacco when she was lifted up for a kiss.

When, one morning a few days after her arrival, she passed Lev Yefimovich on the landing between the first and second staircases, she told him he was right to support the men.

'You are blessed, Miss Livvy, coming from a country that allows free speech.' He spoke English with confidence. Some years his father had engaged an English tutor for him during the holidays, while Esther had had an English governess for a year before the German one. He turned to continue down the stairs.

Lev Yefimovich was a few months younger than her brother Arthur. She was used to brothers. She searched for something to detain him, to know what he really thought. 'Esther tells me you have another year at school.'

He swivelled round to face her. 'That is correct, Miss Livvy.'

'What will you do then?' she pursued.

'I may go to university. My father and I have different opinions. He wishes me to study in the United States, where my uncle is, and return to join him in the oil business.'

Something else they were arguing about that evening? she wondered.

'Your father studied abroad,' she pressed on.

It was as if she'd released a spring. Fervour leapt into Lev Yefimovich's eyes. 'Five years in Paris. But to gain right of residence in Petersburg so he could sit the examinations at the Technical Institute as an extern, he had to register as a *butler*.' Disgust twisted Lev Yefimovich's mouth. Beads of sweat glistened on his forehead. 'That is the sort of thing we Jews have to do. Jews are prohibited from becoming army officers, lawyers,' he counted off the fingers of his left hand, 'civil servants, teachers. Do you know what that Cossack spat as he lashed at my face? "Filthy Yid".'

She realised she was holding her breath. She let it go, trembling.

'Is it any wonder we are vilified as revolutionaries?' Lev Yefimovich asked, as if she might supply an answer. 'What other opening is there?'

Revolution? Was that why Yefim Aaronovich wanted his

son to go to the United States? To keep him away from trouble? There could be more demonstrations like the one the other week.

'Your country had a Jewish Prime Minister once,' Lev Yefimovich's voice was quieter now but hard, 'Disraeli, a favourite of the Queen, I read. And she received the composer Mendelssohn at the Royal Palace, where he played the piano and even wrote music for her to perform. In Russia, we have some way to go before reaching such tolerance.'

Father had regarded Mr Disraeli as an opportunist, she remembered, and had a solemn portrait of Mr Gladstone on the parlour wall.

Lev Yefimovich clicked his heels, went downstairs.

⁓

The train slows, shudders to a standstill. Shouts rise and die outside. Footsteps bump on hard earth. Somebody is unfastening the door. She clamps her eyelids against daylight.

'Room for some more,' the scarred *bolshevik* soldier orders.

Half a dozen peasants climb aboard. People press against each other, force a gap. The *bolshevik* steps up into the wagon, leans out, yells to his comrades words she does not understand, the *argot* of men roughened by war. He turns round, bringing with him the sharp odour of Woodbines. It reminds her of the man who used to deliver her family's milk in Norwich; she wonders if he is still alive; and why this *bolshevik* has British cigarettes.

Somebody is securing the door from outside, an imprisoning. Her skin tingles with the threat of harm. The *bolshevik* opens the top segment of the door, allowing light and the smell of black, fertile earth into the wagon, but the scent of danger lingers in her nostrils. She rests her cheek on George's bonnet.

It is freshly washed. She hopes the frill and embroidery do not make him too conspicuous for a worker's baby.

'Where are you going?' the *bolshevik* demands of one of the peasants.

A new fear joins the others. Peter must not speak, betray his Caucasian accent. Their *bolshevik* permit bears the official stamp of the Astrakhan *soviet*, a town neither she nor Peter has been to, beyond the Caucasus and more than four hundred miles north of Baku.

'Where are you going?' the *bolshevik* repeats, voice harsh.

Is he Lev Yefimovich? for she remembers that same harshness in his voice and how it frightened, shocked her, as he was only sixteen, two years younger than her; and his strength, how her arm hurt where he'd held it. That was on the corner of Baku's crowded Mikhailovskaya one August morning in 1914, the war in Europe a few weeks old. Food was still plentiful and she was returning from the bazaar with baskets of chicken, smoked ham, grapes, quinces, pomegranates for Cook. The air thick with smells of raw onion, bodies, expectation, she lingered to watch a procession. At its head was a priest in the gilded robes of the Orthodox Church, mitre shining with jewels. Behind him, a man carried a gold-fringed purple banner, his companion holding high a portrait of the Tsar. Dozens of men in working suits were walking five abreast, singing with rich, deep voices, *Bozhe Tsarya Khrani*: *God Save our Tsar, strong and all powerful, may he rule to confound his enemies and render glory unto us.*

As the priest passed, people crossed themselves, striking the forehead, right shoulder, left, and the chest, before dropping to their knees. When they joined the marchers and the procession moved on she stayed, enthralled by melodious yet mournful singing, then stepped into the road without looking. Someone grabbed her arm, propelled her back to the pavement out of the path of two neighing horses pulling a phaeton: Lev Yefimovich, hair dishevelled, blue *gimnaziya* tunic unbuttoned, sweat trickling down the scar on his face; just expelled from school for arguing with the Director.

'I can't go on playing the role of obedient son and student, Miss Livvy,' he told her. 'That's all it is, a,' he ground the word out of his mouth, '*role*. I suppose my father has set you all to spy on me.'

'Of course he hasn't.'

'So what was my stepmother doing snooping round my room? That book she found was by Prince Kropotkin. Some of the highest in the land believe there has to be change. My father ripped it to pieces in front of me.'

'Your father loves you, wants to protect you.'

Lev Yefimovich was dismissive. 'Love is a bourgeois word.' He touched his ravaged face. She winced in case it was hurting him. 'That whiplash didn't just wound me here, it struck through to my soul, the roots of my being. I have to *do* something.'

'Where are you going now?'

'I don't know.' He gestured in the direction the procession had gone. 'Everybody is patriotic. For the moment. The priest will bless the men and they'll go to the Front. But there is still injustice. Remember that.'

She didn't know where he went that morning for he never returned home. A week later a note came from him telling the family he'd joined the Army. Grief that he'd not said goodbye, and was under age, struggled in their hearts to find room for pride that he was defending his country. She, too, had left home without saying goodbye; nobody had come after her. She took herself to the barracks to reclaim Lev Yefimovich. We have nobody of that name, *baryshnya*, a pimply-faced orderly informed her. Which meant Lev Yefimovich Markovitch must've changed his name to enlist. Disowned his family.

Is this *bolshevik* really him, different without his spectacles, taller than she remembers, brutalised by five years of war and revolution? she keeps asking herself, a nagging scrutiny. And if it is, will he recognise me? And if he does … ?

A weatherbeaten old man in the wagon, defiance lighting pale eyes, is saying, 'We're going where there's bread.'

'And no fighting,' adds another. 'We don't belong to any party in our village. We organise ourselves. We don't trust the Whites; they'll take our land back.'

'We have to fight to defend what is right,' pursues the *bolshevik*. 'We're building a new world without tyrants and slaves. When all our enemies are defeated, the country rid of foreigners and their wars, you will have bread, peace, freedom to work your land. This baby will grow up in a Russia free from oppression, that belongs to Russians - '

She sees blood-smeared hands, with torn, dirt-encrusted nails, reach towards George as their owner is speaking. The scarred side of his face is nearer to her, the broad forehead and widely-spaced eyes so dark a brown as to be black just like Esther's and those of the young twins, Jacob and Anton. 'No!!' she shrieks in English, pinning George to her chest, wishing she could push him back in the womb, his only place of safety.

Peter is standing up. She is trembling in the silence. What have I done? What will happen now? It is Lev Yefimovich.

George is whimpering. She wants to comfort him but dare not speak.

Lev Yefimovich shakes her shoulder. 'Papers?' he demands.

She turns to him, to eyes staring at her under thick brows, the same as his sister's, above a hard, unshaven face. The film of stale breath clogs her nostrils. His teeth are no more than stumps; when she knew him they were whole, white. She nods to Peter.

'Are you responsible for her?' Lev Yefimovich demands of him.

'I'm her husband.' Peter is reaching into his pocket for the *bolshevik* permit. Lev Yefimovich snatches it from him, tearing a corner of thin, crumpled paper.

George is regarding Lev Yefimovich's hands holding the permit.

She has never learnt to read Russian, a script which makes her think of lines of stick men and garden forks. When Peter told her he'd blackmailed Masha to obtain the permit, he translated it for her, placing a finger under the print as one would for a child. It gives permission for Pyotr Tomashevich and his wife Olga Feodorovna to travel to Moscow about shipments of oil. Peter's father is indeed Thomas. Her own father is Walter not Theodore. She'd given Peter the name for the marriage application. Either he'd since forgotten it or there wasn't a Russian equivalent so he made one up for the permit. And Olga is not the same as Olivia, inducing in her even more the feeling of an impostor, so she invented an identity for Olga Feodorovna: daughter of an Astrakhan factory worker, she kept meeting Pyotr Tomashevich on the staircase of the block in which they both lived, until she realised the encounters were not accidental.

Now, however, is not the moment for fantasy. She closes her eyes: please, let there be nothing about the way the permit's worded or printed that'll be unsatisfactory, that'll give us away.

'Astrakhan?' Lev Yefimovich is saying. 'Shipments of oil to Moscow.'

'Oil is Russia's lifeblood,' Peter asserts.

'You speak with the accent of the Caucasus.'

She opens her eyes. 'So do you,' Peter answers him. 'I worked there for years.'

'Where?'

'First in Grozny - '

'Which company?' Lev Yefimovich interrupts.

'Beylin.'

'I know it well, trained a self-defence unit of their workers. Perhaps you were one of them. Was in Grozny for two years until the Whites drove us out in the spring. This morning's work has done something to avenge that.'

So we're to have reminiscences about Grozny! Lev Yefimovich must've gone there early in 1917, one of thousands who elected their officers after the abdication of the Tsar, demobilised themselves, trekked back to Russia with their weapons. Deserter! Her flesh stings with revulsion. She twists her mouth, wants to scream: traitor! Lev Yefimovich is looking at her while speaking to Peter and she wonders what he means about this morning's work.

'You have a wife who cries out in English?' Lev Yefimovich says to Peter.

'I was born in England,' she tells Lev Yefimovich in Russian. She glances at Peter: just be quiet, can't you? She doesn't want Peter concocting some story about her background; if Lev

Yefimovich has recognised her, it will make matters worse. Even though her own identity is unmasked, there's no reason why Peter shouldn't be the Pyotr Tomashevich on the permit.

'The British,' Lev Yefimovich spits his contempt. 'No friends of ours. Did nothing to prevent counter-revolutionaries shooting Comrade Shaumian and twenty-five commissars in Baku after forcing them to dig their own graves.' He regards her, as a cat might a bird it is toying with. 'When did you come to Russia?'

His stress on the word 'you' makes her feel she is another inconvenience, expendable. She shivers at Russian brutality, remembers a crowd shouting in Baku years ago for Shaumian when he was still in exile. He'd been one of Yefim Aaronovich's foremen until sent to Siberia. Kerensky, who ruled Russia for a few months after the Tsar abdicated, freed all political prisoners. Shaumian returned to Baku, became chairman of the *soviet* and director of the military revolutionary committee.

Can she say she came to Russia when she was a child? No. When she first went to Baku, when Lev Yefimovich knew her, her Russian wasn't good. 'In 1914,' she tells him.

'Why?'

'To work.'

'You also speak with the accent of the Caucasus. The Caspian area, I would say.'

She doesn't answer. Lev Yefimovich jolts her foot with the toe of his boot and the prickle of danger breaks through her skin. 'Where did you work?'

She swallows. 'In Baku.'

He tilts his head back, eyes on hers. His lips move in a twisted smile.

She looks away. The other occupants of the wagon are peering at the splintered floorboards; two and half years of revolutionary Russia have done nothing to remove the subservience ingrained in the Russian soul in the presence of authority and interrogation.

'Why did you leave Baku?' Lev Yefimovich wants to know.

This she can invent, she decides. Lev Yefimovich has just said he was in Grozny for two years until the spring. He may never have returned to Baku. As long as she says nothing to associate Peter with the city, perhaps they will be all right. 'It wasn't a good place to be.' She feels her way into a story, fingertips in the gloom. She notices a five-pointed star on Lev Yefimovich's stained, grey tunic. Have even the *bolsheviki* devised a system of ranks? 'The Turks were approaching the city. Many people left.'

'Where did you go?'

'To Astrakhan,' she lies.

'Why?'

'People said it was safe. Others were going there.'

He bends towards her, prises her left hand away from George, examines the palm then the back. His dirty, roughened skin makes her catch her breath. She looks at her hand and stained, ringless fingers, nails long, chipped, untended since leaving Baku, earth from the Voronezh stationmaster's garden still embedded under them; those of a working woman not a bourgeoise used to being waited on.

He drops her hand as if it is something useless. 'Why are you afraid?'

'Only for my baby.'

'He has nothing to fear. He is the future.' Lev Yefimovich rests a hand on George's bonnet and George smiles. 'As I was saying when you interrupted me, he will grow up in a Russia free from oppression, with a good Russian father who works with Russian oil, sold for the benefit of the Russian people. And a mother who is loyal to her adopted country, where everyone toils side by side each respecting the rights of the other. Isn't that so, Olga Feodorovna?'

Shaking and then the warm balm of relief, her reply a strangled squeak. 'Yes.'

SEVEN

The train steams into the night, stopping at villages, dots on a map, grey log cabins separated by their yards and cart sheds. The *bolsheviki*'s singing becomes more raucous: *Goodbye, Nicolas* ... and she wonders if the Tsar really is dead.

Only when she and Peter are alone in the wagon does she speak.

Peter whistles his surprise. 'Lev Yefimovich! Probably as well his father will never know. Better if Yefim Aaronovich goes on believing his son was killed in Europe.'

'And Nadia Ephraimovna. She was fond of her stepson, of both children. Esther used to say Nadia Ephraimovna called them her squirrels when they were young. They'd snuggle up either side of her and read to her from their schoolbooks. I can remember her calling him Lyovushka even when he was sixteen, before it all went wrong.'

Peter shakes his head, then brightens as if something has just occurred to him. 'Lyovushka,' he repeats. 'Russian names seem to have no end of possibilities, don't they? depending on the level of affection. That was something I always liked.'

'His teeth, Peter. Did you notice?'

Peter nods, puts his arm round her, kisses her forehead.

'Just Esther insisted he might not be dead,' she adds. 'Sometimes she'd say letters had gone astray in the chaos of war and revolution. Other times it would be, he was injured but somebody was caring for him, or simply that it had all been too ghastly for him to scrawl even one line. She was right about him still being alive, but for the wrong reason.'

'They weren't close, were they, even though they were twins?'

'They were different. Esther was educated at home, had few friends. Her passion was the piano. That's why she and her father were in Petersburg in 1914, so she could audition for the Conservatoire. She was given a place.'

'She was fortunate, as a Jewess.'

'Among a clutter of photographs on her bedside table in Baku she used to have a tiny, faded, head and shoulders of Isabella Vengerova, a young Jewess who'd studied piano at the Conservatoire. Esther said that for the wealthy and well-connected there were ways around the restrictions on Jews. Yefim Aaronovich knew people on the Board of the Conservatoire: he'd lived in Petersburg as a young man for several months when he sat his technical examinations.'

'He probably had to pay the Board a lot of money for them to take Esther, however good she was.'

'She would've started the following year when she was seventeen if it hadn't been for the war. The Conservatoire was probably closed by then but in any case Yefim Aaronovich would never have allowed her to travel all that way. Can you imagine, on a crowded troop train? There was a terrible scene when she realised she couldn't go. She wept for days, insisted she was dying, until I told her she wasn't and to come downstairs.' Peter is smiling. 'When Lenin made peace with Germany after seizing power she raised her hopes, but then the *bolsheviki* and the Whites started fighting each other.'

'I never heard her play,' Peter said.

'She'd stopped by the time I met you. A couple of months earlier, the *bolsheviki* requisitioned Yefim Aaronovich's Rolls Royce, the one he bought in Petersburg and drove the two thousand miles to Baku. Esther was worried that her majestic chords of Tchaikowsky, Lizst, Chopin, heard from the street, should mark out the house and its contents.

'I'll never forget the first time I heard her play, the day I arrived in Baku. She and I had done the last stretch of the journey by train with Nadia Ephraimovna's brother and sister-in-law from Ekaterinoslav. I was hot, tired, head aching. Yefim Aaronovich arrived after us, in the early evening. He and Lev Yefimovich argued, shouted, about Lev Yefimovich's taking the men's side in the demonstration. Esther was crying in my room until she left me to rest before dinner. I was lying on my bed wondering what I'd come to when this music exploded through the house. I'd never heard anything like it. Crashing chords urging each other up the keyboard in a … ' she gropes for words, 'in a frenzy, but not managing to reach what they were searching for, and then tumbling as if pursued by a demon. Mama used to play *Pale hands I love beside the Shalimar* and Schubert's *Marche Militaire*. But Esther -' She shakes her head. ' -it makes my flesh tingle even now, remembering. An *étude* by Chopin.'

That first year in Baku, she'd stand in the doorway watching Esther, who practised for hours on the Steinway oblivious to anybody or anything. Esther might sigh over something she wasn't pleased with or wince at a wrong note, shoulders hunched, as though somebody had hurt that hand; she'd repeat passages over and over, body swaying, head back, lips parted, eyes closed almost as if she were praying. Doctor Bagratuni went to the house once a week to give her a forty-five minute lesson. The Conservatoire had been his idea.

Sitting in the wagon talking to Peter, something long forgotten, deep inside her, opens like a desert flower, the realisation whenever she heard Esther play that she was in the presence of something other, something that must still be there, beyond the shabbiness, the making do, the preoccupation with survival that became everyday life; something that has been there since the beginning of time, belonged to others before it was given to Esther, was Esther's for a while then passed on.

Tears are prickling her eyes. She rubs the knuckles of one hand across them, turns away. 'It's all such a waste, all that has happened since.'

Peter reclaims the hand. 'They were different, Esther and her brother, when you think that her last few weeks in Baku she was running anti-*bolshevik* messages.'

'She hated the way *bolshevik* laws were crushing her father. Shaumian – he was director of the Council of People's Commissars by then, wasn't he? The Lenin of the Caucasus, they called him – he'd told Yefim Aaronovich somebody had to take charge of law and order in Baku before they were all murdered in their beds; that *bolshevik* laws would continue until people of his class were eating grass, and he'd be paid a salary at the oilfield till he was no longer needed.'

Esther's friend Maria – daughter of Doctor Bagratuni, the piano teacher - had found a job as typist at the Council of People's Commissars and could spread information. Esther would deliver a few lines scribbled on a scrap of paper, rarely the same address twice; would rummage in people's rubbish, knock on kitchen doors as if begging.

'I passed her one evening after I'd left you at the house,' Peter recalls. 'She was rushing home to beat the curfew. She looked a real mess, shawl round her head, pins escaped from her hair. Yet, it was as if her face were lit from within.'

'I used to think she was meeting a young man. I said as much to her once but she denied it, told me she'd been to visit Maria and Doctor Bagratuni. She was so loyal.'

Only after Yefim Aaronovich and the family had gone to Persia, and the *bolsheviki* on the Baku *soviet* had abdicated rather than ask for British help defending the oilfields against the Turks – what a climbdown for the *bolsheviki* to relinquish three months' power to Socialist Revolutionaries and *mensheviki*; the first British battalion was in Baku a week or so later – only then did Maria Bagratuni admit what Esther had really been doing.

Peter concedes, 'It's for the best, Livvy, she'll never know about her brother. She did care for him. When we said goodbye to them the day before they left, she said if he returned, to tell him where they'd gone, didn't she? She even talked about France and them all being reunited there.'

'She had a photograph of him by her bedside, taken when he was two. He was standing on a chair in a white dress and suede boots, dark curls reaching his shoulders. She told me she cried when his hair was cut because they no longer looked the same.'

'She hoped they'd be able to return to Baku if things settled down.'

'Small chance of that now, if the *bolsheviki* really did murder the royal family.'

'It could just be talk.' Peter sounds reassuring. 'No bodies have been found.'

'Let's hope so. Why didn't the King give them a home? The Tsar and Tsarina were his cousins, after all. And the Tsar helped save the western Front.'

'You mean Tannenburg?'

'Yes. It drew Germany away east but cost thousands of young Russian lives.'

Peter shrugs. The last she knew of Yefim Aaronovich and his family they were in Teheran. This she learnt last year from Mr MacDonell, Britain's former vice-consul in Baku; after he'd sent his wife and baby son home to England in 1917 he came and went, often away for weeks. Nobody was sure what he was doing. In July last year, he had to get out of Baku for a while, having been hauled before a tribunal, accused of anti-*bolshevik* activities. They let him off but he was still under suspicion. He took Yefim Aaronovich and the family with him to Enzeli, the Russian-built port at the southern end of the Caspian on the Persian coast – the same port to which she and Peter were evacuated a couple of months later in September – in calm weather an eighteen-hour boat journey from Baku. In Enzeli, Mr MacDonell borrowed an army car and drove the family to Teheran before returning to Baku alone.

Peter is stroking her fingers, 'You were inspired, darling, all you said to Lev Yefimovich about going to Astrakhan.'

'The thing is, has he recognised me?'

'Probably. Your accent, and then when you mentioned Baku.'

'Should I tell him what happened to his family?'

Peter's fingers stay their caressing and grip hers as if to emphasise what he is saying. 'No, Livvy. Certainly not, in spite of Esther asking us to. The past, good and bad, has to be left there. He's accepted you've married a Russian and have a new identity. All that matters now is getting to Moscow safely. He may not come back in here.'

'Perhaps I have more to discard than you have.'

Peter has turned away. She retreats from him into her memories, too many to abandon all at once, for Lev Yefimovich's father became like a father to her, filling the void created by her own, who'd replaced her mother with Rose and let her come to Russia.

℮℥

She first met Yefim Aaronovich at Esther's invitation to tea in their suite at the Astoria, Petersburg's largest and most modern hotel. His black hair, parted on the left, was streaked with grey at the temples, olive skin taut over high cheekbones. He was cleanshaven except for a trimmed moustache above thin lips. His English wasn't as fluent as Esther's but he had the same way of rolling the r's. Esther had ordered tea to be served the English way: instead of a glass, Yefim Aaronovich had a gold-rimmed cup on which were painted pink daisies. He held the handle between thumb and forefinger as if afraid of snapping it off.

In Baku, Yefim Aaronovich continued to address her in English until one morning, *Dobrayeootra,* she greeted him. He returned her salutation, the fine lines etched at the corners of his eyes and mouth creasing as he smiled. After that, he would speak to her in Russian, careful sentences in case she might not understand, a quiet courtesy which warmed her to him. Around him always lingered the aroma, like liquorice, of Turkish tobacco. They'd taken boxes of it to Baku with them from Bagdanof's in Petersburg.

In August that year, the war in Europe wasn't expected to last more than a few months but Yefim Aaronovich was willing to pay for her return to Britain: twenty-eight days on a steamer from the Black Sea port of Odessa, the other side the Caucasus mountains, to her an unthinkable prospect after her sea-sickness on the few days' voyage from Tilbury to Petersburg that May. Or she could go back to Petersburg: Petrograd they had to call it as Petersburg sounded too German. He would make available to her sufficient funds until she found another job, but the journey would likely be long, with trains delayed and carriages full of soldiers.

She was sitting opposite him at the leather-topped desk in his study. On the wood-panelled wall hung portraits of the Tsar and Tsarina, the Tsar with a faint smile on his lips, the Tsarina coldly distant. She said, 'I don't really want to go anywhere.'

He nodded, as if that was the answer he'd been hoping for. 'I would like you to continue as companion to Esther until Fräulein Lesser can return from Berlin.' The German governess had accompanied her employer and Esther to Petersburg and travelled on alone. 'Also, Jacob and Anton will need a *nyanya* when Anna leaves us to marry later in the month. They already know and love you.' He paused. She waited. 'I would increase your salary from one hundred to one hundred and twenty roubles a month.'

'Thank you, Yefim Aaronovich.' She'd found somewhere she belonged.

Years of war, food shortages, grief at the assumed death of his eldest son, engraved frown and worry lines into his face. People came to the kitchen door beseeching, hoping for scraps. Most evenings, the same scrawny woman rummaged through a sack of rubbish Cook had put in the corner of the courtyard, then pulled out the remains of the fish spine boiled for the evening soup, clutched it to her chest, scuttled away. A horse was found lying in their street. The head and shoulders had already been hacked away and people were gouging out the flesh.

When the grain ration was cut yet again, she suggested going with Esther to villages beyond the oilfields with clothes to barter for food the peasants were suspected of hoarding.

'It's out of the question, Livvy,' Yefim Aaronovich told her. 'There are bandits. Each village is a law to itself, ignores anything from Baku. You could be taken prisoner, even murdered.'

'Isn't it worth a try?' she persisted.

'No!' She flinched against his anger. 'And I will thank you to remember your position in this household, and do nothing to endanger my daughter's safety or your own.'

As if to compensate for permanent hunger by physical closeness, she and Esther used to sit with him and Nadia Ephraimovna at one end of the mahogany dining table in a room where walls were covered in gold silk. Jacob and Anton were also there; Russian parents didn't follow the English practice of shutting children off at the top of the house. The rosewater Esther dabbed behind her ears each day had been eked out until there was none left. Yet, everybody still changed for dinner, into faded clothes mostly bought in Petersburg in 1914 – the suits Yefim Aaronovich had had made by Knabe in as good shape as the day they were lifted from their boxes - and ate from the Limoges service Yefim Aaronovich had given Nadia Ephraimovna at the time of their wedding in Paris in 1906, every piece decorated with her initials. Nadia Ephraimovna had been a medical student there, her father a friend of Yefim Aaronovich's uncle in the boulevard Malesherbes where Yefim Aaronovich had taken his motherless eight-year-old son and daughter for a spring holiday and Esther had her first piano lesson. On a mahogany chest of drawers in her room, Esther had a wedding photograph of her father and stepmother, Nadia Ephraimovna a vision of beauty in a dress from Vionnet.

In Baku, Nadia Ephraimovna divided her time between the hospital and the Red Cross, helping orphaned children who cowered in a corner if approached, and Armenian refugees who'd struggled into the city hoping for sanctuary from the Turkish Army. She, Livvy, thought of the love between Nadia Ephraimovna and Yefim Aaronovich as a living entity encircling them. It was there all the time in glances, the touch of a hand, still a glow in eyes that had become sad and tired, as if whenever Yefim Aaronovich looked at his wife he was struck afresh by her beauty, full lips and creamy skin unblemished by privation, and by the blessing bestowed on him that he should meet her and make her his wife.

She thought how lucky Esther was to have Nadia Ephraimovna. Mama Nadia Esther had called her stepmother when she was a child, having little memory of her own delicate mother. Nadia Ephraimovna consulted Esther about new curtains. The age difference between the two women was about the same as herself and Rose. Judging by the quantities of photographs of Esther's mother's family, and of Nadia Ephraimovna's, that covered the drawing room walls and mahogany or rosewood side tables, she didn't think Nadia Ephraimovna would put any in a drawer as Rose had done.

By the time the *bolsheviki* took power in Baku, Yefim Aaronovich's hair had become sparse and white, his complexion like candle wax. The *bolsheviki* do not have people's support, he said; where they're in power is where they've seized it and the law exists to protect them; I've always longed for peaceful reform but this is monstrous.

At the table, English and Russian conversation outlasted the food. Yefim Aaronovich's thin hands, veins distended under wrinkled skin, occasionally moved to emphasise a point when he spoke. The *bolsheviki* are ruthless, he said; I don't trust them; I remember as a student in Paris over twenty years ago, émigré revolutionary groups plotting, burning with idealism, loathing people of our class making money.

His shoulders had grown stooped, his walk slower. She hated to see him so diminished.

'They have committees for everything,' Yefim Aaronovich said another time. Yet again, the meal was late: pancakes of minced vegetable peelings fried without fat, preceded by soup that was little more than spiced water. Yefim Aaronovich had been dealing with a deputation from the three thousand-strong oil workers' union in the hope of avoiding another strike. That evening the young twins were feverish. Nadia Ephraimovna had painted her sons' throats with glycerine and iodine, and put them to bed.

'The lower orders can't rule,' Nadia Ephraimovna opined. 'They're not educated or qualified. They work well if we show them who is in control. If we display weakness, they take advantage.'

'Everybody who's never been anybody is now somebody, member of a committee, Livvy,' Yefim Aaronovich turned to include her, 'but what do they know of statesmanship?'

'What does the new regime mean for us?' she asked her employer.

'It means the end of all we have, of life as we know it. The *bolsheviki* will take everything into common ownership. They believe working men should share the profits from their labour. They have many enemies, have started training all men aged eighteen to forty. In some parts of the country, Russian is already fighting Russian. It's like a gangrene spreading through the body.'

She remembered the discreet hush of commerce in her father's department of the Co-op in Norwich and wondered how he would be in this situation. It was impossible to think of it happening in England.

She continued to buy what she could in the bazaar for Cook and hid a few roubles under her mattress each week. Families were leaving Baku, Armenian women and old men humping bundles to the port, pushing carts piled with bedding, utensils, children sitting on top, all hoping for space on one of the steamers leaving daily for Krasnovodsk, across the Caspian. Every time she went to the bazaars, another shop was boarded up. She told herself that as long as she and the household continued their daily tasks, they might keep at arm's length anything happening outside the heavy wooden door of the house. Each of them was bound to the others by their work and the comfort of routine.

The *bolshevik* government in Baku nationalised the oil industry and gave it to the Council of People's Economy. Yefim Aaronovich no longer had right to own the family home. A couple of days after their wedding, she and Peter had a visit from Esther at Charlotte's house, where they were spending their honeymoon. Esther had come to tell them Yefim Aaronovich and the family were going to Persia. Other oil families were planning escapes, too, across the mountains to the Black Sea, people Yefim Aaronovich and Nadia

Ephraimovna used to entertain to dinner in the days when you did that sort of thing, five-course meals, not one inch of the lace tablecloth visible beneath plates, bottles, glasses, and playing charades afterwards.

She and Peter called at Yefim Aaronovich's house to say good-bye. They had to make themselves heard over strange voices, slammed doors, wailing babies. The housing commissariat had allocated thirteen refugees, Russian Armenians fleeing homes near the Turkish border. Whirls of dust had settled in corners and along edges of the marble hall. Smells of stale fish, washing, people, pervaded the air instead of polish and spices. Two rifles rested against the bottom of the staircase. Three stairs up, a child in a shift that clung to her like rags to a stick was holding onto the banister, picking her nose, watching.

Jacob rushed into the hall from the kitchen. Cook no longer shooed him out, for there was no food for him to wheedle from her. We're going on a boat tomorrow, Miss Livvy! he announced, as though it were something nobody had attempted. How much would he remember of Baku?

Yefim Aaronovich raised her hand to his lips, an unaccustomed gesture of intimacy that spiked her heart. Thank you for everything, Livvy, he said.

She didn't know how to reply. Sorry, because of what was happening, didn't seem enough. She looked at the frayed collar round his scraggy neck, the absence of hope in the eyes of this man who'd always believed the day would come when men of reason advised the Tsar, and hard work and integration into Russian life were the ways to have restrictions against Jews removed; in Petersburg in 1914, he'd taken his daughter to hear Chaliapine at the opera, and to the Imperial Ballet at the Maryinsky; he was not an orthodox Jew, confining reverence to donations of money to the synagogue. He wanted the newly-weds to live in his apartment in the best quarter of the Black Town, a wedding gift to himself and his first wife. The couple who'd been living there had left that morning. If she and Peter went straightaway, the housing commissariat wouldn't know the difference. Tears were prickling her eyes. Who was going to give him and his family refuge? the only family she'd had for four years. She blinked at the ceiling. This was what revolution did to you, stripped you of your self as well as what you possessed.

☙

The train judders to a stop. Footsteps outside; somebody unfastening the wagon. Lev Yefimovich is holding a hurricane lamp and a khaki greatcoat. He climbs into the wagon with the stink of latrines. In spite of Peter's opinion that Lev Yefimovich has accepted her new identity, uncertainty is making her heart bang about.

'Moscow will be colder than the south,' Lev Yefimovich says, handing the coat to Peter.

'Thank you, *tavarishch*,' Peter responds in the revolutionary manner. He takes off his jacket, places it round her shoulders, puts on the greatcoat.

'The Whites didn't think a tree might be blocking the line this morning,' Lev Yefimovich adds. 'What a haul we captured from them: boots, overcoats, rifles, ammunition! Our comrades in Moscow should be well pleased. We shan't stop again till then, providing the fuel lasts.'

That explains Lev Yefimovich's reference to this morning's work, she thinks; and the Woodbines, stolen from the Whites, who were given them by the British, perhaps some of the cargo she and Peter travelled with from Rostov. Peter is shrugging himself into the coat, buttoning it, and a shaft of gratitude to Lev Yefimovich pierces her, that all humanity has not abandoned him.

Esther's sad face when they parted last year, lips that had forgotten how to smile: tell him where we've gone, Livvy, Esther said of her brother; richness had deserted her voice; war had deprived her of parties and dances, and Sasha Nicolaevich, her one admirer, son of another oil industrialist. Pianist's fingers bony, skin roughened, Esther had been sewing money into hems and making pockets for jewellery and small valuables: a mother-of-pearl box for hair pins, which used to belong to her mother, and lapis lazuli, diamonds, emeralds, pearls, rubies, pink tourmaline earrings; gifts on name days, birthdays, the sale of each would be an amputation of the old life. Esther's thick raven hair – twisted into a coil for the first time in Petersburg in 1914 - had lost its lustre, cheeks and eyes receding into her skull as if she were withering, a plant without water.

How is Esther coping, she wonders now, even further from Petrograd and the Conservatoire? Are the family still in Teheran after more than a year? With the war in Europe over, perhaps they did go to France. How long would Esther keep hoping to see her brother? his absence each season permeating her, a rancid, cumulative sadness.

Why should she, Livvy, be cowed into silence by these *bolsheviki*? Nobody has elected them to power. Who do they think they are? The gratitude of a moment ago is plucked out.

Lev Yefimovich pulls a chunk of bread from his pocket, passes it to Peter. She reaches over, takes the bread. Hard, scarred fingers brush against hers. She defies the raw rankness, the male otherness of him, and, casting aside Olga Feodorovna, says in English, 'Thank you, Lev Yefimovich, or whatever name you go by now. When I went to the barracks to persuade you to come home at the beginning of the war, they knew nothing of you.'

He looks at her, a glare of irritation, as if she is somebody with whom he shouldn't have to concern himself.

Peter cautions in Russian, 'Darling. No.' To Lev Yefimovich he says, 'Excuse her, *tavarishch*, it's her nerves, she saw her neighbour blown up by a bomb in Astrakhan.'

The strangeness of the endearment on Peter's lips in Russian, as when they were waiting at Baku station last week, and the story he has fabricated, determines her further, the first time she has disobeyed Peter.

Her eyes hold Lev Yefimovich's. 'You don't have to pretend,' she tells him. 'Perhaps you recognised me, the same as I did you. My husband knows I used to work for your family.'

'Recognised you?' Lev Yefimovich repeats in Russian. 'Should I have?' He barks, 'Speak Russian!'

She does as he demands. 'Do you hate your family? Don't you ever wonder what happened?' Her voice is steady, eyes never leaving his in spite of Peter's restraining hand on her arm, the other hand loosening her grip on the bread and rescuing it. Convinced that she is in the presence of great wrong and cannot, must not, ignore it, she reminds Lev Yefimovich, 'You castigated your father once to me for not finding out the fate of *his* family, Moscow money lenders who were expelled from the city and herded south when your father was a student in Paris. You're no better.'

Lev Yefimovich's hand is on the door of the wagon. 'Enough!' he roars.

'Your family mourned you,' she pursues, 'believed you killed on the European Front defending your country.' George is whimpering. Hand across her mouth, Peter turns her face away from Lev Yefimovich but she breaks free, voice rising. 'Only Esther never stopped hoping you might still be alive. Before she left Baku, she charged me to tell you, if you returned, where the family were going. They're in Persia, Lev Yefimovich, driven away by what the *bolsheviki* did. Your father's a porter in a Teheran hospital, broken, old before his time.'

Lev Yefimovich is moving towards her.

'You used to talk to me about injustice,' she hurls at him. 'The *bolsheviki* are just as guilty. Your sister served her country well, carrying messages.'

Lev Yefimovich seems to be looking through rather than at her, as though part of his mind is numb, even dead. He raises his hand. 'I said, enough!'

'Esther is the patriot, not you! I just thank God she never knew the truth about you.'

The blows to her cheeks knock her into Peter's lap. George screams.

'I'll leave you to give her the next one, Pyotr Tomashevich!' Lev Yefimovich yells from the doorway. 'See to her. She has a lot to learn.'

EIGHT

In a Moscow station, a train snorts, belches steam, subsides like a great beast lying down to rest or even die. Blinking in late morning light after the gloom of the wagon, Peter notices Lev Yefimovich slapping a back or arm in greeting, soldiers in long overcoats, and cloth hats with pointed top and folding earflaps, unloading crates, legs and feet bound with birch bark and pieces of old tyre. They'll be glad of the boots, he thinks.

In the cobbled street people scurry, eyes lowered, avoiding holes several feet deep, skeletal hands tightened round bundles. Two soldiers approach him and Livvy, blocking their way. 'Your papers, Comrades!' one of them demands; he has spots on his face, earflaps down against the chill.

He produces the *bolshevik* permit, grubby from Lev Yefimovich.

He glances at Livvy. The greasy sleeves of his jacket half cover her dirty hands holding George to her chest. There is still a redness on her cheeks where Lev Yefimovich hit her. She spent most of the journey to Moscow sobbing, hands against her face, as if only the touch of her own skin could heal the outrage. He rocked and caressed his son until George fell asleep in his arms. He let Livvy weep, for was it not only the hurt, the affront, of Lev Yefimovich's attack but also mourning, an outpouring, for the Markovitch family?

Later, when she'd blown her nose and quietened, he said, 'I

told you not to, Livvy. He could've arrested us, separated us. That five-pointed star on his tunic means he's a commissar. He can do what he likes. These people are dangerous. For the first time in their lives they have power and nobody can say no to them.'

'I couldn't let it go, Peter. He has to know there are consequences. If it keeps him awake even one night it will have been worth it.'

'Leave the moralising to somebody else, for goodness' sake. We're more than halfway to Archangel. I want to get us there safely. Is that too much to ask? No more risk taking, Livvy. Understand?'

'The whole journey's a risk.'

'To which we're committed. But we'll have no further outbursts.'

She nodded but he knew she wasn't convinced. She could be very stubborn.

In the Moscow street, the soldiers return the permit, walk away. A motor car splutters past, disgorging clouds of pale blue smoke, then falters to a halt. Three men jump out; one cranks the engine, the other two protesting, gesticulating. He cannot understand what they are saying. The car starts again with a bang like gunfire, bumps along the cobbles. He twists his mouth. Kerosene. No wonder they want the Baku oilfields.

Across the way, on wooden hoardings taller than a person, are three posters: a red triangle wedged into a white circle; a bespectacled man, bushy moustache and mane of black hair - that would be Trotsky - astride a red horse, killing the dragon of the Whites; and the third, a round-faced, balding character with piercing black eyes, snub nose, wide mouth – Lenin - sweeping the world clean of Tsar Nicholas and an Orthodox bishop.

He stops opposite an open gate on the other side of the road. 'Yaroslavl station,' he reads aloud. 'Yaroslavl's a town on the way to Archangel,' he tells Livvy.

'Let's hope a train's going there. Yaroslavl, I mean.' Livvy slows her step. 'Peter. The permit. It's only as far as here, isn't it? Moscow.'

'Yes. We'll have to think of something.'

Hunger gnaws at him. They have had only bread and water in the twenty-four hours since leaving Voronezh. A different ache creeps over his skin, clinging, one of danger because of the permit. 'What's this?' he flared at Masha in the street outside the apartment in Baku, trying not to gag at the odours of sweat, fish, unwashed female, that always lingered around her. 'Only as far as Moscow?' He pointed to the printing on the permit she had just given him. 'I told you we need to reach the north coast.'

'My father has drunk much vodka into the night, *baryn*,' Masha impressed on him. Desperation blazed from Russian eyes, calloused, work-reddened fingers clutching the ridiculous frayed green shawl Livvy apparently bought for her years ago. Beneath it, hair was scraped back fit to tighten the scalp. 'He was shouting about British Imperialists who did nothing to save Shaumian. At first he refused to print anything until I told you were getting impatient, that the papers of his you took, the Russian translation of the article, were burning a hole in your jacket.'

Was there a trace of mockery in Masha's repeating his words? He wondered who was supplying her father with vodka, and why father and daughter persisted in addressing him as *baryn*. They must work out their own destiny. He cared nothing for their politics. All that mattered was getting Livvy and George away.

'I reminded him he has worked twenty years at the oilfield, *baryn*,' Masha went on. 'I cannot see him go to prison. But he will not change the permit.'

He was determined that *bolshevik* toad, her father, wasn't going to have the last word. 'I've already given you half the money we agreed, Masha.' He counted out the remaining Azeri notes before pocketing three of them. 'That is all, Masha.'

He crossed the road to the apartment. Time to tell Livvy.

❧

Inside Yaroslavl station people stand, looking like me, he thinks: tired, thin, unwashed. He gravitates towards a crowd gathered round a train. Livvy follows. Across the wagons has been painted a larger than life head and shoulders of the same balding man as on the poster in the street, with words printed top and bottom.

'Lenin,' he says, then reads, '"He who knows wins. The defence of the revolution is the duty of the working classes." Well,' he adds with forced nonchalance, 'that's us.'

George has started bleating. It could ripple along for half an hour, like shallow water over pebbles, or might erupt into outrage. 'He needs changing,' Livvy says.

They push through a fug of armpits and cheap tobacco. Two soldiers are remonstrating with a man who has a sack slung over his shoulder.

'No, *tavarishch*!' the man screams. 'For my family. Eight children to feed.'

'Rules and rations are the same for everybody,' shouts one

of the soldiers and pulls the sack to the ground. 'No speculating. No private trading.' The soldiers look inside the sack. 'Everything is the property of the people, and to be shared.' They hit the man across the face, march him to the station exit.

Across his son's whimpers he hears the crack of a pistol shot, and reels at rough justice. He checks on Livvy. She's rocking and kissing George.

Beyond an open wagon doorway, he finds what is holding everybody's attention, a film projected onto a screen: Lenin walking in the Kremlin grounds in Moscow, for eighteen months now the *bolshevik* capital, safer from German interference than Petrograd, the commentator behind the projector explains before exhorting his audience: workers of the world, unite! you are saviours of the homeland; all is for a new world.

He remembers Lev Yefimovich's determination: we are building a new world without tyrants and slaves. He looks at people's faces: lined, pale, sad and, for a few minutes, held by the promise of a better future.

Lenin is still addressing a crowd when the screen hums, crackles into darkness. The commentator continues reading the speech, then looks up, realises what has happened. People are losing interest, moving away. Soldiers huddle round the projector.

He touches Livvy's shoulder. 'I'm going over.' George wriggles in Livvy's arms, smiles at him.

The fear in her eyes reaches his heart. 'Be careful,' she whispers.

He knows his safety has nothing to do with being careful. The permit, his accent, simply the edgy, disjointed times in which they are living can result in his being arrested, or shot on sight. After his stricture on unnecessary risks, Livvy wants to maintain some appearance of normality in their lives, and he loves her for it.

As he approaches the *bolsheviki* around the projector, fragments from childhood hover in his mind. Even then, he was fascinated by machinery, how the different parts worked, moved together: Papa, can I go to the factory with you? he'd ask, and Father agreed, holding him astride the bicycle crossbar along the Stratford Road. He learnt that if he kept quiet, didn't touch anything, he could go again to Father's bicycle factory, to stare enthralled at spokes, wheels, pulleys, the smells of grease, sweat, leather, the banging of metal against metal, and the gruff *argot* of men used to each other, so that although he didn't understand much of what they were saying, he felt he belonged.

'Let me take a look!' he exclaims to the soldiers, little more than boys. They stand aside, sensing authority. Yards of film lie on the floor.

The tallest among the soldiers, in a belted black leather coat, challenges him. 'Have you worked this machine before, *tavarishch*?'

There's always one in charge, he thinks. Like Lev Yefimovich on the train. This lad appears to be Jewish, too, enjoying his first experience of importance.

He knows about oil machinery. And he drove a car last year for the first time, between the field dressing station and the hospital in Baku, a Model T Ford from the Hotel d'Europe where the British had set up HQ in August. Father had had no time for motor cars, considering them noisy contraptions that churned up clouds of dust, preferring his beloved bicycles or pony and trap. 'When you work with machines, as I do, you find one is very like another,' he assures the *bolshevik*. 'The first thing is to disconnect the source of power.' A pasty-faced soldier does this.

He retrieves the escaped film. He rewinds it, straightening out a kink which is most likely the problem, checks none of the moving parts has become detached. 'Connect the power,' he orders. Numbers count themselves down on the screen. A few seconds of grey fuzziness and Lenin flares to life in the grounds of the Kremlin.

'We are grateful, *tavarishch*,' the *bolshevik* tells him. 'We can't afford mishaps which lose us the attention of those we seek to educate. Moscow province is to be placed under martial law. The traitor Denikin is advancing north towards the capital. People have to be instructed in the benefits of our rule. We must reach as many as possible. We have orders to take the train as far as Yaroslavl. We should already have left.'

What of the millions who live far from any railway line? He suppresses a smile at the *bolshevik*'s way of speaking, as if every utterance is a speech to an audience. Did he detect a note of panic in the lad's rising voice? Yaroslavl. Another two hundred miles? 'You don't want further problems with the projector,' he ventures. Is there a chance?

'Exactly! You will come with us to maintain the equipment. Your papers, Comrade?'

ຕ

Every time the train stops, she watches Peter stand by the projector. Before the Lenin film is a cartoon: German bulldog snarls at British lion, the King in a sailor's cap; a *bolshevik* bayonets both and throws them aside. People craning through the open doorway of the wagon laugh, while some applaud. The two films are rewound, repeated. She shudders. Are there

113

bolsheviki in Britain? It couldn't happen there the same as here. Could it?

It is years since she saw a moving picture, those innocent days before the war when Esther used to take her to the cinema on the Olginskaya in Baku and swoon over Moszhuhin, his painted mouth and eyes, flashing eyes, filling the screen: he's so romantic, Livvy, Esther would sigh.

Esther knew little of romance. Sasha Nikolaevich used to visit, that summer of 1914. He was always dressed in the dark blue, high-collared uniform of the military school in Tiflis, where he'd been despatched after failing his examinations at Baku's *gimnaziya*. If Esther was practising the piano, she didn't stop but left him lounging in the open doorway, between ferns in terracotta tubs, and palms as tall as he was, twisting stems like aged veins rooted among small stones.

'You're awfully good, Esther,' she, Livvy, heard once at the end of a piece.

'I'm going to be a concert pianist. I start at the Conservatoire next year.'

She always made sure she was within earshot whenever Sasha Nikolaevich called, with a book or piece of paper in her hand on the pretext of fetching something. She didn't know if Yefim Aaronovich was aware of the visits but was sure her employer wouldn't want his daughter left alone with Sasha Nikolaevich. Not that she herself knew anything of romance then. It was all a mystery. It doesn't count if you do it standing up, she remembered Polly Carter informing a hushed group walking home from grammar school in Norwich. But Polly Carter stopped coming to school and weeks later they learnt she'd been sent to live with an aunt in Felixstowe.

Do what standing up? she used to wonder. Kiss him?

Yefim Aaronovich liked her to accompany Esther out of doors. They always went around six o'clock, smells of garlic and coriander percolating into the hall from the kitchen and promising the imminence of food. Before going out, she and Esther would've read a few pages of *Great Expectations*, the book they'd both been looking for - the title fitted her frame of mind at the time - when they collided, literally, at their first meeting in Petersburg's English shop that June. She'd let Esther have the book, the shop's only copy; Esther gave it to her before the family's departure for Persia last year. And now she's had to leave it Baku. She wonders what Masha has done with it.

Walking out with Esther in Baku, street smells of horse dung and sweat could, if she closed her eyes, make her believe she was back in England, wagons and carts rumbling past. But there was the sweetness of acacia, and other odours and sights of the orient: donkeys weighed down by panniers of silk, cotton, fruit, wine, rice, unloaded at the port from Persia and further parts of Asia, to be transported by train throughout the Empire. And always the wind, making her eyes water, so she'd hold her hat in place to avoid repeating the indignity of seeing it tossed along the street. In her bazaar canvas sandals, she tripped once where the cobbles were more widely spaced and knobbly; Esther caught her arm just in time. Her cheeks and nose glowed under protective cream Esther had given her, which she smoothed on with the tip of her little finger, not to waste it.

Six o'clock was the hour to stroll, to see and be seen along the Marine Boulevard. Here, the only shade was from their parasols.

Esther, in an ivory voile dress bought in Petersburg, arm slipped through hers, would return the salutations of several young women and their companions as they rounded the curve of the bay, the ornamented yet austere seven hundred-year-old wall of the Tartar Quarter on their right, while she would muse about those who'd settled in Baku: running away from something; or seeking adventure or a fortune, like Esther's *dedushka*.

And about the ease with which she'd been accepted into the household. Even while they were still in Petersburg, Esther had progressed from Miss Turner to Olivia to Livvy, and insisted she drop the patronymic Yefimovna. In Baku, Yefim Aaronovich and Nadia Ephraimovna were addressing her as Livvy within a fortnight of her arrival. By contrast, Esther's German governess was still referred to as Fräulein Lesser after seven years in the family's employ. Esther showed no sign of missing the German woman, never mentioned her except to say once: she smelt, Livvy. In one corner of her room languished a trunk, the name ANNELISE LESSER painted in black gothic script on the lid. It was still there when she left the family to marry Peter last year.

Another time when Sasha Nikolaevich called, he was bearing a box of *marrons glacés* and asked Esther if he could write to her.

His letters were full of parades, and polishing boots with petroleum jelly. And, after the war began, of the wonder, the glory of fighting for Russia.

'What can I write to him, Livvy?' Esther had received three letters, all unanswered.

'Tell him we're knitting.' They were: socks, wristlets, gloves. 'And about parcels for the men.' Each one contained socks, soap, square packets of cheap *makhorka* tobacco. *For glory and honour*, Esther wrote inside, unmindful that many of the men wouldn't be able to read.

'And tell him you work with Nadia Ephraimovna at the hospital.' Esther helped her stepmother roll gauze bandages but, revolted by blood, refused to do anything messy or risk damaging her fingers; which excluded caring for Armenian refugees, their blood-encrusted shoes in holes, or for women who gave birth and had only rags to wrap their babies in. The war might end at any time, Livvy, Esther insisted, and then I can go to the Conservatoire.

But within a few weeks civilians learnt of the destruction of the First and Second Armies at Tannenburg, where General Samsonov shot himself after losing two hundred thousand men in ten days, many killed. Sasha Nikolaevich's family were informed of their son's death. Esther wept: where's the glory, Livvy? He was just nineteen.

₫

For the first time since leaving Baku they are travelling in comfort. She can stare from the train across an expanse of fields to patches of fir forest, with linden, silver birch, and alder in an immense helmet of bronze. She holds George upright on her lap for him to see out of the window at rooks hanging on the bare arms of grey poplars. She's aware of Peter moving across the wagon to sit with the *bolshevik* who reads the film commentary.

'Course,' Peter expounds, 'Lydia Borisovna runs the docks at Astrakhan.'

'Indeed?'

'Hair cut down to her scalp. Was in the attack on the Winter Palace back in '17. They say her husband died in her arms and

117

she vowed to carry on the fight. Wears his jacket day and night. Escaped south.'

A smile flutters in her mind. Peter's coarsened his voice. He should've been an actor. She glances round. He's leaning forward, arms resting on knees apart.

'And her authority is accepted?' the *bolshevik* wants to know.

'Everything is put to a vote at the *soviet* but everyone knows Lydia Borisovna calls the shots. She has that manner of speaking, persuading you it's the only way.'

'A model government, it would seem.'

'Men and women. Shoulder to shoulder. All that's needed is a strong pair of arms and one good leg. Or even one arm and one leg. Can't be fussy these days.'

She presses her lips together to hold in the smile, concentrates on outside. She can sense the sun behind the forest, the crowns of the tallest firs brushed with a transparent gilding. She gazes at the reds and golds of autumn, not seen for six years when she left home for London, a carpet of fallen birch leaves, others yellowing, clinging to branches. She longs to be back in England, rid of these *bolsheviki*, their crude ideas, hateful films and posters; to know that Father, Arthur and Victor, are safe and well; yes, and Rose, because she made Father happy. But first she must think of something to detain herself and Peter when they arrive in Yaroslavl as the train will be returning to Moscow.

A rearrangement of the air around her; nasal breathing and the odour of strong tobacco. She turns from the window. The *bolshevik* is standing beside her.

'We're grateful for your husband's help,' he tells her, sits with her.

She settles George so her son can see who she is talking to. 'We're glad to assist.' George considers the *bolshevik*, decides he is worth a smile.

The *bolshevik* ignores George, eyes resting on her hair; he's probably wondering why I haven't cut it like the fearful Lydia Borisovna. Now he's studying her face. 'Your business must be of some importance for you to be sent to Moscow,' he comments.

Her brow furrows at his way of speaking, different from that of the Caucasus. She remembers what Peter said to Lev Yefimovich: 'Oil is Russia's lifeblood,' she repeats.

'What happens to the oil at Astrakhan? It has come from Baku?'

He's testing me. Unlike Lev Yefimovich, he won't know that she speaks with the accent of the Caucasus, not Astrakhan. She injects authority into her voice. 'Course, Baku's Azeri now, for the moment, so it's necessary to persuade port officials to release the oil to Astrakhan.' Peter is watching her from across the wagon, nodding, and she warms to her role. She rubs thumb and index finger together. 'They usually do. The oil has been refined into petroleum and kerosene. At Astrakhan it's pumped into barges and tugged up the Volga.'

'Ah, the Volga!' the *bolshevik* rhapsodises. 'The artery of our Motherland.'

They sit in silence. Raw red of the low sun streaks with shadow the fleeting curves of a lake, and sets ablaze the willow leaves and columns of rushes around it.

The train draws them towards the night and Yaroslavl. The separate world beyond flickers under an inky sky pricked with ageless stars.

Think of something, she nags herself, to get us off the train

❧

'At Yaroslavl we shall stay until first light, then return to Moscow,' the *bolshevik* announces. 'We have to defend the capital against the traitor.'

She puts an arm across her forehead, lies back in her seat, a sigh of frustration on a long outtake of breath. In two strides Peter is at her side.

He bends over her. 'Good girl,' he whispers. He straightens up, addresses the *bolshevik*. 'My wife is unwell. A little air, perhaps the stationmaster's wife can help. We don't want to risk being unable to make the journey back to Moscow in the morning. Our *soviet* sent us there, remember, to discuss shipments of oil. We have work to complete.'

Someone is opening the door from outside. The autumn night chill bursts in. The *bolshevik* jumps down to the platform. Peter follows him. She hears them explaining to somebody.

'Bring her indoors,' a man suggests. 'I will tell my wife.'

NINE

In the stationmaster's *izba*, she lets his wife settle her on her bedroll; watches Peter spreading his hands at the clay stove. She fingers the ridges of her wedding ring through her blouse. Will I have to give it in payment for food, shelter, the rest of the journey? Will I be able to? The same longing as in the train overwhelms her with its weariness, to be free from disguise, from the need to bargain and reliance on people who themselves can see no further than their own survival.

She notices Peter has in his hand the packet of Woodbines from the British soldier in Rostov last week. He removes the cigarettes, offers them to the stationmaster. 'We have no money for your kindness,' Peter lies. They still have the tsarist roubles.

The stationmaster takes the cigarettes. 'One of the few pleasures left in our troubled times.' He pushes his cap back across thick white hair.

'We need your help,' Peter ventures. The stationmaster has not addressed him as *tavarishch*. Is there a chance he's not a *bolshevik*? she wonders; but he doesn't know we're not; he's taking a risk.

'For your wife?' The stationmaster is looking at Peter in the glow of the candle. 'Or something else?'

'What sort of something else?' Peter dissembles.

The stationmaster lights two of the cigarettes from the

guttering candle, gives one to Peter and draws on his own. 'I'm an old man,' he says. 'Russia has suffered many things. I don't want to fight, just peace. The *bolsheviki* have come here. They control the town, the railway line and countryside either side of it for perhaps forty *versts*. What am I to do? I accept what they say, keep my job and a roof over my head. If anybody else had come I would have done the same.'

Unlike the stationmaster at Voronezh, she remembers, who lost his life for objecting to the Whites. She watches Peter inhale smoke from his cigarette then cough. The smell, stabbing into her nostrils, reminds her of Lev Yefimovich, who had also been smoking Woodbines. She dabs her fingers against her cheeks. They are still tender.

'You are not from these parts,' the stationmaster says to Peter. 'You no longer seem in a hurry. Your wife is sleeping. And these are not Russian cigarettes.'

She closes her eyes, wills Peter to trust the stationmaster as if, in the silence, she can push him to the decision.

'We need help to travel north,' Peter tells the stationmaster. She opens her eyes, every muscle, fibre, alert for his reaction.

'Petrograd?'

'Further north.'

'A train may come tomorrow morning which will go to Vologda.'

Peter jerks his head in the direction of the track. 'We need to get away before they return to Moscow. Yet, we don't want to put you in danger.'

'That is something we all live with. Shoora can take you to the next station. He has a cart. Vologda's too far for the horse. But he will need payment.'

'We have things he can sell. Shoora?'

'My cousin.' The stationmaster gets to his feet. 'I'll fetch him.' He indicates the door. 'If they stop me I'll say I'm going for a handywoman. Women's matters.'

The stationmaster's wife, a canvas apron over her clothes, has taken a steaming bowl of tea to the *bolsheviki* in the train. Now she urges her two visitors to drink, with hard crusts of black bread to dip into it.

∾

She undoes the top two buttons of her blouse, fumbles for her wedding ring, the fourteen months of her marriage. Peter, kneeling at her side, whispers, 'Keep it.' He fastens the buttons, kisses her forehead. 'It's all we have, with the tsarist roubles, to get us to Archangel.' The stationmaster has returned with Shoora, entering the *izba* through a rear door. As payment, Peter has ready a silver ashtray and a cigarette box with Petrograd's Petropavlovsk fortress engraved on the lid. There's still his watch, graduation gift from his father. On the back is recorded: *Birmingham 23rd June 1912*. She hopes they won't have to let it go, so he'll be able to wear it in England as he was always meant to.

She clasps Peter's fingers over her ring. 'I will part with it, when I have to.'

'I know you will.' He kisses her on the mouth. 'I'll make it up to you in England. I'll buy you another, and more jewellery. We'll have our marriage blessed, with the new ring and our families.'

She smiles. Our families. She will write to Father. It'll be the first thing she does back in England.

∾

He shows Shoora the ashtray and cigarette box. 'They are yours when we arrive.'

'Very good, *baryn*,' Shoora bows. The Russian's lanky frame is covered by a coat that looks and smells to be made of sheepskin; below the coat, as far as the tips of his toes, are leggings bound by straps of birch bark; his beard is grey, his hair cut in the shape of a pudding bowl and topped by a dark peaked cap. 'We start at once, *baryn*.'

He and Livvy with George follow the stationmaster and Shoora along a path to the cart. The night air slices through his clothes.

'I'll tell them in the train you escaped while I was out,' the stationmaster assures him. 'If they want to waste time looking for you that's up to them. You'll be long gone.'

'Thank you for your help,' he says to the Russian.

Above dark forest treetops, the September sky has a milky pallor. Under a hazy moon, the powdery soil of the path is silvery and soft. He is coughing. He was coughing when they were in Rostov, because of the coal dust. There's no coal dust here.

He feels Livvy put her free arm through his.

❧

Lying on foul-smelling straw that lines Shoora's cart, he holds his corner of the blanket over his mouth to stifle the cough. The coarse fabric prickles his nose. Chest raw, like sandpaper Father used in the factory. Eyes aching, two holes. Sleep … he wishes he could reach out to it, lose himself in its sweet depths but it swirls beyond him and he tries to steady his breathing to pace with the creak of the cart, the jolt of wheels, horse's hooves on hard-baked earth. His greatcoat is round himself,

Livvy and George. The blanket covers them, even their heads. Nearly there. How far? To Archangel. To England. The name hangs in front of him like a talisman, a beacon.

Father and Mother will want to talk about Will. He wrote to them about Will last year. He wonders if his letter made Mother cry. He doesn't remember her ever crying. When he left for Russia in 1913 there were tears in her eyes but she hugged him: be happy, my darling boy, she said against his shoulder with the faintness of lavender water he has always associated with her since he was a child and she would bend to kiss him goodnight in the nursery. A motor taxi was waiting by the gate to take him to the station, first stage of the journey to Petersburg. Mother waved him off, back straight, head held high.

He never went to war but war found him. He'd been in Grozny a few weeks when it started five years ago thousands of miles to the west. It won't last, people said, just months. Yet, it caught up the whole of Europe. Then the Dardanelles, Gallipoli, Palestine. Should he leave Russia? he used to think, trek hundreds of miles to find British HQ to enlist, Baghdad, or where? He stayed put, convincing himself that in helping keep Russia supplied with oil he was playing his part, yet the war a comfortable distance away. Until it found him last year, several British battalions, a few hundred soldiers sent from Mesopotamia to defend the Baku oilfields against the Turks. When the first Turkish attack began that August, British civilians in Baku were expected to pitch in. Livvy and other wives were given nurses' uniforms and told what to do at the hospital: no time for squeamishness or protesting lack of training. He spent the day driving injured soldiers, two at a time, from the frenzy of the field dressing station, coaxing the Model T Ford along the sandy track to the hospital then back for more. At the end of the afternoon he returned the Ford to HQ and, forcing each step through a wall of exhaustion, made his way to the hospital to see if Livvy was free to leave. Inside, the sting of disinfectant caught his nostrils and throat, making him cough. A nurse told him Livvy was in the first room upstairs.

There, he stood in the doorway. From about twenty beds some men were moaning, one sobbing into his pillow. Yet, everything appeared under control. Livvy was sitting at the nearest bedside leaning towards a man. The light from the lamp above glinted on a narrow strip of her hair, the rest of it covered by a starched, nunlike thing. He closed his eyes as if so doing might help his love and pride in her expunge the day's horrors: faces half shot away, guts spilling down legs. He wanted to take her in his arms to a far place of beauty without violence, suffering. They'd been married six weeks.

He opened his eyes. As though sensing someone's approach, Livvy turned, glanced at the man in the bed then back at him and whispered, 'He was one of the last to be brought in. He thinks I'm his mother.'

He put his arm round her shoulder. Something had been fitted under the sheet to raise it off the man's stomach. Livvy was holding the man's left hand. Man? The face he saw in the lamplight was more that of a boy. He thinks I'm his mother, she'd said; the same chestnut hair, Livvy and Mother. 'No,' he breathed. 'Not this.' He moved his arm from Livvy's shoulder, knelt by the bed. 'Will?'

Will's eyes were closed; he was breathing in gasps.

The last time he saw Will the boy hadn't even started shaving, was looking forward to finishing school and joining Father making bicycles. Five years.

Will opened eyes that were the same hazel as his own. 'Will?'

Will's eyelids were drooping again and he inched his other hand along the sheet to Livvy, lips parted, a sound escaping from them with an outtake of breath. 'Ma ...'

Kneeling at the bedside, he turned to Livvy. Her eyes widened in realisation. 'Oh ... my poor darling,' she breathed. Tears clustered like pearls on her eyelashes. She put her arm round him, kissed his hair, lay her cheek there.

Deep in his belly a cracking began like ice on the Neva in Petersburg at the end of winter, moving up through his body, rending him apart, taking something of him with it, and he feared, knew, he would never be the same again.

Will looked at Livvy, lifted his hand just above the sheet. 'Ma,' he implored.

Livvy took the hand, bent towards Will. 'God bless you, Will;' her lips touched his forehead.

He'd never seen anybody die. Will just stopped breathing, one moment there the next gone, the beginning of a smile on his face, body left behind like a casing.

After closing his brother's eyes, he laid his face against Livvy's apron, tears mingling with the day's blood stains, making them larger.

Work helped sublimate both shock at Will's death and guilt, for Will had enlisted in August 1916, a month after his seventeenth birthday, according to the diary Will's officer, a captain in the Ninth Royal Warwickshires, gave him afterwards. In pencil-written copperplate there were several references to

Baghdad boil, a sand fly bite rubbing against Will's shirt collar: *Thank you, Mespot.* Will's battalion had been the last to arrive in Baku; he'd only been in the city a week when he was killed. He, Peter, kept imagining some situation where he and Will might've come across each other during that week. He'd been attached to Colonel Rawton as interpreter at HQ, and spent much of his time organising the men's billets at the Métropole, fixing the rations: soup, fish or meat, and water melon; and installing the officers in Mr MacDonell's flat.

As well as the diary, there were two drawings of the desert, dusty with grit and bits of masonry that littered the captain's desk after the shelling. Father, also, was an artist.

I've been out of it and I shouldn't have! he raged around the apartment, hating himself for the look he caused – surely not of fear? – on Livvy's face as she stood wondering what to do with him, castigating himself for not staying in England, not joining up with his brothers, for escaping, like cheating, being in Russia all those years when other men his age were fighting. The Baku Army never turned up! he shouted, as if Livvy didn't know, or might've forgotten; they expected the British to be everywhere, doing everything; six hours of battle and no reserves. The Turks were prevented from breaking through that part of the line but at the cost of many British dead and wounded.

Sometimes she'd grab his arms, enfold him in her own, sooth, reassure him and, weeping, ghastly wrenching sobs of grief, fury, frustration, he'd push her to their bed, lose himself in her sweet oblivion.

A hatred for Baku began to pervade him: why should his young brother die saving Baku? Or trying to save Baku, for ultimately the British mission was abandoned, the battalions withdrawn three weeks after the battle in which Will died. With unreliable local troops, retreat was considered preferable to certain annihilation by the Turks in their final attack. He and Livvy were evacuated to Enzeli with other civilians, a twenty-four voyage down the Caspian, six hours longer than usual because the sea was so angry. Livvy, poor darling, was sick the whole time. Turkish control of the city lasted six weeks until an armistice at the end of October with Britain and her allies. He and Livvy made the return journey in November, another agonising twenty-four hours for her, especially as by then she knew she was expecting George.

His bitterness towards Baku festered, intensifying after George was born, and he knew he must go back to England.

He wonders how long George will be alone, how soon there will be another baby. He never experienced what it was to be on his own: there was always Nell, and then their brothers. When they were children, she used to write plays for them to perform. He was always the villain; Jack, handsome even as a toddler, the prince; Tom had to carry the crown, while baby Will was bolstered on the floor by cushions, cajoled with a biscuit. When they were older, she used to hate it if he called her Nellie: don't, she'd say in her rich voice, you make me sound like the maid. After she left for Canada he missed her cheerfulness and fruity laugh. Jealousy of Patrick de Montfort raked him with its fingernails when she wrote that she was to marry a mounted policeman. A few months later he applied for the job in Petersburg.

After saying goodbye to Charlotte before they left Baku, he and Livvy walked down to the headland and the British cemetery, where Will's grave was by the wall. On a wooden cross had been carved:

Private W.A. Boulton, 9th Royal Warwickshire Regt.
Killed in action August 26th, 1918. Aged 19.

He will have no peace until he is home in England with his wife and son, his parents and other brothers safe, all the family together. Nearly there. How far? Sleep ...

જી

Under the blanket, she moves her hand until it rests on Peter's arm. Damp. She finds his cheek. Wet and burning. He stirs.

'Are you all right?' she whispers. 'You're sweating.'

'Better now than during the night. Nothing a good cup of English tea won't put right – ' A spasm of coughing imprisons him, deep, a disturbing of passageways roused to anger.

Her thoughts race back in time, leaping over all the shocks, changes, privations, she and Peter have suffered and shared, stopping at the first conversation she had with him their last evening in Petersburg in June 1914, when she didn't know his name or that she'd see him again: one winter of bronchitis has nearly done for me; off to the Caucasus and some mountain air. He shouldn't be here, she thinks; we're going further north than Petersburg and it's already late September. The urgency of their situation, the need to reach Archangel and a ship to Britain as soon as possible, for Peter's sake, strikes her with a clarity that has so far eluded her. Why on earth did I agree to this journey?

જી

Shoora is reining in the horse. She hears him talking to the creature as the cart jerks to a halt, and then his feet on the ground. He pulls back the blanket. She puts up a hand to shield her eyes from low sunlight. 'We have arrived,' he announces. 'Please come with me.'

She and Peter climb down and follow the Russian to an *izba* at the side of the railway track. A breeze snips at cheeks and fingers. In front of the *izba* a man is kneeling tending a strip of garden, orange flowers that make her think of English marigolds. He turns, gets to his feet. He is bearded, grey hair cut in the same pudding-bowl style as Shoora's. He and Shoora speak in an accent she cannot follow. The man goes indoors.

She watches Shoora take off his cap as he enters the *izba*, make the sign of the cross, bow from the waist. Inside, she sees an ikon in a metal frame on a stand in the corner, a candle spluttering in front of it. The only other furniture is a table of thick, cracked planks, and benches lining a wall. The smell of freshly-baked bread fills her nostrils. Steam spirals from a cauldron over the stove.

She cannot remember the last time she ate an egg. A woman - sallow, weary face framed by a scarlet and blue kerchief – has placed wooden bowls in front of her and Peter, ladled hot liquid into the bowls and broken an egg in each one. She savours the egg's stickiness on her tongue, licks the corners of her mouth in case a scrap has escaped.

Peter is coughing. When they have eaten, she takes the ashtray and cigarette box from him, gives them to Shoora, who glances at the undersides and hands the man the box. The woman offers Shoora bread and apples, which he pushes into his pocket with the ashtray.

The woman brings bread and apples to her. 'For this evening.' The woman smiles, revealing few teeth.

With a voice like a gate that needs oiling, Peter asks Shoora, 'Can the train take us further than Vologda?'

Shoora speaks to the man.

'The line is single track,' the man says. He extends soil-stained, gnarled fingers vertically, hands an inch apart. 'And narrower. In any case, drivers are afraid to go far.'

'Why?' Peter wants to know.

'Fighting. Sometimes the line is blocked. We don't need war or anybody to tell us what to do. We look after ourselves.'

The train to Vologda arrives an hour or so later: a single wagon of women, children, bundles and baskets, men beyond fighting age. Peter wedges himself against his bedroll, eyes sagging with sleep, coughing every few breaths. For him, her heart aches, a real hurt across her chest. How many more days like this, nights in an earthen floor *izba*?

~

At Vologda the late afternoon sun has thrown the shadow of the stationmaster's *izba* across the line. Her eyes are with Peter approaching the bearded stationmaster after the other passengers have drifted away, showing him the tsarist banknotes, reds, greens and browns faded into crumpled softness.

'We need to get to Archangel,' Peter says.

The Russian glances at the money from under hooded lids. He pulls off his cap, crosses himself, bowing. He takes the notes from Peter, ushers them both indoors.

At the table, she is aware of the Russian and his wife standing waiting with dark lowered eyes, and realises she is eating food they would have had themselves: *kasha*, buckwheat porridge which was simmering over the stove; the woman portioned it out then crossed herself, bowed. Hard ryebread completes a meal eaten in silence. She offers the woman the bread and apples from this morning. The woman places them on the table.

'How can I help you, *baryn*?' the man asks Peter.

'We need to reach Archangel.'

The Russian frowns, strokes his beard, thumb and fore-finger meeting. 'It is nearly three hundred *versts*. There has been fighting. They force their way down the line, sending reinforcements south.' Defending the capital from Denikin's advance, she thinks. 'This station was once a junction for Siberia and Petersburg.'

She glimpses a life reduced in importance, a man now obliged to obey less impressive masters.

'Do trains still go to Archangel?' Peter persists.

'Very few.'

Three hundred *versts* to Archangel: two hundred miles, she calculates. If we can just get moving! What will persuade the stationmaster to help us?

'You would be doing us a great service if you could let us travel north.' Peter pursues. He looks at the ikon in the corner of the room then at the Russian. 'What is your name?'

'Vladimir Ivanovich, *baryn*.'

'Vladimir Ivanovich, for the memory of your Little Father, who loved all Russians until there was no longer breath in his body … ' Peter pauses.

Vladimir Ivanovich crosses himself. 'They tell us he's dead. We've always hoped he will return. Now you bring his money. If, by helping you I am serving him, *baryn* … ' Vladimir Ivanovich stands up, shoulders himself into a shaggy sheepskin. 'I will go and load fuel on the train. The Red Army requisition everything. They say they will be back when they have secured Moscow against the Whites.'

She wants to hug Peter. Brilliant Peter.

❧

He slumps on the wooden seat against the wall of the *izba*. An iron file has lodged in his chest. He closes his eyes, puts his hands over his face, each breath breaking on a cough, searing the inside of him front and back. His mouth fills with sour-tasting liquid and some trickles against the palms of his hands, thick, warm, but he clenches his fingers, presses the fists against his chest as though the iron file is better held in, contained, than allowed to tear itself free.

His breathing steadies. He opens his eyes, uncurls his hands as if they are sheltering a butterfly he is reluctant to release yet knows he has to. Blood. The Caucasus will do you good, the doctor told him the one winter he was in Petersburg: mountain air, mare's milk, lots of meat and fish; northern climate's not for you.

He swallows the stuff in his mouth, wipes his hands on the sides of his greatcoat. Mustn't be a burden … still some way to Archangel … how far? … Livvy … must walk … sweating again, like last night …

He fumbles with the top button of his coat, drags his fingers down the rough cloth to the next one.

TEN

In the autumn twilight she and George follow Vladimir Ivanovich and Peter along a sandy track to the train. The moon, half lost in broken clouds, plays hide and seek with trees which appear in ghostly whiteness then fade into shadows. Peter droops with coughing and night air after the fetid warmth of the *izba*. On the bench in the wagon, he sleeps.

He needs to see a doctor, she forces herself to admit. There'll be one in Archangel. A British doctor; the thought inspires confidence. There weren't enough doctors in Baku in August last year. They could've done with Nadia Ephraimovna, who'd left only the previous month. When the Turkish assault on the city began, everybody had to help, British wives like herself who'd had no training, no experience other than tending children's cuts. Stretcher cases were brought into the hospital and, uncomfortable in the white gown and starched headdress she'd been given to wear, she repeated like a litany what she'd been told: don't expect miracles; first, pain killer; second, clean up the mess. Above shouts of the orderlies, groans and screams of the wounded, nobody could hear her.

One of the local nurses, syringe in hand, called out: as soon as they've had morphine, get their clothing and dressings off; cut, tear if necessary, they won't feel it; soak gauze in iodine; swab wounds with Lysol; don't cover too tightly; leave room to breathe.

All the arrivals had a coating of dirt: the Turks had attacked at the Mud Volcano, ten miles north of the centre of Baku, where subterranean gas bubbled up. She swallowed, mouth and nostrils dry with the stench of man in his extremity. She bent down to a youth whose lips were hanging apart, eyes half-closed. Two, three times he repeated in a whisper, between gasps: please. Blood was congealing at the top of his trousers. She unbuttoned the sturdy khaki, pulled them away, thought of her brothers: Arthur, twenty-one; Victor, nineteen. Were they like this in a foreign hospital? She peeled off the sodden padding put on at the field dressing station. Blood, raw flesh, pus, oozed from where the man's private parts had been; married six weeks, she knew what was missing.

She forced back a rush of bile, reached for muslin, Lysol. Her hands were shaking. It's all right, she soothed the man, and again, to reassure herself as much as him.

The whole day, exhaustion seeped into her bones, finding her furthest corners; the stink, howls, mangled flesh, became part of her. She wondered if the day would ever come when, even behind closed eyes, she wouldn't see twitching tendons, sinew, splintered bone. By sunset, any movement felt as if she were made of lead. Ambulances stopped arriving. An uneasy calm was settling on the hospital.

Gas lamps cast an eerie glow, throwing shadows on the walls and floor. She held the tin basin while a nurse picked shrapnel from what had been a young man's stomach. Sticky flesh glistened among dozens of veins spread like tiny roots; the nurse swabbed the rawness. She immersed strips of gauze in iodine, helped the nurse place them across the wound and then a frame to lift the sheet. The chloroform would wear off in a few minutes. Morphine was rationed; supplies had to come through Persia, with no railway and poor or non-existent roads. The man wasn't to have any more for two hours, if he lasted that long. When morphine ran out there'd only be aspirin and vodka. Then vodka.

After the nurse had gone, she sat with the man, took his hand. Sweat and mud had flattened his light brown hair. A patchy English stubble covered his face. He looked Victor's age. His eyelids flickered. Unfocussed hazel eyes gazed in her direction. He opened his mouth, the voice that came from it no more than a whisper. Ma?

For the first time that day, her lips moved in a smile. She told him her name.

Ma … Ma … He closed his eyes, breath coming in short gasps.

*

Why did we come this way? she asks herself. Because Mrs MacDonell did, with a baby, in 1917. And there will only be five days at sea, on a British Navy ship. The alternative was south to Persia, the same as Yefim Aaronovich and the family last year, then west to the Mediterranean. Through Mesopotamia? Palestine? Or across the Caucasus, as some of Yefim Aaronovich's friends were planning, to the Black Sea. Whichever way you did it you'd end up at the Mediterranean, which itself could take weeks from east to west. In May, when Peter first mentioned leaving Baku, she refused to consider it, made a scene. Cursed seasickness! The journeys to and from Enzeli last year, while she wretched over the side of the boat Peter held her as if to prevent her from disintegrating. It must've been terrible for him to see her like that. So he worked out a plan to get them back to Britain with the least possible travel by sea, and she just gave in to him.

She covers her face with her hands, draws them down her cheeks as if she were revealing the truth. Peter being ill is my fault, coming north to the shortest time at sea because of me. I should never have let him do it.

She brushes tears with the back of one hand, then the other.

He'll be able to see a doctor soon. A week from now we could be at his parents' home, less than a month after leaving Baku. His parents will want to talk about Will, the young man she sat with in Baku hospital last year. Not that she knew who he was until Peter came to collect her. What a shock for Peter, on top of a day driving injured to the hospital; since then he hasn't been quite the same: still affectionate, loving, but at the apartment in Baku he might pass hours without speaking, a harshness in eyes from which the sun used to radiate.

If we'd gone another route we'd have taken a lot longer, she reasons. Peter might not have got a bad chest but could've picked something else up. Or I might have. Or George.

But she is not reassured; sits reproaching herself, each minute taking them further into the silent northern landscape, miles of aspens fifty, sixty feet high, leaves trembling. Autumn browns, tarnished gold, bright scarlet, once more make her long for England, which will only be assuaged when she arrives. With Peter. Safe.

The forest becomes dense, deep indigo, trees taller, like an austere gothic building. A mournful howl reaches them. A wolf? Bear? She shivers, hopes the train will not break down or the line be blocked.

Twice they stop at a station and are invited with Vladimir Ivanovich into the stationmaster's *izba*. She has no choice but to trust these strangers. She washes and changes George, eats and drinks what is offered her, hardly tasting wheat porridge, black bread, coffee made from roasted oats, looking all the time at Peter as if she would share her strength with him, willing him to keep going. The women chuck and dandle George, who beams at the attention.

At the second stop, the stationmaster's wife brings Peter a bowl and urges him to drink, steam rising from it and the odour of, maybe, eucalyptus. The woman gives her something round, the size of the palm of one hand, wrapped in cloth. 'For his chest,' the woman tells her.

She opens the cloth. Inside is a ball of fat; the same aromatic smell invades her nostrils and the back of her throat. In England, we used goose grease, she thinks.

In the wagon she cradles Peter, unbuttons his coat and shirt. She smears some fat onto two fingers, rubs it on his chest.

He smiles up at her, a shadow of the gaze that dazzled her when she first knew him. His voice is weak, rasping. 'I'm no more use to you than a baby, darling.'

'We'll find a British doctor in Archangel, get you well again.'

'I'll make it up to you when we're home,' he promises, 'the hunger, discomfort. But it was the only thing to do, wasn't it, Livvy? We couldn't have stayed in Baku.'

'I know.' But we could have, should have, gone another way.

Peter is already asleep. She watches his chest rising, falling, as if she would coax each breath from him. She does up his shirt and coat, holds him to her with George; lays an arm across her eyes to compel a retreat of tears she wishes were only from the grease fumes.

❧

She peers out of the stationary wagon, sees nothing, catches – or is it imagination? – the snapping of a twig; rustlings and silences. Vladimir Ivanovich has gone. The line is blocked.

'How far are we from the next station?' she asked Vladimir Ivanovich before he left to look for a path through the forest. 'Can we continue along the track on foot?'

'It could be dangerous, *barynya*, a trap,' he cautioned.

He has been away a long time, yet perhaps only a few minutes. She hears a trickle of water, then rain drumming on the wagon roof.

Someone is unfastening the door. She stands up. Vladimir Ivanovich is a dark spectre against the night landscape, sheepskin coat and hat sodden and reeking, feet muddied to the ankles.

'It is all right, *barynya*,' he assures her. 'I found an *izba* a couple of *versts* along a path. Two women live there. They were asleep, so very nervous when I disturbed them. They said Red Army soldiers were here until last week. I explained everything to them and they will escort you through the forest to Obozerskaya, where you will be safe.'

She nods. 'Thank you.'

Woken by the return of Vladimir Ivanovich, Peter is coughing. They take their leave of the Russian, who crosses himself, bows low to them in turn, bids them '*spokoinoi nochi*'.

Peter insists on carrying the bedrolls. She leads the way over a waterlogged track covered in russet leaves and undergrowth. Mud clings to her Baku sandals, making each step heavy. Rain is running down her face and neck, pasting her clothes to her body. She holds George inside her jacket – Peter's jacket - her shawl protecting her baby's head. But it is Peter she thinks of:

what have I done to him; what further damage is being wreaked on his fevered chest, out at night in this?

ℭℴ

'We have interrupted your sleep,' she apologises; and muddied your scrubbed wooden floor. Rain drips from unwashed hair and clothes. The smell fills the room.

'It is of no importance,' a young woman says; the candle she is holding reveals a sad face framed by light brown hair gathered into a plait down her back. The woman bows. 'My name is Olga Petrovna. You are welcome in our home. You must take off your wet things, and eat and rest.' Olga Petrovna moves the shawl covering George's head. 'So young. Six months?'

'Five, next week.'

Olga Petrovna and her mother-in-law prepare bread, slices of cold, smoked ham, and mottled cranberries in a wooden bowl, which they lay on a table covered with a cloth embroidered in red leaves and berries and edged with lace shaped like window frost. The same pattern has been worked on a linen towel draping the ikon in the corner of the room. On the wall are two rectangular spaces, wood paler than the rest, as if pictures have been taken down. The window is hung with muslin curtains and has carved wooden surrounds. The two women sleep on the stove, which is several feet square.

Within an hour, she checks on George in the cradle in the other room; his thumb, as always, is against his mouth. Next to him, she climbs into a bed large and high with iron posts, unused since Olga Petrovna's husband joined the White Army in Archangel. She lies on her back alongside Peter, head supported by a square pillow. The *izba* creaks as if it, too, is settling for the rest of the night. She closes her eyes, feels her bones dissolving into the feather mattress, the discomfort and anxiety of the last two weeks absorbed by softness. Peter's stertorous breathing and the wind hissing in fir treetops bear her towards sleep.

ભ

'Tonight, I'll take you through the forest to Obozerskaya,' Olga Petrovna tells her in the morning. 'It's safer after dark. Obozerskaya's in the hands of the Whites. No Reds have been seen for more than a week, but you have come such a long way to be caught at the end of the journey.' The Russian woman is helping her clean and change George. Clothes have been washed and are flapping in wind that blows from the White Sea. Olga Petrovna has found a skirt and blouse for her, and the husband's full-sleeved shirt, peasant-style, for Peter.

Doves fuss at an open window. A smell of resin fills the *izba* from pine floor planks Olga Petrovna has scrubbed white with sand. She remembers another odour of cleanliness, diluted Lysol, which she used for scouring the hospital floor with a block of brown soap in Baku, getting the place ready last summer before the first Turkish attack.

Peter is sitting under a dazzling sun on the bench fixed to the outside wall of the *izba*. Next to him, Olga Petrovna's mother-in-law is peeling a basket of large mushrooms.

'Your husband must have fresh air with that cough,' Olga Petrovna says. 'Two weeks of smoky dwellings and train wagons can't have been good. If only we had some mare's milk to give him!'

'We'll be able to see a doctor in Archangel,' she tells Olga Petrovna.

She settles George in the cradle and goes outside. The only reminder of yesterday's rain is glistening grass. Willow leaves glitter, slivers of gold against an intense blue sky. Behind the *izba* the Russian women grow root vegetables, beetroot, lettuce, radishes, bordered by late roses and a row of geraniums. At the far end, she recognises cranesbill, golden rod, and bushes of cranberry and large blackberries, unknown in Baku. Red-breasted bullfinches are devouring crimson rowan berries. Beyond these rise larches rustling in the breeze, and black branches of trees stripped of their leaves, etched into the sky, forest which stretches to the White Sea.

Peter has moved over to birch and pine wood piled beneath carved gables of the rye-straw roof. He picks up the axe, staggers as he grips the wooden shaft. She draws in her breath, wants to call out to him to stop, but waits. He lifts the axe as far as his shoulder, starts to cough. He turns to position the axe behind him but twists, bends double, heaving coughs, and she rushes to him, clasps him as the axe clatters to the ground.

かわ

George is crying in her arms, fists flailing with outrage. 'My milk's drying up,' she tells Olga Petrovna.

'Let's see if he'll take some soup.'

Olga Petrovna dips the smallest wooden spoon into broth made from vegetables picked this morning and puts it against his angry mouth. He closes his lips over the edge of the spoon. Olga Petrovna fills it again, brings it to him. He is watching, fury forgotten.

She kisses the down on the top of his head, then looks at Olga Petrovna, sees grief in pale Russian eyes, thinks of the cradle in the bedroom: George is not the first baby here.

'He's the same age as my son when he died last winter,' Olga Petrovna tells her.

'I'm very sorry.' Such inadequate words, and she remembers Masha in Baku, whose baby also died. We adults have learnt to go without food, she realises. George will cry until he is fed, or else become weak. The possibility that he, too, might not survive nags at her, hurting her chest.

'You're lucky,' Olga Petrovna adds. 'We pray this war will end and my husband return. There will be more babies.' Olga Petrovna indicates the spaces on the wall. 'Perhaps the day will come when we can once more show portraits of our Tsar and Tsarina.'

She pulls her wedding ring from its string, gives it to Olga Petrovna. 'We have no other payment. You're very kind to us.'

Olga Petrovna holds the ring. 'You needed help. Would you not have done the same for somebody in your country?' She wonders if she would. 'We don't understand this fighting,' Olga Petrovna adds. 'We don't want *bolsheviki* or Whites telling us what to do. We have our home and land. Some of what we grow used to be for market. Soldiers have taken our horse and cart.' Olga Petrovna gives her back the ring, folds her fingers over it. 'I can't keep it. If I tried to sell it people would wonder. Could be difficult.'

She puts the ring in her pocket.

All afternoon they rest. The sun dips towards the horizon, sky pale and transparent, evening light lingering in a tranquil dream.

They change into their own clothes. Olga Petrovna leads them along the edge of the kitchen garden, past the fruit bushes and into the forest. A slice of moon illumines sky and white birch trunks. They walk in silence, conserving what energy they have, the only sounds Peter's cough and the squelch of feet in mud, bracken, dead leaves. Mist from their breath rises in the cold air towards sombre pine branches. In all directions, tracks veer away from theirs through thickets and hills. They cross a half-rotten footbridge over a dank peat bog, a strong marshy smell ruffled by a sea breeze.

Olga Petrovna comes to a halt. The track slopes down. 'Obozerskaya is this way. There are no other paths to confuse you. I'll wait here until you're out of sight.'

She offers Olga Petrovna her hand in farewell. Olga Petrovna bends to kiss the shawl covering George's head, makes the sign of the cross over him.

Peter takes the Russian woman's hand. 'I'm sorry about the logs,' he rasps.

'My husband may be home soon,' Olga Petrovna tells him; says to them both, 'take care of those you love. That's all we ask to be allowed to do.'

Peter goes first so she walks at his pace. He stumbles over roots hidden under leaves, leans one arm against a tree trunk, panting for breath. She places her free hand across his back, breathes with him, damp earth and pine.

The forest thins. They pass an *izba*, another, and a third. The track widens enough for a horse and cart. Obozerskaya is in darkness; the moon has disappeared. In the distance, the glow of a fire penetrates drizzle.

Peter stops. 'Livvy, the town may be under curfew.' His voice sounds as if it has to scrape his throat. 'Patrols.'

Soldiers hunch round the fire, a few squatting, a couple sitting on camp stools.

'I'll speak to them,' she says.

'Can you? I don't seem to have the breath. Give George to me.'

145

She does as he asks, approaches the soldiers. In the gloom she can't make out the colour of their uniforms. 'We're British,' she says. 'We need food, shelter, and transport to Archangel.'

The soldiers turn to look at her. Nobody answers. One of them slurs something she doesn't understand, spits in the direction of the fire.

Unease claws at her belly. In Russian, she repeats what she has just said.

'You're too late, British,' the same soldier sneers. 'There're no British here any more.'

'No,' she protests. 'No!' Her cry rises into the darkness. 'That can't be true.'

Peter has joined her. 'We've come from the south,' he croaks, 'more than two weeks, for a ship to take us home.'

The soldiers glance at him then away. 'They abandoned us four days ago.'

'Surely not,' she insists. 'They've been helping you: clothes, weapons. We saw the crates, even sat on some part of the time.'

The soldiers lift grey shoulders, concentrate on the fire.

She clutches the arm of the nearest soldier. 'You must help us. Can't you see my husband's sick? My baby's hungry. Help us!'

The soldier throws off her arm, mutters to his companions, tapping the side of his head.

She takes her wedding ring from the jacket, grabs his arm again. 'It's all I can give you. You must help us.'

He puts the ring in his pocket.

George begins to cry. She lifts him from Peter's arms, hugs him. 'You must help us,' she pleads, touches the tip of her little finger against George's lips. 'Have any of you got sons, a baby even? Perhaps one you haven't yet seen.'

The soldiers simper, smirk, until one of them stands up. 'Come,' he says. 'A supply train might be going back to Archangel at the end of the morning.'

ELEVEN

She and Peter walk along the wooden block pavement of Troitzki Prospekt by the river Dvina, which winds like a silver ribbon along the shore of Archangel. The taste of the soldiers' cold soup and hard bread lingers in her mouth. The rain has stopped. The cobbled road glistens in the late afternoon, church domes golden against a sky of polished metal. Imposing, pastel-coloured houses face the river. She knocks on a door which looks heavy, inhospitable.

The *dvornik* opens the door a few inches. 'One bedroom and living room,' he states. His eyes are crossed, nose runny. 'Plus water. You buy food. My wife will cook it. One hundred roubles for one night.'

She stares at him. The amount Yefim Aaronovich paid her each month in the summer of 1914.

'Eighty,' Peter counters.

The *dvornik* slams the door.

She and Peter huddle on the pavement. 'What have we got we can sell?' she wonders.

'My watch,' Peter suggests.

'Let's keep that as long as we can. It's special, from your father. I know, my hair. We passed a barber's.' She indicates along the street.

Peter shakes his head. 'That's special, too. No, darling. Your lovely hair.'

'It'll grow again. What else is there?'

They retrace their steps to the barber's shop. Peter sits with George by the door. The barber agrees to three hundred roubles for her hair, washed outside Olga Petrovna's *izba*. 'But what can I do with it?' he laments as she removes the pins. He reaches for his scissors. She winces. No man except Peter has touched her hair. However, it is no longer part of her; she has sold something of herself.

'Many Russians left Archangel with the British,' the barber informs her. 'The Red Army will be here soon.'

'They won't,' she retorts. 'They're defending Moscow against Denikin.'

'Nobody's interested any more in hair pieces and beautiful styles.' Yet, the barber wraps the hair in silk, lays it in a drawer at the back of the shop.

She and Peter return to the house. The *dvornik* shows them to rooms full of dark, solid furniture, parquet floors scuffed. The ceilings are embossed with gilt wooden carvings of foliage and grinning elves.

Peter is coughing. 'Can we have fuel for the stove?' she asks the *dvornik*.

'It's too early. The house is made of wood to keep warmth in.'

'We're from the south and feel the cold,' she persists.

'It will cost extra,' the *dvornik* decides. 'Thirty roubles a day.'

She follows him downstairs to go for a doctor.

လ

Seated on a padded, upright chair, the Russian doctor crosses his legs at the ankles, places the fingers of both hands in the shape of an arch. He raises his face to meet her searching eyes. 'Your husband has consumption, Mrs Boulton. He tells me he has been coughing blood for several days.'

And not spoken of it. The wind moans, beats against the window. She sits unable to move, smothered in wretchedness, staring at the doctor's pale blue eyes, the left covered by a monocle, the right bloodshot; wanting him to go on talking, offer some encouragement, some remission, a glimmer of hope to warm and dissolve her misery. But she does not see how he can. They are in the wrong part of the country at the wrong time of year.

Consumption, the scourge everybody hopes to escape. An aunt died of it, and two cousins, one barely twenty years old.

'It may have been dormant for some time, years perhaps,' the doctor says. 'The southern climate will have been beneficial. The conditions in which you've been travelling, and poor diet, won't have helped him, of course. With such a chest the patient needs fresh air, good food.' He separates his hands in a gesture of helplessness. 'You say you had hoped to board a British ship.'

Her mouth feels parched, although the room is not warm for the *dvornik* has not brought any wood. 'We had no idea the British were leaving Archangel for good.' Her voice sounds reluctant to venture out.

The doctor strokes his goatee beard. 'News travels slowly, if at all, in these times. One village doesn't know what's happening in the next. Politics and common sense make strange companions. No doubt your country's government had reasons for withdrawing their troops just when we most needed help.' His voice shows no bitterness. His hands resume their arch position. 'There's nothing to be gained by regretting what's happened. We must consider what's best for your husband.'

'Yes?'

'You have little choice. We're not in a position to talk about ideal climates, mountain air, nourishing food. He should have plenty of protein. It isn't difficult to buy fish here; but milk, mare's milk …' He shakes his head. 'You have money?'

She puts her hand to the nape of her neck, conscious of the lack of hair despite her Baku shawl over the back of her head and round her shoulders. 'Enough for the moment.'

The doctor nods, indicates the other room, where Peter is lying on the bed. 'Your husband must rest. The bouts of fever will be most frequent at night. If he bleeds internally or has diarrhoea, I can treat him with morphine. I'll give you a preparation to ease his cough. Yet, whether his lungs will withstand the assault they are under, in this climate … ' He spreads his hands in that way she has seen so many times in Russia and which now has an air of finality. 'It depends on his constitution. But one thing I would advise is not to undertake any further travel, especially by sea.'

❧

Arguing with a British private in Rostov or the soldiers in Obozerskaya, even her altercation with Lev Yefimovich, was one thing. But sitting in the office of General Miller, Governor General of this northern region controlled by White Russians, and commander-in-chief of their army, and Russian in spite of his name – perhaps he had an English father - she wishes she hadn't left her straw hat in Baku.

The office is one of several rooms in a long wooden structure. On the wall behind the General's desk hang portraits of the Tsar and Tsarina, like the ones that were in many Baku shops until the Tsar's abdication, and on the wall of Yefim Aaronovich's study but never removed.

From another room, she can hear the clack of a typewriter as if the person using it is coaxing every letter from a reluctant machine; the clangorous carriage sounds like the electric trams that thunder past, the same as in Petersburg before the war, a noise she is becoming used to again after more than five years. A telephone is ringing, shrill, insistent.

While she was explaining her and Peter's predicament to the General, he listened, pale northern eyes on her face, no apparent acrimony at the British withdrawal from Archangel, or annoyance that he was being asked for help by a British woman. But neither did he smile. Seated at his desk, slim upright frame encased in a khaki jacket with gold-lace tsarist epaulettes, he remained immobile.

His long cavalry moustache and trimmed beard, light brown streaked with white, give him a mournful appearance. The backs of his hands are mottled, fingers stained with nicotine. After a few moments he clears his throat. In Russian, he says, 'I have to congratulate you and your husband on your resourcefulness, Mrs - '

' – Boulton, sir.'

'It is indeed regrettable, Mrs Boulton, that after such a long journey, successfully accomplished, you should arrive here only to miss the opportunity of a speedy return home with your countrymen. For us, the struggle against Germany, allies of the *bolsheviki*, is not yet over in spite of the peace settlement coming from Europe. And we considered Britain our ally and active supporter in that struggle.'

She shifts in her seat. So he is bitter. Who can blame him? Perhaps he will ask her, quietly, courteously, to leave.

'I do not consider this Lenin,' he draws out the two syllables as if they are an affront to language, 'capable of consolidating *bolshevik* forces and uniting the whole of Russia behind him. And so he has to be defeated. For Russia must be united, indivisible ... '

She remembers the White Russian officer on the train at the Azeri border using the same words.

' ... Russia will restore her boundaries to what they were before Lenin signed that iniquitous treaty with Germany last year at Brest Litovsk. No true Russian would have done such a thing. It is for the people of Russia to decide whether there will be a tsar once more ...'

The cadences, the clusters of language flow over her. Yes, yes, but what about Peter? Can you offer me work? What are we to do?

' ... but whatever they decide they will be united, be Russian, under a leader who loves Russia.' The General places his right hand across his heart, and she thinks of what Esther said last year: the Russia we knew and loved. Does she feel the same way about Britain? Could she talk of her country with love? She did not think twice about leaving and coming to Russia with the Claytons, and has been in no hurry to return.

'Be that as it may, it seems to me that for you and your husband there are two paths to choose from. You can try to catch up with your countrymen in Murmansk. For another couple of weeks one can still make the journey by sea. After that, the river and White Sea freeze over but it will be possible, though longer, by sledge and railway.'

'The doctor has advised no further travel for my husband,' she tells the General.

He nods. 'The alternative is to stay here for the winter, although I doubt if the British will still be in Murmansk next spring.' He stands up.

She remains seated. Is that all? Have you no help to offer? She remembers her strident: you're not going to leave us, are you? to the soldier at Rostov station. Can she speak like that to this man and still hope for his co-operation? She must, even though she has the feeling of taking on the whole of the White Army.

'You lived in the Caucasus a long time, Mrs Boulton?'

'Over five years, sir. I would have stayed - '

'I do not know the region. But it strikes me you have a feeling for our country. I'm sorry you have been driven away by bolshevism and nationalism.'

'I was in Petersburg for a few weeks in the spring of 1914. I loved it, the straight streets, and lacquered horse-carriages with livered coachmen. And the smells: leather and sunflower oil, and sweet, spicy hawthorn blossom. It was a city of enchantment.'

The General allows a quiet smile as if he, too, is revisiting memories. 'I fear we would find it much changed now.'

'I need to work here to support my husband and baby, sir,' she reminds him.

He inclines his head towards the sound of the recalcitrant typewriter. 'Can you type, Mrs Boulton?'

She gets to her feet, gratitude and relief escaping through parted lips. 'I'm sure I can.'

☙

While they were still travelling, Archangel a target, she feels that Peter summoned reserves of strength, forcing himself to keep going. Now all energy has left him, no longer required. At night she wipes fever from his brow and face, snatches sleep on the floor. In the mornings she washes him with water brought in from the river, takes the ferry under leaden skies across to General Miller, George strapped to her chest with her shawl.

She never admits to the General she cannot read Russian. Paper does not seem to be in short supply. Once she has mastered the use of the typewriter, she matches the shapes on the papers she is given with the symbols on the machine and for three hours works in a small room with one window high in the wall, thinking only of another rouble, another five, ten, earned to add to the others, to enable a further night at the lodgings. She doesn't know what she is typing, lists of some kind, but nobody complains. No-one speaks to her. She collects her wages at the end of the morning, crumpled grubby notes incorporating the image of someone's face although it is impossible to say whose. The clerk counts out the notes as if the country's future depends on his not making a mistake and hands them to her with a nod of the head.

At the house, the *dvornik*'s wife, bloodless face, forever pulling her cardigan over a flat chest, offers to look in on Peter, and the second day to buy food, this said while glancing round as if fearful of being overheard. Their living room, like the staircases, reeks of the foul-smelling cabbage soup the woman brings them.

She sits by the wooden bed in the afternoons, watches the face she loves, white where the beard doesn't cover it. His lips appear thinner, with a tinge of blue. 'Peter,' she says, two syllables dearer than any other, 'p' the beginning of a kiss. His eyes are half open but he doesn't answer. She takes his hand. Like a wounded bird, fingers lie loosely against her own.

She lifts under his arms to sit him up, the way she learnt in

Baku hospital last year. He has the weight of a child. A bluish wisp of smoke thickens the air, and the fragrance of a second pine log burning in the stove; one more will have to last until bedtime. Rain lashes the window, rivulets making a strange shape of light from the street gas lamp. This is their third day here. Peter focuses on her, as if seeing her for the first time.

❧

Livvy, my darling Livvy. How will you be on your own? The family will look after you and George. Go to them, just as we would have done together.

Coughing attacks, shakes him like a dog with a rat. Each one gets a bit nearer to carrying him off. Livvy helps him put to his mouth a bit of his other shirt she has cut up. She is so resourceful. How much more blood and muck can come out? He slumps back. Not much breath left now. Every one an effort … hurting. His eyes are closing. He forces them open … the address … Livvy doesn't know where to go … should've done it before. She is balling the rag … ghastly red and grey. She throws it in the stove.

He reaches up to her hair, that exquisite hair seeming to go on forever which he used to twist round his fingers; she leans to him and he moves his hand through it, stopping at short edges. 'Lovely colour.' His voice is hoarse, faint. Is it really him?

'It'll grow,' Livvy says.

Yes, it will, but he won't see it.

No more breath … not enough strength for another.

'It's my fault you're ill, darling,' Livvy says. 'I'm sorry, so sorry.'

Don't be sorry, my darling. It might not've happened. Anything could've.

'If only we could put the clock back. Do you remember when we met on the Marine Boulevard?'

Yes. How can I ever forget? But I've no breath to tell you.

'Yet, it was before that, wasn't it? In Petersburg. You gave me the hatband. And now I have both, with their gold lettering. Esther left me hers inside her copy of *Great Expectations*.'

She's chattering, poor darling girl, doesn't know what to say. The address … before it's too late. 'Livvy,' he manages. 'Paper … ' He moves his hand as if writing.

She isn't here. Perhaps she's gone to the other room. Yes. A scrap of paper. It'll do. She holds the inkpot. He dips the pen and forms spidery uneven letters: *34 Laurel Road … Lightmoor* … There. It's done. He hasn't put Birmingham. She knows it's Birmingham.

'Go … to … the … family, Livvy … '

She places the pen and ink on the floor, and the paper, which she has crumpled. She holds his hands. 'We all will, when you're better,' she promises.

No, my darling. He rests against the pillow. Don't you understand? His eyelids are drooping. Just one more breath. One, or two. She is leaning close. 'I … love … you … Livvy.'

✥

The dullness in his gaze makes her feel he isn't seeing her. He is gasping, fighting for every breath. Inside her chest something hard is forming, like rock; and fear, born of an awful certainty. Tears are gathering, burning, behind her eyelids. 'I love you too, darling.' Don't leave me … please don't leave me.

He parts his lips, the dawn of a smile. 'Tell … George … his father … loved … him … '

She escapes from the present into the past, when they were

happy. 'Do you remember, darling, the March Days last year …
I already loved you, was terrified you might come to harm …'

He's breathing from his throat, tiny intakes, as if each one
is rationed.

'… and then you called at the house … you'd got a red band
round your arm, the only way to keep safe on the streets, you
said … you'd brought some flour for Cook … you were waiting
for me in the lounge … I was in the nursery with the boys,
came running down when Nadia Ephraimovna fetched me …'

He only seems to be breathing every third breath.

'…do you remember Yefim Aaronovich's lounge, darling?
… those double doors … polished parquet floor … Kirman
carpet … and that mahogany sofa in crimson velvet and satin
… the potted palms … crystal chandelier … and you kissed
me … I'd never been kissed by a man before … you kissed my
lips, face, neck, almost as if you were worshipping … '

He has stopped breathing.

' … and I felt I was falling, floating away in tiny pieces …
and that's the way it's always been …'

His body is still, no longer needed, like an effigy on a tomb,
the essential Peter not there. But she goes on talking, for
minutes, perhaps longer, until tears choke the words.

PART TWO

If you dwell on the past, you'll lose an eye.
Russian proverb

Forget the past and you'll lose both eyes.
Alexander Solzhenitsyn

Perhaps some day the sun will shine again,
And I shall see that still the skies are blue,
And feel once more I do not live in vain,
Although bereft of you.

Vera Brittain - *Verses of a VAD*

TWELVE

Thomas Boulton rests the scissors on the green leather desk lid of the bureau where he is sitting at home in Lightmoor. He picks up his pen, writes at the top of the article he has cut from the *Times*:

Monday 13th October, 1919.

He returns to the newspaper, looks at the next page and the following one, arrives at the advertisements. So that is all for today, he thinks. He folds the paper in half.

Until a few months ago he would never have dreamt of buying the *Times*, finding the *Daily Express* easier to read; and he always has the *Birmingham Post*. It is a longing for news, any news, about Russia that has driven him to search the columns of the *Times* every evening. Only part of him has been able to rejoice with an exhausted Britain getting used to peace and promise of a future, when in Russia this has yet to come. There has been nothing from Peter for a year: two letters, which arrived within a few weeks of each other.

The second letter carried details of something he and May already knew from the War Office telegram: Will's death. The telegram is in a box with the newspaper cuttings and the letters, which he keeps in the bureau. He takes out the black-bordered brown envelope, runs his finger over it before removing the thin piece of paper inside although he knows the contents by heart:

Regret to inform you Private W.A. Boulton killed in action Russia August 26th.

It was not the first telegram he and May received. He touches another War Office envelope in the box, pulls up the flap, draws out:

Regret to inform you Private J.R. Boulton killed in action France July 23rd.

Three years ago. He arrived from the factory to find May sobbing, which shocked him as much as the message lying between her fingers, for the only time he could remember her crying was after the death of their baby Annie. When the second telegram came last year, May left it staring unopened from the mantelpiece until he was home, and he thought: Tom or Will?

How many were sent during the war? he wonders now, to remote cottages, city terraces, titled mansions; impersonal, identical except for name, place, date. He wishes he knew the times of his sons' deaths so he can think of what he was doing then.

He takes from another envelope a letter written by Will's officer in Baku – strange name. … *I hope it will be of some comfort to you both to know that Private Boulton's dying words were of his mother …*

He puts the two telegrams and the officer's letter back in their envelopes; looks at the last one from Peter, pencil writing small, sloping to the right, on a sheet of paper about nine inches square so delicate that it crumples to the touch, already splitting along its fold. He has left the letter out of its envelope lest the paper disintegrate with too much holding. He smooths it with the side of his hand, marvels at the strange coincidences of life, and war, that Peter's wife should nurse Will when he was dying, and Peter be there, too. *Livvy was wonderful,* he reads again, *showed such care for Will, and for me afterwards. I'm the luckiest man in the world and hope one day you'll be able to meet her ...*

Peter had written of his marriage to Livvy in a previous letter a few weeks before.

He brings to mind a spring evening in 1913: *I've applied for another job, Father.* A flush of excitement lit Peter's heart-shaped face, so like May. *In Russia,* Peter added. He had the feeling Peter was eking out the details, not to load his father with too much at once: *it's a British-owned company in St Petersburg, the capital.* Peter had been living at home since leaving university a year earlier, working in the city centre as an engineer. Nell, Peter's twin, had already gone to Canada. Peter wanted to travel, too: *it'll be a wonderful experience, Father, a remote and ancient country.* You have to let them go, he remembers thinking. How soon did Peter leave St Petersburg? And why?

He reads again what he has just cut from the newspaper: *Bolshevism in Russia ... Lenin is a dictator ... farther removed from the people than the Tsar was ...* There is also a paragraph he spotted on an earlier page, a report from Archangel: *White Russians are pushing back the Red Army.* Archangel? He frowns, looks inside the box, takes out other paragraphs and articles he has cut from the *Times.* Archangel has been mentioned on several occasions: *withdrawal of British troops ... opposition in parliament to involvement in Russia now the war in Europe is over... last steamers with allied troops on board left on 27th September.* He remembers finding Archangel in the atlas.

He stands up, goes over to the small table alongside his

armchair. The flames of the coal and log fire Mrs Brent built up while he was eating his evening meal throw shadows on the walls and are reflected in polished fire irons. The weather has turned cold since Saturday. He picks up the atlas, takes it back to the desk. The only light he has on is the electric lamp on the bureau. He opens the atlas, finds northern Russia. He puts his finger on Archangel, turns to the next page, southern Russia, locates Baku where Peter wrote he and Livvy had been living until they were evacuated down the coast to Persia. He looks from one page to the other: Archangel is the opposite end of the country from Peter. Even so, he will keep the cuttings. They are a link with that vast land, and Peter.

In Friday's newspaper there was an article about Baku. When he first saw the title, *A Year's Work in the Caspian*, he exclaimed: ah! - although there was no-one to hear - excitement rolling towards him that Peter might be mentioned. He read every word, and a second time in case he'd missed something, disappointment mounting that there was nothing about Peter. He takes the cutting out of the box, glances through. Baku was under British occupation for six months from November 1918. Did Peter and Livvy return there?

He sits back in his chair at the desk, raises his eyes to the photograph on the bureau of beloved May, which was taken on her fortieth birthday two years before the war began. Chestnut hair is piled behind her head, clusters of tiny curls framing her face. Hazel eyes appear to be looking only at him, full lips parted a fraction as if she had been about to speak when the photographer captured the moment.

He always suspected that Peter, the eldest of her five sons, was the closest to her heart except when she was exasperated by his obstinacy, a trait inherited from her. Overjoyed last year, after hearing nothing through the war, to know that Peter was not only alive but well, happy with his wife, May sang round the house, throwing herself with renewed vigour into her current causes: petitioning Members of Parliament – which meant writing carefully-worded letters – over inadequate pensions and separation allowances for the dependents of servicemen; raising money for the families of his employees at the factory where the breadwinner had been killed or returned unable to work; organising meetings, recruiting munitions workers to Mrs Pankhurst's new Women's Party, for whom a crusade against Bolshevism was high on the agenda.

He can still hear May declaring in her rich, modulated voice: we must educate women, Thomas! Mrs Pankhurst has been to Russia and seen how things are because of the Bolsheviks; we don't want British workers tempted down the same road … Mrs P believes it is Germany who is fomenting Bolshevism in this country, trying to mislead and exploit our workers … we mustn't emerge from victory only to be caught by Bolshevism.

After the Armistice last November, May involved herself in the forthcoming General Election. For the first time, women over thirty were able to vote. Mrs Pankhurst's daughter, Christabel, was to stand for the Women's Party against a Labour candidate in Smethwick, a new Birmingham constituency. May turned out each morning, followed Christabel Pankhurst along narrow, cobbled streets of back-to-back houses, knocking on doors, mindless of fog, rain, cold.

May fulminated one evening, 'Parts of Smethwick are beyond description! A frozen tap serves the whole street, and just two wash houses, and dry closets for lavatories. The Council *must* pull everything down and rebuild with a toilet and running water for each home.'

He went over to where she was sitting, in this same room, across the fire from him. He took her hands in his, kissed the top of her head, breathed in lavender water. 'And you won't rest, my love, until it's finished.'

She looked up at him, hazel eyes making his breath catch. 'We can't risk giving Labour the chance to do it, Thomas.'

Mrs Pankhurst, he remembers, condemned all Labour candidates as Bolsheviks.

One December evening, May arrived home tired, aching, shivering, those lovely eyes red and watering. Disinclined to recount the day's events, she excused herself from the evening meal and went to bed. Bolshevism wasn't the only danger threatening Britain in the last weeks of 1918. Influenza was also stalking the streets. May stayed in bed – the one in which she'd given birth to all her children apart from Peter and Nell – unable to get up, just managing a few sips of water past parched lips. The doctor called, prescribed aspirin to reduce fever, urging warmth and quiet; not that there was much danger of noise: with him and Joe, his youngest son, out all day, there were only May and Mrs Brent at home. Mrs Brent rationed the coal, delayed lighting fires in other rooms so there was always plenty for May.

As soon as he arrived from the factory, he would bound upstairs to her bedside. Unfocussed eyes stared at him. The hair he'd loved since he met her as a girl of eighteen at the Cyclists Touring Club, now with a few threads of white, lay damp and lustreless on the pillow, framing a face that was turning violet like a polished precious stone.

Once or twice, her lips moved as if she were trying to speak. 'Thomas,' she managed, the sound faint, reluctant to leave her.

He lowered his face close to hers, clasped hands the weight of a fledgling; whispered, 'Dear May.'

The thought that she might not recover hovered around the edge of his mind, like a spectre, waiting, and the memory of it still encloses him.

May died on the Sunday before the election. Christabel Pankhurst lost to her Labour opponent by only seven hundred and seventy-five votes. In the *Post*, he read of a female electorate in Smethwick of nearly thirteen thousand, over eight thousand of whom had voted for Christabel; she had the second largest number of votes of all female candidates in that election, after the one successful woman, the Irish Countess Markiewicz. May would've considered it a noble defeat for Christabel Pankhurst.

He puts the newspaper cuttings, telegrams and letters back in the box; looks again at the envelope that contained Peter's last letter, curling at the edges, smudged by grubby fingers and littered with at least half a dozen unreadable postmarks. He wonders how many hands touched it between leaving Peter and arriving here. Peter didn't include an address. He wishes he could've written to tell Peter of his mother's death.

Still at the bureau, he drums a rhythm on the atlas with the fingers of one hand, the other fiddling with the watch chain against his waistcoat. He turns his head, aware of another sound: rain splattering the window. Whatever the weather, Joe spends most of the evenings with a crystal set in the shed at the bottom of the garden. His eyes stray around the room in light cast by the lamp and fire. It has always been known as the morning room, facing east, catching the rising and early morning sun. It was at this bureau that May used to do her morning correspondence. She admired the designs of William Morris, so the room has none of the Victorian heaviness of many homes. Although the furniture is mahogany, the chairs are covered with flowered chintz, doors and other woodwork enamelled cream, walls papered with patterns of pale green, blue, yellow. On all four hang drawings and watercolours he, Thomas, has done over the years. Since May's death, however, he has neither drawn nor painted.

Three bangs of the front door knocker disrupt his thoughts. Visitors at this time of evening? The only people likely to call are his brother and sister-in-law but never without arrangement. He hears Mrs Brent panting along the hall. Bolts clanging back on the two porch doors. Female voices. Renée home from school for half-term? He is not expecting her for another ten days.

A few taps, uncertain, on the morning room door. Mrs Brent appears in the doorway. The fire flares, crackles, with the draught from the hall. Mrs Brent is breathless. 'Oh, Mr Boulton, sir! I'm sorry to disturb you. But, it's Mrs Boulton, sir … Mrs Peter … with … and … oh … ' Sobs overtake her as she fumbles in the pocket of her pinafore for a handkerchief. 'Please excuse me, sir,' she begs, then disappears.

He has leapt to his feet, is halfway to the door. Peter's wife! And Peter. Home at last. His face relaxes into a smile, arms outstretched. Then he stands still, lowers his arms as a young woman arrives in the doorway. She is wearing a brown coat and gloves. A hat the same colour sits uncomfortably on short dark hair. She is carrying what must be a baby, although all that can be seen is the shawl enveloping it. A baby?

'I'm sorry to arrive unexpectedly,' she begins, as if unsure of herself and what she is going to say. 'But it seemed the simplest way.'

He looks at her as she speaks and two thoughts hit him with equal force: she is alone; and her eyes, although sad, are set in one of the loveliest faces he has ever seen.

THIRTEEN

'A good brush down, ma'am, half an hour in the fresh air and it'll be good as new!' Mrs Brent declares next morning; her speech has the Midlander's hard consonants, nasal vowels; her breathing is laboured after manoeuvring the perambulator down the stairs from the second floor attic. Mrs Brent's mob-cap lies askew grey hair framing a heavy, flushed face, perspiration glistening on forehead and upper lip; she pushes the perambulator through to the scullery. 'Hasn't seen the light of day since Miss Renée was in the nursery, must be ten or eleven years.'

Eyes aching with lack of sleep, Livvy follows Mrs Brent, breathing in the tang of beeswax and turpentine polish, and the housekeeper's sweat; touching walls, door handles, of Peter's home, as if they will give her something of him.

In the garden the housekeeper glances at her with friendly blue eyes beneath thick, dark brows; sleeves rolled up reveal a smattering of fine dark hair while practised hands wipe the perambulator, shake the mattress, arrange a clean sheet and pillow case; a smile and, 'There now,' and, 'That's it,' as if to keep silent could be misconstrued as annoyance.

She's causing extra work. 'Thank you, Mrs Brent.' She settles George under a blanket that smells of camphor. On the pillow sits a small brown bear.

'Barney, Miss Renée used to call him,' says Mrs Brent before going back indoors.

A defiant sun has chased away last night's rain. Blackbirds are enjoying another singing day. She lingers by the perambulator near the golden canopy of an ornamental cherry in the top corner of the lawn. The oblong garden is bound on three sides by brick paths. A snaking mass of wizened stems – wisteria? yes, Peter talked about it – clutch side walls in the same warm brick, the height of a man. Borders have been dug over, fresh, chunky soil absorbing autumn air. A few mignonettes cluster around chrysanthemums and Michaelmas daisies. This is the first year since before the war, Mrs Brent told her, with flowers in the garden as well as vegetables. Onions and red green leaves of beetroot stand proud in the bottom border. Yellow and copper foliage cling to trees and bushes bare of fruit. Here is a garden that has been mastered, part of someone's home and family. She wonders if Joe and his father share the work; if she will ever have such a place.

Joe is Peter's youngest brother, apprenticed to a printer in the city. She looks towards the shed in the bottom corner of the garden, replays in her mind her first hour in Peter's home; she spends most of her time now revisiting all that has happened in the last couple of weeks as if this is the only way to take it in; other times, part of her wishes she would let it go so she can pretend it didn't happen but the rest of her doesn't seem to understand this. The wound of Peter's death is raw, visceral, every bit as hideous as Will's in Baku hospital last year; only this one can't be seen so nobody knows it's there and it doesn't seem as if she'll die of it, this craving for him, the smell, the feel of him. Him. How can he have gone and not be coming back? They were going to grow old together. No casting off. Just a few days he was ill; when did it start, the coughing and fever? In Shoora's cart after Yaroslavl.

After her arrival last evening, Peter's father went out to Joe. When they returned to the house, she was sitting at the dining room table with her supper - Mrs Brent had been quick to prepare soup, cold ham, cheese, pickles - and a fresh lump of coal on the embers in the grate. Joe brought to the doorway the smell of damp wool. He hovered, holding his cap, the flat sort worn by workmen, not what you would expect to see in this prosperous home. She stood up, held out a hand.

'Hello, Livvy.' He took her hand. 'It's very sad about Peter. I'm sorry.'

A man's voice but he had a boyish look, thick dark hair with a reddish tinge, and Peter's hazel eyes. He was wearing a jacket patched at the elbows, trousers with crumpled knees, collarless shirt. She searched for something to say. 'You remember him, I expect.'

'I was eleven when he went to Russia. He was always busy, ready for adventure. I'm sure there was a lot of that in Russia.'

Adventure: how Peter thought of their journey. 'You could say,' she replied. What does he want to know? Her voice blocked, as though someone had placed a stopper in her throat. She lowered her eyes.

'George?' Joe said his nephew's name as if getting used to it.

She looked at Joe long enough to tell him, 'In bed asleep.'

Joe let go of her hand. 'I'll leave you to eat. See you both tomorrow.'

Mrs Brent had warmed some milk for George. 'I'll just go and get the nursery ready, ma'am. Will Master George be all right on his own up there?'

'Don't light another fire at this time of night.' She wished to cause as little work as possible. 'I'll have him with me.' But also,

172

she couldn't bear separation, risk of harm, of losing George as well as Peter. 'It'll be easier if he wakes,' she added.

'I'll bring the cot down to your room.'

Before she carried George upstairs, Peter's father held his sleeping grandson, gazing at him, repeating: George; as if her son were a miracle, and she realised Peter hadn't written after George's birth. Because he didn't expect to stay in Russia?

❧

In the kitchen later in the morning, she sits on a ladder-backed chair at a long white scrubbed table with George on her lap, watching Mrs Brent mince meat, onion and carrot into purée for him. Mrs Brent has agreed to her suggestion they feed him in here but has laid a place for her in the dining room. She would prefer to eat with George.

'In the old days, the children ate in the nursery, but we had Nanny and Dora - '

She cannot remember Peter talking about Nanny. She looks at rows of sparkling copper pans ranged on shelves in order of size. Rose in Norwich was proud of her pans. On another shelf are bottles of cooking wines: sherry, port, and labels she does not recognise. Alongside them, stone jars of homemade preserves, things she hasn't seen for years, labelled with dates. Implements dangle from racks.

She drags her attention back to what Mrs Brent is saying.

' - Dora was a good parlour maid. She left during the war, became a munitionette. Nanny had already been gone several years, as soon as Miss Renée went to school.' Mrs Brent turns George's purée over in a bowl. 'Dora was getting two pounds a week filling shells. Don't know what happened to her after.'

'You've been here a long time, Mrs Brent?'

'Since '96, when Mr Tom was a baby. My man had been killed in the Sudan, fighting the fuzzies. Thought I'd never get over it, realising I wouldn't see him again, or hear his cheerful 'Hello' as he came through the door in the evening; that I couldn't even visit his grave. I was kitchen maid at Hay Hall, the other side the railway. Mr Boulton wanted a cook to live in so I came here, and life went on. We were busy with the young family. Suited me better, having my own kitchen, not being forced to wear a bonnet to church and sit in the servants' pew. Mr Boulton's a good employer, never questions what I spend with the tradespeople.' Mrs Brent hands her the purée, chucks George under the chin, 'Who's a bonny lad?' and is rewarded with his smile; 'You're Papa's boy, indeed.'

The look of Peter in George's smile shakes her breath. She doesn't think she will ever be like Mrs Brent, able to say 'life went on', and talk about her husband's death as if it were an illness or spell of bad weather. Further along the table waits Mrs Brent's thick wooden pastry board next to the oval tin for storing flour, salt and pepper, lid on each side, handle across the middle. Nearby, stands a crock of dough covered with a white cloth. Here she is again, holding up Mrs Brent's work. She touches George's lips with a spoonful of purée. Like a bird, his mouth opens – 'into the tunnel,' coos Mrs Brent – closes over the spoon. She catches some on his lower lip and thinks, Mrs Brent doesn't have to carry responsibility for her husband's death.

George wriggles. The spoon slips. Mrs Brent gives her a muslin napkin. 'There now. It must be a bit strange for you, ma'am, so recently – '

'It's all right, Mrs Brent.' She doesn't want to hear the words widowed, bereaved. She wipes a spot of purée from her skirt, a thick one women from the Salvation Army in Liverpool gave her. She hasn't spoken of Peter's death to Mrs Brent; in that way, it won't be true. But at night she cannot escape reality, so retreats into it, wearing under her nightdress the shirt he had on at the end, burrowing where she can be alone with him in her sleepless world, making love in the stationmaster's cottage in Voronezh, his face against large melon-like breasts now dried up and useless.

಄

Her room overlooks a park across the road. Crimson velvet drapes frame white lace curtains at the bay window. The narrow wardrobe has an outside mirror. She has hung up her two Baku skirts and blouses, Peter's jacket, trousers and greatcoat and, on another hanger, the blue shawl. As well as warm clothes, the Salvation Army women also let her have a buckram suitcase with string webbing on the outside of the lid; it lies open on the single bed, which has a chenille cover the same colour as the drapes. In the cot beside the bed, this first afternoon, George is asleep.

The three drawers in the mahogany chest each have two metal handles the shape of a lion's head. She opens the top one, releasing a faint whiff of tobacco, and wonders which of Peter's brothers had this room. His, Mrs Brent told her, faces the back garden. In the drawer, she places George's other Baku shift and bonnet, muslin squares, and the white silk stockings from her wedding day, wishing she could have parted with them rather than her ring. She holds the *Princess Royal* hatbands, one in each hand. Was it this one, or the other, from Peter in Petersburg? the first thing he gave her; no way of knowing. She puts them in the drawer, and the paper with the address, large inky loops on l,t,d, the only writing of his she has.

Also, Peter's passport, a much folded piece of paper signed by Sir Edward Grey, Foreign Secretary in 1913, in which he personally required and requested in the name of His Majesty all those whom it may concern to allow Peter Thomas Boulton to pass freely without let or hindrance. *Peter Thomas* ... and her mind goes back to the English church in Baku last year, the Chaplain's Adam's apple bobbing above his stiff collar as he intoned: Peter Thomas, wilt thou have this woman to thy wedded wife? And Peter replied with confidence, that same assurance which took him north across Russia: I will.

The *bolshevik* permit is so thin she's sure it will separate into pieces. Pyotr Tomashevich and Olga Feodorovna. 'You helped us through,' she says into the silence. She leaves both papers with the other things, unable to throw away anything to do with Peter. She closes the drawer, handles rattling in their mountings.

All that remain inside the suitcase are the sepia photographs of Mama and the boys. She takes them out. Mama is looking at the camera with an expression that says: this is how I am. 'Mama, you would understand, wouldn't you, this terrible aloneness, although you were never alone.' Mama always understood. 'What am I going to do?' Didn't she ask this sitting by Mama's grave in Norwich six years ago? Shortly after, she went to London. Can she do the same again, start somewhere new?

She turns to the photograph of the boys seated on either side of her when she was eleven, Arthur nine and Victor seven. Time has faded Arthur's freckles, and the thick, dark, springy hair of Victor. Arthur's hair is drying untidy, even though she ran a wet comb through it before they went to the photographer's;

as she did every time they went out. 'What happened to you both in the war?'

As if she would neaten Arthur's fine hair, she moves her finger over the photograph, puts it with the other one on the chest. Perhaps Mrs Brent has some frames. She fastens the case, lifts it on top of the wardrobe.

She steps onto the landing where two rugs overlap. There are six bedrooms on this floor. At the end is a bathroom; last evening, she turned on both taps at the washbasin, let water, luxury, run over her fingers before reproaching herself for a small secret pleasure. To the left is Peter's room. She holds the door knob, closes her eyes, sees his face: we'll have our marriage blessed, with our families, he said. She opens her eyes, goes inside.

A musty, unaired smell greets her. The curtains, same crimson velvet as hers, are faded at the edges. There is a bed, table and chair, mahogany single wardrobe, and a tallboy with rectangular mirror above. The wardrobe door creaks as she opens it. A black suit hangs there. She touches the sleeve, clutches it to her face, breathes it in, hungry for Peter, but all that fills her nostrils is camphor. The tallboy is empty. She opens the table drawer, finds just a pencil with the lead broken off. She holds the pencil against her cheek, puts it in her pocket.

She sits on the bed, pulls at the soft bumpy chenille, rests her hand on the shape of the pillow beneath. She draws back the cover. The white pillowcase is edged with lace, entwined initials B and C embroidered in the top corner. B for Boulton; C? She lays her cheek on the pillow, encircles the pillow with both arms, closing her eyes.

☙

'Thomas,' Peter's father says that evening.

A smile plays around her lips, which surprises her for she cannot remember the last time she smiled, or imagine she ever will again. Does he see the two of them as equals, survivors? She is standing with him in the morning room. When they came in, he put a couple of logs on the fire from a full wicker basket. Their resinous fragrance makes her think of the rationed pine ones at the Archangel lodgings.

She blinks, looks at the chintz, which in Norwich she hated because it was Rose's choice. Here, however, it goes well with pale enamelled woodwork and a Persian carpet surrounded by dark varnished boards. Near her, a bookcase holds a Bible, an atlas, *Household Medicine*, some Dickens, a row of yellowback novels, and Longfellow's *Complete Poems* in the same maroon cover Father had at home.

They have eaten their meal of steak and kidney pie, with Joe, who has gone to his shed. Aren't the evenings getting dark and chilly? she asked his father, alarmed that Joe's absence might be to do with her arrival.

He has a lamp and stove in there, Livvy. I don't push him; he's had a lot to accept, with all that's happened.

Thomas, rather than Mr Boulton. She likes the sound of it in her mind. His Midlands accent is not as marked as Mrs Brent's. Peter didn't have one; she wonders if he ever did or when he lost it, something she doesn't know about him.

Thomas has not asked her to sit down and it occurs to her that, used to being alone, he prefers her to go to her room. Yet his eyes, periwinkle blue, regard her with a kindly expression as if he wants to know how she is. She can find no resemblance between him and Peter. Thomas is the taller by a couple of inches. His hair doesn't flop in the way that Peter's used to but is thicker, as though it stays as it was when combed in the morning, a darker brown than Peter's with streaks of white at the temples and in the full moustache reaching down the sides of his mouth. A sombre green tie, knotted loosely below a winged collar, disappears beneath a waistcoat in the same black worsted as his suit. The material has a white stripe fine enough not to draw attention to itself or the wearer, jacket fastened by a single row of buttons. There is a faint odour about him, of the world outside the house.

Her eyes stray to a photograph on the wall: Peter, in academic gown at his graduation from Birmingham University, right arm curved, hand resting against his waist holding a scroll, hair contained by the mortar board. He is staring at some point beyond the camera. She tries, fails, to connect this person, a dummy, with the husband she knew.

In a frame alongside is Nell, a larger copy of the one Peter had in Baku. She lets Thomas explain, however, to fill silence. 'And these,' Thomas turns to three photographs on top of the upright piano; she wonders if Peter used to play, doesn't ask, afraid to ruffle the air, the life Thomas has made for himself alone; her arrival and the news she brought are sufficient disturbance. 'Tom, Jack and Will, in order of age.' They are wearing the khaki serge Private's uniform of the Royal Warwickshire regiment, one she saw on Baku streets last year, that she cut and ripped from mangled bodies of crying soldiers. Thomas has picked up the middle photograph and is holding it so they can both see. His fingers are long, nails clean. Yet, she imagines making bicycles a dirty job. Perhaps he employs a lot of men as did Yefim Aaronovich. 'Jack was always impulsive,' Thomas is saying. Her eyelids sag with exhaustion. She tries to concentrate on a handsome face beneath a peaked cap. 'He was only three months past his seventeenth birthday when he enlisted in 1915; had a mission to be a doctor among the poor but broke off his studies.'

Thomas goes to the bureau, pulls down the lid. He moves with ease, returns holding a box and piece of paper. 'Jack's VC,' he says, offering the box to her, 'and the citation. His mother and I went to London to receive them from the King.'

She looks at the Maltese Cross and purple ribbon nestling in their case. She unfolds the paper, reads of a night attack in France, deaths of those in charge of Jack's platoon; of his taking command, shooting a German officer and three men, causing others to surrender, then withdrawing, sniping. *Learning that some wounded still lay in the open, Private Boulton went out, as there were no stretcher-bearers, and carried in three men under heavy fire. It was while bringing back the second man that Private Boulton sustained wounds to the chest and abdomen from which he died a few hours later.*

She remembers the animal sound of screaming. The reek of blood and muck in Baku hospital clogs her nostrils, and she understands how Jack died. Tears are prickling her eyes. 'You must be very proud.' She hands Thomas the box and citation. He returns to the bureau and she focuses on the ceiling, blinks to stop the tears escaping.

'Tom was older,' Thomas tells her, 'and was conscripted that same year.' He walks away from the bureau and his eyes rest once more on the photographs of his sons. 'Will, of course, you know.'

An hour spent holding the basin, watching a nurse clean that stomach wound, then sitting at his bedside until he died. 'For a short time,' she manages to say.

'His officer wrote that Will's dying words were of his mother. May was touched and comforted by that.'

Did Peter tell the officer when given Will's belongings? Was it the same one who wrote the letter? Will had thought she was his mother. 'That's right,' she says.

Thomas picks up a photograph on a small circular table next to the piano. 'Tom and Connie on their wedding day.'

Tom is in uniform, Connie's arm through his, the couple smiling at the camera, seeking to preserve for eternity that moment of radiance. The only brother to come back.

'They married in 1916 just before Tom left for France,' Thomas explains. 'They'd been sweethearts for a year.'

At the word sweetheart, she feels again her mouth try the beginning of a smile: Thomas, all his life used to rituals of courtship, marriage, babies; now forced to make conversation to a stranger, the two of them flotsam of a decimated family.

There were no photographs taken at her wedding. She doesn't have one of Peter.

'Here we all are much younger,' Thomas says. He and Peter's mother are seated. Standing on either side are Peter, in knickerbockers and matching jacket, and Nell in a frock with lace collar and cuffs like she remembers wearing as a girl, hair sporting an enormous ribbon, ringlets falling halfway to her waist. Propped on Thomas's knee is a child in a dress, with long hair. Peter's mother is holding a baby. Two boys in sailor suits sit on the floor, legs crossed. 'Tom and Jack in front, and Will with me, about eighteen months old. This was during Annie's first winter, 1900, which she didn't survive.'

Thomas has lost four of his eight children, three of his five sons; and Nell is in Canada. Even more does the weight of responsibility for Peter's death press on her.

∾

He sits at the bureau as he does every evening. It is as if the half hour or so in here with Livvy was a separate existence and now he steps back into the familiar. Livvy has gone to her room after glancing at the *Daily Express*, turning pages without reading. He asked her if she'd like one of the yellowback Wilkie Collins novels. May used to enjoy those. Another time, Livvy said. She must still be tired, he thinks, after that journey, although she has not spoken of it.

He pulls down the bureau lid, reaches for the box containing letters, telegrams, newspaper cuttings. Stops. The familiar has a new layer since he was doing this last evening, a patina of fresh grief. He has left the *Times* in the hall, has no longer appetite or need for news of Russia; he must remember to cancel the order with the newsagent. A fever, Livvy said of Peter's final days, consumption; she clasped George, her eyes closed so tightly as to crease her face into a frown, and he felt a door closing, and that he may have to wait for her to say more.

She gave him a couple of drawings Will had done. They were too big for the box so he lay them across the top. Now, he picks them up, rough paper with uneven edges, touched by Will. In the bottom right corners are dates: 1.vii.17 and 15.vi.18, and initials WAB. Both drawings are of desert: sand, rocks – he would never have thought of those – mountains in the background, a distant camel and rider; could be scenes from the Bible. He rests one against his cheek, closes his eyes, hears Will's voice: I've signed on, Pa. It is as if the news of Will's death, as much as Peter's, is recent, this engulfing realisation that he will never again see his fourth son, speak to him, feel the lad's hand on his arm. Of all his sons, Will was the most affectionate.

He and Will are the only family members to draw. The drawing still against his cheek, he opens his eyes, looks across at two of his own efforts, framed: a loaf of bread, and the church where he and May were married. Will the day come when he draws again? And what; why would anyone want to look at a bowl of fruit? Did you do these? There was admiration in Livvy's question earlier, and a way of placing the words as if she was unused to speaking English. It occurred to him that perhaps in Russia she spoke Russian. The thought lent her an air of exoticism, and to him amazement that he should have living under his roof someone who had seen places nobody here had heard of. The lamplight gilded her thick hair, the same chestnut as May's, parted on the left, and he wondered when she had it cut; perhaps to travel across Russia. It suits her. Several times she touched the back of her neck and he noticed she wasn't wearing a wedding ring. Surely Peter gave her one?

Peter, with his mother's hazel eyes, always late: sorry, is that the time? he'd say, rushing in or out. Should he have kept Peter here, insisted his eldest son join the business? Some fathers would have. But how could he when there was a restlessness about the boy, yearning for adventure, soul searching for moorings beyond this city? The romance of it, Father, Peter said about going to Russia, the land of Pushkin and Turgenev; and he wondered what Pushkin and Turgenev had to do with it. Romance? And yet, even if Peter had stayed here, he would've joined up in 1914.

He places the drawing with the other one, takes Will's diary from the box. The small copperplate is in pencil, perhaps the one

Will used for drawing. The journal starts in September 1916, from Britain, round the Bay of Biscay to the Mediterranean ... *how small and insignificant one feels to be surrounded by sea, no sight of land for days* ... Port Said, Suez Canal, Red Sea, Persian Gulf, names from a geography lesson or fable. Christmas 1916 spent edging towards the beleaguered town of Kut ... *no Christmas Dinner, couldn't eat a thing, in any case, tummy bad again ... 16th February 1917: Kut is ours at last, rain day after day, ground impassable, what wouldn't I give for a cup of tea. Chalky and Lofty knocked out in the final push. I miss them. Flesh wound in my left arm ...*

He turns a few pages to the last entries, which he read again and again last evening and knows by heart. *10th July 1918: we're to go to Persia – all very hush-hush. 17th August: at Enzeli after riding in motors from Kasvin with loaded rifles and fixed bayonets as the locals were likely to be hostile – fortunately they stayed home. 19th August: at Baku, Russia, after dreadful sea voyage up the Caspian; terribly sick. What a hell-hole! Heat, little water, constant bombardment, stink of oil. How could anybody live here?*

Yet they did, Peter and Livvy. Tears for his eldest son are pushing under his eyelids. He fumbles in his jacket pocket for a handkerchief, closes his eyes, holds the handkerchief against them, as if to stop himself falling apart. Shoulders sag on a sob.

But there is George. He puts the handkerchief back. If he'd kept Peter here, there would've been no George: grand little fellow, spit and image of Peter as a baby. His grandson. He wonders if George has been sent to him to replace his lost sons.

He closes the bureau, gets to his feet. He is always in bed soon after ten. Joe will come in later and lock the scullery door.

They both leave for work by eight on their bicycles. Livvy might like one. He will have to ask her.

Before turning out the lamp, he rests his eyes on the photograph of May on the bureau: do the work of each day, Thomas, look after our family, she seems to be saying. And now he has two new members to care for. He curls his right index finger against her cheek.

He goes into the hall, climbs the stairs. A couple of steps from the top he stops, listens. Through the hissing of the gas lamp, sobbing. In Livvy's room. His heart is bellowing, as if demanding to be let out, free to comfort the grieving girl. He covers the remaining stairs in one step, starts along the landing, past his own door, halts a yard from hers as if at a wall protected with barbed wire. The sobbing is muffled, as though she is crying into her pillow. Sweat is prickling his hands and the back of his neck. The grandfather clock ticks in the corner. He stands, unable to move, staring at the closed door, breath coming in short gasps, chest aching as if his heart has literally broken, pieces forcing their way through.

FOURTEEN

How different, she thinks, uniforms look for ceremonial duties rather than active soldiering. She is sitting on a wooden seat in the park, near the octagonal bandstand. George is asleep in the perambulator with Barney, the small brown bear. The Birmingham Police Band is playing *Men of Harlech*. Her eyes wander over people strolling on this mild, autumn Sunday afternoon; many young women wear their hair short, although she still hates her own.

Apart from the band, there isn't a uniform in sight, everybody apparently without a care. Is this a country that has fought a war for over four years? Of course, it ended nearly a year ago, and here there was no revolution or civil war. No-one has seen people hacking at collapsed horses for meat; there isn't anyone who has lived through the last five years with me, to share memories, good times and bad; nobody has any idea that I've lost Peter. It is as if she is in a foreign country he will never know about, where no-one speaks her language.

The last uniforms she saw were at Liverpool docks; and her mind is off again, back along the road trodden, escape from a solitary present. When she arrived at Liverpool from Russia just over a week ago, legs unsteady on firm land, the rest of her still swaying with the movement of the ship, aching stomach hollow but forgiving, Salvation Army people were on the quayside, bread and hot soup ready. One of the women patted George's head, saying: we pray every ship will be the last carrying refugees. Was it the same woman who put her and George up for the night, and offered winter clothes? She can't remember: they all looked the same in those dark coats and bonnets and strange accents. Somebody gave her money for the train fare to Birmingham and a tram to Peter's home in Lightmoor on the edge of the city. In fact, there was enough for a motor taxi from New Street station, a great extravagance, but it was quick to cover the two or three miles to Laurel Road and she was anxious to deliver the news from Russia. Also, the first drops of rain were starting.

After Peter died, she stayed another night at the lodgings in Archangel. The *dvornik* turned out to be unexpectedly co-operative, no doubt not wanting the corpse of a consumptive in the house. He knew where to hire a cart, who to ask to dig the grave. Archangel is a centre of the timber trade, so a coffin was easy to obtain. Money changed hands: her wages from General Miller; and Peter's watch, for which the *dvornik* told her he'd managed fifty roubles.

Try some soup, the *dvornik*'s wife urged her: a little nourishment'll help. She shook her head, turned away from the foul-smelling stuff. Help? Nothing, nobody could. She sat staring at the opposite wall, unable to bear the sight of strange hands on Peter's skin while the Russian woman laid him out; unable to sleep. When she followed him on his last journey through early morning mist the day after his death, people they passed stood still, crossed themselves, men removing their caps, before bowing their heads. She wanted to say: thank you, he was worth more than this; it's my fault. But she said nothing, carrying George in the drizzle, supported by the *dvornik*'s wife; watched the carter and his boy lower the plain coffin into a muddy grave, yellow leaves whirling in the wind.

She left the bedrolls with the *dvornik* in exchange for a string bag to hold her belongings, and that evening, wearing Peter's greatcoat, embarked a ship transporting timber to Murmansk, a twenty-four-hour voyage of vomit. Evacuation was under way there, too. Another few days and she would've been too late. Unlike Archangel, for centuries a port, Murmansk had been built in 1915 with British aid, somebody told her, to supply the Tsar's army. Because it was near the Gulf Stream, the sea didn't freeze in winter. Murmansk comes from the local dialect, her informant added. It means "edge of the earth". Funny, the things you remember. She thought the name apt as she stared through the rain at miles of quays, scattered huts, ugly groups of brick and concrete buildings.

Next day, she was on a British Navy ship. A sailor handed her a tin mug of tea: all right, luv? Soon have you home. Home? she wondered, huddled with George. Baku. As the vessel distanced itself from port, she stretched out an arm to Russia, home for more than five years, as if pulled by a magnetic force, until sickness obliterated it all.

In the park, tears are swelling round the corners of her eyes. The band has stopped playing. She stands up, feels dowdy all in brown, top to toe; but they were kind, the Salvation Army women, and kindness she needs, more than food or liquid, enfolding, embalming her; numbing her. In the rough wool of the coat pocket she finds a handkerchief, lace edged, with initials VN in the corner. She wonders who VN is, or was. A widow who died? A child?

She does not think of herself as a widow, just without Peter, result of a series of events that could've been avoided. She has looked at the atlas in the morning room, worked out the route west from Baku across the mountains to the Black Sea, then along to the Bosphorus, Sea of Marmara, Dardanelles, to the Mediterranean. Sea, sea. Or south to Persia, and across Mesopotamia to the Mediterranean. Hardly the quickest way of reaching Britain with a baby, not to mention bandits, yet she should've insisted they do it:

We can't go north, Peter. Winter's coming. It'll be bad for your chest.

My chest's fine now, he would've argued.

Because you've been in the south. We must go to Persia.

It'll take months to get home. Weeks on the Mediterranean. You'll be ill.

I'll get used to it.

She would've worn him down until he pursed his mouth and agreed to change the plan. They'd still be on the journey now but Peter would be alive.

She presses the handkerchief against one eye then the other, as if to push the tears back.

A strolling couple stop by her. The woman is wearing a navy skirt cut above the ankle, matching jacket ending at hips emphasising a slim figure, blue felt hat trimmed with red berries. What has happened to corsets? she wonders. The woman's male companion wears a fawn lounge suit, white boater, and narrow laced shoes that have pointed toes.

'Are you all right?' the woman asks.

'Yes, thank you,' she lies. 'I'm going home now.' Home? The woman smiles, walks on, arm through her companion's, head tilted as he talks.

Aloneness jolts her.

She puts the handkerchief away. The tentative autumn sun hangs lower. She has complied with Peter's dying wish but doesn't imagine he expected her to live here permanently. Six days now. Thomas has opened an account for her at the Municipal Bank, yet she doesn't want to depend on him for money.

Only the other week, when Peter talked about having their marriage blessed with their families, she made up her mind to write to her father. She must buy notepaper and envelopes. But she has not seen any shops, wanders into the park each afternoon with George in the perambulator, lassitude and exhaustion round her shoulders like an extra layer of clothing. The years stretch ahead, a future she must make an effort to fill; another forty, even fifty she might live, when to remember the sweetness of having loved Peter will always be accompanied by the ache of loss, pain of remorse, the wound never healing. Without the fears of those last weeks in Russia: uncertainty, risk of capture, lack of food and money, all she can feel now is blankness, a sense of walking in a bare landscape with no signposts.

Father did let her go, didn't he? Never went to London to fetch her home when she wrote that she was going to Russia with her employers, nor sent Arthur; Arthur was sixteen in 1914, old enough to travel from Norwich to London alone; Thomas has told her he came to Birmingham from Cannock at that age. Come back with me, Livvy, Arthur might've pressed her; we all miss you; even Rose has been looking quite pale. Would she have gone? Probably not. She'd discovered a spirit of adventure, a means of escape. Can she recapture that same spirit? She must look for a job.

Father might want her to return to Norwich now. Perhaps he and Rose have children. The idea of settling under his roof, with Rose full of advice on how to bring up George, repels her. If she has a job such as she did with Esther's family, she can live in with George.

The men are packing up their instruments. She pushes the perambulator round the bandstand, severe lace-ups pinching her toes. Her Baku canvas sandals were ruined after the night walk through the forest to Obozerskaya; they'd dried out of shape, tops flapping away from soles by the time she arrived in Liverpool.

Golden leaves cover the path that leads to the gate into Laurel Road. One side of the road borders the park. The other is lined with three-storey brick houses. She stands for a moment looking at number thirty-four, Peter's home, opposite the park gate. A low wall separates the pavement from a small garden. A brick path meanders from a gate in the wall to the porch. Borders on either side of the path have recently been dug by Joe. Wicket side gates open into the back garden. She wonders if Peter used to help outside.

She checks right and left before crossing Laurel Road, not that there is any traffic; it is habit, after cars requisitioned by the *bolsheviki* careering through Baku flying a red flag, and then Model T Fords and other British Army vehicles dashing about. A church spire pierces the sky above the rooftops; Thomas asked her to accompany him and Joe this morning. She declined and he suggested she rest. I can neither rest nor sleep, she wanted to say but didn't; nor that she is unable to worship or pray to a God in whose goodness she no longer believes. When the vicar called one evening last week and talked about

God's comfort in time of sorrow, she gazed beyond him and his phrases at Peter's dying face.

Nathaniel and Maud are expected for tea. They live in another part of Lightmoor. She supposes she should address them as aunt and uncle. It doesn't seem right, meeting them for the first time and Peter not with her. Perhaps she can get away with not calling them anything. She unfastens the gate of number thirty-four, steeling herself to meet Thomas's brother and sister-in-law, the remains of the family coming to look, to see Peter's widow and fatherless baby. People who knew Peter before she did, for longer than she did.

Yesterday, it was Tom and Connie. Tom has been home from the war six months and works with his father at the factory. Nothing prepared her for the change wrought by the three years since the wedding photograph: Tom, corners of the mouth drooping, smoking one cigarette after another, same red brown hair as Joe, blue eyes giving the impression of staring through her, shaking fingers drumming a tattoo on the chair arm.

Every so often, he lurched to the edge of his seat. 'What's that?'

'Nothing, love,' Connie assured him.

'Thought I heard something,' he snapped, turned to the others. 'Sorry about that.'

Connie, petite and pregnant, dark curly hair pinned and tied at the back of her neck, smiled - in resignation? - brown eyes those of one who'd searched for the end of the rainbow and found only darkness.

In the hall as they prepared to leave, Tom said: they don't understand, Liv. He took her hands in his, added: nobody does; you do, don't you? You were there; you were in it; you nursed Will. He bent to kiss her cheek, bringing with him the raw smell of Woodbines which will always remind her of Lev Yefimovich. It's nice you're here, Tom said; we'll see you again.

Liv. Nobody has ever called her that, she thinks now. She rather likes it.

He can't do the work he used to, Thomas told her after Tom and Connie had gone; I've kept on the woman who replaced him during the war; he comes in, does odd jobs and I pay him as before; his hands are too unsteady for any precision work, and it's not safe to let him use machinery; he can't concentrate on anything for long.

Poor Tom, she thinks, living with his parents-in-law, paid by his father for a job he can no longer do, now done by a woman. At least he can make a child.

೪

She opens the brown porch door with the key Thomas gave her, then the inner one, which has panels of bevelled glass, blue, red, green. From the outside the panels appear dull but in the long hall shine like jewels, relieving the gloom. She manoeuvres the perambulator across blue, white and terracotta mosaic tiles, into the hall. The left-hand wall is interrupted by the staircase, underneath which is a table holding the telephone and a small silver tray for post. Alongside is a coat stand. She notices two black coats, one sable the other larger, velour with an astrakhan collar, a homburg hat above it. Quality. Peter's Uncle Nathaniel and Aunt Maud. Here. She wonders if she should comb her hair, wishes she could lie down and sleep, puzzles over a suitcase at the foot of the stairs.

The first door on the right opens into the dining room; the second is that of the morning room, from where there is a murmur of conversation. She turns to George in the perambulator, hears the morning room door open, the voices inside louder. She lifts George, closing her eyes on an intake of breath and the warm, soapy, sleepy smell of him. She stands holding him, looking along the hall. The girl advancing towards her reaches out both hands in greeting.

'Livvy! Papa said you'd be back soon.' The girl kisses her cheek, hand against her shoulder. 'I'm Renée.'

Peter's sister has his hazel eyes. Thick chestnut hair ripples down her back in ringlets, tied loosely at the neck. Renée has the heart-shaped face of young Nell in the photograph; is wearing a white blouse, navy cardigan and serge gymslip. 'I've caused a bit of a stir arriving unexpectedly,' Renée chatters, 'with Mrs Brent out for the rest of the day. Three girls at school are down with scarlet fever, so we're all packed off home early for half-term, except those in the girls' class and dormitory, who're in quarantine. Clara Knight's father's chauffeur met us off the train at Snow Hill. Joe's carried some coal in and is lighting the fire in my room.' Renée strokes the back of George's bonnet. 'Isn't he lovely! With Barney, too! Nice to see him again.'

She turns her son round to face Renée. 'This is George.'

'Can I hold him?'

'Yes … that's right, under his bottom, and put your other hand to steady the back of his head and neck.' She takes off her coat, hat and gloves, leaves them on the perambulator, abandons the idea of going upstairs to comb her hair, runs her fingers through it.

Renée's smile disappears. 'Livvy, I haven't said the most important thing. I'm so sorry about Peter. Papa wrote to Mother Superior, asked her to tell me, said I wasn't to be sent home, that you and Joe were here and he was all right. There was a Mass for Peter that evening.'

She stares, realising Renée boards at a convent school. Her throat constricts. She searches for what to say, falls back on, 'I expect you remember him.'

'A bit. He was always nice, used to pat me on the head and call me Little Sis. Nell was Sis. I was only seven when he went to Russia. I used to imagine myself a princess in fabulous jewels and furs from Peter, and everybody would bow and do as I asked.' Renée's eyes sparkle. 'I never told the boys or they would've teased me.'

Her heart pulls with the memory of the same way Peter's eyes used to smile and she remembers him saying about going to Russia: the romance of it, this vast, remote country of Pushkin, Turgenev. She looks at Renée, happy, motherless girl, secure with dreams and innocence. Everybody seems to have their fantasy of Russia and she wonders what it is that holds people in thrall; thinks of the woman swathed in furs, *Princess in the Snow* reclining in a sledge pulled by three horses, frozen, snow-covered fastness stretching as far as a five-domed church on the horizon, that captured her imagination as a child.

'Last summer, Una's parents – Una's my best friend,' Renée tells her – 'they took us to see the Imperial Ballet dance *Petrouschka* in London. The costumes, music, dancing: they were *wonderful*. I've still got the programme upstairs. I'll show you. Russia must've been a lovely place before the horrid things started.'

Horrid things … and the Imperial Ballet, too, have fled. She wonders if they are still in London. Esther enthused about them after an evening at Petersburg's Maryinsky theatre in

1914. What a long time ago that all seems. How young she was.

'We said a Mass for the Tsar when we learnt he'd been murdered last year,' Renée adds. 'Mère Sainte Cécile told us he'd been a good man and much loved by most of the people.'

'And still is by some.' She thinks of Vladimir Ivanovich, stationmaster at Vologda, his obeisance when presented with tsarist roubles. Is the Tsar really dead, then?

'There've been so many special Masses. Nearly all the girls have lost brothers or fathers. There was one for Jack in 1916, Will last year, and for Mama.'

She can think of nothing to say to Renée, comforted and safe at her convent school, a buffer against the world. Why does innocence have to end and dreams be trampled?

George wriggles, whimpers. 'I think you'd better have him back,' Renée suggests.

'He's hungry. I must warm some milk for him.'

'Uncle Nathaniel and Aunt Maud are here. They'll be wondering what's happened to us. Come and say "hello" and let them see George.' Renée passes him to her, encircles them with both arms, kisses her on the cheek. 'I'm so glad you're staying. It's lovely to have a sister again.'

&

She follows Renée into the morning room, aware of voices, silence. Thomas and two strangers stand up. She feels their eyes on her, swallows to ease the tension in her throat.

'Uncle Nathaniel, Aunt Maud,' says Renée, 'this is Livvy, with George.'

Maud – Aunt Maud? - glides towards her, a rustle of jet beads and black bombazine beneath a cloche hat; no concession to the new shorter fashion or abandonment of corsets.

She feels unkempt, adding to her discomfort in front of these people.

'My dear, so sad.' Maud takes her hand, cold lips brushing her cheek in an aura of cologne. 'You must be desolate.'

Must? How does she know what I'm feeling? How can she have any idea? No! I can't, won't, think of her as an aunt. She wishes she could step back but civility is called for. 'Yes,' she says.

Nathaniel, whiskered, florid in a red paisley tie, and larger in all directions than his younger brother, clasps her fingers, raises them to his lips, his hand soft against hers. He's more how she imagines an uncle. She's never really had one. Her father's elder brother ran away to sea as a boy.

'We heard glowing reports of you from Peter's letters last year,' Nathaniel booms, adds more quietly, 'very sad business.' He pats George's head. 'So this is the little fellow.'

'This is George,' she tells him.

George is looking at him as if trying to decide what to do, then smiles.

'Look, Maud!' says Nathaniel.

'Yes, dear, just like Peter.' Maud is taking her arm. 'It's so nice for Thomas to have *one* grandchild here, with his others in Canada.' She sighs. 'I know how it is, separated from grandchildren; a cross we have to bear, result of the path in life our children choose.'

She is about to ask where they live but Maud, drawing her to the sofa, launches, 'You nursed Will, my dear! What a coincidence! Your own brother-in-law.'

'These things happen,' throws in Nathaniel, sitting down. 'Fortunes of war. Chap in the Quarter: brother in France, walked into a barber's shop and who should be in the next chair but his cousin.'

Maud returns to her. 'So you trained as a *nurse* before you went to Russia?' Maud's emphasis suggests nurses are a breed apart.

Three thuds of her heart, so hard they hurt. She wants to shock, tell of screams, stench, blood and other muck; of the ashen faces of the nurses and helpers as they moved from one man to the next that August day last year, cutting away stinking uniforms caked with mud and blood. But the words stick in her throat, have no place in this peaceful, provincial English home. She swallows. 'No, I was not a trained nurse. When the Turkish attack came, we all had to help. We were shown what to do.'

Maud's eyebrows arch. 'Oh? And how did Will come to be in Russia? The last we heard he was in Mesopotamia. You know, he was in the capture of Baghdad, my dear,' gushing now. 'He wrote such an interesting letter about searching houses. The women live separately, it seems.'

'Mesopotamia is south of Russia,' she explains to Maud. 'Will's battalion, and others, were defending the city of Baku against the Turks, who wanted the oil.'

'Hush-hush mission, no doubt,' volunteers Nathaniel. 'Johnny Turk and the Bulgars; lot of mischief in that part of the world; big threat to India.'

Maud is staring at her. 'So it was a Turkish bullet that killed Will?'

'Shrapnel. Yes. Does it matter what nationality?' she wants to know. 'Or alter the fact that he was killed? I sat with him the last minutes of his life but it wasn't my fault, or anybody's in the hospital, that he died. Not even the most experienced

London doctor could have saved him from such carnage.' Does Maud have any idea what the inside of a stomach looks like? she wonders; or the smell of human blood, lots of it, even though Maud's had children? Of course not. She perches, trembling, on the edge of the sofa. Can she escape to prepare George's milk? He has fallen asleep against her chest. She closes her eyes for one breath of his contentment and dependence on her, opens them, glances at Thomas. Has he nothing to say? He is watching her. She looks away.

'Well!' Maud rallies. 'Put like that, Livvy … '

The door opens and Joe walks in, rubbing hands that smell of carbolic, another reminder of Baku hospital. 'Fire's drawing nicely in your room, Reen,' he says to his sister. 'I've taken your case up.'

Renée raises her face to him, inclines it, a mischievous glint in her eyes. 'Thank you, Joseph.'

He flicks her ringlets. 'None of your fancy convent school airs with me, my girl!'

He seems ill at ease, she thinks, in his Sunday suit. Now is the moment to go. Maud, however, has not finished.

'You'll be engaging a nanny for George, of course, Livvy.'

'Livvy knows all about nannying,' says Joe.

'People say you can't get staff since the war,' Maud pursues. 'It's not true. Beatrice has had no trouble in London. If you're prepared to pay, you can find reliable people as before.'

'I shan't be employing a nanny.' George has woken up, is fixing her with a look that says: I know you. She wants to run away with him. 'We have lost Peter and everything that was ours, so I'm not about to turn him over to the care of a stranger. Now, if you'll excuse me, I must prepare his milk.' She gets to her feet, wills the first tear to hold back until she is through the doorway.

'Understandable,' she hears Nathaniel say, followed by Renée's, 'I'll go and help.'

FIFTEEN

Blinded by tears, she places George in a corner of the kitchen, gives him a wooden spoon to play with, clears her eyes with the backs of her hands. Mrs Brent has left milk in a saucepan, covered by a muslin cloth edged with beads; she has Sunday afternoon and evening off so cycles over to Hay Hall to see a friend from when she used to work there, and they attend chapel together.

She removes the cloth, puts the pan on the range, hears the kitchen door open, close. She turns round. Renée.

'I thought you might like some help ... oh, Livvy ... you're upset.' At the range she moves the pan a fraction, feels Renée's arm round her shoulders. 'Please don't cry, Livvy. Aunt Maud has views but she doesn't mean badly.'

That gesture of comfort, the first since Salvation Army women hugged her goodbye at Liverpool Station six days ago, is enough to push her into territory she is terrified of entering, where she might never be able to stop crying, submerged by grief, as if by a tidal wave. She has left the handkerchief in the coat pocket. She sniffs, heaves each breath.

The wall of water is receding. She rubs a sleeve across her eyes and face, lifts the pan, pours the milk into George's bottle, which probably used to be Renée's, and the boys' before that. Peter's bottle. She clutches it, one Peter must've touched as a baby, perhaps pushed away or knocked to the floor. Was he good?

Renée has let go of her shoulders. 'Your father hasn't once questioned me,' she tells Renée, 'which I've really appreciated. I can do without your aunt's opinions and probing. Tom's right. Nobody understands.' A few tears have escaped down her cheeks but she turns to face Renée. 'Can you try and imagine? The Turkish Army are just a few miles away. For weeks you've been expecting an attack. When it comes, there are hundreds of wounded. Everybody has to help. Peter was ferrying people from the Front to the hospital in a Model T Ford. He'd never driven before! And your aunt's face; to infer that if somebody else had nursed Will, somebody trained, he might not have died. How dare she!'

This dear girl can't be expected to understand, she berates herself. Renée's mouth quivers. It's Renée's brother they're talking about, next above Joe in age. Renée probably remembers him better than she does Peter.

'*These laid the world away,* quotes Renée; *poured out the red Sweet wine of youth; gave up the years to be Of work and joy.*'

'What's that?'

'Rupert Brooke wrote it at the beginning of the war.'

'Who was he?'

'A young officer. He died soon after. One of the girls at school was given a volume of his poems for her birthday. She read some of them to us. I liked that one. That's how I want to think of Jack and Will, Livvy, sacrificing their lives for honour.'

Sasha Nikolaevich, she remembers, and realises she has spoken his name.

'Who?' Renée asks.

'Oh ... a friend of Esther in Russia ... he died in the early weeks of the war.' ... in his last letter he wrote of the glory of fighting for Russia; where's the glory, Livvy? Esther wept, quickly disenchanted. It is not for me, she decides now, to do the same to Renée, still idolising dead brothers.

She brushes an arm across her face, nods towards George, who is playing with his feet. 'Can you bring him over?'

Renée lifts him as if he is a fragile parcel. 'I'm getting the idea.' Renée sounds more cheerful, sits and watches him attack the bottle. 'Aunt Maud and Mama had different views on everything. First, it was cycling. Do you ride?'

'Not since before I went to Russia. Your father had a bike sent over from the factory the other day but I haven't tried it yet.'

'We're practically in the country here and there're some lovely rides. We'll go together, shall we? Talking of Aunt Maud, another thing she used to criticise was the WSPU. Mama worked for the Pankhursts.'

'I remember Peter telling me about a hunger strike in prison and forced feeding.'

'Mama ignored Aunt Maud, did whatever she wished. I think that's the best way to be with her.' Renée giggles. 'Aunt Maud refused to vote in the election, said that to register she'd have to reveal her age, which was nobody's business.'

She feels she has an ally in Renée, a nugget of comfort in this alien world; but it does not stop tears congregating once more. 'And then to suggest I engage a nanny for George. I've nobody, nothing, except him. I can't bear to let him out of my sight. Does your aunt think I'm going to have a stranger look after him, then sit and peer at my fingernails all day?' She is sobbing now, holds an arm across her eyes.

Renée takes a handkerchief from the gymslip pocket and passes it to her. 'It's clean,' she says, stands up, puts an arm round her. 'You've got us, Livvy.'

I can't tell any of them how responsible I feel for Peter's death. She keeps the handkerchief against raw eyes as if it is blood she is stemming.

'The nuns have been praying for you,' Renée tells her.

'Huh!' She takes the handkerchief away, sees Renée draw in a sharp breath, eyes and mouth wide open.

Renée's voice is quiet. 'It does help; it must, praying.'

She tilts the bottle for George to have the last of the milk. 'It's easy for you to say that from within the security of your home and school. You might change your mind if you saw some of the ghastly things people do to each other; destroying lives in terrible ways - ' She stops. Don't disenchant the girl. Yes, but … Leave it.

'We've lost loved ones. The nuns say when God sees the suffering man causes, He suffers too, because we have turned so far from Him to do those things.'

Which comes first, she wonders, wickedness or turning away from God?

'What does George do now?' Renée asks.

'We'll give him a few minutes then put him in his cot.'

'Mrs Brent will have left everything ready for our tea.'

She does not feel hungry. Neither does she relish another round with Maud. Yet, she does not want to be on her own. 'Come upstairs with me,' she says to Renée, 'while I change George and put him to bed. He'll be all right with Barney.'

⁊

She makes a pot of tea and butters the bread rather than return to the morning room with Renée. On the oblong oak dining table, covered with a lace cloth, she finds laid out ham, pork pie, a dish of cold diced mixed vegetables and pickles in mayonnaise which, she remembers, the English call Russian salad; and scones, trifle, jam made from garden plums.

When everybody is seated, she pours tea into cups decorated in the top half with gold filigree.

Maud helps herself to a slice of pork pie. 'You know, Livvy, I'm sure you're better away from that country, such dreadful things we hear about.'

She hands Maud a cup of tea. 'It wasn't all bad.' Heart prodding, she searches for words to defend the country that was her home when she knows Maud – perhaps everybody at the table – cannot imagine there being anything good to say about Russia. She remembers the dark, lowered eyes of Vladimir Ivanovich. 'A stationmaster and his wife who sheltered us on the journey gave us their food, went without.'

'These awful Bolsheviks!' Maud pursues, pronouncing the foreign word slowly, as if it were a garden pest; she passes the salad to Thomas, addressing her comments to him. 'Look how they treated their king. It's such a pity His Majesty couldn't have offered a home to him and his wife. They were his cousins, you know. And those poor children.'

'It would've been very unpopular in this country,' Thomas attempts. 'We were fighting a war for freedom, after all.'

'And the Romanovs were autocrats,' Joe throws in.

She catches her breath, that the Tsar should be criticised here as well; that people are speaking as if there is no doubt he is dead.

'I saw Mr Lloyd George's hand in the decision.' Maud shudders.

'His Majesty was most sensitive to public opinion, my dear,' says Nathaniel.

'The Bolsheviks are nothing but murderers and ruffians,' Maud pronounces. 'Did we tell you what young Henry Rowland wrote to his parents recently?' Maud turns back to her. 'The Rowlands are our neighbours, my dear. Henry's at Oxford. Such a nice young man. Apparently, someone on his staircase took it upon himself to go to Russia this summer. Why, I can't imagine. When the man returned to Oxford, he was asked to leave. People won't look at you now if you're suspected of Russian sympathies.'

She feels a flush rising up her neck into her cheeks. 'Not every Russian is a Bolshevik. And about the Tsar and his family: no bodies have been found.' She looks at Renée sitting next to Maud. Renée winks.

'Our government won't stand for any of this revolutionary nonsense,' says Nathaniel. 'See what happened to the rail strike.' He explains to her, 'If you'd arrived ten days earlier, my dear, you'd have found no trains.' He passes the pork pie to his brother. 'People soon realised the Bolsheviks are supported by the Germans. The strikers received precious little sympathy; same with the Birmingham police in August.'

'But the railway workers did achieve a sliding scale of pay,' interjects Joe, 'so the strike was not entirely unsuccessful.'

'It's these trades unions that are the cause of trouble in the workplace,' says Maud. 'They encourage men to be discontented and that leads to disloyalty. Some people have no moral standards these days. Fortunately, there's nothing like that in the Jewellery Quarter, is there dear?' Maud turns to her husband.

'The men know when they're well off,' adds Nathaniel; 'glad to be in full-time work. No skilled jewellery craftsman worth his salt would do anything to disrupt production: too much pride in the job.' He looks at his brother. 'Do you get any trouble?'

'We're a family business,' says Thomas. 'I know all the men, home situations, war service. I won't see anybody go without. A union wouldn't give them more benefits. People returned from the war expecting their old jobs back. The Prime Minister promised them a land fit for heroes and they're not going to forget it. I still pay the ones who can't work as they used to. They help as best they can.'

Like Tom, his own son, she thinks.

'I've kept on some of the women who worked for me during the war,' Thomas is saying. 'They're often the only breadwinner in the family.'

Joe looks at his uncle. 'Not all employers are as thoughtful as Father. They're only interested in lining their pockets. It's tough on their workers.'

She watches father and uncle raise eyebrows at Joe; there is injustice which one day will have to be accounted for, she remembers from Lev Yefimovich back in 1914.

'Mr McAllister's a good employer, dear, isn't he?' Maud asks Joe.

'He's very fair. But men who work for the other sort have to be protected.'

'And I say employers and loyal workers need to be freed from troublemakers,' counters Nathaniel. 'Fortunately, most chaps are decent and hard-working. The rotten few have to be rooted out. They'll soon come to their senses when they find themselves on the street with no money in their pockets and mouths to feed at home.'

He makes it sound easy, she thinks; how to stop a revolution.

Nathaniel turns to his brother. 'Are you thinking of expanding into motor cycles, or even parts for cars?'

'Like Morris?' Thomas shakes his head. 'We're just settling down after finishing with munitions. It's no time to be going into something new. There're shortages of raw materials, skilled labour, capital. Morris must be a fool. Thinks he's Henry Ford.'

'Men are coming back from the war having learned to drive army vehicles,' Nathaniel points out. 'Motoring will no longer be just a pastime of the rich. Your ordinary chap's going to want his own four wheels. That's what Morris is building on.'

Thomas drinks the last of his tea. 'You mark my words, the man'll be bankrupt this time next year.'

Shall I tell them about Peter driving a Model T in Baku last year? she wonders; decides against it, better with attention away from herself and Russia; grateful for the comfort of Mrs Brent's scones, and a room where her eyes can rest on walls papered in blue and green patterns and Thomas's paintings of street scenes. Two sideboards stand along one wall. The door and skirting boards are cream.

At the other end of the table, Joe is pushing crumbs round his plate with a knife. She looks across at Renée. The girl smiles. Renée is her ally. The others have forgotten I'm here. This week, I'll start looking for a job.

❦

He sits at the bureau, pulls down the lid, but his eyes wander from the box of papers. Even though she has gone upstairs, he still sees Livvy standing by the window gazing at the garden, then drawing the curtains: he liked that, as if she felt at home. She turned back to the room, glancing at the photographs as though searching for something. When he asked her during the week if she'd like a bicycle and she told him she hadn't ridden since before she went to Russia, a faint smile moved her lips, more in her mind; he could have missed it. His heart lifted, that perhaps she was remembering some happy occasion, and he wanted to see her really smile, wondered what he could do or say to make that happen.

She was unsettled, upset even, by some of the talk this afternoon. When she was pouring the tea, a pinkish tinge to her eyelids and beneath her eyes suggested she'd been crying. Maud can be overbearing, yet doesn't mean badly and he thinks, not for the first time, that his brother must've grown an outer shell, like ivy over a wall, always showing the world a bluff, hearty exterior, unmindful of Maud's observations.

Nathaniel was the adventurous one – he, Thomas, used to feel there was something of Nathaniel in Peter – leaving the family home and forge in Cannock at the age of nineteen to make a fortune in Birmingham. When's Nat coming to visit? he'd ask Father; as a boy of eleven, just left school, he tried not to get in the way; with his eight-year-old brother, Ben, he'd steady a carthorse for shoeing, or if Father hadn't given him a job would grab the yard broom to look busy, a slap round the ear having taught him not to spend idle moments drawing horses and people's faces along the edges of the *Daily News*. He might have to repeat the question and even then there'd be the hiss of hot iron in water, or several bangs of the hammer before: next bank holiday.

Come back with me, Nat used to urge: there's money to be

made in the city. So, at sixteen - leaving Ben to Father - he went, apprenticed to James Woodhall, maker of sheep-shearing machinery and parts for bicycles, the old penny-farthing bone-shakers. That same year, Nat married the daughter of Samuel Newman, piano maker and music seller, and later became Nathaniel, senior diamond setter in the Jewellery Quarter, buying a house in Forest Road with bells to summon serv-ants. Nathaniel and Maud didn't lose anyone in the war: two daughters are in South Africa, one married to a banker, the other to a diamond merchant. The youngest is in London with a husband in the Foreign Office.

I expect Renée'll take you out while she's home, he said to Livvy after Nathaniel and Maud had gone, felt he was inter-viewing her, wished she'd sit down; if there are things … for Peter … for George, he corrected himself, stumbled to a halt, not wanting to imply she needed clothes, afraid anything he said may upset her. Renée can show you the sights, he managed.

A log shifts, crackles in the fire. He hopes Nathaniel and Maud do not come again for a while.

❧

An angry sun in the Baku November sky. Along the street, wind plays with fish skeletons, bones that cats and rats have discarded. Now three months' pregnant, she's walking the mile or so from the Black Town apartment to Yefim Aaronovich's house to check that the Armenian servants are safe. An extended family trekked from a village in north east Anatolia more than twenty years ago, seeking refuge in Baku from Turkish repression of Armenians. Dedushka took several of them in, gave them work. Others settled in the city's Armenian Quarter. After dedushka died and Yefim Aaronovich moved into the house with his young family, three

210

of the Armenians stayed to work for him: Serge, who used to be dedushka's *coachman, wife Sonia, and sister-in-law Elena the cook. She can remember the three sitting in the courtyard in the late evenings, the throaty laughs and hard guttural consonants of their Armenian language rising into the warm air while Sonia sewed, and Elena smoked a small pipe.*

Before the evacuation to Enzeli in September, she and Peter left bedding at the house; mirrors, photographs, clocks, ornaments, they locked with their clothes in an oak cupboard in the apartment which, on their return a few days ago, they found undamaged after the Turkish occupation. She can take back with her the pillow cases; Peter can call another time for the pillows and sheets.

Following a summer of booming Turkish guns, the quiet exhilarates her, a certainty of safety under British martial law since the armistice with the Turks at the end of October. She hopes Serge will be pleased to see her, for he was disgusted with the British evacuation plan: nothing will make me leave this house, barynya, *he insisted when she and Peter tried to persuade him and the women to go with them;* baryn *left it in our care and we will fulfil the trust of a family who gave us sanctuary years ago. Argument, reason, proved useless: I cannot believe the British will abandon friends in need. Inscrutable eyes, like black cherries, fixed hers: the British are people of honour, were Serge's final words on the matter. Sonia and Elena clasped and kissed her hands before she left; Elena's once plump cheeks hung in folds. Each day in Enzeli, picking her way along duckboards where the sea had silted up through centuries of gales, she searched wharves and warehouses, shelter for camped refugees, in case Serge had relented.*

'Morning, ma'am,' chorus two soldiers in British army khaki, stationed at an intersection. 'Not too pretty down there,' one

211

indicates. She returns their greeting, crosses the road, slows her pace past unknown houses. Her insides feel as though some demon is twisting, wringing them out, and she fears for the child she is carrying; stares at windowless buildings like sightless eyes, doors hanging on one hinge, shreds of flapping velvet curtain, work not of shells but human hands. It seems obscene to look at the anatomy of someone's home, rooms stripped bare, floors strewn with crumpled paper which the wind lifts only to drop again. A small naked doll sits surveying evil. So it is indeed as she and Peter heard in Enzeli: horror stories from Armenian refugees who arrived there after they did, of the Turks staying outside Baku for two days so Tartars could go in and avenge the massacre of last March, and she and Peter wondered, which parts of Baku? The Armenian Quarter, certainly, but other areas as well?

She turns into Yefim Aaronovich's street, head telling her to go back to the apartment, heart determined to know the truth. She passes one, two, three houses, windows and doors kicked in. She sees a man along the pavement, quickens her step. 'Peter!'

'Livvy!' He is running towards her. 'Stay there.' He embraces her as if he would restrain her but she breaks free. 'Livvy! No!' he shouts. 'You mustn't!'

He catches hold of her arm but she is near enough to see the heavy oak door of Yefim Aaronovich's house, which Serge used to unbolt and open for her the early mornings she went out shopping to the port or bazaars, now hacked in pieces. She pulls away from Peter. Mud and glass litter the marble hall around a gutted rosewood sofa, and the leather top of Yefim Aaronovich's desk, separated from the rest and gouged in random lines. Portraits of the Tsar and Tsarina, which always hung on the study wall, lie at the foot of the staircase, faces trampled. Blood spatters smoke-blackened walls. She presses her shawl over nose and mouth against the smell of decay. Her gaze moves to the top of the staircase where Esther's charred Steinway is missing one leg, as if immobilised in the act of escape. Keys and strings dangle over the side as though they, too, had tried to flee.

'Serge?' she falters, as if he might appear in the hall. She looks along it to where he and Sonia had their room, a gaping space, a mess of bones and ashes, a ribcage split open like a boat frame and in a corner the bowl of Elena's small pipe, all that is left by scurrying rats.

Peter's arms are round her. She gives in, lets him turn her head away, heaving, clinging to him, a moan like that of a hurt animal spewing from her throat.

എ

As if a door has slammed against him he wakes, jerks upright in bed, breath coming in short gasps. Outside, there is a noise, a creature in distress, low, keening. He lights the bedside candle, pads with it in its holder across chill linoleum to the window. He edges open a few inches the velvet drape, expecting to see perhaps a fox, but there is nothing except the park gate, silver in moonlight. The noise seems further away. He goes to his door, hears shouting among the keening. Livvy!

He opens the door, steps across the landing. 'Serge … No …' she is begging, retching. 'We wanted you to go with us, didn't we?' He puts his hand over the knob of her door. He must go in, shake her from this nightmare. But his feet refuse to move, as though they have lost all feeling, legs frozen under the nightshirt. He stares at his hand, cold as if it no longer belongs to him, while the other side the door terror subsides to a whimper.

SIXTEEN

Her eyes loiter on George, settled to sleep in the perambulator along the hall ... child of my body, my love. She puts the fingertips of one hand to her lips, places them on his cheek, watches the infinitesimal rise and fall of the crocheted white blanket, Barney the brown bear in attendance on the pillow.

She joins Renée, who is waiting in the light from the coloured glass panels of the inner door. Renée is in navy uniform coat and velour hat; she needs winter blouses for school and has suggested a day in the city. The girl opens the door, then the outer one.

She turns to look at the perambulator, her first time leaving George. I won't be long, just a couple of hours; Mrs Brent'll keep an eye on you; she's even promised to give you some lunch. As if Mrs Brent doesn't have enough to do; at least she has some help today, washday. A woman from the Stratford Road is chopping vegetables for soup and later will scrub doorsteps, kitchen and scullery surfaces, with boiling suds from the copper.

She crosses the road with Renée, longs to rush back to George, lift him out of the perambulator, but forces herself into the park, where an absence of danger fills the air and her lungs. The morning is dry and cold, winter to yesterday's autumn reminding her that in Britain seasons slide one to the other regardless of date. She must buy warmer gloves. What

214

do they cost? How much of Thomas's money will she need to spend before she can find a job?

She and Renée pass the bandstand. Workmen are brushing yellowing leaves, piling them into carts. The men pause, touch their caps. 'Morning, ma'am, miss,' they mumble, before carrying on with their work.

She would like to think Nathaniel is right, that most British workers are decent and hard-working. She inhales as if each breath will push further away revolutionary Russia; yet, she doesn't want to expel Peter. The nightmare yesterday brought a numbing sleep, and she thinks now, with helpless dread, that one may always accompany the other, and she must wake alone only to remember all that has been lost. The nightmare hadn't visited her since before leaving Baku, when Peter would shake her, clasp her the length of him as if he would squeeze the memory out like poison and prevent any more evil reaching her.

'Oh, Livvy, the luxury of a day off!' exclaims Renée.

'You've got two weeks, coming home early.'

'Yes, but there's work to do. Those of us in the Study can't afford to get behind: loads of reading, with exercises and essays.'

'The Study?'

'We're expected to take the Oxford Junior exam in two years' time. The nuns'd like me to sit the entrance for Oxford University. I'd love to go, even though women aren't awarded degrees.'

'Is your father in agreement?'

'He says I can if it's what I want to do.'

Thomas is generous towards his daughters, she thinks, not only with money but freedom, for Nell went to Canada. She tells Renée about studying for matriculation before she went to Russia.

'What made you stop?'

'My mother died and I was needed at home with Father and two younger brothers.'

'And then you went to Russia.'

'I found a job with an English family and they took me with them. Father had remarried.' She might have been talking about a stranger, this edited version of her life.

Renée slips an arm through hers. 'I hope you stay with us a bit before going to see your family. Perhaps when George is older you can continue studying.'

'Perhaps.' The ten and a half years between herself and Renée seem an unbridgeable gulf. Go to see your family? It's as much as she can do to drag herself into the park with the perambulator each afternoon.

❧

The far side of the park opens onto the Stratford Road, one of several arteries linking city and countryside. A tram shudders towards her and Renée, bell clanging, overhead cable flashing blue sparks. She has not been on an electric one since before Russia. The few weeks in Petersburg she walked everywhere, absorbing sights, sounds, aromas. Once, she hailed a *droshky*, an uncovered one-horse vehicle looking like a bath chair; the driver's shoulders seemed about four feet across because of his padded coat, even in June; when the horse reared to a halt, her face was pushed into the driver's back. It smelt of bad tobacco and sweat.

'We'll sit upstairs,' decides Renée.

She feels the casual glances of women in shapeless brown or black coats and hats, wonders how many have lost husbands.

The air is heavy with the odour of unwashed wool, Birmingham speech strange to her ears. She peers out of the window at a terrace of shop fronts with bay windows above. On the second floor are smaller windows shaped like an inverted V, built into sloping rooftops. A horse-drawn milk cart passes in the opposite direction, and butchers' and bakers' delivery carts. She reads names from the past: Oxo, Fry's Chocolate, Player's Cigarettes, Jeyes Fluid. Rose always used to set great store by Jeyes; and Keatings powder, although to have got to the stage of needing Keatings Rose would've seen as a failure of hygiene.

They pass a gap in the terrace, entrance to a side road, the name Hovis, with its small 'o' and green background, on the end wall; less than three weeks ago she was eating hard black Russian bread.

'Mr Willis's preparatory school is down there,' Renée tells her. 'All my brothers went. Peter and Jack won scholarships to the Grammar School. Papa paid for the others.'

She imagines the Boulton boys at narrow wooden desks in the schoolmaster's front room. I was a lazy little tyke, Peter once admitted; Mr Willis walloped me a few weeks before the Grammar School entrance exam: there're two paths in life, Boulton, he said; either you push the barrow or you tell somebody else to push it; which will it be for you? Tell somebody else to push it, I said, thinking that was what he wanted. Which means hard work, he came back at me, if you're to make something of yourself. Then, wham, on the open palm. Ouch! she can hear Peter.

The Stratford Road narrows, shop fronts less spacious, first floor windows small and set in grimy brick walls. When the tram clanks under a railway bridge, Renée says, 'There's the Grammar School on the right.'

He must've worked in the end. As if it will release something of Peter, something new, she gazes at the soot-blackened exterior from which he left top of his year with the Governors' Leaving Exhibition of thirty pounds. How can the boys concentrate on their lessons with the squeal of trams, and the railway goods yard opposite?

The tram veers away. Men in shabby suits and cloth caps are rolling barrels off drays. Others, hands in pockets, slouch against a wall.

'They'll be waiting for the pub to open,' Renée comments.

'Why is it closed?'

'After the war started, opening hours were restricted and haven't changed back.'

She has been away a long time.

A man limps on crutches, one trouser leg pinned up. Others have a sleeve fixed to a coat pocket. Small children play and fight, tumbling in the gutter. Terraced streets stretch off the main road, each house opening onto the pavement, one window downstairs, two up, some drainpipes ending feet from the ground. Paths run between terrace backs, across which are strung lines of grey washing. She remembers Masha's tenement in Baku's Black Town, stink of stale fish, mattress on the kitchen floor; wonders if the conditions these people live in are any better.

☙

'We'll go to the Bull Ring first,' Renée says as they get off the tram.

She and Renée push their way through the crowds - many people are wearing gauze masks against influenza, she realises - past stalls selling greengrocery, clothes, sweets, toys, crockery.

Barrow boys are calling, 'Knives to grind?' 'Salt, penny a block!' At the fish market, rows of shiny herring, whiting, cod, peep at her in beady reproach, scales glinting like stars, alongside plates of whelks, mussels, oysters, and eels writhing in slime. Crates packed with straw leak melting ice, shiny and thick, onto cobbles and gullies; costermongers' leather aprons stiff from other days' dealings, fingers raw red with cold and streaks of blood, the smell taking her to the Baku trawlers.

'Do you remember Woolworth's?' Renée asks; 'everything sixpence or less.'

She does. Some things have not changed.

They pass Chapman's, where hundreds of parrots, finches and canaries are singing, twittering, and rabbits and mice scurrying inside cages. She points to the centre of the Bull Ring. 'Who's the statue of?'

'Nelson. Shall we go and see?'

A man is banging a drum. 'Thruppence a time!' another is shouting at the foot of the statue. 'Get rid of those painful teeth! Only thruppence a time.'

'Aah!' she grimaces, turns away as a man steps forward to have a tooth pulled.

'Joe says Saturday night's best,' Renée tells her. 'He teases me, thinks I don't know about anything outside the convent, says when I leave he'll bring me here to see everywhere lit with tar torches and paraffin flares. There are Italian accordionists and always somebody preaching politics or religion. I never know whether he's exaggerating.'

A man passes them with boards across back and front, proclaiming *The end is nigh*. Another has a tray hung round his neck displaying columns of matches, laces, buttons, razor blades, hair slides. A third peers with white, sightless eyes at the foot of the market steps, hand on a cracked mug. All are dressed for the office, suits, hats, collar and tie. Men limping, men on crutches, old before their time; with only one arm, one eye, no nose, no lips, half a face, or a tin mask as if on a tomb. She is aware of Renée glancing at her; remembers those she nursed in Baku hospital, the smell of fish recalling that of blood, vomit; thinks of eyes holding pain and fear, contortions and cries of men pushed beyond their limits; of Will, unfocussed gaze, hair stuck to a sweat-bathed face, dying. The smell becomes one of decay and death: Serge, Sonia and Elena butchered in Yefim Aaronovich's house. Horror is threatening to push all breath from her.

She watches a man kneeling, drawing on the pavement with coloured chalks the church across the Bull Ring. A purple scar has gouged the side of his neck. Three fingers on his left hand are missing. A message declares: *All my own work*. A dog lies beside an upturned cloth cap. Will's pictures of the desert, she thinks; if he hadn't been killed, might he have come home like this man, unable to work for his father, or do anything except draw on the pavement for a few coppers?

She whispers to Renée, 'Have you any change?'

Renée takes a brown leather purse from her bag, offers a threepenny bit.

She bends and places it in the cap.

'Thank you, ma'am.' The man's eyes stay on his work. 'God bless you.'

Renée puts an arm through hers to move away, but she lingers. She spreads her free arm. 'These are supposed to be the lucky ones because they survived, came home.' She turns to Renée. 'Why, Renée? Why? Why did it all have to happen?'

They climb round into New Street, then Corporation Street, past gold-lettered, etched glass shop fronts. Throops, outfitters for, among others, Convent of the Sacred Heart in Acock's Green, is their first stop. Not since the English shop in Petersburg over five years ago has she been in such a place, where people speak quietly and nothing is hurried. Oak floorboards, wall panelling, spacious counter with a yard rule along the edge, give an atmosphere of solidity, changelessness.

Renée asks for three long-sleeved white calico blouses, black cashmere stockings, calico petticoats, liberty bodices, and navy blue knickers in heavy cotton with fleecy linings. They will be parcelled up and delivered to Laurel Road. The sales assistant presents the invoice for signature.

'Can you, Livvy, please?' Renée prompts, 'for Papa's account.'

She writes her name slowly, *Olivia Boulton*, as if each pulse of her heart will, this first time, secure the letters to the page. This is who I am, will always be.

They call at the Municipal Bank. Eight guineas a month! She catches her breath. Thomas didn't have to do that. It's the amount Mr Clayton used to pay her in Petersburg, for hard work and little time to call her own. Again, she signs her name, getting used to it.

Outside, she examines the new brown and green notes, ten shillings and a pound. 'I don't want your father to feel he has to go on doing this,' she tells Renée. 'I must find a job, support myself.'

'But you've only just arrived. Stay with us a while. Think of it as holiday.'

She has not had one for years.

They look at the end of Broad Street where the council propose building a Hall of Memory to honour the nearly thirteen thousand Birmingham men killed in the war.

'Jack's and Will's names will be there.' Renée sounds comforted.

But not Peter's, she thinks. He has no memorial.

Into her coat pocket she has put the money in a purse one of the Salvation Army women gave her. She takes the purse out, pulls away a ten shilling note, crumples it in her hand. The purse once more in her pocket, she's running, tight shoes never so swift, back down Corporation Street past blocks of offices with elaborate façades, Peter's dear dying face hovering in front of her and his last words: tell George his father loved him. 'Livvy!' she hears behind her. 'Wait! Where are you going?' She is elbowing her way along New Street, the smell of fish like a compass point.

In the Bull Ring she rushes over to the man drawing on the pavement. 'I want you to have this,' she tells him, breath rasping. She tucks the ten shillings in his upturned cap.

He is bent over, working on a wall of his church. 'Thank you, ma'am,' he says. 'God bless you.'

She stands, all energy dashed from her, willing him to see the note because there is nothing else she has or can do.

'Livvy!' Renée is panting towards her.

She turns, looks round the Bull Ring: a blank landscape and Renée reaching out both hands.

The girl ushers her away. 'Let's go for something to eat.'

❧

'Put the headphones on, Livvy. Now, can you hear anything?' Joe is twiddling knobs of a crystal set beside her at the table in his den. Arthur used to have one in the kitchen. Rose complained about the mess.

Through crackling in her ears, she makes out military music followed by an indistinct male voice. 'Did you do all this yourself, Joe?' She takes the headphones off and places them on the table.

'Tom helped me carry everything in and fit the aerial outside but I did the rest.' He hands her the headphones. 'Try again. Tell me what you can hear.'

She does as he asks, grateful for a simple task away from the sight of wounded, mutilated men. Yesterday, after catching up with her in the Bull Ring, Renée kept hold of her arm until they arrived at oak-panelled Barrow's restaurant, where they had tea and hot buttered crumpets: pikelets, the waitress called them. In Edward Grey's, pushing herself through a daze of exhaustion, she bought a green skirt and cardigan, and two blouses, cream and pink, as well as gloves and warm underwear. They were delivered to Laurel Road after she and Renée came home but are still upstairs in their box and brown paper; there is comfort in the familiar, even indoor clothes from the Salvation Army.

Renée had urged her to add a pair of low-heeled, black leather shoes with a strap across the front, and button fastening: they'll look nice in the house, Livvy, the girl enthused, and are flat enough for cycling. All right, she conceded, but a coat can wait; the only time I go out is to the park and I don't need a new one for that. She did put the shoes on this morning rather than the tight lace-ups.

She spent the rest of the money on George: calico shifts, woollen vests, and a coat, bonnet and mittens; plus a pattern and wool to knit for him. Something to do in the evenings.

This evening, however, she is with Joe. A stove warms them.

Two cane basket chairs are piled with cushions. Books fill a shelf at chest height along half one wall. Golden light from a paraffin lamp on the table is enough to read by, although not the titles on the bookshelf. The sultry smell of the stove and lamp mingles with Joe's intensity. He is adjusting the controls again, turns to look at her. He has the same heart-shaped face as Renée and Peter, and their mother.

'It's louder but no clearer,' she tells him. She takes off the headphones.

'Accumulator probably needs recharging,' Joe says. 'Job for Tom next time he's here.' He sits on the edge of his chair. 'Just think, Livvy, if this could be improved so that it sounds as clear as I'm speaking to you. What a wonderful way of communicating if everybody had one at home.'

'It might put newspapers out of business. You wouldn't want that.'

'They can carry a lot of information, and pictures. People will always buy them.'

Joe strikes her as older than his seventeen years, someone who thinks about other things than going to the Bull Ring on a Saturday night. She picks up the newspaper lying on the table, the *Town Crier*, proclaiming itself Birmingham's first Labour Weekly. Friday 3rd October, 1919. The day Peter died.

'This is the first edition,' says Joe. 'It's got a great future.'

'Why's that?'

'Mr Chamberlain, the founder, fortunately no relation to the Tory family, is a pacifist and Socialist. The paper will educate people in Socialist beliefs.'

She remembers talk at the tea table on Sunday about trades unions. 'Beliefs you sympathise with?'

'Very much. You know, Livvy, I'm glad I was too young to be in the war because if I'd been older I wouldn't have gone. It was all wrong. When I heard the maroons crash at Greet, near Father's factory, to announce the Armistice, I didn't think: we've won the war! I thought: thank God it's over.' He points to the paper. 'Mr Chamberlain, and Mr Rudland who used to be a compositor where I work, led the anti-conscription forces in Birmingham during the war. I think that takes as much courage as going to fight.'

'Your brothers were of a different opinion.'

'They were swept along! Everybody cheered, waving flags, throwing flowers at soldiers as they went marching off. I bet you half the lads didn't even know what they were going to fight for, just vague notions of honour and glory, adventure, *Boys Own* stuff. They certainly hadn't any idea what it was going to be like - '

Leave your sister her dreams, she thinks, watching passion light Joe's eyes.

' - Jack didn't wait, nor Will, off down the recruiting station as soon as they thought they could get away with lying about their ages. You had to be nineteen for Kitchener's Army. Tom didn't really want to go but was conscripted. And look what happened. Two killed, and Tom, well, you've seen him. He'll never be the same again. He's just twenty-three, Livvy. That war was a quarrel, between Austria and Serbia to start with, then other countries fell in behind their friends and relations; but the human sacrifice needed to settle it, thousands upon thousands, millions. You only had to see daily casualty lists in the *Times*.'

'The *Times*?' she queries. If Joe is a pacifist and Socialist, what is he doing reading the *Times*?

'Father started taking it months back. It gave reports from Russia.'

Thomas, hungry for news. She wonders if her father sought mention of Russia in spite of the ease with which he let her go.

Joe is looking at her, uncertainty rippling his ardour. 'Do I shock you?'

She shakes her head. 'It wasn't just in this country. It was the same in Russia. We all wonder why when we see death, suffering, shattered lives. We lose sight of what it's all about and long for the end. Yet, refusing to fight will only work if everybody does and is prepared to be without armies and weapons.'

'It's about having to conform,' says Joe, 'and I was never a conformist. I hated school. I wasn't any good at lessons and had the achievements of four brothers to live up to at the Grammar School. Tom didn't do any exams but the others did. Then along I come, the runt. I had to have two goes even to pass the entrance exam. When the war began, a school cadet corps was formed. Everybody thought I should join, so I had to. There were over a hundred of us: Camp Hill Company of the Fourth Cadet Battalion, Royal Warwickshires. The only things I enjoyed about those years were working on the school allotment in Hall Green, and fruit-picking in the Vale of Evesham; and once we were sent flax-gathering in Scotland. At least I felt then we were doing something useful.'

Joe indicates the books on the shelf. 'I'm not just a pair of hands out of doors. I read as well but not the sort of rot the school fed us.' He picks up a pamphlet from under the newspaper on the table. 'Have you heard of this?' He gives it to her.

She reads *Labour and the New Social Order, by Beatrice and Sidney Webb.*

'Nothing can change the fact that the war has happened,' Joe tells her; 'that life, society, as we knew it, has gone for ever. It's up to us how we shape the future. This is where Socialists and the Labour Party can play such an important part. Tories and Liberals just hang onto their old interests, the rich getting richer, poor staying the same. I don't doubt Father's very fair but you heard him and Uncle on Sunday, not wanting anything to alter in the workplace. Working people have to be listened to now, which is why unions are essential.'

She puts the pamphlet back on the table. 'Do you belong to one?'

'The Typographical Society, for printers.' Joe sits on the edge of his seat again, excitement in his eyes. 'Livvy, I'm going to join the Labour Party. The Birmingham branch started last year and Mr Rudland is secretary. Trouble is, people like Father, and my aunt and uncle, think it's full of Bolsheviks. It isn't. We're not out to fight or murder. Parliament's the thing: get trades unions involved and more Labour MPs elected. They won fifty-seven seats in the election last year, which is a start. Who knows, in a few years' time we could have a Socialist government.'

We are building a world without tyrants and slaves, Lev Yefimovich said. Is Joe any different, with his wish for change? British Socialists will do it peacefully; Russian Bolsheviks are using force. Suddenly, she feels old, weary of the struggle of ideas. Her head is aching. 'Does your father know you want to join the Labour Party?'

'Not yet. Mr Rudland's a good man. All this year he's been in the Hands off Russia campaign. He's going to chair a conference in the city centre next month. You'll be able to go if I can get you a ticket.'

She looks at him, her forehead creasing. 'What do you mean, Hands off Russia?'

'Don't you think it's wrong that nearly a year after the Armistice, and the peace treaty with Germany signed, British soldiers are still in Russia *and* helping one side in the civil war fight workers? Mr Rudland calls it the greatest crime of capitalism and I agree with him. Some people are making a lot of money continuing to manufacture weapons and supplies for the Russians.'

She stares at Joe. 'So it's *Socialists* who pressured the government to withdraw British soldiers from Baku. Well, it didn't do me and Peter any favours. If the Army hadn't left Baku we'd probably still've been there. Peter would be alive, nothing changed.' She looks away from Joe, bites her lip. They couldn't have stayed in Baku for good, could they? An oriental city, where westerners were less and less welcome.

Her head feels as if two small drums have installed themselves, one under each temple, and started pounding, competing. Joe is looking down at the table, mouth pursed in the way Peter's used to when faced with a situation he didn't like.

'I've upset you, Livvy,' he says. 'I'm sorry. I didn't want to. Father said I wasn't to ask you about Russia. I haven't done but I've still managed to ruffle you.'

How kind, sensitive, Thomas is, she thinks.

'Could you just tell me this, Livvy, now the subject's come up?' Joe pursues. 'I can't believe the Bolsheviks are all murderers and ruffians. Mother had no time for them. She was so pleased to hear from Peter last year, that he was safe and had married you. She sang round the house for days. Did you know any Bolsheviks?'

'Two,' she says, imagining May singing and how Thomas must miss it. 'The family's maid. She was sacked because of her disrespect after the first revolution, when the Tsar abdicated; she started working for Peter and me at the beginning of this year when I was expecting George. The family's eldest son was also a Bolshevik.' She tells Joe about the encounter with Lev Yefimovich on the train, yet feels detached from what she is saying, as if she never experienced it, conscious only of her aching head.

'And his parents never knew?' Joe asks.

'It was better that way, to think he died fighting for Russia on the European Front. War and revolution had brutalised him.' In spite of the stove, she is shivering. 'A lot of ordinary people, those who showed Peter and me kindness when we crossed Russia, didn't want to fight when the civil war began. They'd had enough. But young men had no choice. Some of the older ones just went along with what was easiest, to keep jobs or a roof over their heads.'

She puts her hand against her forehead, has to get away from the smell of paraffin. The walk back along the garden path, into the house and upstairs seems an insurmountable obstacle. She closes her eyes.

Joe is on his feet. 'Livvy, are you all right? I shouldn't have asked you about the Bolsheviks. I'm sorry I've upset you. You don't look very well.'

Holding onto the table, she opens her eyes, stands up, begins to walk to the door, each limb throbbing to its own rhythm. 'It's not your fault, Joe,' she says. 'I feel very strange. I'll have to go and lie down.'

SEVENTEEN

Seven-thirty a.m., early March 1917, wind whipping smells of oil and fish round her as she hurries down to the port ... men and women standing talking in groups, something you don't normally see, especially since the oilfield and factory strikes ... two men and two women walking towards her, arms linked, holiday smiles on thin, pale faces. 'You look worried,' one of the women says through a miasma of vodka; 'nothing can worry us now.'

'Is there any fish?'

'Trawlers didn't go out last night. Everybody's celebrating!'

'Celebrating?'

'Revolution!'

'In Baku?'

'Petrograd, so we follow.'

... Yefim Aaronovich assembling his household in the drawing room, reading from Kaspii *the news from Petrograd: the Tsar has abdicated. 'Hurrah for the Revolution!' they hear in the street below and the call is taken up by dozens of voices: 'Hurrah for the Revolution!' What does it all mean, for her, for Yefim Aaronovich and the family?*

He folds the newspaper in four as he does every day. 'There's been trouble before,' he reminds everybody. 'It won't last. The Tsar will return.'

... she ties her shawl round her head, steps into the street and a stream of people, many holding hands, carrying red flags made

from shirts, strips of cloth … in the Olginskaya even more throng the pavements, bringing with them odours of armpits, garlic, determination … what has happened to portraits of the Tsar and Tsarina in the fashionable shops? Just red bunting in the windows … three men have climbed the façade of City Hall, are tugging at the gold-painted Imperial eagles. 'Come on! Get on with it!' shout the crowd, pausing to watch. The men hold the eagles aloft before hurling them down. They clatter on the cobbles a few yards from her feet and a cheer of 'Yes!' pulses through the crowd …

… she squeezes into the courtyard of City Hall, dozens of red flags bobbing like kites, men and women in coarse working clothes, talking, nobody listening, a day's holiday, smells of vodka, tobacco, making her want to gag …a man and woman are clasping each other, the woman's skirt pulled up, legs round his as he jerks against her, face on her neck until the woman throws back her head and shouts: 'Yes!' She turns away, ignorance and embarrassment a burn on her skin … on a platform at the far end, a man in soldier's uniform, faded and hanging on him, screaming at the crowd: 'Comrades! I am an old convict! Freedom has dawned on Russia. Down with the Romanovs and their representatives! Hurrah!' and hundreds of voices merge into one hurrah! as if they would be heard two thousand miles away in Petrograd … 'We are the common people,' the soldier continues. 'Land must belong to workers. Land and Freedom should be our motto.'

'Land and Freedom!'

'No more can we be made to join the Army as many of us at Nobel were for going on strike … we don't need Constantinople … if Nicholas Romanov does, let him get it!'

'Land and Freedom! Give us Shaumian!' …Shaumian, a foreman at Yefim Aaronovich's oilfield, exiled to Siberia years ago

for subversion ... 'Land and freedom! Shaumian!' and across the courtyard flashes a green shawl – we'll see you in a crowd, she said to Masha when she gave it to her nearly three years ago - and Masha's arms held high, waving something red that might once have been a blouse ...

The images follow her, swaying in front of smarting eyes, head restless on the pillow, one side, the other, Peter's pillow she took from his room her first afternoon here.

Daylight insinuates itself through velvet curtains. She can hear the clop of horse hooves, the rumble of a delivery cart. Her limbs are throbbing as if to the beat of a demon dance master, heart pounding in competition with pulses at her wrists and neck, mouth parched. She swallows, wonders what nails and other ironmongery have become lodged in her throat; closes her eyes but has no relief from the ache that bores through them.

The sound of a baby crying is pulling her ... tugging ... louder, nearer. George! A sour smell wafts from his cot. She tries to sit up but the pain in her head pushes her down. She lies shivering, panting, fear crawling over her.

A knock at the door. Slowly, painfully, she eases her head towards it. Renée is standing in the doorway.

'Livvy! What's happened? I heard George crying. He doesn't usually make such a noise ... ' Renée is approaching the bed, a scowl of terrible understanding breaking onto the girl's face. 'Oh, Livvy, no!' Renée turns away. 'I'll go for help.'

What do I look like? she wonders, gasping, listening to her baby crying. Is it minutes later, half an hour, when the door opens?

Mrs Brent steps inside. 'Mr Boulton has telephoned the doctor, ma'am.' As if observing another world, she watches

Mrs Brent skirt the bottom of the bed, lean over the far side of George's cot. 'I'll see to Master George, shall I?' Mrs Brent lifts him up. The crying becomes a whimper. 'There now,' Mrs Brent soothes him. 'We'll soon have you changed and fed.' The housekeeper pauses at the foot of the bed. 'Can I bring you anything, ma'am?'

'Water,' she mouths.

The door closes. Silence.

A man in a black suit is walking towards her. Is it still today?

'Doctor Hollis, ma'am,' says Mrs Brent from the doorway.

He brings with him a whiff of carbolic … Baku hospital? No, Peter at the sink at home after a day's work … takes her damp hand, touches a wrist pulse while he is talking. 'Does it hurt to speak, Mrs Boulton?'

She nods, lurches with pain.

'And swallow?'

Nods again.

He feels both sides of her neck. His fingers are soft, warm. 'Painful?'

She winces, screws up her eyes.

He unfastens a black leather bag, takes from it something small and flat. 'Open your mouth as wide as you can,' he says, placing the thing on her lower lip, then the tip of her tongue.

She tries, wider, forces herself through pain.

'Good, good,' he encourages. He removes the thing from her tongue, throws it on the fire. 'Relax again, Mrs Boulton. It seems very likely you have scarlet fever. We shall know for certain tomorrow if the rash appears. I understand Mr Boulton has already taken steps to engage a nurse for you. I'll call again soon.' He closes the bag. 'Try to rest. With any luck, and good care, you should be over the worst in a few days.'

Rest? 'George,' she keeps repeating. 'My baby.'

... through the night, balalaika, drums, cheering ... by day, people laughing, talking, arguing, shaking hands, where has fear gone? ...red-bound histories of the French Revolution in the bookshop window: red, colour of blood and revolution ... she finds flour for sale in the bazaar, buys as much as she can carry in a sack. Two men, shrunken, desperate, jostle her: 'What's in there?' and she steps back from fumes of stale wine. Wine? 'We've been in prison for five years,' they say. 'Kerensky's amnesty set us free.' She tells them she's British. 'Our great friends!' They clasp her hand in comradeship, calloused, bony fingers round hers. 'What say we share the flour?' One of them reaches inside his jacket, produces filthy sacking ...

The curtains remain closed. What day is it? What time? She drifts, like bits of wood and rubbish she used to see on the beach as a child, left lying until caught up, swept away by the sea, only to be brought back, abandoned once more.

A figure moves around the room, clothed in white, faceless except for two dark eyes over a gauze mask. Cool, fluent hands sponge her with lavender-scented water, hold a cup to her mouth as she tries to force liquid past a burning throat, lift sweat-soaked nightdress up scorching body and over her head to replace it with a soft, clean one; help her sit on the chamber pot.

Her limbs, feet, hands are blotchy red; tongue swollen, heavy, fills her mouth. Shivering, she sinks into the pillows. 'George,' she repeats; 'my baby.' She cannot hear her voice, and the white-coated gaoler makes the indignant chatter of a small caged bird.

ဆ

'How is she?' He watches Eleanor seated the other side of the fire from him, and wonders if the nurse is picking out what to tell him, discarding what not to say.

Eleanor's large, dark eyes regard him; her mother's eyes, if he remembers well from his last visit to Rednal, out in the countryside, where he has a cycle agent. 'Poorly,' Eleanor begins. 'Delirious. Calling for George, but also Peter, and somebody named Serge.'

Serge. The person Livvy was shouting to, or about, in her sleep the other night: we wanted you to go with us, were her words. What horrors did the poor girl suffer, witness, as well as losing Peter? he wonders. I didn't mention Russia, Father, Joe said as if defending himself; Livvy brought it up; we were talking about war. Joe stopped and he felt his son had more to say but Joe didn't want to give it voice, refused to meet his eye. You mustn't blame yourself, he told Joe. The lad's growing up, seems preoccupied these days. At least Joe'll know a peaceful world. What did Livvy say about Russia? he muses.

'The fever should reach its height in the next twenty-four hours,' Eleanor adds.

And then? He trusts Eleanor. Nice girl, although she must be thirty now; but it's as a girl he remembers her before the war when she was still at home, and he used to call on her father, a customer of his, the village doctor in Rednal. Then she came to Birmingham, trained as a nurse and when the war started joined the Army nursing service, was sent to London's East End. He heard there was a fiancé killed on the Somme. He looks now at the wide unsmiling mouth, dark hair streaked with grey, the calm stillness of a face for whom life has no surprises.

૮૪

... along the Norfolk beach where Father used to take his family every summer, magical morning light glowing on the water, smell of seaweed in every breath, derelict boats and sagging mooring ropes among purple marsh flowers and muddy creeks, taste of salt on her lips, gulls wailing into the air. Yet, it is the relentless Baku sun that is burning her. She has to reach the end of the beach in spite of this sun slowing her down. A man is walking in her direction. She strains to see his face ... Peter, that terrible day last November in Yefim Aaronovich's street: stay there, Livvy! Don't come any nearer. No, Livvy! No! You mustn't! The sun is going to ignite her but still she keeps walking. Peter! On her right, waves are crashing on the sand, each one nearer. She must embrace Peter before the tide comes in, engulfs her; before she catches fire. Peter! A wave larger than the others breaks against her, knocks her onto the sand; and then another, the sea rolling over her and back again, taking with it the burning.

∽

She opens her eyes. The ache drilling through them has gone. She turns her head towards the curtains, finds this hurts less. A whiff of carbolic and antiseptic stings her nostrils. She hears the door open, moves her head again. The white-coated gaoler is coming towards her.

'Ah, Mrs Boulton. You're awake. Good.'

She regards dark eyes. Why didn't the gaoler speak like this before, instead of those silly little sounds?

'Your eyes have lost their fevered look,' says the gaoler; rests a cool hand against her forehead. 'Feels better.'

She tries to smile, twists her mouth with pain. 'Where am I?'

'At home in your own bed. The fever must have broken in the night.'

Home? Where is that? 'What day is it?'

'Friday morning. You became ill on Tuesday evening, your brother-in-law says.'

Brother-in-law? Tuesday evening? Friday morning! Not sickness now but panic burns her. No cot! 'Where's George?' she gasps. 'Where's my baby?'

'He's safe and well. Nanny's looking after him in the nursery.'

Nanny. So Maud prevailed. The doctor said she'd be over the worst in a few days. 'No nanny,' she says. 'I can take care of George.' Her face twists with pain.

'Mrs Boulton, you're far from well and still extremely infectious. It'll be weeks before you can see your baby. At the moment, he's in ten days' quarantine.'

Weeks! The doctor only told her half the truth. She turns away. Is this a punishment for Peter's death? Tears push through closed eyelids and roll down her cheeks and neck. Might it not have been better if I had died, too?

∞

The gaoler has a name, Nurse Mackenzie. 'My father married a Sassenach,' the nurse adds in speech sounding very English, 'much to my grandfather's disgust, and settled in Birmingham.'

'How's George?' she asks Nurse Mackenzie each morning.

'He's fine.'

'Nanny is nice with him, isn't she?'

'Of course. She's busy knitting, sitting in her old chair, delighted to be back and a fire burning in the nursery ... except for your being ill, that is.'

She never hears crying, tries to take comfort in George being looked after by somebody who knew and, she hopes, loved his father as a little boy.

Renée is also in quarantine. 'Probably a carrier, bringing it home from school,' says Nurse Mackenzie. 'I leave her meals on a tray outside her room.'

She remembers the hugs, comfort, the handkerchief – it's clean - Renée lent her when she was sobbing in the kitchen that first Sunday afternoon.

Before going out of the bedroom, Nurse Mackenzie removes her long white overall, head covering, face mask, and hangs them on the back of the door; brings from the kitchen soup made from marrow bones, vegetables, lentils, pearl barley, and the scrambled egg, jellies, blancmanges, that Mrs Brent produces.

She wonders what has happened to Peter's shirt she was wearing under her nightdress.

Nurse Mackenzie arrives with a glass of dark liquid one morning. 'Toast tea. Mrs Brent assures me it's her grandmother's recipe.'

She takes the glass from Nurse Mackenzie, tries the boiling water infused with burnt toast, cool enough now to drink; finds the acrid taste strangely refreshing.

Red spots disappear and peeling starts. 'Quite normal,' Nurse Mackenzie assures her. 'Shows the illness is taking its course.'

She hates the slivers of dead skin that litter her bed every morning, and wonders what her face must look like. When Nurse Mackenzie fetches a hand mirror, she recoils from a pale mask framed by lank hair touching her shoulders. The moment it is long enough for pins, she will put it up again. She cradles the thought in the palm of a scaly hand, holds it to her chest, a pearl of comfort.

Doctor Hollis prescribes a mixture of thymol and Vaseline for her skin. Nurse Mackenzie rubs it in, sprays her throat with another antiseptic. What is all this, plus the doctor's visits and the work of Nanny and Nurse Mackenzie, costing Thomas? she wonders. What trouble she is causing. He probably wishes she hadn't come here.

~

One afternoon, she persuades Nurse Mackenzie to let her sit in the chintz-covered armchair by the fire. She enjoys wiggling her fingers in front of the flames. Conversation is becoming more comfortable as the soreness in her mouth and throat lessens. She learns Nurse Mackenzie was in the east Mediterranean during the war, on *Britannic*, one of the hospital ships bringing sick and wounded to Britain from Mudros on the Greek island of Lemnos; somebody who knows another part of the world and has, what Tom calls, been in it.

'Mudros,' she repeats. 'Peter said the Armistice with the Turks last year was signed in the harbour there. On board HMS *Agamemnon*.'

Nurse Mackenzie is nodding. She wishes she could see the rest of the nurse's face and wonders what horrors the nurse witnessed during the war.

'I lost the man I loved,' Nurse Mackenzie tells her. 'On the Somme, the first day more than three years ago. It was months before the news reached me. We were going to marry. I forced myself through each shift, to the point of exhaustion, so tired I couldn't even think. After the war, life was a blank page. It was up to me to write on it.'

'A bare landscape with no signposts.'

Their eyes meet in understanding. The fire crackles. Of the journey to Archangel and Peter's death, however, she says nothing. It remains like an obscene growth, her hand unable to cut it out.

'You didn't go back to hospital nursing here?' she asks Nurse Mackenzie.

'I'd only been home a couple of weeks last winter when I caught influenza. Mother had it as well. She came through but has never recovered her strength. It made me realise my parents were getting older, and how the war took its toll of the older generation: shortages; constant anxiety and waiting for news which, more often than not, was bad when it did come.' Nurse Mackenzie pokes the fire. 'They were afraid I wouldn't be up to the rigours of hospital shifts so I stayed home. There's plenty to do there and in the village, and I can help Father.'

'They'll be missing you now.'

'Somebody's giving Mother a hand. They'll manage.'

A flicker of warmth is curling in her heart. She is not alone.

∽

'Do you think you can cope with some toast?' asks Nurse Mackenzie the following afternoon.

'I'm determined to.'

'One of the things I longed for when we were abroad was toast.' Nurse Mackenzie pushes bread onto a steel fork, holds it near the fire. 'Funny, the things you miss.'

'And what you have to get used to again, like having your own key, making tea, new bank notes. And the weather as a topic of conversation, and how quickly it changes.'

'I thought Russians were great tea drinkers.'

She tells Nurse Mackenzie about heating water in a samovar, talks about Yefim Aaronovich and the family, skips from one random memory to another, then the few weeks nursing in Baku hospital last year. 'We were given white dresses to wear. I always think it's a silly colour for a nurse, with all the blood and mess.'

240

'You were lucky.' Nurse Mackenzie cuts a piece of toast in half, spreads it with butter and some of Mrs Brent's plum jam, hands it to her. 'We had a seven-piece uniform: cuffs, collars, belts, plus studs and clips to hold it together. Nothing had changed since Florence Nightingale's time.'

She chews every mouthful a dozen times; braces herself before swallowing, winces against pain; licks, with a tongue that still feels too large, the corners of her mouth in case a crumb has escaped, retrieves a spot of jam. 'This is delicious.'

When they have eaten all the toast, they drink cups of Horlicks. She breathes the malty smell from years ago. 'Tom's right,' she says, 'people at home don't understand. How can they?'

'I couldn't talk about what I'd experienced, especially to the family,' Nurse Mackenzie admits. 'Some of us nurses went down with typhus. We had to have our heads shaved. I've never told Mother that. It was a long time before I could admit it to Father. Then there was the fear of torpedoes. I'd lie awake at night on *Britannic* listening to the thresh of the screws, wind whistling above the masthead, water rushing against the side. And they did get us in the end. For the rest of my life, I shall remember that cry: all hands off the ship! She sank in three quarters of an hour. Everybody was in the lifeboats, Matron last. The worst was seeing the ship go. The propeller cut one of the boats in half.' Nurse Mackenzie looks away.

She imagines the shattered lifeboat, screams of friends. Nurse Mackenzie turns back to her, dark eyes searching, as if she, Livvy, may hold new answers.

'What happened to you then?' she asks the nurse.

'We cared for our own sick and wounded in the Russian

hospital in Athens, then went on to Malta to nurse. So you can see it was difficult, impossible, to come home and talk about this to people whose main preoccupation was the meat and milk ration, and whether they'd have enough fuel to see them through the winter.'

'I keep everything to do with Peter bottled up. It's the only way of having him with me, memories, happy times. To share him, let others have a bit of him, would mean less for me.' She looks at Nurse Mackenzie, at brown eyes caring again; is conscious of the release of a latch, a dam breaking, a force she is powerless to hold back. 'I feel so bad about it. His death … it was all my doing;' and out it all tumbles, the journey from Baku to Archangel and the approaching winter, in spite of his weak chest, because he didn't want her to have a long sea voyage. 'I should've insisted we go a different way, south. It's with me every waking moment, like a piece of lead inside that won't move.'

'I can't tell you not to think that way because at this moment it won't help you. Guilt can be part of grief. It's how you feel.'

'You mean I might not always?'

Nurse Mackenzie shakes her head in a smile, opens her hands palms upwards as if to utter: what can I say? 'It's possible. You may see things differently, in time.'

'It doesn't alter what happened.' She looks at the nurse, who is neither judging nor agreeing with her. Like a dim light at the end of a tunnel, she glimpses the possibility that one day the lead will have shifted. But that would be to let go of Peter and is something she is not able to do. 'I can't tell his father,' she says. 'He'd hate me.' Tears are filling her eyes.

'He's very concerned for you. I can't imagine him hating you or anybody.'

The tears seem reluctant to move. She dashes at them with the back of a hand. 'Before it all happened, I used to talk to God: when things were difficult, or something I wanted. I felt, somehow, He was there. I don't now. I blame Him for allowing it. I shocked Renée, snapping at her when she told me the nuns were praying for me.'

The dark eyes smile. 'For some time after Edward was killed I was the same as you. If you want God to be there again, He will be. We are the ones who move away.' Nurse Mackenzie stands up, comes over to her, puts a hand on her shoulder. 'Do you want me to help you to bed?'

She eases herself to her feet. 'I can do it.' She starts to walk, holds onto the back of the chair to steady herself, wonders how she is going to push George round the park or get a job, when talking and eating toast have drained her strength. Pain, grasping, ripping at her abdomen, forces her to clutch the chair. 'Aah!' she cries out.

Nurse Mackenzie takes her arms; soothes, 'Steady.'

She bends over with the cramp invading her legs. 'Don't let go of me,' she gasps. Warm, sticky liquid is gathering on the inside of her thighs. Nurse Mackenzie is guiding her towards the bed, pushing at the bedclothes, helping her onto the mattress.

She sees blood trickling below her nightdress towards her ankles. She sinks into darkness.

☙

She opens one eye: by the door a blood-flecked towel wrapped round a bundle as if sheltering the contents. 'More work for Mrs Brent,' she says.

Nurse Mackenzie is sponging her face. 'How do you feel?'

'Exhausted. All the lower half of me aches.' She looks at troubled eyes, brows puckered above the mask.

'You've lost a lot of blood.'

'I haven't had a monthly since George was born. I was feeding him until a few days before we left Russia.'

'This wasn't a monthly,' Nurse Mackenzie begins. 'It's stopped now.'

'Not a - ?'

' - no. I've seen women in the village the same. You must've got caught around the time you weaned George.' Nurse Mackenzie clasps her hand. 'You've miscarried.'

A second baby? 'Oh, Peter, no,' she falters. 'I'm sorry.' Tears swim inside her eyes and this time they do spill over. 'I couldn't even do that for you.'

Nurse Mackenzie is kneeling, cradling her.

She thinks of the stationmaster's cottage in Voronezh, of new life conceived there; and weeps for her double loss, double punishment: hard, jagged edges of grief which only Nurse Mackenzie's arms keep from sweeping her into the abyss.

EIGHTEEN

He holds Renée's hand as she steps into the trap; tucks the tartan travelling rug round her legs against November chill. Renée tries a smile, face pale after quarantine. She's had a cold but thrown it off. 'I'm all right, Papa,' she assures him, 'and I did all my schoolwork.'

He climbs in beside her, takes the reins, breathing in their comforting smell against his gloves, leather on leather. Copper, faithful bay gelding, begins the few miles to Renée's school. He does not hurry the creature, as if he would stretch out the time he still has with his daughter. In a few years, he will have to relinquish her to Oxford.

'I put a note under Livvy's door,' Renée tells him. 'I feel responsible.'

'She might have become ill anyway,' he says. 'She was quite run down when she arrived.' He brings to mind candid blue eyes, light glinting on chestnut hair, the promise of a smile playing around her mouth once or twice. Just an hour or two for eight evenings was she with him. Yet, she has never been out of his consciousness. Her devotion to George brought once more the reality of love into his silent house. He has taken *Household Medicine* from the bookcase, looked up scarlet fever: *advisable to keep the patient in bed for three weeks and guard against possible chills ...*

Three weeks. But that doesn't apply to George. Perhaps

Nanny will bring him downstairs this evening. No. Better still, he will go up to the nursery.

೮೨

'When can I see George?' she begs Nurse Mackenzie.

'Not until the peeling has stopped, nothing coming from your nose, probably at least another month.'

She looks at hands rough like unironed cotton. How much more skin can come off without leaving her raw?

'You must rest, in any case, because of the miscarriage,' says Nurse Mackenzie.

She retreats from at the word, will never use it, never talk about what happened. After George was born, she marvelled that he was hers to keep; but this one, no. She has asked Nurse Mackenzie not to tell anybody downstairs, adding: I don't want their pity.

She reads Renée's note again ... *Nanny is fussing over George just as she used to me and the boys* ... Fearful of draughts, Nurse Mackenzie didn't let her stand at the window to wave Renée off last week. She listened to the clop of horse hooves receding along the road, hating the four walls enclosing her, loathing ugly skin, constant smell of disinfectant and antiseptic, everything to do with the scarlet fever that robbed her of Peter's child. The first she knew she was expecting George she was with Mr MacDonell in Enzeli after the evacuation from Baku last year. They were checking for anybody who should be in hospital. Inside a shack rigged up by Armenian refugees they opened a wooden trunk to be met by the fevered eyes and blotchy skin of measles, and she fainted.

Nurse Mackenzie sits with her as maroons burst with a clatter, start of two minutes' silence on the first anniversary of the

Armistice, although in her room there is a lot of silence. She asks Nurse Mackenzie to sharpen Peter's pencil from his table drawer. On the back of Renée's note she makes a calendar for the rest of November. Every morning she marks off the day. As soon as she is allowed out of bed she walks the perimeter of her room, touching the four walls. Twice at first is plenty but she perseveres. George is the only child she will ever have. For him, she must grow strong again.

In her top drawer she finds Peter's shirt, ironed; Mrs Brent lost a husband young, understands about keeping a shirt. She slides her finger over the starched cotton where the stitching is loose in one of the shoulder seams. She lifts her nightdress over her head, puts the shirt on and the nightdress on top, hugs herself to press the shirt against her skin.

Every dry afternoon, she stands by the window, raises a hand as Nanny, stout in navy hat and coat, holds up the shapeless bundle of George cocooned against winter. She watches Nanny put him in the perambulator; sees them cross the road and into the park, until they pass the bandstand, disappear from view. She wonders if George will recognise her; walks three, four, times round the room. Under her calendar she composes an advertisement she hopes will lead to a job. … *four years' experience caring for and teaching two boys* … She remembers Maud saying: people won't look at you, and decides not to mention Russia, but feels ashamed, as if she is abandoning Peter.

One day she can walk round the room twenty times. The peeling and mucus have stopped. If it's the same in the morning she'll be free: to go up to the second floor, hold her son, see Thomas and Joe downstairs. She is not going to ask Joe if he has joined the Labour Party, or about the Hands off Russia

Conference which will have taken place by now. Will he and his father regard her return as an intrusion? She was only with them eight days before becoming ill. They have grown used to being without her.

That evening, she reads Renée's note for the last time: *love from your friend and sister…* She throws it on the fire, looks at the pencil. That must go, too. Peter's pencil. When did he last use it? She cannot keep it and risk infection staying in the room. She drops it into the flames, watches them jump, welcome and absorb it.

☙

Next morning in the bathroom she wets her face, smoothing soft skin with her fingertips and the Lembena soap Nurse Mackenzie has given her.

Back in the bedroom she tells her nurse, 'I shall miss you.'

Nurse Mackenzie has stripped the bed and is bundling the sheets. 'Write to me, tell me how you're getting on. When Mr Boulton goes over to Rednal, why not join him, call and see us?'

Something to look forward to. A signpost on the bare landscape.

Fumbling with stiff buttonholes, she dresses in her cream blouse, new skirt and cardigan, inches to spare. 'There's a bit of weight to put back on,' she comments. The skirt length, well above her ankles, feels strange, even bold.

'It's very fashionable, the slim, drapy look.'

With a whalebone brush that used to be Renée's she tidies her hair, washed yesterday.

'There's almost enough to put up,' encourages Nurse Mackenzie.

'It would need a lot of pins not to break free. I'll leave it another week.'

She climbs the stairs to the nursery, dismayed by a veil of tiredness. Outside the door she listens to George gurgling, Nanny soothing. Heart clamouring as if heralding her arrival, she opens the door, steps inside, pushes it shut behind her. George is lying on the floor trying to pull himself into a sitting position, arms and legs kicking like a crab wanting to right itself. He is wearing a blue dress with circular rows of pleats above the hem. Boxes of bricks, toys, dolls, stand along one wall, the cot against another, a rocking chair in the middle of a worn Persian carpet. The room smells of beeswax and turpentine polish, the same as downstairs, and she realises she has missed it all these weeks.

Nanny, changing the mattress sheet, looks towards the door. 'Why, ma'am! This is indeed a good day!' Nanny's speech has none of Mrs Brent's hard consonants. Nanny bustles to her, holds out both hands in welcome.

She takes them, meets grey eyes, feels she's known Nanny a long time. 'Thank you for all you've been doing,' she says.

'It's a pleasure, ma'am. I remember Mr Peter when he was a little boy. Even then he was fascinated by how machinery worked. "Can I go to the factory with you, Papa?" he'd ask and Mr Boulton would take him sometimes. Didn't surprise me when I heard he became an engineer.'

She feels a glow spreading from her belly to warm her, as though she might turn and find Peter in the room. 'That's a lovely memory, Nanny.'

'It's only natural to look after his son.' Nanny's face becomes still, as if she is no longer calling on memories, or words of any kind. 'I'm sorry, ma'am, about Mr Peter.'

I'm sorry ... I'm sorry ... everybody's sorry ... I've let down all who knew and loved him. She says what is expected, 'Thank you, Nanny.' She lets go of Nanny's hands. 'And how's George?' She bends, picks him up, panting with exertion as she has lifted nothing heavier than a hairbrush for weeks, and he has grown. He wriggles, yells a protest. She struggles to steady him, turns him towards her so she can look at his face, at Peter's hazel eyes. 'What a pretty dress! Did Nanny make it?' A frill edged in dark blue covers chest and shoulders. 'Two teeth! You *are* a clever boy!' He smells of soap. The down that used to cover his head has thickened into hair, the same light brown as Peter's. Love for them both explodes inside her. She hugs George, closing her eyes as if returning to a lover, tears mounting. 'Oh, my baby! My baby!' She gazes at him again to imprint every detail on her mind, kisses him on the cheek. 'How's George?'

A cry of indignation gathers force. He stretches out his arms to Nanny. George, her baby, content for her to carry him much of the journey from Baku to Archangel. She rocks, kisses him, but nothing calms him until he is back with Nanny.

❧

She stands in the doorway to her room, brushes tears from her cheeks with the back of a hand, holds it under her nose against the reek of disinfectant.

Nurse Mackenzie comes over to her. 'Didn't it go well? Nanny was looking forward to meeting you.'

She covers her face with both hands, as if to restrain engulfing aloneness. 'I've lost him,' she says on a sob. 'He didn't recognise me. And he looks so like Peter.'

'Let's go to the morning room,' suggests Nurse Mackenzie. 'Mrs Brent's lit the fire. I'll take this mask off.'

She drags her hands down her face, sees for the first time

Nurse Mackenzie's calm expression, wide mouth with full lips. She takes a step towards the nurse, as if to touch her, ensure she is real. Nurse Mackenzie has unfastened her overall, rolls it up, drops it on the floor; she is wearing a black skirt reaching almost her ankles, and a white blouse bereft of frill or adornment.

She rests in the nurse's embrace, a voice against her hair saying, 'I think you can call me Eleanor now.'

In the morning room they sit by the window. She looks out at the garden fast in winter sleep under a blanket of frost such as she has not seen for nearly six years, branches stark against a blue sky.

'George can't be expected to recognise you at his age after all these weeks,' explains Eleanor. 'Crying was just his way of saying: this is different; I don't understand. You and Nanny can work out a routine, help each other: you're not strong enough to take complete charge of him, while she's not as young as she was. It's better she goes out with him in cold weather; you could bath him, care for him in the mornings.'

'I don't want Nanny to think I'm the sort of mother who hands a baby over. If I hadn't been ill I wouldn't have needed her. I'll find a job, the sort I had in Russia, then I can take George with me, bring him up myself. He's all I have.'

Doubt creases Eleanor's forehead. 'Wait until you feel stronger. Livvy, I know you don't want to talk about it, but for your body's sake you must remember you've had a miscarriage and not try to do too much too soon. You could damage your chances of more children.'

She stares at Eleanor. 'More children? There'll never be any. How can there?'

She glances at the clock on the mantelpiece, and above it two pictures that weren't there before, framed and mounted behind glass. 'Will's drawings,' she says. 'His captain gave them to Peter at HQ in Baku with Will's diary the day after he was buried.'

Eleanor stands up, goes over to have a look. 'It's exactly how I imagine the desert.'

When Peter came home with the pictures and diary, she asked him what the captain had said, as if words could make any difference. Just that he was sorry neither of us knew the other was in Baku, Peter told her, sighed through his teeth: it's just another death to him, Livvy.

Her eyes return to the clock: a quarter past ten; the rest of the day waits, hers to do with as she wishes. This evening she'll see Thomas and Joe again. Foreboding kicks at her.

✦

Mrs Brent serves vegetable soup in the dining room to her and Eleanor. 'It's good to see you, ma'am,' the housekeeper beams. There's a plate of cold beef from yesterday's roast, Russian salad, bread and butter.

'It's lovely to be downstairs again.' It is, more than she realised.

'I'm hungry,' she admits to Eleanor when they're on their own. She dabs some mustard onto the edge of her plate. 'I was giving George his lunch in the kitchen our first week here. I suppose he Nanny are in the nursery. It's best for him to keep to that now. Russian families used to like English nannies for their orderliness and routine.'

Eleanor smiles; it reaches her eyes, transforms her face. 'I was perhaps a bit hasty, what I said about more children. Not very sensitive of me. But I do think you should rest.'

'There'll never be any more; never be anybody else. You haven't met anyone since Edward.'

'You're young and attractive.'

'So are you. But it isn't about looks, is it? It's feelings.'

After lunch she goes upstairs. She takes off her cardigan, skirt and blouse, lies between soft, clean sheets, drifts asleep. When she wakes, her room is in darkness except for a glimmer from the embers, and the gas lamp outside. She hears the porch door open, close, then the inner door. Thomas or Joe home from work. Thomas is always first; she wonders if he is already back. She gets out of bed, puts on her clothes, checks all the fastenings, brushes her hair, and another ten times, delaying the moment she will speak to him. Apprehension has rolled her stomach into a fist of knots.

She steps onto the landing. The grandfather clock, chimes silenced when she was ill, shows a quarter to six. She walks down to the morning room, takes a deep breath.

Thomas is reading the *Daily Express* in light from the fire, and lamp at the side of his chair. He looks up, throws the paper to the floor, leaps to his feet, strides towards her, both hands held out in greeting. 'Livvy! This is a day for thanksgiving.'

She takes his hands in hers. Her anxiety dissolves in the happiness on his face. There is a clean smell, of soap or even cologne. He seems as if he might bend to kiss her cheek but the moment passes and blue eyes smile at her.

'I wanted to thank you, Thomas, for all you've arranged.' He blinks and she pauses, thinks: he did suggest, didn't he, that I call him Thomas? 'For everything.'

'There's no need, Livvy. To see you like this is sufficient. You look wonderful.'

'I've just slept all afternoon.' She keeps hold of his hands, asks herself how she can possibly have been nervous of him. He's real, no longer a memory or someone in her imagination.

❧

Several days have passed since Livvy's return downstairs. He watches fire- and lamplight catch her hair, which she has pinned up, allowing an air of elegance. There is about her a completeness which brooks no intrusion, and always the faintest catch of perfumed soap. The sound of his name on her lips has reached deep inside him and he wants to hold it there. She is threading navy cotton through a needle, has told him she's agreed with Mrs Brent she can help with the mending in the evenings. On her lap is a shirt of Joe's. Chestnut hair: May, who has been dead a year, used to sit in that same chair, reading a report, or embroidering; all the bed linen she stitched with the initials B, C: Boulton, Cottrell.

The only sound is the crackle of the fire then the rustle of newspaper as he lets it slip to his feet. 'Livvy,' he says. She glances up and he wishes he could look at her face without speaking. He forces himself to continue, 'it occurs to me, you probably don't relish going into the city yet.' Renée told him how upset Livvy had been in the Bull Ring. 'There's a post office at the end of Wood Road. I've opened an account for you.'

'Thank you, Thomas.' She rests her hand on the shirt. 'I left my post office book with a friend in Petrograd before the war. Petersburg it was then. I was only going to Baku for the summer. The war changed everything, didn't it?'

He nods. It is the first time she has mentioned Baku. Eleanor explained to him about Serge, the servant butchered with his wife and sister-in-law, causing Livvy's nightmare. Will Livvy ever tell him herself? Why should she? He certainly can't expect it. Are there yet more horrors she keeps locked away? What can he do to help her settle, to assuage grief?

Should he tell her that Peter, too, went to St Petersburg? It might give her an opening, an encouragement to speak of him. But she has looked down at her sewing, is pushing the needle and thread in and out of a button on the shirt. He wonders how Peter met her - surely not the enthusiastic, fresh-faced boy of his memory with this quiet, self-contained woman? - what their first words were to each other. He sees again her bare ring finger and the idea crosses his mind that she wasn't married to Peter but Peter gave her George to bring to England, the mother already dead. Then he remembers Peter's letter after marrying Livvy, looks away, ashamed of his thoughts.

In a few minutes she will go to her room. He retrieves the *Daily Express* from the floor. Perhaps one day she will talk about Peter.

∾

She considers the park from the nursery window. 'The frost has cleared, Nanny. There isn't a cloud in the sky, no wind, a good afternoon for my first walk with George.'

Nanny stands, waiting. 'If you're sure it won't tire you, ma'am.'

You're the one who could do with a rest, she thinks, dark half moons beneath your eyes. She lets Nanny dress George in his green knitted coat, bonnet, mittens. He reaches out to his mama as he has done every day except that first one. Her heart kicks with wonder, each time like a consummation of love. She takes him from Nanny, inhales the warmth and sleepiness of him as if she must renew a depleted supply yet can never have enough.

Down the path, December air tingles her cheeks. Instead of crossing Laurel Road and going into the park, she turns right, pushes the perambulator round to Wood Road. She finds the post office beyond a terrace of red-brick villas, smiles in her mind at Thomas wanting to make things easier for her. The shop also sells wool, haberdashery, ladies' underwear. She leaves George asleep, opens the door. A bell tinkles.

She withdraws a shilling from the account Thomas has opened, buys stationery so she will not have to use his. At the counter she dips the pen in the inkpot, writes on the first sheet:

Young widow with seventh-month-old son seeks live-in position. Four years' experience caring for and teaching two boys.

Widow. She can remember not wanting to use or even hear the word. But this is how the world will regard her, and she must prepare herself for the scrutiny of strangers. Might *widow* offer protection, a buffer behind which she can retreat? *My husband died in Russia*, is all she will need to say. She adds her name and address, pays a halfpenny, aware of curiosity in the postmistress's glance; thinks, every time I open my mouth people know I'm not from these parts.

On the step outside she breathes the air of achievement, looks back the way she came, then in the other direction. Houses line both sides of the road until fields, hedgerows. She releases the brake of the perambulator, sets off. At the end of Wood Road are more fields to her right, houses beyond. She glances left: a farm, in the distance a church. Careful to avoid cowpats, she walks past the farm and outbuildings, where a cart languishes as if abandoned to damp-smelling air. Geese hiss a warning from the ends of outstretched necks. A cow wails and she wonders if the creature is bereft of her calf. Behind the farm she notices an orchard and copse, an oak tree imposing in its bareness. It is easy to forget the city centre is no more than three miles away.

She passes a blacksmith's forge, perhaps where Thomas stables the pony and trap. She slows her step, listens to the chink of hammer on iron, the fizz of steam as a horseshoe plunges into water, sounds she has not heard for years. A wagon trundles towards her, a man perched at the front holding the reins of a weary-looking horse. The man has a battered cap on his head, a dusty jacket and corduroy trousers. A cigarette end hangs in one corner of his mouth. She stands with the perambulator at the side of the lane. He raises his cap an inch, mumbles something.

The gate to the churchyard is open, inviting entry. Unthinking, she pushes the perambulator along the path. Many of the grey gravestones are new. She finds herself looking at black lettering which tells her:

Here lies May Alexandra Boulton,
wife of Thomas Herbert Boulton,
who died on 8th December 1918, in her 47th year.
Also their daughter, Annie Margaret Boulton,
who died on 4th January 1901, aged 3 months.
Thy Will be Done.

At the base, in a stone vase, two pink chrysanthemums have shrivelled after this morning's frost. She recognises them from among those cultivated in pots on the kitchen windowsill at Laurel Road.

She thinks of other Boulton graves: Jack in an unknown corner of northern France; Peter and Will at opposite ends of Russia, Azerbaijan now in Will's case; nobody to visit or tend them. And here, Annie, the dead sister. Her own baby, conceived in the stationmaster's cottage in Voronezh, was flushed away before developing to take even one breath. Another boy? She would've been feeling him kick by now. George was a great kicker. Peter used to adore lying with her, stroking her bump and his unborn child, sure it would be a boy, while she wondered about twins.

Thy Will be Done: she wonders if Thomas really believes this. And if so, how?

Weariness, sadness born of futility and an inability to change anything, weigh her down, the earlier sense of achievement vanished. She shivers. Soon, the daylight will be going. She turns the perambulator round, walks to the gate, starts back along the lane.

ↄ৲

Next morning, she sits at the bureau, lid down, with her writing paper. She dips Thomas's pen in the ink, writes *34 Laurel Road, Lightmoor, Birmingham. 10ᵗʰ December, 1919. Dear Father and Rose …* She puts the end of the pen in her mouth, whisks it out again: it's not hers to chew. How to start? Her last letter to her father was from London early in 1914 to say she was going to Russia in May with the Claytons. He replied, formal sentences that did nothing to close the gulf between them: *… one always imagines that in foreign countries the ways are different, and therefore deleterious to health and wellbeing. Do think again, Livvy, about moving to St Petersburg with this family. The distance is too great to imagine and three years a long time to separate yourself from your country and family, not to mention your books.* She ignored his request, never wrote back.

She writes: *I* ... ; crosses it out. *This* ... This what? I what? She stares at the paper waiting to be filled. Like her life. There are no words. Tears drip onto the page, crinkling it, the crossed out *I* smudging, illegible.

She rests her head against the bend of her arm on the desk.

❧

'Livvy!' She is coming out of the park that afternoon when Maud hails her. 'I'm glad I've caught you. I don't want Thomas to be bothered with this.' Maud, in black hat and sable coat, is holding a piece of paper. 'I've just been to the post office with letters for South Africa. What are you thinking of, Livvy?'

Her advertisement. 'You've removed it, Maud?' It is the first time she has addressed Maud by name: Maud looks at her, as though a boundary has been breached, a new one established; and then at the paper. 'How dare you! I have to support myself and George, therefore I need a job.'

'You don't have to do any such thing!' Maud's cologne mingles with the air, ice on ice. 'Thomas can provide for you: you're his responsibility.'

Like a belonging. 'I worked until I married Peter. I must do so again.'

'Boulton women do not work. Think of your social standing, Livvy. What you did before you married has nothing to do with now.'

'Connie continued to help her father in the shop after she married Tom and he went to the war.' She moves the perambulator a few inches forward, back.

'That was family. It's not the same.'

'May worked,' she points out. Her feet are chill. She wants

to sit down with a cup of tea but is not going to invite Maud into the house.

'May had … interests.' Maud chooses the word carefully. 'No payment.'

'And I am *interested* in looking after children, for which I have experience - '

' – but no qualifications,' Maud jumps in. 'Neither can you supply references.'

She has not thought of references. The Claytons will be unlikely to give her one, assuming they have returned from Russia. 'Thomas has been very kind,' she concedes, 'but I can't expect him to pay for everything for me and George indefinitely.'

'It is exactly what you *can* expect. His duty. Have you forgotten that, Livvy, in your selfishness?'

That last word stings her. She takes the creased paper from Maud, clutches it like a permit to a new life. 'My duty is to look after George and myself.' She stamps her feet to keep some feeling in them.

'Thomas helps his employees in time of need, also men who come begging for work, people to whom he has no obligation. Even more will he give to you and George, his family. It's doing him good having you both here. He's looking happier.'

'What do you mean, men who come begging for work?'

'Just that! Ex-officers, people who should know better. For example, one man a few weeks ago, had set up a business after coming back from the war, used all his savings and victory bounty, and the whole thing had gone wrong. He hadn't a penny.'

'What did Thomas do?'

'Pressed on him five pounds and his overcoat.'

Five pounds. A man can keep a family of six on one a week.

'Thomas's resources can't be endless, Maud. He might be glad if I provide for myself and George.'

Maud glances in the perambulator but little can be seen of George wrapped against December. 'When he's in the nursery, he tries to sit up,' she tells Maud.

Maud appraises her. 'At least you're not totally one of those modern women with short hair I thought you were when I first met you. It does look so nice now it's up.'

'I had it cut to pay for lodgings. Peter was dying.'

'Ah, yes. Peter. You know, we remember him as a charming boy, my dear. His mother's son. Not easy to think of him married and a father.'

Boy? They never knew my Peter.

❧

In the morning room he listens while Livvy explains to him, a cramping dread coiling inside him. Maud again! Yet, it is not what his sister-in-law has said that is wrenching him but that Livvy wants to leave. After she has finished speaking, he continues to look at her, imagining the house without her and George. The silence. Never to see the promise of her smile and one day, he is sure, its fulfilment.

Her eyes meet his. He must say something. 'You're not happy here, Livvy?'

'I shall never forget all you've done, Thomas.' He has the impression she is selecting words. 'And I don't want you to feel I'm ungrateful.'

'The house has come to life since you and George have been here.' He goes over to the bureau, wonders why he hasn't shown her before, rifles through papers, moves the box of cuttings, and some writing paper Livvy must have left there as if she were

261

at home; good. Yes! He picks up a small brown leather album, scuffed at the edges, takes it back to where she is sitting. She has turned round to see what he is doing. He opens the album. On the inside cover, ink faded brown, is May's writing: *Autumn 1893*. There they are, the first page, he and May, proud parents, each with a baby on their lap.

He shows Livvy. 'Who do you think that is?'

She puts a finger against his younger self in dark suit and winged collar, looks up at him with that promise of a smile. His breath catches in his throat. She returns to the picture, touches a baby. 'Like George,' she says. 'Peter? And Nell?'

'Taken at the age George is now. You've brought me a miracle, Livvy. I see Peter every time I look at George.'

'If I find a position locally, we can visit you.'

He nods, cannot dispute what she has said, has no hold over her, is unable to put into words what he really means, as if it is something unapproachable, impossible for the mind to encompass; only that the thought of her not being here is too much to bear.

∽

I have discussed the matter with Thomas, she writes to Maud. *He has not forbidden me to look for a position. I have taken my advertisement back to the post office. Please leave it there.*

She seals the envelope, recalls the stricken look on Thomas's face when she told him what she planned, as if a giant fist had punched him powerless. He regards George as a substitute for Peter, perhaps for all his dead sons; holds George high in the air, his grandson kicking and screaming with glee; jumps George up and down on his knee, lets his grandson pull at his tie, adoration lighting his face.

You're not happy here, he said, doubt in his voice making it a question. Happy. How easily we use the word. She has security but does not think she will ever be happy in the way she once was.

Selfishness, Maud said. If she had thought about Peter's chest, insisted they go south rather than north, regardless of her seasickness ... Now she has a choice to make. Like a seed planted in moist soil after spring rain, the realisation takes root that she does not want to hurt Thomas.

NINETEEN

Preserving jars twelve inches high begin to appear in the larder, crammed to the stopper with garden onions and pickling vinegar. Smaller jars hold jelly made from cranberries bottled in the summer. Threepenny bits nestle in muslin-wrapped puddings. This morning when she goes into the kitchen, she finds Mrs Brent pushing apples and raisins through the mincer. On a plate are chopped suet and nuts, with a second one of raisins. One jar has already been packed with this mixture, which will fill mince pies.

'Shall I stone the rest of the raisins?' she offers.

Mrs Brent looks up, sweat glistening on her upper lip. 'If you've the time, ma'am.'

Time? She has plenty. Each morning her waking is a slow dawning and acceptance of a new day. She breakfasts alone downstairs. Thomas and Joe have long since eaten porridge, bacon and egg, toast, and left for work. She manages a cup of tea, perhaps a piece of toast with Mrs Brent's marmalade; the habit of small breakfasts in Russia is hard to break. She goes to the nursery, baths George, plays with him while Nanny sits in the rocking chair, knitting, sewing, crocheting. She wonders how much time May used to spend with her children.

'The job I never liked was peeling chestnuts for stuffing,' she tells Mrs Brent, 'scratching my fingers, and all the bits catching under my nails.' She pulls out a chair.

Mrs Brent smiles. 'Miss Nell was always one for raisins.'

She opens the first one, breathes in the rich smell of fruit. 'Do you miss her?'

Mrs Brent reaches for the bottle of cooking brandy. 'We all did. Mr Boulton was sorry not to give his daughter away when she married.' Mrs Brent unstops the jar of mincemeat, feeds it with a teaspoonful, secures the top as if sealing in talk of the past. 'And now the first family Christmas for years.'

Tom and Connie will be here on Christmas Day, and Nathaniel and Maud. So as to treat them the same, she greeted Nathaniel without 'uncle' when he and Maud called last week. She wondered if he even noticed, raising her hand to his lips with: I'm pleased to see you restored to full health, my dear.

'Of course, last Christmas Mr Tom still wasn't home … ' Mrs Brent sits down, stones some raisins; whenever Tom is mentioned she goes quiet for a few moments, ' … and with Mrs Boulton not long buried, Mr Joe and Miss Renée went with their father to Mr and Mrs Nathaniel Boulton.'

The porch door slams at the far end of the hall, followed by the inner one. 'Miss Renée home from school,' Mrs Brent volunteers.

Thomas took the horse and trap to the station to meet his daughter. 'Livvy!' she hears from Renée, and the girl opening and closing the dining and morning room doors. She stands up licking her fingers, scraping the chair on the red-tiled floor. In the kitchen doorway Renée enfolds her in a hug as if afraid of mislaying part of her. She has missed hugs, the feeling of belonging.

Renée eases her to arm's length. 'You look wonderful, better than before you were ill.' Renée holds her hand and they move into the kitchen, closing the door to keep out the chill of the hall. Renée kisses Mrs Brent on the cheek, still talking: 'Papa's gone back to the factory.' The girl sighs, a smile of delight. 'And this holiday you and I, Livvy, are going to do all the lovely things we didn't manage at half term.'

☙

She helps Renée clip metal holders with wax candles onto branches of the Christmas tree in the morning room; the tree nearly reaches the ceiling. There and in the dining room they put up streamers of crinkled paper. Joe brings home bunches of holly and mistletoe from a stall in the Bull Ring. Presents appear round the bottom of the tree. From the haberdashery part of the post office, she buys Lembena soap, initialled men's handkerchiefs, others with a rose in the corner, gifts for all who people her world.

Inside a Christmas card of a frozen lake and bare trees, she writes *from Livvy and George*, sends it to her father and Rose. It's a start.

A few days before Christmas, a parcel arrives from Montreal. She looks at large black writing: MRS P. BOULTON, reminding her who she is, that somebody outside the house is thinking of her. Renée prompts, 'Open it, Livvy. There might be a letter.' She fumbles with string, rolls it in a ball to keep. Father used to do that. She realises she didn't put her address on the card to him, and they will wonder who George is. She peels away layers of brown paper to find a cardboard box containing gifts for all the family, wrapped in Christmas paper.

'I'll put these under the tree,' she tells Renée.

There is indeed a letter; ... *has Papa told you,* Nell has written, *I came here on the* Lusitania *with a school friend to visit her*

266

aunt and uncle and found work as a floor walker in one of the big stores. I'd seen people looking at stuff, slipping an item into a bag or pocket and nobody taking any notice. I said to the manager, 'You need someone to keep an eye on things,' and he gave me the job. I was only eighteen! The following year I met Patrick at a dance. ... Dear Peter, brilliant, handsome in striped blazer and flannels. I'm so glad we named one of the twins after him ... She examines a photograph taken in October: Nell, a younger version of May; her husband in the high-collared jacket of the Mounted Police, their sons, ages four, two, and twins of six months. The letter is an invitation to friendship, exchange of confidences. She has nothing to offer.

Striped blazer and flannels? He never wore those in Russia.

಄

On Christmas morning she finds George sitting in the middle of the nursery floor, a grin on his face that says: I've done it! When he sees her he gurgles excitement, jiggles his arms, too much for his precarious balance, keels over, chuckling.

'Well done, darling!' she cries, scooping him up. 'You *are* a clever boy.' She hugs him, kisses the side of his head, the softness of his cheek, which is always red: he has four more teeth, others showing beneath angry gums. She wallows in the feel of him clinging to her shoulders, poking her hair and face, depending on her. Only with him does she laugh, when they're on their own, a softening of grief to see Peter in his eyes and smile, and she wonders how she would've been after Peter died if there hadn't been George, the link between her two lives.

A bat for beach cricket stands in the corner. She carries George, clasps her free hand round the handle, pictures Peter and his brothers by the sea. Where? Pebbles and shells litter a shelf, and Ludo, Snakes and Ladders. Above are Andrew Lang, and Grimm's Fairy Tales, Hans Andersen, *Alice in Wonderland*, *Treasure Island*, annuals, adventure stories by Henty.

She takes George to the window, looks across at the park. Frost covers ground, railings, and branches of trees reaching up to a clear sky. Church bells are rejoicing. Thomas, Joe and Renée may already have left for the service.

'Will you come with us, Livvy?' Renée asked after breakfast.

'I'll help Nanny,' she dissembled. 'It's Christmas Day for her, too.'

Later, Nanny and Mrs Brent, friends since girlhood, will be sharing a capon in the kitchen.

She moves away from the window. Plumbing pipes are clanking. Nanny is running George's bath.

❧

After Christmas dinner - a suckling pig with a red apple in its mouth, which Thomas carved at the table - she joins Tom and Connie by the morning room window. It is the first Christmas Connie is not spending with her parents; they were invited but Mrs Phillips had already asked some widowed members of the chapel to Christmas dinner.

Jealousy curls round her as she looks at her sister-in-law's distended abdomen. The baby is not due for two months but Connie moves heavily and has difficulty getting in and out of armchairs, so Joe has brought in one of the dining chairs. Peter's child would have been more than three months inside me now, she thinks, and me glorying in my swelling body. She recalls last Christmas, the only one she and Peter had together, a sybaritic celebration in the Black Town apartment, much of the day in bed; they'd been

268

invited to Charlotte's house; Peter had written to excuse their absence with a white lie: *Livvy tires easily.* She wonders how Charlotte is and remembers earlier Christmases with her, singing carols round the piano.

She is wearing the single string of pearls Nathaniel and Maud have given her: you look wonderful, my dear! Maud exclaimed as she put it on; fresh air, good food, I knew you'd be better away from that dreadful country. In her hair, a bright blue comb from Joe, which made her relieved he wasn't thrusting more Socialism on her with a book; he hasn't mentioned Russia or the Labour Party since her return downstairs, saying little beyond: all right, Livvy? each evening, as if wary of disturbing her. Connie has knitted gloves for her. From Renée she has *Martin Chuzzlewit* and a marker sewn in cross stitch. From Thomas, a writing case with fountain pen, stationery, stamps.

Her gifts from Nell were a pale blue knitted coat for George, with matching bonnet, bootees, mittens; and lipstick and rouge for herself in little metal tins.

'Isn't it rather *fast*?' Renée giggled. 'I thought cosmetics were only for actresses.'

'Nell was never fast,' Maud observed.

She looked at Maud, who was sitting up straight, staring into the distance, and it occurred to her that perhaps Maud missed Nell; Maud's daughters were in London and South Africa, so many women gone from the family. For a moment she glimpsed a different Maud, a lonely woman, as was she herself. Might we ever become friends?

'There's a note,' she said. 'Nell calls it make-up, says it's becoming popular with women on their side of the Atlantic.'

Maud drew in her breath: in disapproval? Or was there a hint of sadness?

She has taken the make-up to her room and put it in her empty third drawer. She cannot imagine wearing it in the house or out in the park and Wood Road, the boundaries of her existence.

❧

She stays with Tom and Connie by the window, away from the rest of the family. Renée has suggested charades but everybody seems content with lethargy. Nathaniel is already snoozing.

Fingers shaking, Tom lights another cigarette, leans forward on his chair, mouth still drooping at the corners. 'I don't know where he is, Liv, the Tom who used to live here.' He glances across at his wedding photograph on the small circular table next to the piano, then back, blue eyes looking through her as if for an answer. He jerks his head towards the family. 'They don't understand! Nobody. Lot of bloody armchair patriots! Don't 'spose they've ever seen a dead person 'cept at home, all peaceful. Like Mother last year.' She remembers May would already have been dead four months by the time Tom returned. 'No-one but you knows what I mean, Liv. It should've been me, not Jack, Will, Pete.'

'Tom!' whispers Connie. 'Not on Christmas Day. And you'll upset Livvy.'

Tom turns. 'Be quiet, Con! You don't understand. Liv's the one who does.'

An ache in her chest pushes away clinging jealousy: she wishes he could be more considerate of Connie She wonders what he was like, the young man who fell in love before he went to war. Perhaps the new baby will make a difference to him.

Tom returns to her. 'I was in the burial party once, Liv. It's quite a sweet smell when bodies have lain out for some time. We couldn't always get the wounded back from no man's land. That was the worst part, hearing their cries in the night. Then we'd have weeks with not much going on, living like rats, an' with them, in those stinking trenches. Big as otters, some of 'em, grey greasy things staring at us from white bloated faces.'

She knows about rats: the hall of Yefim Aaronovich's house November last year.

Connie has covered her mouth and nose with her hands.

'You run a lighted match down your seams, Liv, kill the lice.' Tom pinches the air with thumb and forefinger. 'Course, it was different for the officers. I took the dead men's pay books to their dugout, once. There were parcels from Fortnum and Mason on a table. They gave me tea and cake. Didn't seem right. I was glad to escape to my mates. You know, Liv, in the end we just thought of each other in the platoon. We'd lost sight of what it was all about.'

Companionship, chance friendships. A line from Will's diary comes to her: *Chalky and Lofty knocked out in the final push. I miss them.*

Tom is telling her, 'Every time we went over the top I'd think: this is it! Now they'll get me … I'll be with Jack, only without glory. I'm a coward you see, Liv. Could never've done what Jack did. I used to grit my teeth, screw up my eyes and dash for it. Once, I even shouted, "I'm here, you bastards! Come an' get me!" Nobody heard, of course, through all that racket.' He draws on his cigarette.

'Tom!' breathes Connie again.

She sees tears in her sister-in-law's eyes, remembers the rattle of

271

artillery fire during the Turkish attack on Baku and feels sympathy for Tom, too. He has buried friends; she and Peter watched Will and others lowered into sandy graves in Baku's British cemetery. Screams in Baku hospital echo in her mind and she puts both hands to her ears, fingertips resting against the lobes.

Tom glares at Connie. 'I've told you. Quiet! Let me be, always nagging.' He looks across the room. 'Wonder if Father's got any whisky? Christmas Day, after all.'

Whisky in the afternoon? She has never seen any here. They had sherry before dinner, and home-made elderberry wine at the table, the melting feeling reminding her of her wedding day last year. She puts her hand round Connie's, feels warm fingers squeeze hers then settle like a bird in a nest.

'All that happened,' Tom continues, 'was one in the arm when we attacked Vimy Ridge. Then, back in France from Italy, spring of last year, they did the other arm. Clever, wasn't it?' With the enthusiasm of one trying his best at everything, he takes off his jacket in the rankness of sweat, flings it on the floor, pushes up his left sleeve to reveal an indentation between shoulder and elbow, purple skin puckered, shiny, where flesh was cut to remove shrapnel.

'Italy,' she repeats, something to say.

'Helping the Eyeties after Caporetto. Bloody waste of time! Like a holiday compared with France. Country's nicer, too. Hillsides covered in vines.' He grins at his wife. 'Have to try that, Con. Grow some up the back wall in the sun.' He blows through his lips, a rumble of amusement. 'Don't 'spose your father'd agree.' Then to her: 'They turned us round for France as soon as the big Hun push started.' Tom rolls his sleeve down, reaches for his jacket.

She places her other hand across Connie's. A tear is struggling over each of Connie's cheeks.

'Funny thing was, Liv,' says Tom, jacket on his knee, 'one Christmas we met the Hun in the space between the trenches. They were just like us. Thin and filthy.' He creases his mouth in the rictus of a smile. '"Tommy," one chap called me. He couldn't'a known it was my real name; had hair the colour of ripe corn. "Fritz," I said. We shook hands. Our side let them come out and mend their wires and they did the same for us. We began to wonder why we were there at all. Things changed when we had a new company commander. He ordered us to fire on them. It was like we were killing our mates.' Tom puts his jacket on. 'They should've got me, Liv. Done the job properly. Pity the one who's least use should be the only survivor. Jack would've been a brilliant doctor, and Will far better with Father than I am. Pete, well, he always came out on top.'

'Tom!' Connie implores.

'Not in the end, he didn't,' she reminds Tom. 'I wouldn't say you're of least use. Connie needs you, and there's the baby to think of. You're a lucky man, Tom.' He is watching her, listening. 'Even if Jack and Will hadn't been killed they may not have returned as they were before the war. Have you seen men in the Bull Ring selling things off trays, drawing on the pavement?'

Tom's eyes are darting round the room. 'I get this dream, Liv. I'm in the trench, head down, hundreds, thousands of boots, marching past at eye level. It's the dead leaving me behind. I worry I've been forgotten, that I'm still there. Then I wake up in a cold sweat and find I'm next to Con.'

'I had a nightmare that kept coming back,' she tells him. 'It got less.'

Tom looks at her but doesn't answer or ask her to explain, and the words she might have said shrivel. He turns to Connie, sighs in exasperation. 'You're always crying, woman! What's the matter?'

She defends her sister-in-law. 'Women do, Tom, when they're expecting a baby. I was the same.' No you weren't, she thinks, but it'll help Connie.

Tom pats Connie's knee, swivels round to the rest of the family. 'What's Aunt Maud into now?' he wants to know; 'always on about something.'

She strokes Connie's hand, follows Tom's gaze to see what has aroused Maud's voice to carry across the room in indignation.

'Thomas! You don't mean to tell me you're condoning this?'

'Who am I to stand in their way, Maud? It seems an excellent arrangement. She's a hard worker, just the sort of wife he needs.'

'But they're not even from the same class!'

'I'd say that's the last thing on their minds. His own haven't done much for him.'

'It's dreadful,' objects Maud. 'Some people have lost all sense of social values. I think you should sack her at once, wash your hands of the whole sordid situation.'

'And what would that achieve? I'd lose an experienced worker and they'd neither of them have a job. She paid her rent all through the war, learnt how to solder when we were making shell fuses. She can use that skill now we're back producing bicycles. There's no point in offering the job to him. His hands were far too unsteady.'

'And they're living on her wages?'

'Until he finds a job. I can't take him on but somebody may.'

'I blame Mr Lloyd George for this sort of thing, encouraging women to do men's jobs. They get ideas above their station.'

'We'd have been in a poor position without women during the war, Maud. We wouldn't have been able to survive, and they needed work, with homes and families to keep going. Remember, the Queen herself said: prevention of distress is better than its relief; employment is better than charity.'

'Thomas, really! You sound like May.'

She hears Tom snort next to her. She glances at him.

'Liv, that ex-officer,' Tom says, 'who came to Father a while back; he's gone and married Florrie at the factory whose husband was killed a few weeks before the Armistice, lives with her in a two-up, two-down near the railway line.' Tom shakes his head. 'Poor Aunt Maud. Never had to cope with anything worse than that. Must've ruined her Christmas Day.'

Renée has drawn the curtains and is raising the piano lid. 'Looks as if Reen's going to give us a tune,' Tom observes. 'Spose I'll have to wait till the pub opens if I want a whisky.'

She is regarding Thomas, who has turned towards his daughter. How infinitely understanding of people he is, not judging. Her heart lifts, as if fanned by warm air.

TWENTY

She peers out of the morning room window at each snow-flake floating, landing, merging into a white blanket over the garden, something she hasn't seen since before she went to Russia. Every evening, Joe clears a path to his shed. 'Come and join me, Livvy,' he offers. She never does, but gives him her job advertisement to put in the *Birmingham Post* as there has been no reply to the one she left at the post office.

She sits with Renée by the fire, strengthening buttons on shirts; in Baku, when she ran out of black cotton she had to use white to darn black stockings then paint the patch with ink after each wash. Renée huddles for the first time with the curse, concentrating on the drawn threadwork border of a tray cloth. Hers started the year after Mama died; she ran to her friend Pearl's house, convinced she was dying. Pearl's mother gave her rectangles of cloth and a belt, showed her how to attach them. You're a woman now, pet, Pearl's mother hugged her. Later, she stopped by Mama's grave and cried.

'I keep thinking of Mama,' says Renée, glancing across at the photograph of May. 'She was prettier than that.' Renée rethreads her needle. 'Papa might marry again.'

'Would you mind if he did?'

'Not if he was happy.'

If he does, she hopes Renée has a friendly stepmother, like Nadia Ephraimovna.

Another day Renée plays a Mozart sonata, careful to be accurate, a shadow of Esther's brilliance. Renée stands up, closes the piano. 'Peter and Nell used to do duets.'

She drops her mending, goes over, lifts the lid. She touches the keys and Peter's fingers are soft against her skin, the delirious forty-eight hours of their honeymoon at Charlotte's, late breakfasts, afternoon siestas, early nights as soon as they could politely excuse themselves from the sitting room. *Can I really go on living without him? How?*

When the snow stops she cycles into the countryside with Renée, enjoying the tick-tick of the wheels, and the sprung saddle of the new bicycle. The air whips her face; as a girl she would pedal to Blakeney Point and watch avocets searching for worms with their upcurved bills, marsh harriers swooping low over reeds and stunted larches, and seals staring back at her with soft eyes. She skates with Renée on the lake in the park, wearing May's boots which fit as if bought for her. *I feel the breath of normal life, without fear of danger*, she writes to Eleanor.

A photographer comes to the house. Tom and Joe carry dining chairs into the morning room. She is seated on Thomas's left, George on her lap, Connie next to her, Renée the other side of Thomas, Tom and Joe standing behind. Is this photograph, too, destined for an album? *Family group, New Year 1920*, Thomas might label it. The start of a new decade, fresh hopes. A future?

She imagines Peter standing behind her in the photograph, next to his brothers; going to work in a suit each morning, an engineer in the city. Thomas says there is a housing shortage, so they might still be living here, sitting with Thomas in the evening, reading and sewing, until making love upstairs.

Her fingers are trembling as she pushes black wool through the heel of a sock, taut over the wooden darning mushroom, Joe's scornful voice during the evening meal ringing in her head: the government promise to build a hundred thousand new houses this year, but it's *now* people need homes!

Discontent. People taking the law into their own hands. It can't happen here, she tells herself. Can't it? Why not?

Thomas has brought home the news that Tom and Connie have left her parents and gone to live on a canal barge. Tom has told his father he will stay at the factory for the moment but insists on the same payment as other unskilled workers, no more charity off Thomas, or Connie's parents. He's going to get an allotment and grow enough to sell.

A barge. In January. And the baby due next month. No-one but you knows what I mean, Liv, Tom said on Christmas Day. She tries to navigate his damaged mind, his desperation to prove himself: pity the one who's least use should be the only survivor. Yet, nothing any of the family does should surprise her: Nell to Canada, Peter to Russia, two brothers enlisting under age, another a Socialist.

After sounding off about the government's housing policy, Joe stomped out to his shed. In the morning room, Thomas unfolds, refolds, the newspaper, lets it fall to the floor. Never has she seen him so unsettled, ruffling the fabric of her security, the warp and weft of the last three months.

'Is there nothing we can do,' she says, 'no way of making Tom think again?'

Thomas allows a smile, sighs, shaking his head. 'My children have always known their own minds. It's a trait they get from their dear mother. Even Tom, the most docile, sensitive – he was thirteen when his mother was arrested yet still cried – could never be persuaded against something he was set on.' Thomas picks up the paper, smoothes it across his lap. 'He has a high regard for you, Livvy, feels you understand what he went through in the war. He listens to you, I've noticed. Could you go over to them, say on Saturday afternoon when they're together? Take them one of Mrs Brent's potted meats. See that at least they've got running water and warmth. I suppose they're living on bread and cheese and kisses. I'm not going to get anywhere with him the mood he's in, and if you visit just Connie he'll accuse us of interfering behind his back.'

'Of course I will. He's stupid! Why all this just before Connie's time? She'd have been better with her mother. How near are they to any help? What are they going to do when the baby starts?'

'I put all that to him, you can be sure. Apparently, there's a row of six barges some man has made habitable and is renting out at three shillings a week each. Three shillings! All the others are occupied by families. Connie'll have plenty of help, Tom says.' Thomas purses his mouth. 'She's only ever lived with her parents above the shop, their one child, a sheltered life.'

'I'd like to know what she thinks about this. I don't suppose she had much say, poor girl. Perhaps I'll find out on Saturday.'

೧

By then, just a few patches of snow cling to the grass. She ties her Baku shawl round her hat, pulls on Connie's Christmas gloves, leaving Mrs Brent and the Monday woman making marmalade, the sticky, bitter smell of boiling fruit and sugar penetrating even the second floor. She cycles across the park, turns left onto the Stratford Road, and left again, past terraced houses. On the cobbles children are playing in ill-fitting pullovers, patched trousers hanging over knees above matchstick legs thrust into clogs.

'Like yer bike, Miss!' one urchin shouts.

'Thanks!' she calls back, concentrates on her balance, mindful of Mrs Brent's potted meat tied with muslin in the metal carrier. She peers ahead, uneasy in such a street on a new bike.

She passes a sign to Boulton Cycle Works, sees the canal and beyond it the railway line. She gets off the bicycle and pushes. From the canal bridge she looks at murky, grey-green water, a towpath on the left, fields along the other bank. She walks the bicycle down to the path, which turns under the railway bridge. Black, wet moss clings to stone. She waits while a train trundles overhead; as a child she would've made a wish.

Like a canopy, catkins hang from winter branches along the canal. A robin pauses by her before flying away. Six barges are moored, once painted different colours. Two girls in frocks that are too big, drawers reaching half-way down their legs, are running wooden hoops along the towpath. Another is skipping with frayed rope. A girl and boy are playing hopscotch, pushing a pebble over lines scored on flattened earth. They stand aside and she feels their eyes following her, a lady with a new bicycle, past a low, wooden construction, corrugated iron roof, three doors secured with padlocks. A scrawny cat crouches in suspicion. A woman's voice raised in anger, children crying, float on air sharp with the smell of sewage, one she remembers from years ago with Masha in the poor quarter of Baku's Black Town, hauling to Masha's tenement a sack of flour.

Each barge is connected to the towpath by a footbridge.

Seated on a three-legged stool at the end of the first, a man is whittling wood, cap back off his forehead, jacket and trousers crumpled, streaked with dirt and shavings.

'I'm looking for Tom and Connie,' she says. 'They've just moved here.'

The man stops. When he glances up she clutches the handle-bars of the bicycle, wishes she could turn away but can't while he is speaking to her. One eye is missing, the lashless lid pulled down. In some frenzied field dressing station, were the two lids stitched together? The skin has gathered, angry, sunken. Several days' stubble covers his face.

The good eye stares at her. 'We'm all jus' moved 'ere,' the man answers out of one corner of his mouth, a cigarette lying undisturbed in the other. ''Er expectin'?'

'Yes.'

With a jerk of the head, he indicates, 'Las' one along. Red 'un.'

'Thank you.' She pushes the bike, heart beating faster, wondering what she is going to find. She passes another wooden hut alongside a vertical pipe with a tap at the end, sees a battered copper and mangle through the open door.

She hesitates to walk across Tom and Connie's footbridge without them knowing she is there. 'Hello!' she calls. A tin bath is leaning against the covered area of the barge. 'Hello! Tom! Connie!'

The door opens and Tom emerges. 'Liv!' He bounds over to the towpath, hugs her. How thin he feels, compared with Peter. Tom kisses her cheek. 'Come aboard,' he urges, mouth still drooping in one corner but happier than she has ever seen him. He is wearing a shapeless brown pullover turned back several times at the cuffs. He takes the bicycle from her. 'We'll bring this. Don't want to leave it lying around. Not like my old thing. Nothing but the best for you, Liv,' he chuckles. 'Quite right, too.' He puts a hand on the carrier. 'What's in here?'

She follows him. 'Potted meat from Mrs Brent.'

'She doesn't have to, you know, Liv. We're all right.'

'Let's call it a present for your new home.'

'Mind the bucket,' he points. 'Rainwater for Connie to wash her hair.'

He guides the bicycle through the scratched red door. 'On yer feet, Con! Our first visitor.'

She crosses the threshold, stands for a moment in the dimness and smell of paraffin until Connie's arms are round her. She hugs her sister-in-law, unable to avoid pressing against the hard abdomen, shelter for the unborn Boulton. Fingers of jealousy prod her, teasing. She kisses Connie on both cheeks.

'It's nice of you to come,' says Connie.

'Welcome to *chez nous*, Liv,' says Tom. 'That's French. You don't spend all the time I did there without picking up a bit of the lingo. It means our house. The government promised homes fit for heroes. Well, I'm no hero so I don't deserve much of a home, but it's ours and we're proud of it. And I've signed the pledge, Liv,' he adds. 'Not another drop'll pass my lips. It's old toast water for me now.'

He wanted whisky on Christmas afternoon. 'That's good, Tom.'

Connie takes the basin. 'Do thank Mrs Brent. Tom always liked her potted meats.'

'Come on, Con,' Tom chivvies. 'Get water on for tea. Liv's cycled all the way from Laurel Road: thirsty work. You sit here, Liv.' His hand is on her arm. 'Best chair.'

She does as she's told, watches Connie bend to scoop water into a pan from a bucket on the floor. Connie straightens as if afraid of disturbing the air around her, puts the pan on a hotplate over a paraffin stove. The other armchair is padded with cushions. An oilcloth covers the table, beside which wait two ladder-backed chairs. In the middle stands an aspidistra, and a paraffin lamp with a blue china bowl. A tin basin perches on a stool. A couple of rag mats lie on the floorboards.

Connie reaches for the tea caddy from a shelf which also holds cups, plates, sugar, biscuit tins. On the one above are ranged candles, jugs, paper flowers. A faded, green velvet curtain flops from a rail nailed alongside for there is no wardrobe. On the opposite wall hang a mirror, Tom and Connie's wedding photograph, a *Home Sweet Home* sampler, a print of the Bubbles advertisement for Pear's soap, a drawing of fruit with Thomas's initials in the corner.

Connie spoons tea into the pot. 'Tom's going to put paper on the walls.'

'Mix a bit of flour and water,' he enthuses from the patchwork quilt on the iron-framed bed. 'Done in no time, eh Liv?'

'You've made it cosy,' she says. It is, in January. How stifling will it be in summer?

'We're all right,' says Tom. 'Dirty water, out the window into the canal.' He sits forward, jerks his head in Connie's direction. 'Old man Phillips was getting up my nose,' he murmurs, 'full of the good old days when wars were fought on horseback. Then it'd be how wise Lloyd George was to call the election before most soldiers were home, and the government's sense taking a tough line with the railwaymen in October. Enough to drive a chap to drink! He thought I might be a revolutionary 'cos I'd been in the Army. Better for us to get out to our own place.'

'Are you a Socialist, Tom?' She wonders what she can say or do if he is.

'I'm not anything. For nearly three years, I was Private Boulton, Fifteenth Battalion, Royal Warwickshire Regiment, *sir*! Now I'm nothing. Just Tom. Governments can do what they like, long as they leave me alone. I've got an allotment up Hay Mills. Come spring and summer we'll have good stuff. What can be better than that? If I grow enough, I'll sell some.'

Connie hands them tea in thick cups without saucers, lowers herself against the cushions and puts her feet on a footstool.

She notices swollen ankles. 'How are you, Connie?'

Tom nods towards her belly. 'She'll be glad to drop that lot, won't you, girl?'

Connie flashes him a smile, a shadow of the one on the wedding photograph. 'I'll say. Were you this big, Livvy, with George?'

'Yes.' She's sure she wasn't. 'The last weeks are always the worst.'

Connie looks across at Tom, then away.

They drink their tea.

'Are the other women friendly?'

Again, Tom answers. 'Oh, yes. Couple of babies on the way, but Connie'll be first.' He grins at his wife. 'We were quick off the mark, weren't we, girl?'

Connie smiles, lowers her eyes, finishes her tea.

'There's a woman this side the railway line helps with births,' says Tom.

Dimness is thickening into darkness. She thinks of the blackness and wet under the railway bridge, clinging moss, and wonders how soon she can leave.

'Have to light the lamp,' says Tom. 'Can't see where we're looking.' He goes over to the table, trims the wick, peers inside the bowl. 'Need more paraffin soon.'

She stands up. 'I'll come and see you again.'

'I'll take your bike out, Liv,' Tom offers. 'Thank Mrs Brent for the meat but you're not to bring any more. Understand?'

'All right. But there are George's things he's grown out of. They're no use to anybody lying in a drawer.'

Tom is through the door. Connie hugs her. 'We could have a cup of tea, Livvy, when Tom's at work. The days go rather slowly.'

'We will,' she promises.

∽

It's a trait they get from their dear mother: did he really say that to Livvy about his children's stubbornness? He hopes it didn't sound disparaging to May. In the lamplight, he sits back in his chair, looks at the photograph of her. He would never deprecate her. He was indulgent at first when she began to accompany her elder sister to meetings of the Midlands branch of Mrs Pankhurst's Women's Social and Political Union, in Birmingham. The boys were at school, Renée in the nursery; it couldn't hurt, he thought, an outing once or twice a week with Enid.

The Liberal meeting at Bingley Hall in September 1909 changed everything. Prime Minister Asquith was speaking on Mr Lloyd George's People's Budget and had only gone a little way to explain that an increase in death duties and those on tobacco and spirits, and income tax up to one shilling and tuppence in the pound, would all pay for new Dreadnoughts, old age pensions and labour exchanges, when he was interrupted by women shouting and waving placards. Ten protesters, including May and Enid, were arrested, sent to Winson Green prison. When they refused to eat, they were fed by force, the first in the country. The WSPU sued the Home Secretary, unsuccessfully.

May returned home, pale and thin, yellowing bruises on neck and cheeks. 'No more meetings,' he stipulated.

'But Thomas,' she pleaded, voice faint, scratchy, from the feeding tube; 'the cause. I promised Enid.'

'Well you can unpromise Enid. She has neither husband nor children.' Nor likely to; a plain bluestocking if ever there was one.

So May made do with two afternoons a week at HQ in John Bright Street, folding pamphlets, addressing envelopes. Nell helped her, in between parties, tennis, theatricals. When, less than two years later, his daughter announced she wanted to go to Canada he remembers relief that she wasn't following her mother. Enid moved to London before the war when the parents had died; he's had no contact with her since May's funeral.

Livvy seemed tired this evening after her visit to Tom and Connie, though insists they're warm and happy. She's going to see Connie again; perhaps they'll become friends. Is there nothing we can do? Livvy said to him when he first told her about the barge. We. A hand reaching into the aloneness.

↜↝

Connie eases herself onto the chair. 'Does it hurt a lot, Livvy, when the baby comes?' Foreboding clouds brown eyes.

'Yes. Even though you know it's going to happen, it catches you unawares. It's best to lie on your side.' She had

Masha, someone who'd been through it advising a novice. 'You have to take deep breaths, relax between the pain,' she tells Connie. And then *baboushka* Agafia crooning through toothless gums, greasing her with something aromatic. She points in the direction of the other barges. 'The women will help you.'

'Elsie next door's very kind, and Tom'll run to fetch the handywoman from Collett Road. Elsie's had twelve: six died, two are here, the rest she had to put in Doctor Barnardo's. She's started another, scraping the pot, she says, for her baker's dozen.'

They drink their tea. She has brought George's shifts. The bonnet from Charlotte he can wear again this summer. Before Connie put the shifts under the bed, she touched the embroidered edges: bees, vine leaves, in red, green, yellow. 'Beautiful! Did you do it, Livvy?'

She shook her head. 'A Russian friend.'

Connie smiled, as if encouraging her to say more. I can't, she thought, not to Connie; where to begin? It was Esther's Armenian friend, Maria Bagratuni, who'd embroidered the shifts; who used to work for the Council of People's Commissars during *bolshevik* Baku eighteen months ago, and passed information for Esther to deliver. As evacuees in Enzeli, once she realised she was expecting George, they would sit together sewing.

Connie rearranges her weight on the chair, confides, 'What if it's in the night? I wish you could be here, Livvy.' Connie prods her middle, anxiety on her face reflected in, 'It's such a tiny button. Going to have to stretch an awful lot.'

'Button?'

'Tummy button,' says Connie.

Elsie hasn't told Connie everything. 'The baby isn't born through *there*!'

Fear replaces anxiety. 'How, then?'

'Between your legs!'

Connie stares at her. 'The way it went in?'

'Yes.'

Connie sighs. 'Mother never explained *anything*.'

'How did you feel about leaving your parents and coming here?'

'We were more comfortable there, but Tom was getting so depressed, kept saying nobody understood. Of course, Father and Mother didn't. How could they? And Tom couldn't bear the telephone: he'd run out of the room, hands over his ears. Father used to like Tom to have a game of dominoes with him in the evenings so Tom did, but then he'd go to the pub, play cards, come back drunk. I don't remember him drinking before the war. It started when he was in the trenches, he told me, to pass time with the other men, help them forget. The French used to sell them whisky, and they had a winter rum ration to keep out the cold, then beer in the pubs.'

'Does his father know?'

Connie shrugs, opens both hands in a gesture of helplessness. 'So you can imagine the atmosphere at home, with Father and Mother teetotal. Lunatic soup, Father called it. Better for us to come away. We can manage. The family in the end barge have to take their clean clothes to the pawnshop on washday to get through the week. We don't.'

She remembers the ravaged eye of the man she spoke to on her first visit.

'I want Tom to be happy,' Connie says. 'He still has the

nightmare. He's so different from before the war. It was like living with a stranger when he came back.' Tears trickle down Connie's cheeks. 'You know, one morning he peed at the corner of the lane where his father has the factory; didn't even turn away, same as he used to in France, I s'pose. Mrs Beddows was outside her grocery. She was really upset. Mr Boulton had to go round and apologise.' Connie fumbles for a handkerchief, brushes the tears away. 'Don't be cross with me, Livvy, for crying. Tom always is, but I can't help it. I feel so sad, because he's gone, the man I loved, even though he's here.'

She pulls her chair nearer to Connie, takes her hand. 'I've done a lot of crying.'

'That's what I tell myself,' Connie sobs, holding the handkerchief against her eyes. 'Thousands of women really have lost their men and I should be thankful I have Tom.' She wipes her eyes. 'I keep thinking how he used to be. He'd come into Father's shop every morning for his tobacco at the beginning of the war. Sometimes I served him. He was shy, gentle. One day he asked Father if he could call on a Saturday afternoon. We used to go for walks. Then Sunday as well. He told me one of his brothers was in France. I was terrified he'd go, too. He did, of course, but we got married first.' Connie gazes at the wedding photograph on the wall, a smile playing around her lips. 'He didn't want to leave. We'd just heard Jack had been killed. On our wedding night we clung to each other, and as for the rest ... ' Connie allows the smile, ' ... well, you know. We were so innocent, so much in love. We had two nights together. I prayed I'd be pregnant, have something of him in case he went the same way as Jack.' Connie blows her nose.

… something of him. I have George, she thinks. The lost baby would've been the child of our return, start of a new life. One day she will tell Connie about it. She takes Connie's hand again. 'I expect he wrote to you.'

'Yes. Sometimes there'd be weeks with nothing, then two or three letters together, or a couple of lines scrawled in pencil, or just field postcards confirming he was still alive. I don't think he could write about it. There grew a barrier between us because of what he knew and had seen that I would never know or see.'

'There are things I don't want to put into words,' she tells Connie. Yet, with Peter there was never a barrier, just that small one of her making when she didn't tell him Masha had said the British would be leaving Baku; we endured everything together: bombardment, Will's death, evacuation, seeing the horror at Yefim Aaronovich's house, crossing Russia.

'It helped him, talking to you on Christmas Day,' Connie says.

'I understand something of what he went through.'

'A lot of the time now he's silent, never chats about his day or asks me about mine. There was no love in his letters, but I've kept them all, even the field postcards. After he came home, he said I should throw them away.' Connie starts to cry again, tears of hurt. 'That was the worst part. I was so happy to see him.' Connie manages a misshapen smile beneath puffy cheeks. 'He was in a demob suit. It was too big, trousers turned up, but he said if he'd waited for the right size goodness knows when he'd have got home. I thought after a rest he'd be all right and everything the same as before.'

Connie blows her nose, rubs her eyes. 'It was dreadful, that first night. I mean, I really did want him after years of waiting; I'd pushed my nightie up and opened my legs. He was like an animal, didn't say anything, just lay on top of me. There was no love with it. He didn't even look at me when he was doing it. I wanted it to be like before, eyes on each other, enjoying it together, the miracle of it. When he'd finished he rolled off, ignored me until he was ready again. I felt used. Every time. Are you with me, Livvy?'

'Yes,' she lies, for she can only imagine. With Peter there was always love.

'He'd say he was no use to anybody, and it was Jack and Will who should've come back, not him, and that *that* was the only thing he could still do. I felt he was determined to make me pregnant, to prove himself.'

Heat rises through her thighs: Peter's soft lips, fingers against her skin like a whisper of butterfly wings, rough morning face as he kissed her awake. Her throat constricts but she manages, 'So he's pleased about the baby.'

'Yes.' Connie bunches the cushions behind her. 'But he still wanted to do it. Not now, though. Says he can't get near me, that I'm like a fortress. But after the birth he'll expect to start again. I'm afraid if ever I tell him no he'll take it out on the little one.'

'Wait and see,' she suggests. 'A baby affects men as well as women. Peter was very emotional.' His voice comes back to her, the way it caught, that hot Baku afternoon in May last year: I'm so happy, darling, so proud of you.

Connie sighs. 'I wish you were nearer, Livvy. Will you come often?'

'As much as I can.'

She pushes her bicycle along the towpath, tears running down her cheeks that Connie's baby, born out of Tom's loveless thrusting, will forever be a reminder of how she has failed Peter, miscarrying their second child. Then there is her advertisement: no reply. Doesn't anyone want a young woman to care for their children? Every day before Thomas comes home, she has been looking in the newspaper at positions advertised. Is she never going to take George away, make a new life? At night, she weeps for Peter: I love you, he said even as he lay dying. She reaches now for the sound of his voice … I love you … this time it has gone.

∾

When she visits Connie on a Monday, washing flaps from lines strung along the barges. Through the open wash house door, between squeaks and groans of the mangle, comes a lusty off-key rendering of *My Old Man said Follow the Van*. 'The men fill the copper on Sunday nights,' says Connie, 'and light the fire, so water's hot for the morning. The other women let me use it first in case I start.' Clean clothes lie folded in a pile on the table.

She calls on a Saturday afternoon so Tom won't feel she doesn't want to see him. He is out digging his allotment.

One evening, banging on the front door reverberates through the house in Laurel Road. In the dining room she is cutting the first portion of steak and kidney pie for Thomas, releasing beefy steam. She hears Tom's voice in the hall, and an excited 'Oh, Mr Tom!' from Mrs Brent. Thomas and Joe are on their feet. She puts down the serving knife, pushes back her chair, stands up as Tom rushes in.

'Connie's had twins!' he exclaims. 'Isn't she wonderful? *Two* babies! Boys.'

She hugs Tom. 'Congratulations!' she manages, face pressed

into his shoulder to conceal a sob. She lets him go, wipes the back of a hand across her eyes while Thomas embraces his son and Joe claps him on the arm.

'Early this afternoon,' Tom says. 'They're both crying well. Going to be dark, like Connie.' He takes her hands, clasps her to him. 'I'm so proud of her, Liv.'

She feels him heaving, cannot stop her own tears, mingling joy and loss; she walks towards the sideboard, pulls out a handkerchief, flicks them away.

'Stay and eat with us,' says Thomas. 'Or do you want to get back to Connie?'

'Hardly room for me there.' Tom rubs a hand across his cheeks. 'Place full of women, washing, crying babies.' He sits down. 'I'm best out the way.'

She opens the cutlery drawer, takes out a knife and fork for him.

'We've decided on Peter and Jack,' he says, 'in memory.'

Peter. A nephew I can love? She cuts some pie for Tom.

He gobbles his meal, anxious to return. She goes with him into the hall. 'You'll need extra of everything. I'll be over tomorrow.'

Tom puts his arms round her. 'Thanks, Liv.'

She eases him away. 'Tell Connie you think she's wonderful. Make her happy.'

He kisses her forehead, squeezes her hands. 'I already have, Liv.'

TWENTY-ONE

'A penny bone, Livvy, and a penn'orth of carrot, turnip, leak and parsley make a good dinner,' chatters Connie. 'Tom said he never wanted stew again, it's what they had in the trenches, but if I only put a little meat in, and lots of veg and broth he doesn't mind. In a few weeks we'll have what he's grown.' Connie lowers her voice, looks round as if ashamed of what she's about to say. 'The French, they even charged the men for water.'

Whenever she goes to the barge, she always inhales the promise of food simmering on the hob. She looks now at the babies lying facing each other in their wicker cradle, noses and foreheads touching. She will be like a maiden aunt to them, dry, alone, separated from eighteen months of passion by years of emptiness. Connie lifts Peter out, suckles him, his tiny fingers splayed across a porcelain breast threaded with blue veins; contentment radiates from her. She, Livvy, remembers the feeling.

'You were right about Tom,' Connie says. 'Fatherhood has changed him. He's happy beyond belief, proud of his sons and me. He still wants to do it all the time, greedy for more babies. But if I say no he doesn't sulk.'

'As long as you're feeding them yourself you're unlikely to get caught.' Yet I did, she thinks, when I was weaning George … the stationmaster's cottage in Voronezh …

Connie sighs. 'So there's a breathing space. I don't think I could cope with three.'

She holds Peter while Connie changes Jack on the table. Peter is the smaller of the two, skin red and mottled, eyes closed, the sleeves of George's shift reaching his fingers. There is a sour, milky smell from him. He could be a doll, and she wonders why she cannot summon the same love felt for George when he was this young. She closes her eyes, clenches her teeth against the ache of longing, the tidal wave rushing at her, for her own Peter, lovemaking, children she will never bear to be brothers and sisters for George.

The threat of drowning recedes. It always does, just when she's about to go under. She opens her eyes. Perhaps, with time, she'll find love for this Peter. He and Jack will be playmates for George.

ᘓ

Renée, home for half term, goes with her to the barge. Renée holds and kisses the twins, but with none of the enthusiasm shown for George last autumn.

'I don't know how Connie manages,' Renée says when they are wheeling their bicycles back along the towpath, where yellow and mauve crocuses have cut a swathe of colour. 'I think Tom's selfish expecting her to live here.'

'He's happier than I've ever seen him.'

'He will be!' Renée counters with a flash of asperity. 'He's got everything he wants. He wouldn't find me putting up with these conditions.'

'You won't have to. Your sights are on Oxford.'

'It's wrong, women without much education having to live like this.'

But it's the way things are, Renée, she thinks. She pictures

Masha – how often she's thought of Masha these last few weeks in relation to Connie - moving around Yefim Aaronovich's old apartment in Baku's Black Town, keeping house for her father, and perhaps some of her brothers, comfortable somewhere once owned by the man who used to employ them all. Does it take a revolution to change life for people like Connie?

✧

She has asked Joe to retain her advertisement in the *Birmingham Post* for another week. She receives a reply from a Mrs Pearsall, with two sons aged one and three. *Before we bring you all the way over here for interview, could you please supply references. Also, you give no indication of why you are leaving your present position.*

She fetches from upstairs the leather writing case Thomas gave her at Christmas. In the morning room, she sits at the open lid of the bureau, forming and discarding sentences in her mind, fingers on a small cardboard box. She's seen it before, when writing to Eleanor. It has no lid and contains newspaper cuttings. Now, she takes out the top one: *Bolshevism in Russia* … The others are also about Russia last year. How desperate Thomas must have been for news! She comes to two black-edged War Office envelopes: *Mr and Mrs T. Boulton*. From one, she eases out a piece of paper: notification of Jack's death in 1916; formal, impersonal. She glances at the contents of the second envelope just enough to see the wording is identical except for name, place, date.

There is a flimsy envelope covered in smudgy, illegible post-marks. A single sheet of paper is dated 30th August, 1918, written in Baku. She reads the letter, as if staring at her own ghost.

… I expect you have been informed of your son's death in Russia.

296

He was a fine soldier, and died with honour and dignity, without suffering long. I hope it will be of some comfort to you both to know that Private Boulton's dying words were of his mother.

Yours sincerely,

Tristram Barcroft (Lieut)

She wonders how this Tristram Barcroft knew about Will's last hour, when only she and Peter were there; feels the intrusion of a stranger.

At the bottom of the box is some paper, folded once, and her fingers, independent of discomfort at trespassing further, are opening it out. Her heart seems to shift. It is as if Peter is in the room here, for she held and read this letter telling his parents about Will. Peter wrote and sent it from Enzeli, after their evacuation from Baku. ... *Livvy was wonderful, showed such care for Will; and for me since. I'm the luckiest man in the world and hope one day you'll be able to meet her ...*

'Do you really think we shall go to England?' she asked Peter.

'Who knows?' he said. 'We might.'

The nonchalance in his voice closed the matter for her. But for him, that was never the case. He didn't write to his family again, sure he'd soon be with them. George was only a few weeks old when Peter first talked about leaving Baku. She cried, pleaded, refused to consider the idea. Months passed and she thought he'd forgotten; but he hadn't, presenting her with a plan, a *bolshevik* permit ... and I let him journey north instead of insisting on the warm south.

Could she have persuaded him, though? My children have always known their own minds, Thomas said of Tom in January.

She looks away from the bureau, across the room to the piano, chairs, small tables, bookcase, photographs, nothing different. Yet, it is as if she has entered the room for the first time, starting something new. She sees not the confident Peter whose smile dazzled her along Baku's Marine Boulevard with Jacob and Anton; not the workman in shabby suit and cap who sheltered with her in the Tartar Quarter two years ago, lips soft against her fingers; not the lover on their wedding night, those same lips kissing every inch of her, setting his seal upon her until she was ablaze; simply someone who clung to the dream of going home to England, humming a tune around the apartment in the Black Town as they prepared their bedrolls for departure.

Her hands are sweating. She wipes them down her skirt, returns the cuttings and letters to the box, opens the writing case. *For four years, I was employed by a Russian family in Russia*, she writes to Mrs Pearsall, *until revolution forced them into exile. I married a British engineer. The following year we, too, left but he did not survive the journey. Our son and I are living with his family.*

ↁ

The next Saturday, after Joe has gone to work, Thomas glances up from spreading marmalade on his toast. 'I think we both deserve a free day, Livvy.' He passes his cup to her for more tea. 'Can Connie manage without you?'

'I'm sure of it.' She fills the cup, wonders what he plans. We? 'I'm not really needed there.'

Thomas raises his eyebrows as if the possibility has never occurred to him. 'How are they going to be next winter?' he muses; 'two babies starting to walk, the damp, the canal mists. I'm wasting my breath offering them a home with us.'

'Tom's content, master in his own place,' she points out.

'He's a different man from when I first met him.'

Thomas nods on a sigh of concession, turns towards the window. 'It's going to be a fine day. We could cycle out to Rednal and call on the Mackenzies. Would you like to see Eleanor again?'

'Yes.' But her parents? Strangers, questions.

He wipes his mouth on the table napkin, stands up, finishing his tea. 'If you'll excuse me, Livvy, I'll see if I can reach them on the telephone.'

She carries the breakfast things to the kitchen, something else she has agreed with Mrs Brent. She puts the plates on the deal table, goes over to the window ledge where trays of seeds have germinated, safe from night frosts until the plants can go outside. She likes watching new life develop, now no more than an inch high, stems the thickness of a cotton strand, supporting two leaves the size of a teardrop. On paper in the corner of the first tray Thomas or Joe has written *Tomato*; in the other trays, *Cucumber*, *Lettuce*, loops on the *b* and *l*.

She looks through the window. Daffodils, red and yellow tulips, nod in the breeze. Blossom, white and pale pink, covers fruit trees, ornamental cherry, flowering almond; and new leaves, that delicate green only seen at this time of year. Spring she is unable to share with Peter. Each season there will be something she cannot enjoy with him. Tears cluster under her eyelids. You wanted England, Peter. She rests the backs of her hands against her eyes, sees only his heart-shaped face, light brown hair. Tomorrow is his birthday. Should she mention this to Thomas? She decides not to: it must be seven years since Peter's last birthday in England. Thomas may not even remember.

She pedals alongside him; he is wearing a tweed suit instead of his weekday black. She takes deep breaths, as if she must cleanse and refill stale winter lungs; past fields, a farm, patches of copse, buds forcing colour into trees and hedgerows. Birds squabble and sing. A dog is barking. A milk float passes them in the opposite direction, a clinking of metal churns and the whistle of the milkman, who touches his cap in greeting.

Eleanor has insisted they go for lunch; what did she say at Laurel Road about the parents? Yes: …main preoccupation was the meat and milk ration, and whether they'd have enough fuel to see them through the winter. Unease that she is to be with people who never knew Peter or anything that happened, and her disinclination to talk about it, frets around her. People don't always know what to say and so tell her how she must be feeling, like Maud last October, but it doesn't work. She wonders what they'll think of her hat and coat from the Salvation Army in Liverpool. She'll have to buy new ones, thinner for the summer.

They stop, rest the bicycles against a gate. She takes out of the carrier two apples from Mrs Brent and hands one to Thomas. She bites through red and green skin into white flesh, still crisp after being stored for months, catches juice down her chin with a finger, watching cows lowing and munching grass. One trundles over to the gate, gazes at the visitors with mournful eyes, rubs the underside of her jaw against the rough wood.

The land rises ahead, trees covering the top of a hill. 'That's Lickey,' says Thomas. 'The view's worth the climb.'

They throw the apple cores into ferns growing above ankle

height. After pedalling up the incline for a few minutes, Thomas halts. She looks where he is pointing along a path away from the road. 'We'll wheel the bicycles,' he says. She follows him past blackberry and bilberry bushes, green shoots pushing from new stems.

The path steepens. They lay the bicycles on the bracken. She takes the hand he offers. It is warm, strong. She picks her way over stones and tree roots. When they arrive at the ridge, he lets go of her hand. She turns, gazes across miles of fields, the occasional village, to a range of hills in the distance. 'It's magnificent,' she says.

'Those are the Malverns,' he tells her. 'Too far to cycle in one day.'

Behind, the path meanders into trees she saw from the road. Beyond, the mass of buildings that is Birmingham lies like a toy town on the horizon.

His hand is on her arm, his touch light. A few yards away, a pheasant is stepping over the uneven ground, unaware of the perfection of chestnut plumage marked with cream and black. It stops, jerks its head in enquiry. She holds her breath, fearful any movement will destroy the magic. Did Peter come here in his striped blazer? With an ache of longing, she wishes it was him sharing this moment. That it is not, shatters the happiness opening in her heart.

A clatter and squawk, a sheen of green and purple in midday light, and the bird rises towards the trees.

Thomas is pointing to a village below. 'There's Rednal. I could stay here all afternoon but the Mackenzies will be expecting us.'

She wants to say: tell me; tell me all about him, everything, those years he was yours; in Russia he was mine.

301

She takes his hand down the path.

❧

Steak pie is comforting, familiar, as she listens to talk about those who have, or not, survived influenza and scarlet fever, people Thomas knows; speculation about how long sugar will stay on the ration and whether bread will come down again to less than a shilling. She feels Doctor Mackenzie's dark eyes appraising her from under bushy brows; his red hair is sprinkled with white. She tenses in anticipation of a question from him, loosens when Thomas tells their hosts about the garden, the new babies.

'Connie's a very capable mother,' she contributes. Mrs Mackenzie, frail, pale-faced, turns to smile as if enjoying the sound of a new voice.

She glances across the table, finds Thomas looking at her. She studies the arch and sweep of a bridge on her Japanese willow pattern plate, takes the dish of vegetables Eleanor passes to her.

After lunch, Mrs Mackenzie retires upstairs. Thomas wants to see his agent. 'I'll walk with you,' Doctor Mackenzie offers.

The dining room is at the front of the grey stone house, overlooking a path winding from the lane, lined with daffodils. 'Come through to the back, Livvy,' Eleanor suggests.

She follows Eleanor to a sitting room opening into a conservatory bright with afternoon sun, where vines have snaked up the corners and across the ceiling. At one side of the house are stables bordering a lawn and garden.

'Did you ask them not to say anything about Russia, Eleanor?'

'I told them you'd lost your husband and had a bad time. They wouldn't pry.'

She and Eleanor sit in chintz-covered chairs. A man is digging

302

the garden. 'Frank was gassed at Loos,' Eleanor explains. 'He puts in an hour or two when the weather's fine. It's as much as he can manage. He loves fresh air.'

'Like Tom.' She talks of his allotment. A maid brings tea things on a tray and Eleanor pours into gold-patterned white china cups.

She tells Eleanor about the pheasant on Lickey ridge. 'I'm happy when I'm with George, in fact I don't know how I would have been without him. I don't feel bad about that because he is part of Peter. He *is* Peter.' She drinks some tea. 'But any other joy seems wrong. Were you like that after Edward was killed?'

'Yes. For a long while.'

'Are you still?'

'Sometimes.' Eleanor leans across, takes her cup to refill it. 'Have you told Peter's father how you feel?'

'No. I don't want to upset him. He's lost so many people.'

'He's probably experienced the same, yet doesn't want to sadden *you*.'

She thinks of smiling eyes, wonders how soon he'll be back with Doctor Mackenzie. How cautious we are with each other. It would be better if I wasn't living under his roof, then he wouldn't have to be concerned about me. I can still take George to see him. When he's older, George can visit his grandfather by himself.

There has been no response from Mrs Pearsall.

&

They return the same way, without the stop at Lickey. The ridge was his and May's favourite place. He was in his third year of apprenticeship to James Woodhall when he met May at the Cyclists' Touring Club. The new safety bicycle, no crossbar for

303

ladies, had resulted in cycling and the freedom it gave being very popular among young women in spite of the hazard of nails from horses' hooves. May, in a divided skirt reaching her ankles, was always accompanied by her sister Enid. He would spend hours lying awake at his lodgings on the Stratford Road - only a few hundred yards from where May's father kept a grocery – dwelling on chestnut hair, hazel eyes, a ready smile, wondering how he could prise the sisters apart, make her notice him.

One April Saturday on the Club excursion to Lickey, some farm workers, who appeared to be lying in wait, started throwing clods of earth at the ladies, and comments, the least harmful of which was: got yer leg over then? They should all have ridden on but May, her sister, and a few friends, hit yet not injured, stopped on the other side of the road, which was just a surface of stones left to work themselves in. He was off his bike, jacket thrown down as he laid into a freckled, dun-faced youth who had bucked teeth and smelt like a pigsty. Rough hands separated them to opposite hedgerows. He saw blood on his fingers.

Oh, Mr Boulton, are you hurt? He stood panting, gazing at May's eyes, aware of a hand against a bruise forming on his cheek, and a whiff of lavender water.

That summer and autumn he became a regular visitor for Sunday tea in the parlour above her parents' shop. Sometimes he and May cycled out to Lickey, and it was there he asked her to marry him.

But they never saw a pheasant. And he has still to see Livvy smile. The bird's plumage was the same chestnut as her hair. He has the feeling of a blank sheet, something new to be written, which strikes fear into him, for not only does he not know what to write, he cannot even form thoughts, just impressions.

The young lassie, Doctor Mackenzie wanted to know as they walked down the lane after lunch: how long has it been? When he replied: five and a half months, the doctor shook his head, added: time, it just needs time.

She does seem more settled and has not talked recently of leaving Laurel Road. Tomorrow would've been Peter's twenty-seventh birthday, yet Peter will be forever in his mind the boy who set off for Russia, radiating excitement, anticipation. He thinks back twenty-seven years to the cramped bedroom in Farm Road and, when the handywoman finally let him in, May cradling a baby left and right, hair still damp with sweat: one of each, darling, she smiled at him, and he thought there could be no greater happiness.

∽

'Livvy, you have not had George baptised?' Thomas repeats.

Never has she found him so serious, sitting in his usual morning room chair across the fireplace from her. She imagines investigation of some misdemeanour at the factory; thinks of Yefim Aaronovich at his most intractable; feels a bristle of irritation that Thomas might call her to task. A few days have passed since their visit to Rednal and he has been telling her the twins are to be baptised on the Sunday after Easter.

She darns half a dozen stitches into the heel of a sock before saying, 'Peter and I stopped going to church. It was a mile from where we lived and trams were infrequent because there were so few horses,' she notices Thomas's eyebrows move in surprise, 'and then the heat, and I was expecting George.' And, and, and … 'In any case, does it make much difference? When you see men screaming, dying in agony and muck, you think God

305

can't possibly be there, then realise life's going on whether He is or not. I am unable to believe in God's goodness, if He exists at all. If He is not good, or is indifferent to our plight, then it would be better if He weren't there. I expect I shock you. I'm sorry, but I cannot pretend - '

'You don't shock me, Livvy. It grieves me that man has in him such a capacity for wickedness as to cause war and suffering. It is the work of evil forces in the world, and I believe our only response can be to turn to God.'

'How?' she flashes. 'You lost three of your sons! And May. Tom has altered beyond repair. Don't you feel angry that God allowed it to happen - ?'

'No.' Again he interrupts, as if he would rescue her from herself. 'We shouldn't blame God for man's wrong-doing. I have had great sadness, Livvy;' he looks at her as though she cannot have been aware of this. Fury that he might think so, twists inside her searching for a way out. 'With each death I mourned,' he adds. 'And Tom: if I could hold him, reshape him to the Tom you never knew before the war ...' He glances away, as if groping for words. 'All our lives are fragile. We could any of us, at any moment, be changed or taken. The time and manner of death are not ours to arrange. It is faith that has stopped me drowning in my own despair. To trust in the goodness of God, that He is not indifferent to our ordeal, is the only hope for man, otherwise we are all at the whim of evil. We have to hang on to good, for that comes from God. There is still goodness in this world.'

'If you'd seen some of the things I have, you might speak differently. I've never told you about the Russian house where I worked. Over four years I was with them. The family left because of the Bolsheviks but three Armenian servants stayed, believing their employers would come back. A few weeks later, all British and Armenian civilians were to be evacuated before the Turks took the city. This was after Will died. Peter and I tried to persuade the servants to go with us but they refused. At least, Serge did. The women had to do as he said. When we returned two months later, we went to check they were all right.' In words that hammer the air as they escape from her head, she describes the scene at the house, the blood, the stench of decay. A parched voice catches in her throat. 'All that was left of them was ashes and bones. Simply because they were Armenians.'

Thomas is staring at her, mouth open, face a rictus of horror. 'Livvy - '

'They used to go to the Armenian cathedral in Baku every Saturday evening. What good did it do them?'

'Livvy, faith is not an insurance against bad things happening.'

'So what's the point?'

'It is belief that in spite of terrible evil, good will prevail.'

'Will,' she ploughs on. 'Your own son. I held the basin while the nurse picked shrapnel out of his stomach. I watched him die.' Thomas has closed his eyes and spread a hand across the rest of his face. 'The vicar comes here and talks about God's comfort but it isn't true, I tell you. It isn't true!' She flings the darning on the floor as if it is contaminated, rushes to the door. 'Oh, I can't talk about this any more.'

'Livvy - ' she hears behind her but she slams the door, makes for the stairs.

❧

He stands at the morning room window, sky shot with scarlet and crimson on the horizon, trees in his garden taking on night shapes; feels like a shell of a man floating in oblivion, as if his heart has been cut from him by what Livvy said about the servants. He should've told her that he, too, had a crisis of faith: after Will's death, a second son lost to war. He hadn't been able to protect his sons - surely the right of any father - caught up as they all were in something too great to comprehend, a creature sucking people into its maw. But casting away from God was even worse than questioning, doubting Him yet clinging on. If Peter had come home, would he have been a stranger to his father, no longer a boy yearning for adventure? He has always wanted Livvy to talk about Baku. Now, he can only think of it as an alien, hostile place. A backwater. Horse-drawn trams? They went out of use in Birmingham years ago.

He draws the curtains, picks up her discarded darning, leaves it where she was sitting. He switches on the bureau lamp, pulls down the lid, sags onto the chair.

❧

She expects to cry, craves the release of tears but her eyes remain dry. Still dressed, she sits on her bed, takes off her shoes, swings her legs up and hugs her knees. She reaches behind for Peter's pillow - Mrs Brent never returned it to the other room - shoves it between knees and face, rests a cheek against it, clasps it as if she would squeeze out the horror of Russia, all she said to Thomas.

How could she have spoken to him like that and banged the door? she chides herself. Thomas, who has shown her nothing but unquestioning kindness. There is still goodness in this world, he said and she cannot dispute it thinking of unexpected help: in Russia, Shoora transporting them in his cart through the night, respectful Vladimir Ivanovich, Olga Petrovna in the northern forest, even the *dvornik*'s wife in Archangel; back in England the Salvation Army, Eleanor. Thomas himself. Most of all. After the way she's just behaved, he cannot want her to go on living under his roof. He won't say so, in which case it will be better for her just to leave.

That Mrs Pearsall hasn't replied to her letter can only be because of Russia. People won't look at you if you're suspected of having Russian sympathies, Maud said last October. Is that country always going to be her burden, an umbilical cord? There must be somebody who will employ her. The alternative is a return to Norwich. But that will deprive Thomas of George. Which is going to be more upsetting for him: no George, or continuing to have her in the house?

She clutches the pillow, stares through closed eyes at the balance sheet of her life: ignoring her father's last letter and going to Russia against his advice; leaving the Claytons in Petersburg, yet now as a mother, even with Nanny's help, she can see the support Mrs Clayton needed. And Peter: letting him make that journey across Russia instead of another route. It was all to suit her.

She lies on her side, knees drawn up against the pillow, doesn't want to sleep. What if the nightmare comes back? It hasn't done for weeks but everything's swirling around the cauldron that is her mind. She dwells on Peter, goes back to the start, meeting him along Baku's Marine Boulevard. We love Miss Livvy, Jacob said, and he replied: that's not difficult to imagine.

Peter … Peter … let me rest with you … yet, it is Serge's implacable stare she sees, hooked nose, sallow pitted complexion. 'No, Serge, not you. Go away.' Peter … Peter … we believed the British to be honourable, *barynya* ... 'No, Serge, no ... go away,' and his face disintegrates until there is just a skull, then that, too, separates into fragments. 'No!' she screams. 'Serge!' Someone is shaking her shoulder, skeletal fingers from which the flesh is melting. She pushes them off. 'No!' Whichever way she turns, the carnage in the hall of Yefim Aaronovich's house goes with her. 'No!'

'Livvy!' Hands grip hers. She opens her eyes, finds she is sitting up, pillow behind her. The gas lamp outside projects watery light across the bottom of the bed. She forgot to draw the curtains. 'Livvy. It's all right. You're safe at home.'

Thomas is in a striped nightshirt. She closes her eyes, horror draining on a sigh.

೮๑

She wakes to a silent street and house, no notion of how many hours have passed, or recollection of lying on her side again. She opens one eye into the faint glow of a candle on the bedside cabinet, does not remember lighting it. Someone has closed the curtains. She turns onto her back, realises she is still dressed and that something is over her like a blanket. She touches the rough wool of her coat. It always hangs on the hallstand downstairs.

Thomas must have fetched it.

TWENTY-TWO

Polish forces have invaded Russia, he reads in the *Daily Express* on the twenty-sixth of April, 1920, and are crossing the Ukraine with their sights on Kiev. He wonders if Livvy has seen this or if he should hide the paper. After what she told him – shouted at him – the other week about the house in Russia and the fate of the servants, he wants to protect her from hurt. He will never speak of that country to her now.

She didn't say anything about the nightmare or his covering her with her coat. She did, however, agree to baptism for George. This pleased Connie, too: all three done together, Connie said, as they stood in the chapel where Mr and Mrs Phillips had worshipped for thirty years, sun glancing through stained glass windows. The twins wore the christening robes May had made for Peter and Nell; George was in the one Mrs Phillips had sewn for Connie as a baby, a bit tight on him. Livvy was wearing a new straw hat, fawn coat and pink dress. The coat didn't have any buttons but a belt in the same material that tied loosely at the front. She didn't look at anyone through the service, yet there was peace in her expression, and he wondered what she was thinking.

He folds the newspaper, wedges it behind a cushion.

☙

Even just flicking over the pages of the *Express*, she couldn't miss it: *Russia*. Is this why Thomas didn't leave the paper on a table? Kind Thomas wanting to keep bad news from her. She closes her eyes, can still smell gold-domed Kiev the one night she stayed there with Esther and Yefim Aaronovich on their car journey from Petersburg, wind bringing a whiff of the Ukranian plains, a mild yet bitter perfume of smoke and rushes that grew along the banks of the river Dnieper, and whorls of yellow dust that cracked between the teeth; can still see the setting sun pale and dull behind whitish clouds, the misty, reddish light of dusk low in the sky over hilly streets, balconied houses, arched windows, lime trees lining boulevards; and the realisation that each day was taking her away from Europe to something other, so that an excited impatience to reach Baku began to spread through her younger, innocent self.

Moira, her friend in Petersburg, had dispensed Earl Grey tea and Garibaldi biscuits when she, Livvy, used to call during her free afternoon. Three months in Baku, Moira had enthused; think of it as an adventure, Livvy. Moira gave English lessons to Russians; had been born in Russia of Scottish parents who'd gone to Petersburg to work at one of the cotton mills owned by Coates of Paisley. Moira must wonder what has happened to her, might no longer be at the same address or even in the city. Write and find out, she prompts herself. You can do it: you wrote to Mrs Pearsall. Otherwise, you'll never know.

She puts the *Express* back, goes over to the bureau, pulls down the lid.

അ

On the afternoon of Thursday the sixth of May, George's first birthday, she pedals with him in the sunshine to meet Connie by the fishpond in Victoria Park; Thomas has had a seat fitted behind her saddle, built up on three sides for George. She wishes Connie could've come to Laurel Road for tea in the garden, but it is too far from the canal with the perambulator. She's pleased with her coat, its softness and the way it moves with her. Mrs Brent told her of a dressmaker in Wood Road, who copied the coat from a picture in the *Lady* and also three dresses. The straw hat, with a small brim, she bought on the Stratford Road, without the need to go into the city centre. She keeps her pleasure locked away and with it, as during the baptism ceremony for George and the twins, the thought that Peter would've wanted her to have new clothes.

In Victoria Park, cowslips, half-opened bluebells, primroses, grow by the path. Two boys are fishing, a net each on the end of a cane. Beside them is an empty jam jar with string handle. Rooks caw above their heads.

'What a smart birthday-boy: dress and bonnet to match!' Connie stops pushing the perambulator, which Tom found second-hand on the Stratford Road, hugs George out of his seat, kisses him on the cheek. 'How many teeth?'

'All except the big back ones.' She stands with her bicycle and looks at her nephews. Both have a covering of dark hair on their heads, more than George at that age; blue eyes have started to deepen into brown, after their mother. Jack is the more alert, moving his arms above the blanket. Peter lies scowling, a red spot on each cheek.

'A bit early for Peter to be teething, isn't it?' says Connie. 'He's had those red patches since last evening. I think he's done himself in crying all morning. I couldn't get him to feed. Jack's had enough for both of them.'

'Try him on a bottle.'

'Lift him, Livvy, so George can say hello.'

'He feels hot and damp.'

'There!' Connie holds George close to his cousin and their cheeks touch. 'Say hello to Peter, George.'

She wants to say: no, keep George away, because she does not think Peter is well, but it might upset Connie and now it is too late. George pokes Peter, making him cry. 'George isn't used to other babies,' she reminds Connie.

'We must meet often. They'll grow up together. Now Jack's turn.'

She puts the wailing Peter back in the perambulator, repeats the ritual with Jack. He has the same hot, damp feel. However, he smiles, kicks, gurgles. What was it her Peter said in Baku about taking George to England? Yes: he can grow up with English children his own age, know the rest of his family. Is it really a year since he was born? since the pain, the musky smell of whatever *baboushka* Agafia greased her with in the Baku heat; the joy of holding him for the first time; Masha boiling water, washing sheets and muslin; Peter arriving home, his happiness.

She walks with Connie the length of the fishpond; thinks, the lost baby last autumn might've been twins ...

'Tom's at the allotment every hour he can spare,' Connie is saying. 'We already have radishes. Soon there'll be spinach, lettuce, carrots, peas.' Connie speaks as if itemising a treasure trove. 'He's going to take on a second one as soon as it's available, then he can grow enough to sell. He resents every hour indoors. Don't repeat this to his father, but he really doesn't like the factory.'

'It can't be easy for him.' She tells Connie about Frank, the

Mackenzies' gardener, and his love of fresh air. … if Peter were here he could have an allotment …

'He's still moody,' Connie adds, 'but I don't take any notice or feel threatened as I did before. If he goes off, I know he'll be back for the next meal. I have something of the old Tom again, and for that I'm grateful. He has the nightmare but not as it used to be.'

… and I would push the babies and George up there with him in the evenings.

ॐ

A few minutes before eight o'clock next morning, he cycles into Conduit Lane, past Mrs Beddows' grocery – where her boy has already swilled the front - Bob Potter's wheelwright's, Joseph Lloyd's stationers' sundries, to his own factory. He gets off the bicycle, removes his ankle clips, notices the pavement hasn't been swept. He glances at the sign above the entrance:

Boulton Cycle Works

Thos. Boulton and Sons

Cycles built to order. Tyres and Cycles repaired.

Could do with another coat of paint after the winter. A job for Tom. When Will died, he thought of painting over the final 's' of Sons but left it in case Peter should come home and decide to join him in the business. He'll get Tom to do it soon.

It was exactly thirty years ago that James Woodhall opened new premises for bicycle parts and repairs, so popular was the safety model and its pneumatic tyres. You've done your three years, Thomas, James Woodhall told him; I'm putting you in charge of the apprentices. Twelve months later, with a loan from Nathaniel, he bought the bicycle stock when James Woodhall separated that half of his business from the sheep-shearing side.

His own boss at the age of twenty! I can marry May, was his first thought. But Herbert Cottrell, canny grocer, made him wait until he came of age a year later and the bicycle enterprise was flourishing.

He and May started in two rooms in Farm Road. After a few years, with Peter and Nell toddling and Tom on the way, he moved his factory here and the family to the house in Laurel Road. They were the bounty times, the last decade of the old century and the first of the new. He repaid his brother. During the coronation celebrations in 1911, six of his bicycles paraded through Greet, decorated with flags, and garlands made by May and Nell. Peter walked with the first bicycle, followed by each brother, then Nell, holding the hand of five-year-old Renée; smells of sweat and flowers that scorching summer, the excitement and confidence at the start of a new reign. All his children together. A few weeks later, Nell left for Canada.

The entrance gives onto a courtyard where Bert, sleeves rolled above the elbow, has already fired the brick furnace. The first of several mudguards lies across the anvil.

'Morning, Thomas.' Bert pulls a metal rule from the pocket of his leather pinafore.

He takes off his hat, returns Bert's greeting. If apprentices or visitors are within earshot, Bert resorts to Mr B. He and Bert have known each other thirty years, since their days in the Cyclists' Touring Club.

'No sign of young Tom,' Bert observes, lips pursed beneath a greying moustache. Bert lost two sons on the Somme and a daughter to influenza, which has added cement to an old friendship, and affection and tolerance where Tom is concerned.

'Past his usual time,' he concedes. Tom should've helped Bert fire the furnace, then would swill and sweep the pavement. A paralysing fear is tightening his gut: that Tom has gone back to drink, had a nightmare from which he can't recover, disappeared with Connie and the babies, a moonlight flit.

He goes into the factory, puts his hat and cycle clips on the chair by his desk in the corner. He walks between the two long worktops and tool racks, greeting his employees. 'Morning, Mr Boulton,' comes back in ragged chorus. The men are measuring lengths of tubing which will be cut for bicycle frames. The two women are still tying on leather aprons, pushing hair under cotton caps. Florrie James, or Florrie Eldridge as she is now, who married the ex-officer before Christmas, is near her confinement. Then what will they do for money? he wonders, for as far as he knows her husband is still without work. Florrie'll probably take in sewing or washing, or card linen buttons. He'll have to keep an eye on the family.

The room is lit by windows that look onto the brick walls of his neighbours. Much of the time, his workforce labours in pools of light from several low hanging bulbs half covered by metal shades. He wishes he could turn the factory round, so that everybody has a view of either the road, or the stream and trees at the back. Nobody complains or even comments, just glad to have a job. Not like his young day when you could buy out your boss at the age of twenty.

It's going to be warm. Odours of leather and grease, swirl in front of him. He returns to his desk, takes off his jacket, stares at the telephone.

❧

'Morning, Tom,' he hears from the courtyard, where Bert has finished all the mudguards. 'Everything all right?'

'No. Is Father here?'

He reaches the courtyard as Tom is loping towards the factory; unshaven, eyes bloodshot, hair uncombed, Tom looks to have slept in his suit. If at all. He puts a hand on his son's arm and they stand by the desk, backs to everybody else.

'Peter has a fever,' Tom says. 'He cried all night. And now Jack won't feed.'

'We must send for Doctor Hollis.'

'You know I've no insurance, Father.'

'I will pay, Tom. Isn't the health of your sons more important ... ?' His voice trails off. More important than pride, he was going to say. What will Doctor Hollis think of the living arrangements? Pride, he upbraids himself.

'The children in the next barge are sick, too.'

'I'll pay for Doctor Hollis to call there, as well.'

'Have to think about that,' Tom says. 'Can't tell neighbours what to do.'

He turns away, closes his eyes for a moment, wonders why Tom has to be so stubborn. George! He reels back to Tom, as if his son might have the answer to the question now burning him. George and Livvy were with Connie and the twins yesterday.

❧

The following morning, she wakes to George crying upstairs. She rushes out of bed, throws the Baku shawl over her nightdress, runs barefoot to the nursery.

Nanny, face pink in agitation, grey hair tumbling down the faded wrap round her shoulders, is holding George, patting his back. He is kicking, flinging out his arms in distress. 'Oh,

318

ma'am!' Nanny exclaims with relief. 'I didn't want to disturb you. Master George woke before daybreak and we've neither of us had a moment's rest since. I've tried him with his milk but he won't touch it.'

She takes George from Nanny. His face is flushed, a red patch on each cheek, canker on perfection. He feels hot and damp, wriggles in one direction then another. She lays him in his cot, helplessness and fear slicing into her. 'Have you looked inside his mouth, Nanny?'

'As much as those little teeth will let me.'

'He hasn't been sick?'

'No, ma'am.'

'I'm going to contact Doctor Hollis, then I'll dress and be back.'

Before the doctor arrives, Mrs Brent comes to the nursery doorway. 'You're wanted on the telephone, ma'am. Shall I make you some tea?'

'Yes, please, Mrs Brent.' She is aware of neither hunger nor thirst, just an ache of dread in the pit of herself.

She runs down to the hall, picks up the earpiece from the table. Thomas's voice sounds clear but distant. 'Livvy, Doctor Hollis has seen the twins and the children in the next barge. They've all been taken to the isolation hospital. He suspects diphtheria. There's a lot of it in poor areas of the city. The neighbour thinks milk she gave her children was bad. I heard George crying this morning. Is he all right?'

The line crackles. She shivers, although the morning is not cold. Her heart is slamming into her ribs as she leans against the wall by the stairs, fingers wrapped round the telephone mouthpiece as though it is the only thing preventing her from sinking to the floor. Diphtheria. Please God, no. It killed her mother all those years ago. Please, not George as well. 'Livvy, are you there?' she hears Thomas say.

'Yes, Thomas.' She tries to steady her voice, weighing each word as she speaks, as if the total might crush him, or her. 'George is sick, too. I've sent for Doctor Hollis.'

'I think we should tell Eleanor, then we can keep him at home. Nanny can't be expected to cope on her own. Will you phone?'

'Yes.' She hears the little clicking sound that ends the connection.

∽

By the end of the morning, she is standing with Eleanor in the nursery watching George. He is asleep following an antitoxin injection in his back from Doctor Hollis. Nanny, insisting she had diphtheria as a young woman, and having been at Laurel Road nearly seven months without a break, has gone to her sister's in Acock's Green.

Eleanor has given her a white overall, head covering and antiseptic gauze mask. Cold, numb with fear, she chases round her mind: let it be me … let it be me, not George; then halts wild reasoning, the idea of leaving him an orphan, to be brought up by Thomas and Mrs Brent. She waits for Eleanor to tell her what to do, the same hardness forming in her chest as when Peter was dying in Archangel. Why, God? she demands. You've taken Peter from me. Do you want George, too? Hasn't Tom been through enough? Are you to have his sons? Is there no end to suffering? She purses her mouth. Thomas can talk about trusting in God's goodness, and order *Thy Will Be Done* on the gravestone of his wife and baby daughter, but she will fight and argue with God. She will not let George go. He is all she has, will ever have, of her own body.

'Put him to your breast, Livvy, as if you're going to suckle him,' Eleanor urges.

She unfastens her overall and blouse, cuddles a whimpering George to her barrenness, his face hot against skin grown unused to human touch. She takes from Eleanor the feeding bottle of warmed milk, taps his mouth with the teat. His lips close over it. He sucks for a few seconds, turns away, milk dribbling down his chin. His cry of desolation stabs at her.

From a medicine bottle with squeezable stopper she releases two drops of glucose and water into George's mouth when he stops crying. Earlier, she tried diluted salt. Every hour she perseveres, three or four spots. Mrs Brent warms some cooking brandy. Eleanor squeezes one drop into George's mouth and says, 'We must keep his throat open.'

Just after half past six that evening, stiff with tiredness and worry, she leaves Eleanor in the nursery. She takes off her overall, head covering and mask, washes her hands in disinfected water, starts downstairs as if with each step she would find a way out of the crisis. There is nobody in the morning room. She looks through the window. Thomas and Joe, in shirt sleeves, are planting seedlings that have germinated in the kitchen. Her chest tightens, tears swelling. Thomas's heart will break if George dies. She dashes the back of a hand across her eyes and goes into the garden. She must not cry in front of him; never has.

She blinks in the light after a day indoors. Joe waves in greeting. Thomas straightens, hurries over to her.

'How is he?' Thomas moves to take her hands, stops, rubs fingers against palms to dislodge clinging soil, and she wants to say: never mind that, just hold mine; we can comfort each other. Etched into his face and forehead are lines that were not there yesterday.

'He's taking a few drops of liquid,' she tells him.

He sighs. 'That's good. What would we do without you and Eleanor?'

She has no answer; asks herself how he can bear hours of waiting for news, wondering, unable to see the grandson he adores. She looks at rows of marguerite and mignonette which will bring colour to the garden. Fairy capes of almond blossom speckle the lawn. Swathes of wisteria, a profusion of sagging blossoms like dozens of miniature blue bells, cascade down the two side walls. Blackbirds carol their joy. Fragrance of lilac, tiny drooping flowers in mild air, fills her nostrils, displacing disinfectant. How long has it been since she enjoyed an evening garden with the promise of summer? She wants to stay but must return to the nursery so Eleanor can sleep.

Now Thomas does take her hands. 'How are *you*, Livvy?'

His fingers are warm, rough from work. She meets eyes eloquent with concern, this man who drew the curtains, lit the bedside candle and covered her with her coat after the nightmare following their quarrel about George's baptism. She frees a hand, puts it against her chest. 'I hurt here all the time.'

He takes the hand back, as if it is lost and he wants to keep all of her together. 'Remember, whatever happens, you will always have us. You know after Will was killed, two sons taken, I abandoned God in my despair but found that was worse than doubting, raging why? yet hanging on if only by the fingertips.'

'George is *not* going to die.'

She craves Thomas's agreement, reassurance, but his lips brush the top of her hair and he says, 'I'll see you tomorrow.'

She stays seven hours in the nursery while Eleanor sleeps in the next room; seven hours watching her son's restlessness and closed eyes, sponging burning skin when he wakes and cries, no other sound except his stertorous breathing, and the yelp of a fox, perhaps in the park. The perfection of his bow-shaped mouth is the same as Peter's. What she and Peter did so many times that stifling August of 1918, while Turkish shellfire made sleep impossible and Baku held its breath waiting for the big attack and wind howled round the rooftops, resulted in this precious child. Which time was it? she wonders. After her wedding night the previous month she wanted to remember every detail, every sigh, tremor, cry. But there were so many nights, stolen afternoons, early mornings, evenings, they all blurred into a single state of being. Could God create this baby only to take him away?

At two o'clock in the morning she creeps downstairs one floor, along the landing silent except for the tick tock of the grandfather clock. Her head aches with tiredness. In her room, the gas lamp outside illuminates the bed. She closes the curtains, puts on Peter's shirt – it's too warm now to wear her nightdress on top - folds back the chenille bedcover, hesitates before climbing in. 'Eleanor said last year, You're there when we turn to You,' she speaks into the night, drops to her knees, lowers her face to her hands. 'And Thomas has doubted, yet still believes. Please God, don't take George from me,' she implores. 'Let him live, for my sake and for Thomas's. Please save all the babies. Is it too much?'

In bed, she lies on her back, hands flat either side. An exhausted peace washes through her. God is here, she feels, with George in his sickness, with me in my despair.

Only Eleanor knocking on the door at nine o'clock wakes her.

TWENTY-THREE

On the fourth day George's breathing quietens, a normal, barely perceptible movement of the blanket. The back of her hand is against his forehead, skin to skin, no burning so she cannot feel where one ends and the other begins. 'He's going to be all right,' she says, as if she has, like him, arrived at a place of sanctuary, and she takes deep breaths, absorbing what she has just said; the relief.

'With care, yes,' Eleanor cautions, 'but there's some way to go.'

We will travel the way and I'll give George all the care he needs. She hears the outside door downstairs open and close. 'Thomas is early. I'll tell him this good news, and bring our lunch tray up.'

Thomas is by the morning room window, gazing out. He turns to face her. She tries to read his expression: exhaustion? defeat? He takes her hands. This time, his are cold, hers warm, the hardness in her chest dissolving. 'I hoped you would come down,' he says.

'George's fever's passed,' she tells him, a lightness in her limbs. Is it really true?

He closes his eyes, sighs, looks at her again. 'We must thank God. If anything had happened to him, too - '

' – too?' she echoes. 'Jack and Peter?'

'Jack's fever has broken, but Peter … ' He pauses. She breathes with him as though strengthening him to say what she is certain has happened. 'He died in the night.'

She shakes her head on a long outtake of breath. 'No.' Her nephew, for whom she could never summon the love she wanted to feel, named after her own Peter. 'Tom. Connie.' She speaks their names as if picking them at random. 'They've lost their baby.' The second Peter Boulton to die within eight months. It could've been George; might still be him. No, don't think that.

'Tom came to the factory to tell me. He's gone back to Connie,' Thomas says. 'I've been at the undertaker's. Tom couldn't refuse that. He hasn't any insurance, of course, but no Boulton will be buried in a pauper's grave as long as I'm alive.'

It is the nearest she has ever heard him to sounding bitter.

He clutches her hands to his chest. 'Thank you, Livvy; for everything. Thank you for being here. I don't know what we'd do without you. You and Eleanor.'

She stands with him, their heads touching.

ৰৎ

The following week, she sits George on the floor; Eleanor is allowing him an hour out of his cot, cautioning strain to his heart if he uses too much energy. He turns onto hands and knees, eyes the door, ready to crawl. His legs fold under him and he flops to one side. A second time he tries and the same happens. After two further attempts, he begins to cry. 'There, there,' she soothes, scooping him into her arms. 'Your poor legs are a bit out of practice, aren't they?' She takes him over to the chair, eases him to standing on the carpet, his hands on the arm. His legs give way and he sinks to his bottom, face creasing with frustration.

'Put him back in his cot, Livvy,' suggests Eleanor.

She lays him down as if he is a piece of china.

'It's a paralysis,' Eleanor tells her, 'not uncommon after diphtheria. The poison which attacked his throat reached the nerves.'

She stares at her friend. 'Paralysis?' she repeats in horror. 'We nurse him through all this for him to be paralysed?'

'It'll pass. A week, two at the most, with rest and care.'

'Tell me, honestly, is he going to be all right?'

'I'm sure he is. He'll just be later walking than he would've been.'

She sets her mouth in determination. Tom and Connie have lost a baby. They will have others. George is all she has. She will not let anything happen to him. For Thomas, as well; George is the link between loss of his sons and hope of the future.

ↄ

In the afternoons, she pushes George round the park in the perambulator. Sun glares warm on her shoulder blades, sole responsibility for him heavy inside her when Eleanor returns to Rednal in the middle of June. Since the beginning of the month, he has been able to crawl from his cot to the nursery door but not back. For an hour each morning she tucks him into the perambulator in the shade of the flowering almond. Mrs Brent brings a sugar teat. 'Just a couple of spoonfuls tied in muslin, ma'am, and dipped in the kettle. He'll be asleep before he's down to the cloth.'

She feels kindness helping carry anxiety. Sugar is still rationed. She sits in a wicker chair near George, shelling peas, cocooned by bees humming and scent of lilac and honeysuckle. Runner bean plants have climbed more then a foot up their sticks.

'Livvy, I'm taking the trap over to see Renée,' Thomas tells her that Saturday lunchtime. 'Would you like to come?' Because of the diphtheria, Renée stayed at school through half-term, preparing for Oxford Junior exams.

'I can't expect Mrs Brent to look after George all afternoon.'

'Another time,' Thomas concedes. He gets up from the table, starts towards the door as if unsure what to do next.

ᴇᴏ

In the airless barge the following week, she clasps hot, clammy hands Connie holds out to her. The open door admits rank canal smells. 'I didn't come before,' she tells Connie. 'I couldn't risk him falling or being in a draught. Mrs Brent's keeping an eye on him for an hour … ' Connie's arms and an unwashed smell are round her, and she feels her sister-in-law collapse on a sob, until Connie eases away. Connie has lost weight, forehead beaded with sweat, front of blouse and skirt stained. Yet again, she thinks of Masha in Baku, whose baby died; her mouth looked as if it had become unused to smiling.

Paper that Tom put on the walls in the winter is crinkling at the edges. She glances at the empty cradle. 'They've still got Jack at hospital,' says Connie. She meets Connie's eyes, which seem larger because of dark rings underneath. She wonders how Connie copes with aloneness after being so busy. 'You understand, don't you, Livvy?' Connie beseeches, as though relying on her to answer questions that torment. 'You've lost a Peter, too. A little bit of me died with mine. He's buried with Tom's mother and baby sister. I go there, or to the allotments with Tom, in the evenings. Elsie next door's had one die in hospital, and her near her time. "You're never a mother till you've lost one," Elsie says; she'd already buried six, knows how it is.'

But Connie and Elsie still have husbands, she thinks. There

will be more babies. She only has George. She tries to square what she sees as an unequal equation, passes her tongue over dry lips. Connie's eyes continue to hold hers and all she can manage is, 'I'm sorry, Connie,' an apology more than a condolence.

௭

By the third week in June, George is able to crawl as much as before his illness. Each morning, she takes up to the nursery a tray of tea for herself, and egg with bread and butter soldiers for George. Later, she gives him his bath. It is the middle of the morning before she returns downstairs, with George if the weather is fine.

One Friday she puts him back to sleep in his cot, sun lost behind rain clouds. She reaches the hall to see Mrs Brent closing the morning room door. 'Mrs Boulton, ma'am,' Mrs Brent walks towards her. 'The postman knocked earlier.' Mrs Brent points to the table in the stairwell. 'He asked if he could have the stamps when it was convenient to you, said you'd given him some before. His son collects them.' Mrs Brent takes the breakfast tray from her.

'From Canada, yes, of course.' She goes over to the table. No doubt Thomas wrote to Nell of the babies' diphtheria and young Peter's death. She senses unease, Mrs Brent hovering as if there is still something to be said. She picks up the letter. It feels stiff. Nell must have sent more photographs. She turns. 'Thank you, Mrs Brent.'

'Very good, ma'am.'

She wonders why Mrs Brent should be worried. She moves away from the poor light of the stairwell, looks at the envelope. Her insides judder. These are not red and brown Canadian stamps, with the King's comforting, bearded profile. They're blue and brown, with pictures of broken fetters. She speculates on the conversation between the postman and Mrs Brent, notices the address printed in black ink and, alongside, a strange script, one she cannot read but saw enough times until last autumn to recognise as Russian.

Relief that Moira received her letter and has replied, tangles with apprehension about what news this contains. She goes into the morning room, takes Thomas's silver opener from the bureau, sits by the window. With shaking fingers she slits the envelope, draws out two pieces of paper folded round her old post office book, which she leaves in her lap. She reads the first page of a letter, small writing sloping ahead.

My dearest Livvy,

Your letter arrived welcome as spring sunlight on the Neva ice. The fact that it got here at all shows the extent to which our poor country is hauling itself back onto its feet after a self-inflicted beating. Russia has few friends abroad, so foreign contacts are encouraged. Lenin craves international recognition. Imagine my surprise when I was summoned to the postal headquarters for this sector of Petrograd and asked to translate an envelope, only to find it was for me! I am so sorry, dear Livvy, that you were widowed after less than fifteen months of marriage, and your little boy will never know his father.

Perhaps you did not hear that Baku was finally retaken by the bolsheviki *this April. The economy there was so depressed that people welcomed the Red Army as the only ones who could help. Lenin's delight at repossessing the oilfields was cut short by the Polish invasion of Russia's western border a few days later, and the loss of Kiev in early May. The invaders have now been pushed back almost to where they started.*

She thinks, so Masha and her father have what they wanted, *bolshevik* Baku, and without the violence of two years ago, which Peter was sure would be repeated.

I am as you remember me, although thinner, result of dried fish, buckwheat and potatoes. Petrograd is so changed you would not know it: roads full of holes several feet deep, eaten out by frost; drains collapsed. People have torn up wooden pavements and demolished houses for firewood. The population is now estimated at three quarters of a million, from two and a half in 1917. Many British homes were commandeered after the bolsheviki *took over, the British leaving with only what they could carry. Having been born in Petrograd and lived here all my life, I was regarded differently, and able to keep my apartment, although I did have Red Army soldiers billeted a couple of years back. One legacy of capitalist enterprise remains: electric trams, until six in the evening.*

She wonders if the Claytons managed to return to London and grimaces at the thought of Mrs Clayton confronted by a *bolshevik*. She begins the second sheet.

I work at the administration as typist and translator. Everything is common property. I long ago had to give away unneeded blankets, for the Red Guard, we were told, but the general belief was they were being sold to the Germans. I confess the clothes you left here I bartered. In exchange for warm garments, peasants were prepared to part with milk and eggs, which they still refuse to sell for a currency only a fraction its former value. The public canteen doles out soup: a brew of boiled fish in which float a few cabbage leaves. The queue stretches interminably. Waiting one morning last summer, I fainted in the heat.

Memories: a dismembered horse on a Baku street corner; meatballs of horse flesh; pancakes of minced vegetable peelings

... She wonders who is wearing her winter clothes, peasants in a village outside Petrograd; skirts she made from worsted suiting the last two winters in Norwich.

Let us keep in touch. In spite of all that has happened, Petrograd is my home and I cannot imagine living anywhere else. There is something about Russia that binds people to her. Perhaps you understand ... yes, I do, she thinks, although Peter didn't ... *or maybe you're glad to be away. Below is my address in Russian script. If you can copy it onto the envelope when you write, I shall be spared further visits to the postal headquarters. The only English word you need is Russia ...*

She puts the letter in her lap; thinks, suffering is universal, yet people have the capacity for survival. She opens her post office book, relic from another era: Olivia Turner, 29 Heather Road, Norwich. The balance of her account in May 1914 when she left England with the Claytons was one pound, seventeen shillings and threepence. The name and address blur. Olivia Turner is no more. She became Livvy Boulton, who has known privation, grief, yet has survived.

Olivia Turner is no more but 29 Heather Road will still be there. Father and Rose must've suffered over the last six years. And her brothers: are they home, making the best of what is left of their minds and bodies, surviving; or buried in some foreign corner like Jack, Will, Peter? She has to know. Father, Arthur, Victor; yes, and Rose. What has become of them?

She looks at the clock on the mantelpiece. In half an hour she will prepare George's lunch. Until then she can make a start on the job which will be put off no longer. She goes over to the bureau, opens her writing case, fills her pen with ink, writes the address and *25ᵗʰ June, 1920. Dear Father and Rose ...*

TWENTY-FOUR

'He's so selfish, Livvy!' explodes Renée, sitting with her in the shade of the almond tree. Marigolds crowd the borders, yellow, orange, copper. 'I don't know how Connie puts up with him.' Renée has been over to the barge. 'Even if *he* doesn't want a holiday he could at least let Connie and Jack come with us. She looks exhausted. Two weeks of sea air would do her the world of good. She says the factory's organising a charabanc to the Vale of Evesham for August bank holiday and Tom's taking her on that.' Renée sighs, a growl of frustration. 'Why do women tolerate the way they're treated? If he'd been there I'd've given him a piece of my mind.'

She senses a difference about Renée since the Easter holiday: chestnut hair still shines in schoolgirl ringlets but a smooth complexion, full mouth, dark eyebrows, and her mother's hazel eyes, make a beautiful woman at the age of fourteen and four months. She doubts if Renée knows that Connie is pregnant again. If it's another boy, Livvy, we'll call him Will, Connie confided last week; then we shall've remembered all Tom's brothers who died.

That day, he came home from the allotments with several lettuces and spring onions which he put on the table. Nice to see you, Liv! he greeted her, kissed her cheek. As well as tobacco, he had a smell of the earth, a rawness, otherness, so different from Peter. Want to take a lettuce? he suggested.

I haven't any money with me, she said; I know you're selling stuff at the factory.

C'mon, Liv. Call it a gift.

She agreed, watching adoration transform Connie's wan face.

He put his arms round Connie, kissing her forehead and closed eyes. All right, Con? he said gently.

And she, the maiden aunt, knew that for both of them she was no longer there. She picked up the lettuce – leaf upon leaf layered round a firm green heart – said goodbye, glanced at Jack asleep and left. All the way home, heat of frustrated desire coursed through her, the sweet smell of crude oil, Peter coming back from the refinery last year and carrying her straight to bed.

In the garden now she reminds Renée that Jack was only discharged from hospital a couple of weeks ago. 'Connie did say she might take him hop picking next summer,' she adds, 'but I can't see Tom agreeing.'

'Good for her! At least she's showing *some* spirit. It's nothing short of imprisonment, Livvy. A few words of flattery and women allow themselves to be trapped into marriage and an endless round of childbearing. They can't do anything to be free.'

She looks at Renée and wonders where the girl has found these ideas. She doesn't remember feeling trapped with Peter. 'Is this what they've been teaching you at the Convent?'

'For Oxford Junior? Hardly! We read together in our spare time, Una and I. We've been through Olive Schreiner's *Woman and Labour*. Have you heard of it?'

'No.'

'In the strongest primitive societies, women always worked alongside men,' Renée expounds. 'It's only right that now they should have the same openings in the professions, which

334

means equal opportunity in education. How much schooling did Connie have? I'm not saying there's anything wrong with working in a shop but she was never given a chance. It was assumed she'd leave school and get married.'

'I left at fourteen, Renée. Somebody has to take charge of the home.'

'But many women have other abilities they're not allowed to use.'

'You wait till you fall in love, then you'll understand.'

'Love has nothing to do with it,' Renée counters.

Love has everything to do with it, she thinks, and remembers when she was only a couple of years older than Renée she, too, took no account of love between a man and a woman: Father and Rose.

Father and Rose. It is nearly three weeks since she wrote but there's been no response. At first she told herself they'd gone to the coast for a holiday; her father had always been fond of Yarmouth. Yet they can't have been away all this time, for he has his work. She put her name and address on the back of the envelope so that if they'd moved from Heather Road it would be returned if not forwarded to them. The realisation they might be ignoring her letter as she did her father's last one to her, and having had nearly seven years without her, makes her chest ache.

I can't believe Father wouldn't reply, she said to Thomas one evening.

Unless it is Rose, so dominating him that he prefers to leave things as they are. What embarrassment, scandal even, did she cause Father and Rose by leaving? When girls of eighteen go away suddenly, it's often to have a baby, like Polly Carter at the grammar school who thought making love standing up didn't count. But then Arthur or Victor could've written. Father might not have told them about her letter, maybe they can no longer write, perhaps they aren't even alive … Every day she tortures herself with possibilities.

… I was ill for weeks with scarlet fever. Last month George had diphtheria. He has recovered but is still not walking alone … did it read like excuses for not writing?

There will be a reason, said Thomas. There is for everything.

When she is with him she finds reassurance. The rest of the time, she wants to know that the reason is not her. Waiting only increases the hurt, a wound that she has opened and now cannot heal. *I'm sorry for the long silence.* She means it. Yet, are they just words? Can Father and Rose accept such an apology?

She dreads the arrival of the post, that there will be nothing.

If a letter doesn't come before we go to Wales, we'll ask Joe to check each day and forward it when it arrives, suggested Thomas.

Before the war, she has discovered, he and May always took the family for two weeks in the summer to Eynon's Bay on the west coast of Wales, near Aberystwyth. The last holiday was six years ago; the war started while they were there. Thomas has written to the landlady, and she has offered several rooms from the twenty-fourth of July. He is including Nanny and Mrs Brent, and Renée's friend, Una, whose parents took the girls to see the Imperial Russian Ballet in London last summer.

'Tom doesn't want to leave his allotments that long,' she explains to Renée now. 'He's also worried Jack might pick up infection on the train.'

'It's the same for George.'

'Your father's sure it'll be all right first class.' However, she is uneasy about this. She peeps at George asleep in the perambulator alongside her. At the beginning of the month he started walking, holding her hands. For days it has been just one hand, sometimes no more than a finger. If anything should happen to reverse the progress of weeks ... 'Connie going with us would leave nobody to look after Tom,' she enlarges. 'He'd have to stay with her parents, which he doesn't relish after last year. Neither does he want the barge unoccupied: somebody might take it over.'

'At this rate they'll never have a holiday. He could go to Uncle Nathaniel and Aunt Maud, like Joe. Or even stay on the barge and fend for himself. I'm sure the neighbours would take pity on him. It's always what *he* wants.'

Her last holiday was in Yarmouth with Father, Rose and the boys a few weeks before she left home. Holidays belong to the days of innocence when she had nothing to worry about except Rose's remarks: isn't that dress pulled in too much at the waist? ... could do with a lace collar ... Now she faces a fortnight away from all that is familiar, with two opinionated schoolgirls whom Thomas may expect her to chaperone.

❧

'Let's have a paddle,' she suggests to Renée and Una when they return the donkey to a swarthy, sharp-eyed child who has bare feet and sandy legs. Every morning this first week, the girls straggle after her to the beach for George's ride. She wonders what happened to Renée's enthusiasm for him; notices other children, smaller, thinner than him, running about. He will not walk without holding her little finger,

The girls wear wide-brimmed hats protecting pale faces from a constant sun. They arrive at the water first, shriek and giggle when a wave splashes the bottom of petticoats clutched around thighs, retreat to the promenade and enormous threepenny ice creams. She will catch up with them, and probably Thomas, at the Punch and Judy show.

Some afternoons, the girls have been drawing. Views of the bay appear, in crayon, from different angles, then vanish just as quickly; nothing to put on the walls at home.

On Thursday, the girls come in for tea laden with books, sharing a joke, averting eyes in disdain until bending over with laughter. 'It was you they spoke to first,' Una reminds Renée. Una takes off her hat, puts it with her books on the hall table. Thick blond hair hangs down her back in two plaits.

'Oooh!' Renée is indignant. 'They asked *you* what we were doing this evening. But I answered we always go to the Music Hall with my father,' Renée turns to her, Livvy, links arms, 'and sister.' Renée wrinkles her nose. 'The dark haired one smelt of tobacco.'

She smiles, pictures young men she has seen lingering on the promenade in straw boaters, blazers, cream flannels. Like Peter seven years ago? Did he talk to girls? Was there anyone before me?

A blush has settled in Renée's cheeks. One day you will meet someone, Renée, she thinks, really someone, perhaps at Oxford.

She spots the name Olive Schreiner on the spine of one of Renée's books, puts a finger against it, raises her eyes in enquiry, remembering *Woman and Labour*.

'She's South African,' Renée tells her. 'This is *The Story of an African Farm*. Poor women! It's even worse for them than for many here. Talk about oppression!'

She wonders where she will be living when Renée meets

somebody, and whether Renée will tell her; likes to think yes, that she and Renée will be friends. She had nobody to confide in, who would've understood, when she met Peter.

On Saturday morning she walks with George still clasping her finger, down the path and along the pavement past three-storey, double-fronted, dark grey stone houses. Ahead are Nanny and Mrs Brent. Nanny wears the same navy blue hat as for walking in the park at home. Mrs Brent, always seen in a mob-cap at Laurel Road, sports a large-brimmed black straw creation trimmed with ostrich feather, tulle, lace, coloured beads and bunches of cherries; she helps Mrs Williams, the landlady, with shopping and preparation of vegetables but otherwise time is her own.

She leaves Nanny and Mrs Brent strolling to the sea and turns back with George. Mrs Williams has set off in the other direction with border collie Tafyn on a lead. 'Fyn!' cries George. Crawling round the house, he has managed to pull Tafyn's coat several times. Now he lets go of her finger, totters after Tafyn. 'Fyn!' He stops, waddles round, stretches out his arms, scampers to her. 'Fyn! Fyn!'

She gathers him up. 'Oh, George!' She hugs him, her eyes wet with tears. 'Well done, darling.'

Mrs Williams and Tafyn are out of sight but George wriggles in her embrace. She puts him down, watches him toddle towards the house. The wonder of it.

He curls his hands on the wrought iron gate, looks at her, waiting.

∞

After lunch she jostles her way with Thomas through bank holiday weekend crowds to the end of the promenade. George was ready for sleep and Nanny offered to stay with him. 'Let's climb the road to the cliff top,' Thomas suggests. His fawn suit, broad-brimmed canvas hat, leather satchel over one shoulder, give him the appearance of an artist or perhaps explorer.

She inhales smells of the sea, of salt and seaweed. Her cheeks are tingling. She feels herself floating with each step, as if someone has removed her worry over George like a cloak that has lain too long round her shoulders and now there is nothing to tether her. At the summit, she and Thomas stand gazing at the cliffs, the curve of the bay, sea shimmering towards the horizon, specks of people on the promenade. Gulls wheel their mournful cry. Waves crash on the beach.

'Isn't it splendid, Livvy?' Thomas wipes his forehead with a handkerchief.

She thinks of Lickey Ridge in March. 'You like magnificent views away from crowds,' she comments. A breeze ruffles the air and she clamps a hand on her straw hat.

'I do indeed.' He puts the handkerchief back in his pocket. 'Let's sit down.'

On the grass, he unfastens the satchel, takes out pencils and two leather covers, page-size, secured to each other with green ribbon. Inside, are sheets of paper which he clips to one of the covers, turning the other back. She watches him look at the bay, then his paper. He selects a pencil, makes several movements an inch or so above the page.

From her string bag, she retrieves the copy of *Martin Chuzzlewit* Renée gave her for Christmas, finds where she left the marker. After a few paragraphs she stops reading, concentrates on the bay. She doesn't want to know about young Martin ill with fever in America, doesn't want to dwell on anything, not even Father and Rose, or Peter and whether he came here seven summers ago before setting off for Russia. She wants only to be in the present with George healthy, walking, as if after a long voyage she, like Martin, has arrived on the coast of a beautiful land but for her all is well. She abandoned searching for a job while George had diphtheria. When they return to Birmingham, she will start again, something not too far from Laurel Road so Thomas can see his grandson. She closes her eyes. The warmth and sea air reach inside her, to all the dark corners.

'There!' says Thomas with satisfaction.

She blinks open her eyes, looks at him.

He smiles, furrows his brow at the sketch. 'I'd like to do it in watercolour when we're home, Livvy, with your permission.'

He shows her a head and shoulders profile of herself, without the hat.

She gasps. 'I'd no idea! I thought you were drawing the bay.'

'I was. But when you stopped reading and turned I had to take the opportunity.' Uncertainty flickers across his eyes. 'You're not offended, are you?'

'Not at all. I'm flattered. It's very good.'

'You looked pensive, yet peaceful. That's what I tried to capture.' He puts the paper down. 'Are you happy here, Livvy?'

'Yes,' she says. 'I never thought a day would come when I could admit that. I've always felt bad about happiness over the last ten months. I remember the time with you on Lickey ridge. I pushed at the feeling, wouldn't allow it.'

'Because of Peter?'

She nods. 'Do you understand?'

'Yes. It was the same for me after May died. After each death. But I do think the dead would wish us to go on, not remain numb to anything except grief.'

'Isn't it breaking faith?'

'It is the only thing to do if we are to be healed and continue living. It doesn't imply disrespect. Precious memories can't be taken away.'

She stares at the bay, and now Peter is with her. He must've known this spot. Can he see her here? He would want her to enjoy it as he did.

Thomas is putting away his pencils. She turns to him, smiles. He looks at her as though he wants to imprint on his mind every detail of her face for the watercolour he plans. His lips part as if he is going to speak. Her smile loosens, weakens, and she lowers her eyes to his hand on the unfastened satchel, nails neat, clean, skin wrinkled over finger joints and knuckles.

He secures the satchel, stands up, gives her his hand as she gets to her feet. They will be expected back for tea. He looks at her face again, as if this is the last time he will see her.

'Shall we go?' he says.

He releases her hand.

ↄⱷ

Early the following Saturday evening, they arrive at New Street Station hot, dusty, exhausted after three changes of train. A porter loads their luggage onto a handcart. She walks alongside Nanny, who is carrying a sleeping George, Renée trailing behind. Una's father met them off the train and whisked his daughter away for a connection to Stratford-upon-Avon, where they live in School House. It will be another week before the girls are together: with Una's family at a guest house in Brighton, followed by their annual stay in London for theatres and museums.

She stops suddenly, drawing in her breath. 'No!' A poster by the news stand carries the headline: CITY DEMONSTRATION AGAINST WAR WITH RUSSIA.

'Undudds in demerstation!' the newsboy mangles his words. A second boy, pile of newspapers a few feet away, is bellowing in competition: ''Nother planned termorrer!'

Thomas has gone on ahead. He comes back with the *Birmingham Mail*. 'What's happening?' she asks. War? she frets, reluctant to let the word into her mind. There can't be another. Against Russia? Because of the *bolsheviki*? Does that mean there are people in Birmingham sympathetic to them? Fear has pummelled her insides into knots.

'We'll read about it on the way home,' Thomas says.

The porter is summoning two taxis. She settles in the second with Thomas and Renée, behind Mrs Brent, Nanny and George; Nanny is going to help with the jam.

Thomas unfolds the newspaper. 'The demonstration in the city centre was organised by the Labour Party,' he begins without looking up. 'There have been more all over the country. London dockers a while ago refused to load a freighter with munitions for Poland.'

'Poland?' she echoes. 'According to Moira's letter, Poland invaded Russia in April but the Russians pushed them back.'

'Yes,' Thomas says, still reading. 'Back and back. The Russians have almost reached Warsaw, the capital. Our government sees Bolshevism spreading west across Europe. Arming the Poles would increase their chance of defeating Russia.'

'And the Labour Party are against it.'

'Not because they prefer Russia to Poland. They don't want war.'

It sounds sensible, she thinks, yet … Bolshevism spreading across Europe?

'Joe's bound to be involved,' volunteers Renée. 'He's a pacifist.'

She watches Thomas raise his eyebrows at his daughter and reply, 'Is that so?'

Renée looks down.

'When did Joe tell you this?' Thomas prompts the girl.

'Before we went away. He was teasing me about my ideas on the poor status of women, so I asked him what *he* believed in, or felt strongly about. He told me he was a pacifist and had joined the Labour Party in April after he was eighteen.'

Thomas is pursing his mouth and she thinks: it's the first he's heard of this. The taxi turns into Laurel Road. She sees the park railings again, the path along to the bandstand; remembers another father's return from holiday, in Russia just over six years ago, to learn of his son's political sympathies and involvement in public demonstration. Where is this going to end? Surely not the same way?

TWENTY-FIVE

'Livvy, what do you think Renée meant by "the poor status of women"?' Thomas asks her.

They have been home a couple of hours. She is sitting with him in the morning room and the last of the daylight, as if to switch on the lamp will illuminate matters they do not want to face. Renée mentioned a headache and has gone upstairs. Of Joe there is no sign although his bicycle is behind the house with the others. That he was here earlier is evident from cake, potted meat, butter and bread Mrs Brent found on the cold slab in the larder, no doubt sent by Maud. The gardens, back and front, have been weeded.

She tells Thomas about *Woman and Labour*. 'Renée feels that if women had better education and the opportunity to enter one of the professions, they wouldn't be so quick to marry and embark on what she calls the endless round of childbearing.'

Head back, he laughs, a single bark of incredulity. 'Whatever next? She realises, surely, survival of the human race depends on women bearing children?' But the laugh evaporates and he frowns. 'Did you know about Joe's interests as well?'

How we can upset, exclude, our parents, she thinks. 'He did tell me he was a pacifist. I'd only been here a week,' she recalls. 'I went to his shed to see the crystal set. We talked about war. He asked if I'd known any Bolsheviks in Russia.' Perhaps pronouncing it the English way will make the meaning, and

Russia itself, more distant, but still the images invade her mind: soldiers searching Yefim Aaronovich's house one Christmas Day … haranguing a crowd in the centre of Baku … Lev Yefimovich on the train: we are building a world without tyrants and slaves. 'He said he intended to join the Labour Party. We've never spoken of it again. I don't want anything to do with politics.'

'He should've been at work this morning.'

'Is he likely to lose his job for taking time off?'

'In many places he would, but the printers have a strong union. The company'd find itself with a strike on its hands if they dismissed men. I expect he'll be disciplined, lose a morning's money. That's what unions do, Livvy: tie the hands of employers so they're no longer free to decide what happens in their own factories. I shall tell Joe when he comes home. If this is what the Labour Party wants, to give the working man power that has always been enjoyed by his boss, then the country's in for trouble.'

'If he continues to belong, knowing your disapproval, might you disown him?'

'No.'

Does Joe realise how fortunate he is? She says, 'I feel that's what my father's done.' There is a letter for her from Eleanor in Rednal but from Norwich, nothing. She wonders what she can do to make things right with her father; sees concern on Thomas's face, brow furrowed.

'I'm sure he hasn't, Livvy. How long is it since you wrote?'

'The end of June: six weeks. Do you think I should go to Norwich? You could say I should already have gone.'

'You were ill for some time … and then George.'

But there were several months between her recovery from

346

scarlet fever and miscarriage, and George going down with diphtheria. 'It was easier not to. There's been no contact for years. I was unhappy when I left, didn't get on with my stepmother, felt unneeded, pushed out. I did send a card at Christmas and realised after I'd posted it, silly me, I hadn't put my address,' she allows a wry smile, 'or who George was.'

Thomas says nothing but sits looking at her, a calm expression on his face as if he is taking time to absorb all she has suddenly told him. He nods slowly. 'Your letter will have been a shock to them. And you don't know how they are in health. There must be a reason for the delay. I'm sure a reply will come.'

She wants to believe him.

❧

Breakfast is silent, Thomas unsmiling, Renée staring at her plate. Joe has not come home. Have I influenced him? she harries herself, remembers telling him last October about Lev Yefimovich. Is he going to do the same, leave home without saying, become a Bolshevik?

After lunch, she takes George to the park, pushes the perambulator as far as the bandstand, sits and listens to *It's a Long Way to Tipperary*, walks towards the Stratford Road. She rests again, reluctant to go back, dreading argument between Thomas and his son if Joe returns, thinking of the day she arrived in Baku: Yefim Aaronovich and Lev Yefimovich that evening, raised voices, slammed doors, Esther weeping. The government sees Bolshevism spreading west across Europe, Thomas said. Will Britain really go to war to stop it? Are the Labour Party Bolsheviks? Is that why there's been this demonstration? Is the same going to happen here as in Russia? She thought she'd brought George to safety, but for how long?

Baku, September 1917...the Tsar gone six months, *bolsheviki* yet to seize power ... twenty minutes' walk to Yefim Aaronovich's house from the tram stop in front of the railway station after a Sunday with Charlotte ... thin, shabby soldiers crowding the square at the end of the Olginskaya ... strained eyes, rough, hard, bewildered faces ... Nicolas Romanov signed secret treaties with Britain and France, someone was shouting; if Austria and Germany are defeated, Russia will gain a lot of land, which is why Kerensky wanted to launch another attack. Did you fight?

No! hoarse roars erupted from hundreds of throats.

She lingered, drawn yet repulsed.

Now she stands up, looks towards the Stratford Road entrance to the park. A young man is walking in her direction. Her insides jump. Joe? Or is she imagining it because she's been thinking about him?

Is it our purpose to defeat fellow workers in Austria and Germany? that eloquent Russian in Baku demanded.

No!

She pushes the perambulator towards the man. Heart and belly collide. Joe.

Baku again: when you heard of revolution in Petrograd, you elected your own committees and officers.

Yes!

Joe's working suit is crumpled and dusty. She wonders where he was last night; if he slept in his clothes. 'Hello, Joe,' she says. A day's stubble covers his sunbrowned face. Perspiration gleams on his forehead beneath his cap.

'Hello, Livvy.' He bends to kiss her cheek, smells of sweat and tobacco, although she has never seen him smoke; Woodbines, which will always remind her of revolution, of Lev Yefimovich on the train. About Joe there is nothing of the boyishness when she first met him ten months ago, but a lean strength, coiled energy, like a creature on a leash. His voice has coarsened, consonants harder. 'You're looking well,' he tells her. 'Nice holiday?'

'Yes, thank you.'

He puts his hand to her hair, touches the comb he gave her for Christmas. She wants to leap away. 'Suits you,' he says, glances inside the perambulator. 'George all right?'

'He's asleep,' she comments unnecessarily. 'He can walk on his own now.' In spite of the warm afternoon and good news about George, she feels chill. 'Your father's worried about you,' she blurts.

'Because I didn't come home last night? I thought he'd assume I was at Aunt Maud's.'

Furtiveness, secrecy. 'Were you in the demonstration?'

'You heard about it, then. Good.'

'It was on the station newspaper stands. The boys were yelling it out.'

'Good.'

'And another this morning?' They start across the park towards Laurel Road. 'There's not going to be war again, is there?'

'Not if we can prevent it. It's madness, Livvy. That ass of a Foreign Secretary, Curzon, told Russia a few days ago if the Red Army didn't stop advancing into Poland we would go to the aid of the Poles. He reminded Lenin it was just six years since Britain had gone to war to support Belgium after Germany had invaded, and we would do the same again.

Would we hell! Millions of people are just starting to rebuild their lives after the last lot and he'd tear the men away, put everybody through it all once more. Working men are *not* going to fight and be killed in their thousands just to line the pockets of politicians and those who make weapons.' She catches the fervour of Lev Yefimovich and feels it is not the first time Joe has said all this.

The Russian soldier in Baku's Olginskaya emphasised: our purpose is to take possession of our own land. Gentry officers will deliberately lead you to your death so they can keep the land that is yours.

'Are you a *bolshevik*?' she asks Joe; realises she has filled her cheeks with the 'l' and 'sh', the Russian way. What if he says yes?

'Of course I'm not. I told you last year I'm a pacifist. I'll demonstrate, argue, even go to prison, anything to persuade people of the wrongness, stupidity, of war.'

'There are many who think the Labour Party's full of Bolsheviks.'

'It isn't. The Bolsheviks call themselves Communists now. There's a small group in this country but we won't have anything to do with them.'

'Your father's not happy about your belonging to Labour.'

'I don't suppose he is. He's an employer. We're interested in the working man.'

'Since April, Renée said.' She has not managed to keep censure from her voice.

'He was going to find out sooner or later.'

'And you took time off yesterday morning.'

'So did many others. The union will support us.' He turns to her. 'Whose side are *you* on in all this, Livvy? Where do *you* stand? You never talk about Russia. Father said not to ask or upset you at the beginning but you've been back nearly a year now.'

… not to ask or upset you … Dear Thomas. She stops walking, faces Joe. 'I'll tell you where I stand, Joe; *exactly* where. The Russian house I'd lived in for four years, ransacked, furniture smashed, broken glass, servants murdered, blood and mess everywhere. The family had already left. Peter and I were married by then but went back and saw it. That wasn't the Bolsheviks, yet a result of war, racial hatred, people taking the law into their own hands. Then Will, your brother; I held the basin while the nurse picked shrapnel out of his stomach. I watched him die. And you ask me where I stand. I never want to experience anything like it again, ever. Demonstrating in the street is the first step.' She looks away from him, at white knuckles clutching the perambulator.

He puts a hand on her shoulder. 'You pack a powerful argument against war. We could do with you at our meetings, Livvy. Will you come? So everybody can hear it?'

She shakes her head. 'I couldn't repeat it all again. It's too upsetting, too recent. When I did tell your father about the house, when … ' She falters, not wanting to admit arguing with Thomas. ' … the nightmare came back. I'd had it for months in Russia.'

They walk some more. 'You and I are on the same side, Livvy. Stop any man in the street and chances are he'll have a horror story to match yours; and you know how Tom talks. That's why we don't want people to have to go through it again. Public demonstration can be peaceful. It's a way of getting the message across.'

'But it means pitting yourself against employers, Joe, and

those who run the country, against the *order* of things. I've seen crowds shouting for the revolution after the Tsar abdicated; heard one man's eloquence holding hundreds in the palm of his hand. "You took up your rifle to defend Mother Russia," the man shouted, "do not put it down again until you have your Mother Earth."'

'And so you don't want anything to change here.'

'Can you blame me? I thought I'd brought George to safety.'

'Not everybody's as fortunate as you, Livvy.'

'*Fortunate*?' An echo of incredulity.

'Yes, in many ways. You've seen streets near the city centre, and some of the people who live there, haven't you?'

She nods.

'I stayed in one of those terraces last night. A lot of the men are out of work. The women take in washing, sew hooks and eyes on by a stub of candle, anything to earn a few pennies. Coal's a luxury. In winter, they burn old boots, orange or fish boxes. The only place they see a flower or blade of grass is the churchyard. Our fancy city centre: New Street, Corporation Street, Colmore Row, all it's done is increase poverty and over-crowding in other areas as people were moved out to make room for new shops and offices. The poor deserve something better, don't they? Not to be sent away to fight.'

She thinks of Masha and the fetid tenement in Baku; the release of revolution.

❧

I shall tell Joe when he comes home, she can't forget Thomas saying. She creeps round her room, as if any sound will result in him and Joe raising their voices downstairs. She has left George in the nursery with Nanny. Normally she would take him to play with Thomas before tea, but this is not a normal day. She opens her wardrobe, stares at the two Baku skirts and shawl, wonders if she will wear them again. The door creaks as she closes it so she leaves it ajar, tiptoes onto the landing. She leans over the banister, can hear ebb and flow of voices, and brief silences.

She is aware of Renée's door opening. She jumps back from the banister, turns round, stands against it, hands behind her.

'Livvy?'

'They don't seem to be arguing, Renée. I couldn't bear it if they were. I'd feel responsible: you see, I told Joe about Esther's brother in Russia … '

'Joe? He's back, then?' Renée sounds as if it was only to be expected.

' … Esther's twin brother, he took issue with his father, you could hear them all over the house,' the words tumble free, 'he'd been in a demonstration, taken the workers' side, his father's men, he left home without saying goodbye and became a Bolshevik.'

'And you're afraid Joe might do the same?'

'Yes.'

'A bit extreme, isn't it?' Renée kisses her cheek, turns towards the bathroom. 'They're probably talking about the garden.'

She grabs Renée's hand; the girl stops, looks back, a flicker of alarm in her eyes. 'You're so lucky, Renée, that your father is as he is. He doesn't judge.'

❧

'I have twenty-five employees,' he tells Joe in the morning room. 'I know all their home situations and what they did through the war. Florrie Eldridge gave birth to a boy the day we went to Wales. I shall go and see them tomorrow, leave an envelope on the table. Her ex-officer husband is still without work. Now,' he challenges his son, 'you suggest what a union can give them that I don't.'

The lad's an idealist, he thinks, facing Joe perched on the edge of a chair; he'll grow out of it, especially if he settles down, raises a family. On the one occasion he went to Joe's den, apart from the evening Livvy arrived, there were titles like *The History of Trade Unionism* and *Industrial Democracy* on the bookshelf. He remembers wondering what industrial democracy meant, and whether he should borrow the book to find out, but never did, not a great reader.

'What about factories with hundreds of employees?' Joe wants to know. 'Morris, Austin. Workers have to be protected. The boss can't take a personal interest in everyone. Your sort is a dying breed.'

'I give people work, security. Demonstrations can mean damage to property, injury to others, and that I will not tolerate. Your mother had political ideals, too, with the Pankhursts. But after the chaos they caused at the meeting Mr Asquith had come all the way from London to address, I forbade her any more activity, and I shall do the same with you, Joe, if necessary. I imagine the unions are hand in glove with the Labour Party.'

'All we want is to put across the case for reason and fairness. Nobody's going to fight, here or anywhere else. That's the whole point.'

'I won't have Livvy upset with this radical talk. She feels safe here, hasn't had a nightmare for months. Let's keep it that way.'

'Livvy's all right. She's stronger than you think. Don't s'pose she'll be with us much longer if she puts another ad in the *Post* and gets a reply.'

He says nothing, not wanting to betray ignorance, tightness in his throat, a tremor he fears in his voice at Livvy's distance from him. Only after several moments does he continue, 'Staying away overnight: yesterday was an exception. It is common courtesy to say beforehand.' His son nods. He feels he has reached calm water so gets to his feet. 'Tea at five o'clock. Mrs Brent's left everything ready as usual. Your sister could do with cheering up. She's missing Una.'

Joe leans back, rolls his eyes, lets out a long breath, stands up.

He walks with Joe to the door, adds, 'I expect there's still some hot water.' Joe, his youngest lad, his and May's little boy now with reddish bristles on an unwashed face; May's favourite, after Peter, who once chased a screaming Renée up to the nursery clutching half a worm and when called down to the morning room said, with wonder in his voice: look, Papa, it's still wriggling, with soil on. He wants to embrace Joe, his only complete, undamaged son. But Joe goes ahead of him into the hall, towards the stairs.

જી

Just an hour each evening, until the best of the daylight has gone. It's soothing, painting, away from the smell of cooked sugar and fruit, yet another jam-making. Last week, after coming back from Wales, he brought his easel down from the attic, and his paints and smock. When he's finished the picture, he'll frame and mount it behind glass. It must be three years since he painted; Jack had been dead twelve months and he did that bowl of fruit.

He has set himself up by the window in Tom's old room,

the lowering sun at the right angle. Tom: always in a hurry now to get to his allotments; next year he'll most likely leave the factory. He uncovers the easel, considers what he has done, looks at the pencil sketch he made in Wales of Livvy gazing at the bay. He no longer needs that one but keeps it with him, reminder of a time when she was happy. She'd been sparkling at lunch that day, speaking of George's first steps alone – how devoted she is - but her smile when he was putting away his pencils on the cliff top was for him, as if she were opening a gate hitherto kept locked, through which he was free to walk into a garden, and all he could do was stare, devoid of speech, at a place of beauty.

Since their return there have been no smiles, worried about her family, unsettled by demonstrations in town and Joe's politics. Dying breed, indeed! So that's how Joe sees him. A few days ago, the government decided against a declaration of war on Russia. 'They'll have to take notice of organised labour in future,' said Joe; 'working men won't be pushed around now.'

They were at the supper table. He saw Livvy close her eyes, clamp her lips as if to hold words in, prevent anything else from reaching her, so he suggested to Joe, 'We could pick the last plums before the light goes.'

And still she's looking for a position, according to Joe, who said of her: she's stronger than you think. He breathes in against the familiar dread that one evening, sitting with him, she'll say: I'm leaving.

Onto his palette he squeezes red, brown, yellow. The tubes of paint have kept well. Can he really ever do justice to her lovely face? How is he to get exactly the right shade of chestnut for her hair? He mixes the colours. Frowns. He dips again the pinpoint end of the brush in water, too small a drop to measure, and introduces it to the mixture. Yes. He shifts in his seat, brings brush to paper.

TWENTY-SIX

A further advertisement in the *Post* yields not one reply. Fortunate, Joe called her. She looks at her hands, smooth, unused to drudgery. It must be more than eighteen months since she shopped, cooked, did any housework, before Masha started working for her at the apartment in Baku's Black Town.

She goes into the morning room late one afternoon, stops a couple of steps past the door. On the chair where she always sits is the watercolour of herself. Last week she opened the door to Tom's room; the covered easel stood in the far corner and she decided not to trespass, the completed picture something to look forward to. Now, she walks closer, sees a young woman: chestnut hair on which light glints, piled at the back of her head; blue eyes, slight smile, unblemished skin; a portrait of beauty and serenity, enclosed in its frame the colour of sand, preserved behind glass, the same person who regards her in the mirror each morning when she has pinned up her hair, yet, is that the real Livvy? He has no idea how I feel.

Thomas comes into the room. She moves away from the picture towards the window, heart knocking against her ribs as if demanding escape. He stands looking at her, pushing the door closed behind him. She swallows to ease a constriction of her throat; Thomas, herself, the picture: a tableau, three points of a triangle, the two people reluctant to invade the space in the middle.

'It's very good, Thomas; very good indeed.'

He smiles, comes nearer. 'Shall we hang it on the wall instead of that dreadful bowl of fruit?' He makes no move to pick the picture up.

He wants to please me, wants my approval. A tear escapes from under each eyelid, trickles down her cheeks. She looks away. 'It's a nice bowl of fruit,' she says. Panic is climbing, handhold, foothold, up through the core of her. Never, in extremes of grief the first weeks here or when George had diphtheria, did she cry in front of Thomas. She brushes her hand over one cheek, but he has seen. He walks over and stands by her.

'Livvy.' He puts one arm round her shoulders. 'You're not offended because of the picture, are you? I couldn't bear you to be.'

The warmth of his arm makes her tremble. She cannot look at him. 'No. Really. It's very good. I don't know what's come over me. Nobody's painted me before.' Only then does she turn to him. There is a clean smell about him, as if he has washed or even shaved since returning from work. Blue eyes are searching her face. She smiles, wanting to reassure him. With him she can smile, because he is … she searches for a word to encompass the realness, the compassion, the certainty that is him.

His other hand is smoothing her cheeks. He rests it at the side of her face and chin. 'You've never shown me tears, Livvy.'

'I didn't want to upset you.'

His lips part in a smile enabling a short sigh, like a silent laugh, as if it has been long bound there, waiting. His voice is almost a whisper. 'Dear, brave Livvy.'

Brave? I don't know. And as for dear ... But speech will not form; his mouth is brushing her damp cheek, and her lips, as if they are infinitely precious, to be treasured.

It is a brief kiss. He continues to look at her face and, as when they were in Wales, she has the feeling he wants to imprint every detail on his mind.

A brief kiss. Yet, she thinks, a kiss need not be measured in length of time. 'I'll go and bring George down,' she says.

'Yes.'

He walks with her across the room, arm still round her shoulders. Only when they reach the door does he release her, leaving an emptiness, more than physical separation.

❧

During the evening meal, she moves her glass and Joe's for Thomas to pour more water. Thomas says, 'Tom's bringing more and more stuff from the allotments to sell at the factory. He's hoping to be self-supporting by next spring. If only they could find somewhere else to live.'

'We need a council whose priority's cheap housing,' Joe reminds him.

'There's still shortage of materials, whoever's in power.'

She says, 'Please, don't argue.' Thomas and Joe turn to her. She drinks some water, stands up. 'Will you excuse me? I don't feel too bright.' She makes for the door.

Through the night she shifts from one side of the pillow to the other, relives Thomas's kiss, curses her treacherous body's response, an abiding warmth between her legs, a flowering, opening, for the first time not by the memory of Peter but the kiss of another man. Not just any man. Peter's father. Peter, what have I done to you? She clutches the pillow, rests her lips against it.

Daylight arrives by stealth, as if aware it is not welcome. She hears doors opening, closing, water pipes clanging, toilet flushing. She'll go downstairs after Thomas has left for the factory. She gets out of bed, looks in the wardrobe, removes Peter's greatcoat, jacket and trousers, holds them to her face, breathes in, in, in, the only way of possessing him now, a faint smell of oil and unwashed body. She lays the clothes on the bed. She puts on a Baku skirt and blouse, fastens each button with care as if preparing for a special occasion, but the skirt pulls tight round her waist. This is what I was wearing the second time we met, darling, really met, in the Tartar Quarter. She ties the shawl under her chin, turns to the mirror. A stranger stares at her. She opens her bottom drawer for the tins of make-up from Nell, returns to the mirror. With her little finger, she smears some across her lips, presses them together. 'Trollop,' she says to her reflection. From the top drawer she takes out the white silk stockings in their crinkled packet; sits on the bed, fits one over her foot, smoothes its softness up her leg, remembers the thrill of Peter's touch on her wedding night, his lips on her skin, when he knelt to take the stockings off.

❧

In the nursery, she can hear Nanny running George's bath, humming *Annie Laurie*. George is sitting on the floor playing with coloured bricks, chattering. He clambers to his feet. 'Mamamama!' He runs to her holding out his arms.

She lifts him up, hugs him, drinking him in, his smell of milk, egg, sleep. 'Mama's going down to have a cup of tea,' she says. 'Then we'll explore the garden.' This evening she will be dry-eyed, as if nothing has happened. There will be no reason for Thomas to kiss her.

A letter waits in the silver tray on the table in the stairwell. She picks it up. *Mrs P. Boulton.* She does not recognise the writing. She looks at the postmark and her heart swerves, jumps. A sweat of apprehension erupts on her hands, forehead, back of her neck.

Norwich.

She takes the letter into the morning room, gasping for breath. Shivering, she sits by the window in the sun's warmth, tears at the envelope, for to have fetched the opener from the bureau would have taken valuable seconds now she has in her hand what she craves yet dreads. She pulls out a single sheet, closely written. A glance at the bottom of the second side shows it is from Rose. She turns back and begins to read.

Dear Livvy,

Thank you for your letter. I am sorry you have lost your husband, but pleased you have made a new life with his family. You understand, I know, that suffering is not easy to write about. Although I have had your letter since last week, only this morning am I able to reply. I have been away for two months, to my sister in Yarmouth. The change and sea air were beneficial. Your letter must have been lying on the mat since soon after I went, and you wondering what had become of us all.

I have only bad news to relate. I will be as brief as this allows. Neither of your brothers survived the war. Arthur enlisted in 1915, when he was eighteen, and lost his life at Suvla Bay. Victor volunteered at the beginning of 1918, before his eighteenth birthday, and was killed at the battle of Cambrai. Their loss, and the realisation you could have come to harm if you were still in Russia, took their toll of your father, although your card at Christmas with the Birmingham postmark reassured him to some degree. He bore his sorrows with fortitude, continuing to do his work.

At the end of April he succumbed to a chill which went to his chest and against which he did not seem to have strength to fight. He died on the sixth of May. You, too, are a widow, Livvy, and I need not write of the agony of such a loss. I have returned from Yarmouth to pack up and then I shall go back, where my roots are, for good.

What I have written will, I know, add to the sadness you have already suffered. I can find no way of avoiding it if you are to be told the truth.

Your stepmother,

Rose.

She lets the letter slip from her fingers into her lap, incapable of movement, thought; shrouded by numbness. The sixth of May. George's first birthday. Tears fill her eyes, spill onto her cheeks. Self-loathing breaks through: she should've written sooner, made herself do it. … *your card at Christmas … reassured him to some degree.* But not completely. If he'd known George was his grandson, might it have given him hope after years of war; a photograph, the promise of a visit: strength to fight and overcome his illness? She heaves with each breath as tears and despair flow out of her.

She drags her arm across smarting eyes, staunches them with her handkerchief, sits back in the grip of an exhaustion born of desolation. She looks out of the window. Mrs Brent is in the garden cutting the last gladioli, bringing them to the house.

Within a few minutes there is a knock on the morning room door. She smoothes a hand over her hair, puts the handkerchief back in the pocket of her dress. 'Come in.'

Mrs Brent pauses in the doorway. 'Good morning, ma'am. I've brought some tea.'

'Thank you, Mrs Brent.' She stands up, takes a saucer and steaming cup.

'If there's anything else, ma'am – '

'No … I've had bad news from my family.' My family: I have no longer any family. 'I have to go to Norwich. I'll leave a note for Mr Boulton in the hall.'

'I'm very sorry, ma'am. If there's anything you would wish me to do – '

'Nothing thank you, Mrs Brent. I'll speak to Nanny and set off. I'll have to be away at least one night.'

She sits at the bureau as soon as Mrs Brent has closed the door; writes, *Dear Thomas. You always said there was a reason. Please read the letter that arrived for me this morning from Norwich. I have left it in the bureau. Livvy.* She folds the paper in half, puts it in an envelope on which she writes *Thomas.* She looks at it uneasily, adds *Mr* before and *Boulton* after. She seals the envelope, places Rose's letter on top of her writing case in the bureau, closes the lid. She gulps down the tea, goes into the hall, leaves the note for Thomas on the table, runs up to the nursery. Only when she is at the top of the stairs does she realise she did not write that she is going to Norwich. He will understand.

❧

Less than two hours later, she is installed in a first-class carriage on an eastbound train. Making the decision to go released energy. After explaining to Nanny, hugging George, taking leave of them before tears returned, she threw into the buckram suitcase things for a couple of days and nights, then left. Her first stop was the post office in Wood Road, where she sent a telegram to Rose: *Very, very sorry. Arriving this evening. Livvy.* She withdrew ten pounds, continued to the Stratford Road for the tram to New Street Station, her first journey into the city since last October with Renée,

She has the carriage to herself. The train gathers speed through flat Warwickshire countryside and she remembers another train journey decided on impulse, paid for with money from her post office account, on her eighteenth birthday almost seven years ago, from Norwich to London. She replays Rose's letter in her mind. Arthur: where was Suvla Bay? Victor: so named because he was born on Mafeking Night, when wars were far-off matters fought on the outposts of Empire, affecting only regular soldiers, not a generation of youth. One of her earliest memories is of Father taking her and Arthur round Norwich that night, when it seemed the whole town was celebrating in the street, and her small hand clung to his with the noise of fireworks and glare of bonfires, while upstairs at home was a new brother who'd be playmate for Arthur. She'll never see any of them again. Her mind tries to absorb this but can't.

What part of the sixth of May did Father die? When she was with Connie in Victoria Park? Perhaps when she blew out the candle on George's cake. Every few minutes she wipes away tears, thinking of the awfulness of it, the finality. ... *you could have come to harm if you were still in Russia* ... She took herself off to Russia believing Father no longer cared for her but it wasn't true, just as Thomas said he'd never disown Joe. It is too late for her to say or do anything to put things right.

Rose had been home several days before writing; will she have already returned to Yarmouth? She pushes the possibility to the back of her mind. Exhaustion combines with shock, weeping, rhythm of wheels on rails, to lull her to sleep.

☙

In between four changes of train she dozes but after Wymondham forces herself to keep awake, sitting on the edge of the seat peering out at fields bare and golden brown since harvest. Under late afternoon sun they stretch as far as she can see, to Norwich Cathedral, spire soaring to a milky sky. She stands up, takes deep breaths in an attempt to steady her nervousness, looks in the mirror above the seats to make sure her hat is in place. Will Rose be at home? What is she going to say to Rose? What if Rose does not welcome her visit? Yet, there was neither bitterness nor recrimination in the letter. She realises nobody who has lived through the last six years can be the same as before and wonders what change has been wrought in her stepmother. She pulls on her gloves.

A porter comes along the corridor. 'Norwich Thorpe next stop! All change at Norwich Thorpe.' He glances through the window to her compartment, opens the door. He has a thin moustache that looks as if it has been pencilled on. 'Norwich, madam.'

'Yes.' She indicates her case.

He lifts it from the rack. She notices the tops of three fingers are missing. A war injury? Where? She sits down, gazes out of the window at the approach to her native city, willow trees lining the River Wensum. Her chest is aching, heart tapping.

The train is hissing, disgorging clouds of steam, doors clunking shut like gunfire. She steps onto the platform. The porter is pushing a handcart loaded with her case and others. 'Can I get you a cab, madam?'

'Thank you, no. It isn't far.'

'Very good, madam.' He manoeuvres the cart ahead of her.

Walking to the house will give her time to decide what she is going to say to Rose. Heather Road is fifteen minutes from the station, on the same side of the city; she remembers the ease with which she could be away from Norwich helped persuade her to leave that September morning seven years ago. She wonders if neighbours will see her today from behind net-curtained windows. There's Walter Turner's girl, might they say? … come back too late … Livvy Turner, went off to London, was in Russia last we heard, broke her father's heart … Was that how they spoke of her? A girl who suddenly disappeared, no better than she ought to be.

She is aware of greetings, reunions, other porters carrying or pushing luggage. She glances at her cream gloves: not a sensible colour for a train journey. There are black specks on them. She sees her porter leave the platform through a doorway on the left.

'Hello, Livvy,' says a woman's voice.

She stops, attention drawn to a large sagging hat of green straw, embroidered with pink raffia. Grey-blond hair hangs beneath it like cobwebs. Sad blue eyes scrutinise her, cheeks marred by a network of fine red veins. 'Rose!' she gasps.

Rose offers a hand in greeting. 'It's good of you to come.'

Trembling, she takes Rose's hand, the first time they have ever touched. 'It was the least I could do. It's kind of you to meet me.' Kind? Rose?

'It makes a nice walk down after tea. They said that coming from Birmingham you'd be on the train out of Thetford and one was due. So I thought I'd wait.'

The East Anglian way of speaking, words slithering into each other, sounds strange after so many years. She releases Rose's hand. They walk towards the platform exit.

'The porter has my case,' she says. They are in the ticket hall. 'There he is!' He is unloading his cart. She takes her purse from her bag. The only change she has is sixpence. She feels it is too much but gives it to him, aware of Rose watching her.

He touches his cap. 'Thank you, madam.'

She picks up the case.

'You've been able to leave your little boy with somebody?' Rose asks.

'Nanny's staying with us for the moment, helping with the jam.'

'Nanny,' repeats Rose. 'You've done well for yourself: a home, enough money, nanny for – ' Rose hesitates.

' – George,' she supplies. 'Father would like to have known about him,' she adds in a rush, 'I mean, to have had a photograph – '

'We did wonder who George was, on your Christmas card.'

' – it's my fault and I'm sorry.'

She waits for a sharp rejoinder, a rebuke, but Rose walks in front, placing each step as if uncomfortable on her feet, along the path to the river. The lowering sun is ahead, then behind when they follow the curve of the Wensum away from the city. After a while Rose says, 'We'll stop by the churchyard.'

They leave the river, go alongside the old city wall for a few hundred yards before turning left. Rose opens a gate secured with a loop of binder twine. She follows Rose along neatly-kept paths until they reach the grey gravestone with black lettering. At the base is a vase of fresh marigolds.

She drops to her knees on the grass, traces with her fingers the mound of the new grave, squares of turf still not knitted together after being dug up in May; seven years ago she sat here when the grave was flat, railing against Rose to Mama. She touches the words on the stone, as might a blind person:

Here lie Victoria Olivia Turner,
died 28th November 1909 in her 39th year,
And her husband, Walter Arthur Turner,
died 6th May 1920 in his 56th year.
May They Rest in Peace.

She bows her head, scalding tears falling on the earth. I'm sorry ... I'm sorry ... She sits back on her heels, fumbles for a handkerchief. *May They Rest in Peace.* It is she who must live with not writing to Father. She starts to get to her feet yet feels weighed down by the prospect of a long, lonely road, and stumbles. Rose's hand is firm on her arm. She turns to look at Rose, notices tears gathering. Never, in the eighteen months they lived under the same roof, did she see Rose cry.

☙

He sits at the bureau as he used to every evening. But now in his hands are not newspaper cuttings, War Office telegrams, letters from foreign parts. Those days seem distant, another life. He reads again Livvy's note and the letter from Norwich. He brushes his fingertips across the note, penned only this morning. Her writing is round, upright, that of someone who has done a lot of it. Studying and writing. There is a faint puckering of the paper near the right-hand corner, as if it has been wet. She must've cried, reading her stepmother's letter, and the thought pains him, eats into his chest. Here, he can do nothing for her, be of no comfort. She hasn't written where she's gone but Mrs Brent assured him she is in Norwich.

He wonders how long she will stay there, and a possibility plays around him like a chill wind, that she will decide to live with her stepmother; or perhaps there's a young man, the families know each other and now he's back from the war. She will return here to collect George – her devotion to George is absolute – and her few belongings, a footprint in the sand of the ten and a half months she has lived in this house, for her soon smoothed over. I have no claim on Livvy, he reminds himself, no right to expect anything. He closes his eyes, can feel their kiss last evening, her lack of resistance. Nothing will loosen the grip of dread that one day she will leave for good.

TWENTY-SEVEN

She takes her suitcase upstairs while Rose is preparing tea. She slides her hand along the banister, something Father might have done. On the landing she stops outside his bedroom, his and Rose's. She curls her fingers round the door knob, not because she wants to go in but because less than four months ago his hand touched it.

In her own room, nothing has been moved, curtains and bedcover the same chintz, now faded but not as awful as she remembers. She looks out at the garden. Father was never a cultivator in the manner of Thomas and Joe but the grass was always cut and borders planted each spring with annuals. Now the lawn grows in tufts, and weeds have settled among the roses. She wonders if her bicycle is still in the shed.

On the table, the inkwell is encrusted, black. She touches the exercise book on top of the pile, the one from which she tore the middle page to write a note before leaving home. The cover is no longer red but pink after years by the window. She opens it. *French Grammar Olivia Turner May 1913* She leafs through pages of sentences, lists of vocabulary, conjugations of verbs, Miss Handley's corrections in red. Yet, when Esther and her family spoke French, she couldn't understand. She closes the book, turns away, trespasser in the room of somebody who has gone out but is expected back.

On the shelf are Dickens and the book with the picture *Princess in the Snow*; Andrew Lang fairy stories, the spine of the yellow cover aged to buttermilk: she read them as a child and later to her brothers, tales of battles between giants and mortals which were her only understanding of war in those years of innocence. Victor used to like the seven-headed serpent and would count the heads in the picture. Arthur always wanted to hear about the Emperor's new clothes: read it again, Livvy, he'd insist. She leaves them, goes downstairs.

After she has eaten salad, cheese, bread and butter, she offers to wash up. 'You've had a long journey,' emphasises Rose. 'Sit yourself down.' She wants to point out she's been seated most of the day, that Rose is the one who ought to rest; she has noticed Rose's ankles, swollen beneath a shapeless, unfashionably long, green tussore dress. However, she does as she's told; habit, threading her to years ago.

Rose makes a pot of tea, eases herself into the rocking chair by the range. No more do the steels have a shine you can see your face in, nor do the pans sparkle. 'They were good boys,' Rose says. 'No trouble, well-mannered. Lads to be proud of. Worked in your father's department until they joined up.' Rose stirs her tea. 'Arthur's body was never found. The place where he and others lay was marked but when the action was over he'd disappeared.' Rose speaks as if reciting a text learnt by heart and often repeated. 'His padre called to see us that winter when he was on leave.'

'Suvla Bay?' She drinks some tea. Rose has remembered she likes it weak.

'Gallipoli,' says Rose. 'Victor's nurse wrote that his last words were of your father and me.'

'Thomas received something similar about one of his sons. He kept it, and the telegrams.' If she could read about her brothers, their deaths might seem more real, and she would be sharing Father's sadness.

Without standing up, Rose reaches to a drawer, pulls out several envelopes, there waiting not pushed at the back. Rose hands them to her.

She opens the black-edged War Office ones:

Regret to inform you Private A.W. Turner killed in action Turkey August 12th

Regret to inform you Private V.A. Turner killed in action France October 9th

Little more than a dozen words to shatter a family. And only a month before the Armistice in Victor's case. From the envelope with a French stamp, she unfolds a sheet of paper.

St Quentin,
France,
15th October, 1918

Dear Mr and Mrs Turner,

I expect you have been told of your son's death. I was with him at the end. He was a fine soldier, and died with honour and dignity. I hope it will be of some comfort to you both to know that Private Turner's dying words were of his mother and father.

Yours sincerely,

Emily Calloway (Nursing Sister)

Private Turner … her little Victor, with curly hair so thick it never moved; her brother, who always smelled of the earth; one day he cycled to Blakeney Point without telling anybody, to see what was there, he said on his return, informing an anxious father and sister that he was going to be an explorer. Sister Calloway's letter is almost identical to the one Thomas had from Russia about Will. Did they always write the same, those officers and nurses? An order, directive, from the War Office? That this should be so, makes the letters seem impersonal, just words, straw for a grieving family to clutch.

There is no mention of Victor not suffering long. She pictures a French field hospital, can smell the stench, hear screams, Victor lingering between life and death. She closes her eyes. Rose does not know she nursed in Baku hospital, that she can fill the gaps in this polite letter. She looks at the ceiling, blinks against tears. Rose is watching her. She puts the telegrams and letter back in their envelopes, offers them to Rose. 'I expect you want to keep them.'

She feels the paper slip from her fingers as Rose takes them, as if she is letting go of her brothers. Rose returns the letters to the drawer. She, Livvy, may have brushed the boys' hair, helped them read, tended cut knees, but it was Rose who honed their manners, saw their transition from school to work, perhaps even kept an eye open for a future wife. In leaving as she did, she abdicated all responsibility for them.

❧

Rose has hobbled to the window, drawn the curtains, switched on the electric light; at the range she mixes cocoa in two mugs.

'Your feet are hurting you, Rose.'

'Arthritis.' Rose pours warm milk into the mugs, hands one to her. 'Always worse in the evening. The winters of the war were long and cold.'

East Anglian winters were always long and cold. And damp. Perhaps Father and Rose didn't have enough fuel during the war. While she had over five years of Baku sun.

Rose returns to her chair. 'I always felt you resented me.'

She drinks some of the sweet chocolate. 'I wanted to continue as we had been: Father, me, and the boys.'

'My sister warned me, you know. "Won't be easy," she said, "taking over a home with a girl of sixteen who's been in charge." I didn't listen, of course. We always think we know best, don't we? I was in love. Your father was in his forties when I met him, but a man that age can capture a woman's heart, make her feel like a princess.'

A sweat of discomfort prickles the back of her neck, to hear Father talked about in such intimate terms. She wonders how well she knew him; she, who used to ask herself if he and Rose were happy. How well do we ever know anybody? 'Had you read Mrs Gaskell's *Cranford*?' she asks Rose. 'When you gave it me for my eighteenth birthday, had you chosen it specially?'

Rose's brow creases, waiting for her to say more.

'It was just,' she flounders, 'the heroine leaves home … ' to escape her stepmother, she wants to say but can't; 'goes to live with her aunts.'

'You were always a bookish person,' Rose comments; adds, 'you didn't mention your husband's mother in the letter.'

'She died the winter of the Armistice: influenza. We have Mrs Brent, the housekeeper.'

'A man needs a wife, Livvy. However much he loved the one who's died, and his children, he needs a wife. Peter's father may want to marry again. How old is he?'

'I don't know. I wouldn't think he's fifty.'

'Like your father when I first knew him. He was a lovely man and a dear husband. We had eight years together and I treasure them. It is my great regret we were not blessed with children. There was one but his birth was not to be. I miscarried after four months the summer the war started.'

'Oh Rose, how dreadful for you. The same happened to me last winter. It was the scarlet fever. I got to two months.' I've never told anyone, she thinks, and now it's Rose I'm sharing it with. They sit looking at each other, understanding.

'You may remarry,' says Rose, 'have more children. You always wanted your own home, didn't you?'

'Yes, I did. But it's difficult to picture being with anyone else.'

'You're young, still attractive enough to turn a man's head.'

She feels herself blushing at this unaccustomed compliment, wishes she could say the same about Rose, whom she remembers young, blond, pretty; Rose, who certainly turned Father's head, perhaps one summer week in Yarmouth. 'When are you going?'

'Soon. It doesn't matter. One day's the same as another.'

She looks round the kitchen, recalls her bedroom untouched all those years. 'Do you want me to help you pack?'

'There isn't much to do. I've no use for this furniture at my sister's. Nor any of the other things,' Rose flaps a hand in the direction of the pans. 'I was going to sell the whole lot to Mr Biggin.'

She remembers the landlord, small with a toothbrush moustache, collecting the rent each month; sometimes he sent his son, a pasty boy in a Norfolk jacket.

'You should have some consideration now,' Rose continues, 'but, in your present situation, I can't see you have room for a houseful of furniture.'

Tom and Connie might move from the barge and need more, she thinks; yet Tom is happy there, and Connie's happy because he is. 'I'm hoping to find a job,' she tells Rose, 'where George and I can live in.'

'Take anything you want,' says Rose.

❧

Next morning, the smell of frying bacon rises from the kitchen through the chill that has settled in the air. She draws back her bedroom curtains to see fine drizzle meandering under grey sky. She looks at the derelict garden, thinks of the flowers, the neatness and care of the one in Laurel Road, and longs to be there. She will pick some roses and stop by the grave on the way to the station. While waiting yesterday, Rose found out times of return trains; one at eleven o'clock will connect with the London and North Western line to Birmingham. Allowing for her case being heavier, and a few minutes in the churchyard, she needs to be leaving by ten-fifteen.

She eats her largest breakfast since returning to England. Back in her room, she packs her books. She opens the wardrobe and drawers, releasing the pungency of camphor balls. She pulls out the few remaining clothes. She can turn up the hems of the skirt and dress. Connie might like them. She moves over to the table by the window. Should she take the exercise books for George? No; he will write his own. She picks up the top one, tears at the faded cover, pulling away the stitching and the inside: one, two, four, dozens of pieces, and the next one and so down the pile, snagging her nails, gasping, a cleansing, pouring out of herself that September morning seven years ago and the person she was. Through the open bedroom door she hears Rose's footsteps on the stairs and breathing in puffs.

Rose comes in, sees the mess on the table and says, 'There's some sacking in the shed. I'll get it.' Rose is holding two photographs in frames. 'You have one, Livvy.'

She looks at the head and shoulders portraits of Father: a solemn expression, just a suggestion of a smile, gentleness in his eyes; how he was ten years ago.

'Which would you like?' she asks Rose.

∽

In the hall, Rose gives her a brown paper parcel tied with string, some looped into a handle. 'I've made sandwiches for your journey.'

'Thank you.' She puts them on her case, next to the roses and a pewter vase from the kitchen, also wrapped in paper. She holds out her right hand. 'Goodbye, Rose.'

Rose squeezes her fingers, smiles. 'Goodbye, Livvy. I wish you well.'

She bends to kiss her stepmother's cheek. It is soft and smells of soap. 'Let me know how you settle in Yarmouth.'

At the end of the road she turns, waves. Rose, standing on the pavement by the gate, raises an arm.

By the time she arrives at the churchyard she is ready to put her case down. She rests the sandwiches on it, arranges the roses in the vase, folds up the paper small enough to go in her bag. She tips into the vase some water from the one containing marigolds. She straightens up, clothes clinging in the drizzle; marshals the words she has prepared in her mind, although nothing she says can ever be adequate. She bows her head. 'I'm sorry, Father … Papa … I'm sorry I didn't write and tell you about George; but I will show him your photograph and make sure he knows his grandfather was a good man.'

∽

The eleven o'clock train leaves on time. She takes off her damp gloves, hat and coat, spreads them over the seat opposite. She should've brought something warmer to wear; in England, fine dry weather comes to an end, not like in Baku. She eats cheese and egg sandwiches Rose made for her, thinks again of the inescapable finality of death, of Thomas's words months ago: we could any of us, at any moment, be changed or taken. She still has George. And Thomas; they must remain friends, while what happened two evenings ago in the morning room has to be forgotten. Whether or not he remarries, she will leave Laurel Road.

She finishes her lunch, rests her head against the back of the seat, closes her eyes. Marry again, marry again, marry again: the rhythm of the train enfolds her in sleep.

In Birmingham, drizzle has become rain. There are no taxis outside the station. She goes over to the tram stop, avoids a puddle. On board, the air is thick with smells of coarse tobacco – Lev Yefimovich again - of unwashed clothes and bodies, and the rattle of urgent, asthmatic coughs. She is glad to get off and cross the park, damp buckram case banging against her leg, the house drawing her like a beacon through clinging cold.

The front gate is unlatched. Her wet fingers fumble to open the outer door, the inner one. She closes both, puts her case down, the minutes lugging it from the tram stop still causing her to draw in deep, painful breaths. The sweet, beefy welcome of Mrs Brent's steak and kidney pie fills the hall and she realises she has missed it. She takes off her hat, coat and gloves, leaves them on the perambulator, shivers in her dress.

The morning room door opens. Thomas comes out. 'Livvy?'

She looks along at him, heart speeding as if it wants to be free to greet him.

'It *is* you!' Thomas exclaims. He is walking towards her.

She smiles, happiness racing through her, joy she has forgotten how to feel. 'Thomas!' She takes a few steps. His arms are outstretched. She gives him her own, clasping him, the warmth of him.

'Thank heaven you're safe, my dearest Livvy,' he murmurs against her hair. 'Welcome home. I didn't know … Mrs Brent said you'd gone to Norwich. I'm so sorry.' He eases her to arm's length; that same look, of wanting to imprint her face on his mind. 'You're wet from the rain, Livvy. We'll get Mrs Brent to light a fire.' His hand under her elbow, he guides her along the hall. 'I'm so sorry … your father … and your brothers … '

∽

That night, euphoria recedes into hours of darkness. I love him, she forces herself to admit. Is this love, less than a year after Peter's death? That she should feel anything for any man can only be a betrayal. That the man is Peter's father makes it more imperative she live elsewhere. She remembers when she first loved Peter, the wonder, the joy of it, the fear that something would happen to let daylight onto the magic and break the spell. But this, if it is love, is something shameful from which she wants to flee. After her reunion with Thomas, she carried her case up while Mrs Brent lit a fire in the morning room. She put on a dry dress, joined George and Nanny in the nursery. By the time she went back down, supper was ready. Afterwards, she returned to her room, unpacked, put the photograph of Papa on the chest of drawers, books in a pile for the nursery, although it occurred to her that if she was going to find somewhere to live she could've left them in the case. A man needs a wife, Rose said. She must go; can't keep retreating upstairs.

When she takes George down in the morning, sun is emerging from behind cotton wool clouds. The spiciness of stewing blackberries and apples filters through to the hall. The last jam-making. Other fruit has already been jammed, or bottled for winter pies and tarts. 'Nanny!' George shouts, pushing at the kitchen door.

'Nanny's busy,' she calls to her son. 'Don't interrupt her.'

He takes no notice, goes through.

Hot pans, fruit and sugar: she rushes after him into the steam of the kitchen. 'I'm so sorry, Nanny ... Mrs Brent,' she gasps, grabs George's hand. Mrs Brent is filling the flour tin from the sack the grocer's boy has just delivered. Nanny is stirring fruit in the preserving pan on the range. George tugs his mama towards the door to the garden. It is Saturday; through the window she can see Thomas in shirt sleeves, picking blackberries. She wants to be there; then, suddenly afraid, wishes she were in the park, anywhere, away. George is pulling at her hand. 'All right,' she concedes, 'we'll say hello to Grandpapa, then we must let everybody get on with their work.'

She opens the door. George frees himself from her hand, runs into the garden. 'Papa! Papa!' He scampers down the path towards Thomas.

She stares at George running to his grandfather, calling 'Papa!' and wrapping his arms round Thomas's legs. Papa. Is this what Thomas was encouraging while she was in Norwich? Peter's thin face, dying in that dismal room in Archangel last October is, for a few moments, all she can see: tell George his father loved him. She *will* tell George. Soon. She walks towards him and Thomas. One kitchen basin is full of blackberries. Thomas has started a second. She avoids his eyes, concentrates on two stained hands he has raised as if in surrender.

'I'd pick him up if I could,' he laughs.

'Good morning, Thomas.' She prises one of George's hands away from Thomas's legs. 'Grandpapa can't lift you up, he's got messy fingers.'

'Papa,' says George, pressing his face against Thomas's trousers.

'*Grand*papa,' she insists. 'Let him go so he can get on. Papa was somebody else.'

'Papa seems easier for him to say,' observes Thomas.

'Of course it is if he's allowed to. He must learn to say grandpapa.' She bends down to George. 'Leave go, then you can give Grandpapá a kiss on the cheek.'

George relents. She holds him level with Thomas's face. When she permits her eyes to meet Thomas's she sees hurt. He kisses George on the end of the nose, a gesture of tenderness from which she turns her head.

She takes the full basin, starts back along the path with George. 'Wave bye-bye,' she says to him. He copies her and waves. Her chest aches. She could've stayed, picked blackberries, enabling Thomas to be at the factory sooner. What has she achieved? Nothing, except to discomfort him.

ᘒ

By lunchtime she is sneezing.

'Looks as if you chilled yesterday, Livvy, getting wet,' says Joe. The evening she was in Norwich, he was helping Tom with potatoes. Earth still encrusts his nails. She thinks of the stationmaster's garden in Voronezh, soil on her hands; of Peter, and making love inside the *izba*.

Thomas is regarding her, concern in his eyes. 'I'll be all right,' she insists, studies her plate, cuts her ham into smaller pieces than necessary.

'There was a telegram from Una's father this morning,' says Thomas. 'They're putting Renée on the train in London to arrive at Snow Hill at three o'clock. Somebody must meet her. Could you, Joe? Take the trap.'

She looks across at Joe. 'Want to come, Livvy?' he asks.

'I must keep George occupied, away from the kitchen.' Find a job, somewhere to live. She remembers a Saturday evening in London almost seven years ago, buying a newspaper, which led her to the Claytons and Russia. And still she is escaping.

In Wood Road, she stops at the post office. An advertisement in the window offers a room to rent. She pushes the perambulator along to the last house in a terrace. The lion's head knocker needs a polish. Brown paint is peeling.

A woman answers the door. From a pale face, grey eyes appraise her. Nondescript hair is pulled into a bun. 'Yes?' The woman stands with arms folded across a nonc-too-clean sacking pinafore over a sagging bosom. Underneath is an over-large, ankle-length, black alpaca frock to which age has given a greenish tinge.

'I've come about the room.'

Reddened hands; a whiff of carbolic. The woman stands aside to let her in. 'Jus' you an' the babby?'

'Yes.' She follows the woman's button-up boots along a hall smelling of cabbage, like the tenement in Rostov last September. They climb four staircases, past splintered banisters, to the second floor. All the doors are painted brown.

The woman opens the first one on the left, draws back brown curtains to reveal a window looking out at fields. 'View's nice.'

Unconcerned about the view, she glances round the musty-smelling room: washstand, wardrobe, chest of drawers, iron bedstead, faded armchair; edges of wallpaper crinkling away from the plaster; strip of threadbare carpet, original colours hard to distinguish, lying on grey linoleum mottled with age. Newspaper covers the fire grate.

'Shillin' a week,' says the woman. 'I'll cook yer food if yer buy it.'

She thinks of the cabbage downstairs, and her stomach shouts: no.

'Gotta job?' asks the woman, suspicion in her voice.

The journey to Norwich has left one pound ten shillings in her post office account. There is money Thomas deposited in the Municipal Bank last November. Can she use this to support herself when she will be rejecting his home? Unease stalks inside her. 'Soon,' she says, with more hope than certainty.

'I'm out all day,' the woman tells her. 'Mam downstairs can look after babby for yer. Where yer livin' now?'

'With my late husband's family.'

'Not workin' out?' A speculative yet knowing glint enlivens the woman's eyes.

She sneezes, and again; blows her nose, thinks once more of the tenement in Rostov, and of the space and light of the house in Laurel Road, the smell of polish, and realises she would miss the house as one might a dear friend. Panic shakes her: ... faded armchair, edges of wallpaper crinkling away from the plaster, strip of threadbare carpet ... I can't do it: take George from there and bring him to this; leave him with a stranger while I go out to work?

'Are yer sickenin'?' asks the woman, without compassion.

'It's nothing. I must get back to my baby. Can I let you know?' She is already out of the room and at the top of the stairs.

'Suit yerself.' The woman closes the bedroom door. 'But if someone else comes it'll go.'

❧

To one like himself, a practical man not given to much reading, there is something accusatory about Reverend Cuthbert Timms' study, three walls lined floor to ceiling with leather-bound books. All that knowledge waiting to be learnt, all those things he doesn't know, never will. The fourth wall is relieved by a large window, with crimson plush curtains, giving onto lawn, rose beds, and a buddleia nodding in the evening breeze. Sweet woodsmoke infuses the room, fire in the grate a concession to September.

Cuthbert Timms, at his mahogany desk by the window, is looking not at the garden but him seated in a chenille-covered armchair; has taken off his spectacles and is regarding him with a kindly expression.

He edges a finger under his collar, uncomfortable in the warm room; feels his way into what he is here to say, to ask. The vicar has become a friend over the years, christening all the children, visiting after Jack and Will were killed, May's death, Peter's; now he is listening, nodding. In understanding? 'I have developed a fondness for Livvy, a deep fondness.' He picks each word, turns it over in his mind as he might handle a pebble found on the beach. 'I wish to care for her, offer her security.' He must now say what has remained locked in his

385

head for days, perhaps weeks, perhaps since the first time he saw her although his consciousness could not then recognise it. 'I wish to marry her.'

Cuthbert Timms crosses one knee over the other, laces the fingers of both hands on his lap. 'Is there a certificate of her marriage, Thomas?'

'I have not asked her. She was still in deep shock when she arrived last October, and suffered nightmares for weeks.' He explains about the destruction of the Russian house and murder of the servants, Livvy's rising shrieks as she told him echoing round his mind.

Cuthbert Timms has pursed his mouth into an 'o' of pain; he shakes his head. 'She still doesn't feel able to come to church?'

'It undermined her faith, that and Peter's death. There are probably other things she's never spoken of. So, whether she had, folded amongst her few belongings, a bit of paper … ' His voice trails away, as if he would expect Cuthbert Timms, only now realising what he has said, to interrupt him, discount the possibility of marriage to Livvy.

But it is the crackle of the fire that breaks the silence. Encouraged, he pursues his course, as though he must lay everything out before a door closes. 'I have not questioned her but sought to give her peace, refuge, stability for her son and herself. She spoke some while back of leaving, finding a position, but has not mentioned this for several weeks and seems more settled. I don't think of her as my son's widow, perhaps because I never knew them together … ' She didn't seem put out, he remembers, when he suggested she call him Thomas that first day; father made it seem as if he were treating her as a child, while Mr Boulton sounded too formal although, he thinks now, even after more than four years Connie still addresses him so. The heat of shame creeps up his neck and cheeks as he recalls, last winter, wondering if George's real mother were dead and Peter gave their baby to Livvy to bring to England. Cuthbert Timms is watching him.

He forces himself beyond unruly thoughts. ' ... perhaps because the Peter I remember was a boy yearning only for adventure, not ready for the responsibility of marriage.' And yet, every time you look at George you see Peter, he thinks. George is his father in so many ways: the same fine light brown hair, that way of placing his feet as he toddles, the look of determination even when he is smiling. If George reminds him of Peter, does that mean with Livvy he would perpetuate May? No. Livvy might have the same colour hair but would never have campaigned for the Pankhursts, has no political interests. She is unique.

'I feel that for Livvy to continue under my roof without marriage is ... ' Is what? He remembers their kiss, the softness of her lips, lack of resistance. But the day after her return from Norwich she seemed distant, annoyed that George was calling him papa. And now he has not seen her for forty-eight hours. Aching eyes and sinuses have kept her in bed, result of getting wet on the journey back. Mrs Brent has been taking up toast tea, and honey and brandy dissolved in warm water.

He realises he has not finished the sentence.

'There was a union with Peter,' Cuthbert Timms rescues him, 'but if there is no record of a marriage ... '

Does everything depend on a written record? Was there a marriage? he wonders again; Livvy has no ring. Peter wouldn't have written as he did if there'd been no marriage, surely?

Would he? A different Peter from the son he remembers?

Cuthbert Timms uncrosses his legs. 'I will consult the bishop,' he says. 'It will be necessary to check with Somerset House in London. Yet, it seems to me that if there is no record there can, in law, be no impediment between yourself and Livvy.'

... in law. But in Livvy's mind? Apart from fear, from which he wants to protect her, and devotion to George, which he shares, he knows nothing of what is in her mind.

TWENTY-EIGHT

Seated next to him in the trap, Livvy turns, waves to Renée left standing in front of ivy-clad convent buildings. He was going to suggest Livvy accompany him and Renée but found his daughter had already arranged it when Livvy felt recovered enough to go with the girl into the city to buy winter uniform. They get on well, Livvy and Renée, he muses. Before the three of them set off from Laurel Road after lunch, Livvy let Renée fuss her, tuck a travelling rug round her knees; you can nurse my hockey stick, Renée said, sounding just like May.

Banks of rhododendron foliage line the drive. He keeps Copper at a steady trot, past tennis courts, the scent of cut grass, until wrought iron gates open to families bringing girls for the new term. Renée wanted to show Livvy round but he was anxious to get away. There won't be many more Sundays as fine as this. Mrs Brent has made a picnic.

He hopes a ride in the countryside will be good for Livvy. She's been quiet, as if preoccupied, since her two days in bed and they've not had any time alone. He settles into the creak of the harness, clash of hooves against stone.

'Thomas, why do you send Renée to a convent school?' Livvy asks.

'They have a good reputation. May and I felt she should be well educated, as Nell had been. That was the main consideration. As she had no other sisters, we wanted her to grow up with girls her own age and from a similar background. You will feel the same for George, surely?' He turns to her with a silent laugh. 'I mean, that he should grow up with *boys* his own age.'

She allows a hint of a smile; the real one has been put away. 'He was the reason for leaving Baku.'

He grips the reins, stares at Copper lest the horse should sense lack of concentration in him now that, suddenly, Livvy is unlocking a door that has been sealed for a year.

'Not the revolution, then?'

'We might have had to go anyway, especially after Baku became Bolshevik once more in April. But this time last year, it was still the independent Azeri capital. Peter had his job. I would've stayed, even though Baku was an oriental city with fewer Europeans. I'd been there for more than five years. Peter was the one who wanted to come to England. "George can grow up with English children, know his family," he said.'

He glances at her but she is looking at the hedgerow and he senses she does not wish to say more, that he must tread carefully. But about George, surely he can speak. 'You were annoyed with me last week for letting George call me papa.'

She is gazing at the road ahead. 'Yes. I don't want him to be in ignorance of his father. Peter's dying words were, "Tell George his father loved him." I shall honour that and talk to George about Peter.'

'Then I shall respect it, too.'

He allows Copper his own pace over a surface of compacted stones; past farmhouses, a terrace of cottages, fields after harvest, then onto a track which rises towards Lickey ridge with its crown of trees. When they come to a curve, he turns to Livvy. 'We'll stop here and walk. Are you warm enough?'

'Yes.'

He climbs down, goes round to her. She gives him her hand, meets his eyes, looks away, as if apprehensive of anything he might say. He lifts out the picnic basket and travelling rug, strokes Copper's neck in a parting gesture.

A path meanders between ferns and blackberry bushes. Livvy follows him. They pick and eat as they walk, a companionable silence amidst birdsong and humming of bees. The path steepens where they left the bicycles last spring. He offers her his hand and she takes it. The sun is warm on his back through the jacket of his Sunday suit. He is sweating, aware of the smell of himself.

When they reach the ridge he keeps hold of her hand, puts the picnic basket and rug down. Fields shimmer below. The Malvern Hills loom in shades of blue and pink. He lets go of her hand, rests his arm across her shoulders. 'I wanted to bring you somewhere you enjoyed,' he says. 'There hasn't been much happiness for you since we came back from Wales.'

Again, that suggestion of a smile. She does not look at him. How can he release whatever she is nursing? Or should he even try? Is it grief for her father and brothers?

He takes his arm away from her shoulders. 'Shall we have tea?'

She turns from the view of the Malvern Hills, opens out the travelling rug, kneels to unfasten the picnic basket. 'There's enough for four!' she exclaims, unwrapping piles of sandwiches, scones, slices of cake.

'Mrs Brent knows people always eat more out of doors.' He sits down beside her, breathes the perfume he has come to associate with her, not the bottled sort, but perhaps soap or just the freshness that is her, in spite of the climb. He takes off his jacket. She is looking at his hands and he wonders if she is thinking of the picture; if he felt it was upsetting her he'd stow it upstairs out of the way but she has insisted she likes it. He pours her a glass of lemonade, puts sandwiches on the two plates she has taken from the basket. They spread white napkins over their laps. She breaks a sandwich in half, nibbles one corner without appetite.

How to begin, or rather continue? 'It was careless, unthinking of me, to let George call me papa,' he says. 'The thing is, to me we're a family, Livvy. I have developed a deep fondness for you ... ' Is it too soon to speak of the things closest to his heart? She is looking at him now, those lovely eyes – did they draw him to her even that first evening when she stood in the doorway of the morning room last October, rain glistening on her shoulders in the dim light? – now regarding his face, unblinking, and he knows he must step into the unknown with no visible foothold. 'You've brought joy into my life, Livvy. I love you, want to take care of you, make you happy, so that all you've suffered becomes a distant memory without power to hurt.'

He puts down his plate, touches her hand. She does not withdraw it and he leaves his hand over hers. She pushes her plate to one side, curls her fingers around his. He feels her taking in breath, as if she would call on reserves of strength. 'I have become very fond of you, too, Thomas. I shall never forget all you've done for me and George, without questioning, probing the past. You just accepted me as I was.'

'This last week we've seemed like strangers to each other.'

'My feelings for you ... ' She shakes her head. 'I do not see how we can stay under the same roof, so I am going to leave

Laurel Road.' Her words hit him, cold steel against his heart, released from where they've been prepared, stored until needed. 'I am looking for a position where I can live in,' she continues. 'Perhaps there is a lady who needs a companion. I've also been to see a room in Wood Road.'

And not told him. But then, why should she? 'I agree we cannot continue as we are,' he says. 'But as my wife, Livvy. Would you remain at Laurel Road as my wife?'

'Your wife?' she falters. 'We are already related by marriage.'

He has never questioned her, and she has just told him she has appreciated this. He searches for the words he needs without appearing to interview her. 'It would seem … it's a matter of … whether or not there is actually a record of your marriage. Under normal conditions, I understand, the British Embassy would be informed. They would register the marriage in this country.'

'Normal conditions!' She gives a short laugh, 'huh', like the report of a shotgun. He clasps her hand to stop himself taking her in his arms. 'A certificate, you mean? I suppose there was one but I was so excited the day of the wedding, anticipating being alone with Peter, we hardly had been up till then, only for an hour or so some evenings, always out of doors. You know how it is.'

He smiles, remembering precious snatches of time with May before returning her to Herbert Cottrell who would often be waiting in the doorway, pocket watch in hand.

'There was a Bolshevik night curfew,' Livvy is saying, looking beyond him as if trawling memories. 'He could see me home by nine forty-five, run up the hill and be back at his lodgings by ten. He relied on the watch you gave him for his graduation.'

The watch: he chose it, had it engraved. He wonders what happened to it. A momentary stab jolts him. Of surprise? Yes: the Peter of his memory was hardly aware of time. And pride, that his son had matured, was behaving responsibly. But it is more than that. It is jealousy of a life glimpsed; of Peter, who knew Livvy before he did.

'A certificate?' Livvy repeats. She shrugs. 'I've no idea if there was one or, if there was, where it was put. It wasn't in either of our bedrolls for the journey across Russia. Peter always said we'd have the marriage blessed in England, with our families.'

Bedrolls for the journey across Russia? He nods, as if he would show understanding when he feels ignorance, strangeness. Bedrolls?

'It was a good wedding, in spite of wartime rations,' she is recalling. 'Friends there, the Russian family I'd been with for four years. Singing.' She removes her left hand from his, indicates the bare third finger. 'I did have a ring, a Russian one. It used to belong to the mother of Peter's landlady. I gave it to White soldiers so we could travel the last part of the journey to Archangel. That was the sort of thing you had to do in Russia, Thomas.' She looks away, biting her lip, and he knows it is time to close this door.

He retrieves her hand. 'Livvy, dearest Livvy. It wounds me to have you revisit painful memories. This is what I want to protect you from. If there is no record of your marriage, then there is no impediment to ours. We have the rest of our lives ahead of us. You're young, lovely, made to be loved.'

'I never planned to marry again.'

'Of course not. But with time, new circumstances … '

'I want to do what's best for George … and for you. I couldn't bear to hurt you. I always seem to, those I love.'

'How so, Livvy?'

'My father: he died without a letter from me, not knowing that George was his grandson. And Peter … '

She is pressing her lips together, as if in fear. He does not know what to say. To keep silent may imply censure. 'Peter?' he echoes, little more than a whisper.

Now she is looking at him, eyes full of pain. 'The journey across Russia,' she begins, focussing again on that point beyond him. 'The route: Peter decided and then told me. The idea was to spare me a long sea voyage because I always get very sick. Just a few days to Liverpool on a British Navy ship, better than a ferry or cargo boat. So we went north towards the winter, in spite of his chest.'

'His chest?'

'He moved to the Caucasus in 1914 because he'd had bronchitis most of that first winter in Petersburg. Didn't you know? The doctor told him mountain air would be better. This was before I knew him. Peter kept well, in Grozny for over three years, and then nearly two in Baku, which wasn't in the mountains but was hot and dry.'

It's there, the boil lanced, poison, guilt, wretchedness, spread in front of him, her eyes beseeching: what am I to do? Peter never wrote of having bronchitis his first winter in Russia. It's nearly seven years ago but he's sure he would've remembered, for May would've been worried.

Livvy is looking at her lap. She closes her eyes. He asks, 'What would've been the alternative to going north?'

She glances up at him, nervousness in her expression like a foal shying from a stranger. 'Persia, Mesopotamia, Palestine, a ship through the Mediterranean. It could've taken months but I should've insisted we do it, for his sake. If I'd only thought …'

Strength is filling every corner of him; strength he must share with her. 'These are just names to me, Livvy. But it strikes me anything could've happened to you there: sickness, the sort of thing one imagines in hot places.'

'I know. But I've felt so terrible about it. I didn't tell you before because I didn't want you to hate me.'

'Hate you? My dearest Livvy … '

' … I don't think you have it in you to hate anybody. But when I first came to Laurel Road I didn't know that, and then you were so kind to me and George and I didn't want you to take against me and the kindness stop, for that was what I needed more than anything. Still do. Eleanor's the only one I've told.'

He closes his eyes, breathes out as if he has been holding his breath. The poor, darling girl, bottling all this up for nearly a year. He looks at her, brings her hands to his lips, presses them there. 'I will give you kindness, Livvy, without measure.' He holds her hands against his cheek. 'It's easy to feel guilty when someone you love dies, especially when it's sudden, out of time. When May died I wondered if I should've forbidden her canvassing for Christabel Pankhurst, demanded she stay at home as many husbands would've done. And Peter: instead of letting him go to Russia, should I have forced him to join me in the business, the eldest son? A lot of fathers would have. After their deaths, I questioned my integrity as husband, father.'

'You give people the freedom to be, which is something I love about you.' She turns to look at the Malvern Hills.

She has not refused to marry him, and he must wait for the bishop's response to Cuthbert Timms. 'Livvy, will you promise me one thing?'

'Yes?' She is still gazing at the hills.

'Not to think any more about leaving Laurel Road.'

✧

A few afternoons later, she walks with the perambulator as far as the church. She leaves George asleep outside, twists the ring handle and pushes open the door; crosses the stone-slabbed floor to the back, where she sits in dusty warmth. She opens the prayer book, turns pages until she finds what she is looking for:

A Table of kindred and Affinity – wherein whoever are related are forbidden by the Church of England to marry together.

There are two columns. She puts her finger at the top of the first.

A Man may not marry his – she moves her finger down the column – *son's wife.*

Then the top of the second column.

A Woman may not marry her – down to – *husband's father.*

She closes the book. Thomas has made enquiries at Somerset House in London. No record has been found of a marriage between Peter Boulton and Olivia Turner. The Russian capital had already moved to Moscow, she remembers, by the time she and Peter married. She doubts if the British established an embassy there; even if they did, news of the wedding of two British people nearly two thousand miles away in Baku would've been unlikely to reach them. And because of that, she and Thomas could marry. His acceptance, without blame, of the journey to Archangel, has left her with a feeling of walking on air, as if anything is possible.

You're young, still attractive enough to turn a man's head, Rose said. She will be twenty-five on Monday. Her body – treacherous thing – is ready, has long been ready, for marriage again; there could be more children, brothers and sisters for George. Yet Peter, her great love, her first and, she thought, only love: even though it is difficult to recall his face, the sound of his voice, I still love him, the memory of a time, our life together. If it were not Thomas but somebody else, would to remarry seem a betrayal of Peter? To marry means to relinquish the past, embark on a shared present and future.

This she knows, as she stands up and goes out into the September sunshine, is the crux of the matter. For it is the past that crowds her memory: last September, the decision to leave Baku, making their way across Russia, each stage like a notch on a long stick.

She returns along Wood Road, passes the house where she looked at the room. She's never told Thomas how bleak it was, that she can't subject George to such a place. He will suppose she's not going there because she has promised to think no further about leaving Laurel Road.

Back home – he's earlier than usual - he comes out of the morning room into the hall. He must have heard her opening and closing the two doors. They stand looking at each other the length of the hall as they did when she returned from Norwich. Neither makes a move, as if afraid, aware that nothing has been agreed, permitted, and she upbraids herself for naivety, an arrogance that imagined the passion she and Peter enjoyed is the prerogative of the young. Father and Rose knew these feelings, too.

She lifts George out of the perambulator. He toddles towards Thomas calling, 'Gappa! Gappa!' She takes a few steps towards them.

Thomas holds George up to his face. 'Grand-pa-pa,' he says with tenderness.

'Ga-pa-pa,' repeats George.

She meets Thomas's eyes over the head of her son.

ભ

Rose, settled in Yarmouth, writes to her with a postal order for five pounds, having sold to Mr Biggin the contents of the house. *Let me know from time to time how you and your little boy are.* She replies with a note of thanks, frowns at its brevity. What else can she say? Everything, and yet nothing, has changed since her return from Norwich.

She accompanies Thomas and Joe to church for the first time the following Sunday when the morning service includes unveiling a bronze plaque engraved with the names of all in the parish killed in action. After the service, Joe stands hands in pockets, his back to the plaque and to people. She reads near the top of the first column:

BOULTON J.R. VC
BOULTON W.A.

Jack, a handsome face in a photograph; Will, whom she watched die; but most of all she thinks of Peter, who lost his life in different circumstances, buried in a corner of Russia nobody will ever visit, his name unrecorded in England.

She turns away, is conscious of glances, one or two people smiling at her. A woman approaches, clasps both her hands. 'It's so nice to see you.' There is sincerity in the woman's voice and she wonders why a stranger should say this to her.

'Thank you,' she manages.

The woman releases her hands. 'Hope to meet you again.'

No questions, comments, just a gesture of friendship. If she stays here, these people could become part of her every day. A new life.

The day before the first anniversary of Peter's death, a letter arrives from Charlotte, whom she wrote to before going to Wales in July. ... *we are still in the little house you remember. Two ageing ladies were not considered a threat to the Communists when they took over but we were told we would have to work. Everybody has to. I agreed with the commissar who came to see us that we would tend the graves in the British cemetery. The church was closed last year. I pointed out to him that although he might regard the British as Imperialists and therefore enemies, there was a time when the British Army were welcomed as protectors of Baku against the Turks and many British boys perished.*

She smiles, picturing Charlotte summoning imperial hauteur, striking a deal with a young commissar. She closes her eyes, can still smell the oil, dust, hot wind on her face; the peace and space in Charlotte's house, white painted walls, a camel saddle of striped red canvas resting in one corner; pewter mugs and ewers in niches. And green tea in china cups. Among the British community, rumour had it that Charlotte had spent years travelling in Persia before settling in Baku, although she never spoke of it. People have their pasts.

So, in the warmth of the evening – you remember, Livvy, the lesser heat – we can be found walking down to the headland in our battered straw hats. Looking after the grave of dear Peter's brother is the last and only thing I can do for you both ...

That Will's grave is cared for only emphasises Peter's: unvisited, untended, known just to herself.

The next day she tucks George into the perambulator after lunch, sets off towards the churchyard, sun warm on her back past fields and cottages; thinks of the rain, the early darkness, that afternoon a year ago in Archangel. She pushes open the churchyard gate, makes her way to the Boulton grave. The inscription on the headstone has the addition:

and their grandson, Peter Thomas Boulton, who died 11th May 1920, aged three months.

She stands with head bowed. I shall always love you, Peter. My Peter. I loved you from the second time I saw you: do you remember, in that alley in Baku's Tartar Quarter? Third, if you count when you gave me the hatband in Petersburg. There will never be such a love again.

She studies George sleeping in the perambulator, hair the same colour as his father's, no wave or curl, and she wonders if it will flop over his forehead as Peter's used to. 'I'll tell you about Papa,' she says to her son. 'Soon. He has no gravestone. He's a memory for those who knew and loved him, and you are his legacy.'

A year; and tomorrow, a year since the first day without Peter. She turns away, pushes the perambulator back along the path, home; she will manoeuvre it through the two doors, has got the hang of it now, and Thomas will come into the hall, and she'll walk towards him, to the certainty, the kindness of him, the clean smell of him when he's freshly shaved. As it's a fine Sunday afternoon he might be in the back garden taking down the bean canes, end of the season, so she'll go out to him. Next year there'll be more beans, a new season, many new seasons. What was it he said in the summer when they were in Wales, about breaking with the past?

Yes: it is the only thing to do if we are to be healed and continue living.

Yes.

THE END

Afterword

All novels are of unique conception. Some have a long gestation. I once read about a young Englishwoman caught up in the 1917 revolution in Baku - which was at that time in Russia – and she wouldn't let me go. Who was she? Where exactly was Baku? How had she come to be there? If escape were necessary, how and which way would she go? A fiction writer can create much out of very little, imagination filling in the gap of ignorance. The Englishwoman blossomed into Livvy.

Russia is a rich and fascinating country. As Livvy wonders after her return to England: what is it about Russia that holds people in thrall? The temptation for the novelist - one to which I happily succumbed in the first draft of *Beyond the Samovar* - is to tell everybody's story through those years of world war, revolution, civil war, when the old certainties and boundaries, geographical and social, were swept away. Livvy, however, kept reaching out to me. This was to be her story.

I finished each draft of the book feeling I had done all I could, but that there was still more to do, although I wasn't always sure what. So there were gaps - sometimes years - between drafts. I worked on other projects, short and long fiction. Livvy was always at my shoulder. Every time I returned to *Beyond the Samovar* with fresh eyes and insight, cutting away at the dead wood - although nothing is ever wasted and some will come to life in another book - shaping Livvy's story, keeping myself out of it.

Sculptors and artists are sometimes asked: 'How do you know when to stop, to leave off shaping here, touching up there?' The answer - and it applies to writers, too - is: you don't, always. In this case, Livvy no longer reached out to me. The gestation was over.

Janet Hancock,
Dorset,
November 2018

Acknowledgements

I would like to thank the North Staffordshire Regiment for material about Baku in 1918.

I am grateful to the staff of the central reference library in Birmingham, who made available to me material from their local studies department. My thanks also go to the Governors of the schools of King Edward the sixth Foundation in Birmingham for material from the Foundation archives concerning Camp Hill School.

My grandmother's house in Birmingham, where my mother grew up, was the inspiration for the Boulton family home. I used to go there as a child and wonder what was behind dark, closed doors on the landings.

Through many edits and drafts, I was sustained, challenged, cheered on, by writers who read a chapter, a partial, a complete draft: Liz Bosanko, Kathy Butler, Clio Gray, Nancy Henshaw, Åse Johannessen, Barbara Large, Tessa McGregor, Diane Morrison, Pam Pointer, Irene Thomas, Margaret Wiwczaryk, and all at Dunford Novelists. Thank you all for your support, encouragement and insightful comments. They helped shape the book.

Thank you to James Essinger and The Conrad Press for bringing the book into the world, and to Charlotte Mouncey for the cover design and typesetting.

Thank you to Margaret Reynolds and Rita Metcalfe.

And to Ken, who would have loved to see the book in print.

Bibliography

Baedeker, Karl, *Russia: A Handbook for Travellers*, London, 1914.

Berman, Leonid, *The Three Worlds of Leonid*, Basic Books, New York, 1978.

Bradley, John, *Allied Intervention in Russia*, Weidenfeld and Nicolson, 1968.

Bradley, John, *Civil War in Russia 1917-20*, B.T. Batsford, 1975.

Bradley, John, *The Russian Revolution*, Brompton, 1988.

Brittain, Vera, *Testament of Youth*, Arrow Books, 1960.

Bunin, Ivan, *Cursed Days: A Diary of Revolution*, Phoenix Press, 2000

Clark, Moira, *Reflections in the Samovar*, The Merdon Marque, 1991.

Coates, W.P. and Z.K., *Armed Intervention in Russia*, Victor Gollancz, 1935.

Dunsterville, General L.C., *The Adventures of Dunsterforce*, Edward Arnold, 1920.

Fitzlyon, Kyril, and Browning, Tatiana, *Before the Revolution: A View of Russia under the Last Tsar*, Penguin, 1992.

Glenny, Michael and Stone, Norman, *The Other Russia*, Faber and Faber, 1990.

Ironside, Field Marshall Edmund, *Archangel 1918-1919*, Constable, 1953.

MacDonell, Ranald, *And Nothing Long*, Constable & Co. Ltd., 1938.

Maclean, Sir Fitzroy, *Holy Russia*, Weidenfeld and Nicolson, 1978.

Maclean, Sir Fitzroy, *To Caucasus*, Weidenfeld and Nicolson, 1976.

Mawdsley, E., *The Russian Civil War*, Allen and Unwin, 1987.

Pitcher, Harvey, *When Miss Emmie Was in Russia*, John Murray, 1977.

Price, Morgan Philips, *Dispatches from the Revolution: Russia 1916-1918*, Duke University Press, NC, 1998.

Price, Morgan Philips, *My Reminiscences of the Russian Revolution*, Allen and Unwin Ltd., 1921.

Shukman, H., ed., *Encyclopaedia of the Russian Revolution*, Blackwell, 1989.

Suny, R.G., *The Baku Commune*, Princeton U.P., 1972.

Swietochowski, T., *Russian Azerbaijan 1905-20*, C.U.P. 1985.

Turgenev, Ivan, *Fathers and Children*, Everyman, 1998

Wood, Gloria, and Thompson, Paul, *The Nineties: Personal Recollections of the 20th Century*, BBC Books, 1993.